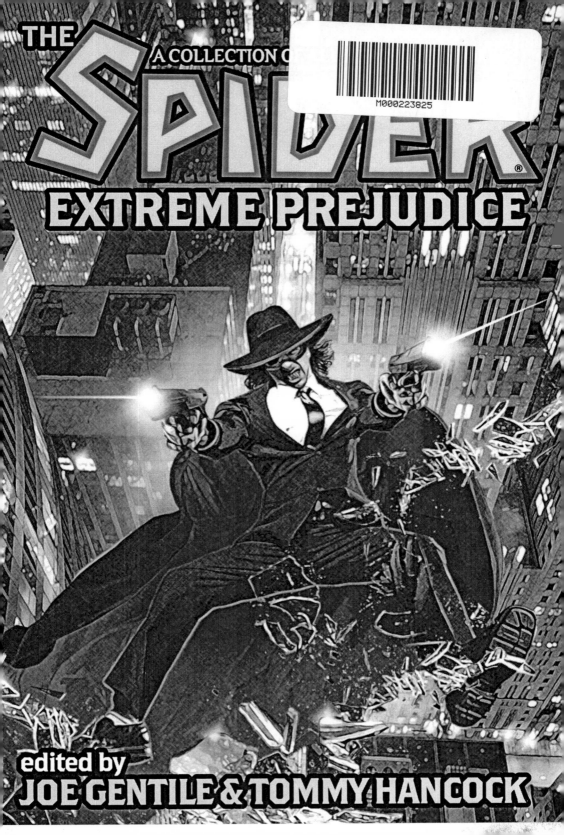

Joe Gentile and Tommy Hancock
Co-Editors

Malcolm McClinton
Cover art

Lewis Chapman
Book Design

Erik Enervold
Simian Borthers Creative
Cover Design

David White
Editorial

The SPIDER: Extreme Prejudice
softcover edition
978-1-936814-46-6

The SPIDER: Extreme Prejudice
hardcover edition
978-1-936814-47-3

Published by
Moonstone Entertainment, Inc.
1128 S. State Street, Lockport, IL 60441
www.moonstonebooks.com

THE **SPIDER**
Extreme Prejudice

Introduction
by Joe Gentile

I first met The *Spider* as a young teenager…at a used bookstore. (You could even trade in books that you didn't want anymore, and get in-store credit that you could use on anything!)

I would spend hours and hours combing the dusty shelves, even standing on a chair when I couldn't reach high enough. I would burrow my way through boxes of "new" arrivals, hoping for an elusive pulp or action title.

While my thirst for adventure drove me to various authors and characters like: Sherlock Holmes, Ed McBain, The Avenger, Zorro, Raymond Chandler, Tolkien…you name it…I came across something I had never heard of before.

It was a small paperback with a cover price of something like 50cents, so even at that time, it was old. There was a drawing of a blond guy wearing what looked like a turtle neck sweater, with some kind of beige-yellow dress pants, and a gun holster on over his clothes. He actually looked like a ski instructor.

The name of the story on the front cover was "Death Reign of the Vampire King".

How could I NOT want to read more about that? So I picked it up immediately and went home to start reading it.

What did I find inside? Well, for one, the main character was described nothing like the "Ken doll look" on the cover, which was good, but confusing. The book described him as a dark figure of the night who wears a cloak, a scraggly wig, fangs, and with a slight hunchback. Couldn't be more different than the cover image if they tried to do so on purpose.

Secondly, the characters in the story were different…unusual for tales of this kind. First, The *Spider* himself…seemed to be the REAL identity, while the civilian identity of "Richard Wentworth" was more of a mask…at least to my way of thinking. Then, we had his love interest, Nita, who not only KNEW her boyfriend's secret identity, but understood it and helped him! What kind of crazy stuff was that? That kind of thing never happened! Thirdly, there was Wentworth's aide Ram, a turbaned Sikh Indian who wielded knives as well as cool colorful sayings? What?

The *Spider* was also different from every other character I read about in a couple other respects. He wasn't welcome by the police, as they thought he was a criminal, and the bad guys feared him like the plague.

The *Spider* also had this intense, deep seated need for justice. He went after it with a passion. Nothing stood in his way. He had no compunction about delivering this justice with his pair of 45's, leaving no room for our court system to earn its keep. Why bother, right? The *Spider* left NO loose ends. He killed his way through criminals and slept soundly after. Wow, this was a far cry from the usual heroes who had codes against killing, and always tried to arrest the bad guys. There's none of that uncertainty in a *Spider* story! How does that not appeal? Justice was served.

Then…the story inside the book covers was revealed. It was relentless from beginning to end. It didn't stop for life's minutia; it rickety roller-coastered straight down, leaving your breath and stomach behind. I had never read anything like it. I needed more the next day, but it was very difficult finding *Spider* reprints back then, so that second book was a long time coming. So long in fact, that when I found it, I was unsure if that was where I should be spending my hard earned cash, but I went ahead and bought it. But once I started reading…it all crashed over to me like a giant wave.

The *Spider's* original run went 118 novels, from 1933 -1944. (as a side note, Moonstone published what was originally planned to be the 119th novel, "Slaughter, Inc", recently, and is interesting in its own right)

We are convinced this character had more tales to tell.

Justice is still something we crave. When that elusive right can be captured, we like it delivered cold, if you please.

Joe Gentile
May, 2013

Scourge of the Giggling Ghouls
by Howard Hopkins

T he skylight imploded as a dark figure crashed through, each gloved hand brandishing a .45 automatic. Glass fragmented, shards spiraling, glittering, lacerating the air. Below, in the great dining room of the Neptune Club, screams punctuated by shivers of inhuman ghoulish giggling rang out. But the screams were not for the cloaked form dropping into the midst of the panicked gathering, though certainly the intruder appeared a thing of darkest nightmare. No, their wailing came for a far more grisly reason. Many of the screams were cut horrifically short, and trailed by the grotesque tearing of human flesh.

Retaining his feet, the dark shape landed with a thud in the center of a large round table formerly occupied by the guests of the political function—a fundraiser under the guise of a masquerade ball designed to persuade a certain Richard Wentworth to throw his hat into the arena for the office of governor. But funds were not the sole entity to be raised this night—Hell was!

The figure's arms swept out, cape swirling about his shoulders, automatics, twin messengers of leaden death, searching the mass of ragged shambling creatures that had once been men. Blue-gray eyes narrowed behind a domino mask, scouring the carnage. Scraggly locks flowed from beneath a low-pulled slouch hat that framed a demonic face with a slash of a mouth, from which protruded gleaming needle-sharp fangs. If possible, the man's grim features became more severe.

Good God, what madness was this? Were those pitiful creatures human any longer? Were they living dead men, as *The Times* had proclaimed?

No! Even should these shambling monstrosities the press had come to label as the "Giggling Ghouls" be human beneath a gruesome façade, he could not hesitate—for he was The *Spider!* The Master of Men! And these creatures, whether created by accident or design, were committing murder, wholesale and ghastly.

The room's occupants were in a wild churning panic, masked politicians and their wives, girlfriends or high-priced escorts scrambling for doors, windows, any opening that would allow egress, escape from certain death. Helpless women were trampled in the mad rush. But the doors and windows had been sealed from the outside, carefully premeditated to trap those within, by a mysterious underworld figure who had proclaimed himself in taunting notes to the police as the Knight of the Living Dead. The villain's target was the very man being sought for office—Richard Wentworth. But in that capacity the ghoul master had miscalculated, for Wentworth, holding no interest in the office, had not attended the function.

Until now.

Now he stood atop the table, seeking the woman he had sent in his stead. He stood with threatening automatics, an insane laugh issuing from his gash of a mouth and swelling horror in his heart.

Richard Wentworth, the scourge of the guilty; Richard Wentworth— The *Spider!*

He'd tested the door and windows before entering, only to find them sealed with some sort of "super" adhesive he could not immediately circumvent. It would have taken time—time he did not have while Death struck down innocent lives. That had left him two choices: the skylight or the method by which the giggling dead men had entered. The Neptune was built upon pylons and extended out over the harbor at the end of a short pier. The *Spider's* gaze swept to the trapdoors located on the ancient timber floor, dual doors flipped open to admit the horrors whom had raided the masquerade function. It was the third such attack in as many weeks, all aimed at opposition candidates to the Romanero family syndicate, who'd made little secret about their intent to rule the state's political machine.

Two more of the monstrosities clambered through the openings, their insane cackling giggles raking The *Spider's* nerves. The sound was inhuman, a grating gibbering thing that rose and fell without rhyme or reason like a demonic death rattle.

"Nita!" he cried, guns shifting, seeking blood. He'd sent Nita to the gathering to speak for him, wishing to remain free to combat the Knight's ghouls, should they attack—and he had had every reason to think they would, for though the police had partially thwarted one raid in the act, they'd discovered the supply of ghouls nearly inexhaustible; scores had met doom at the hands of the living dead men.

The *Spider* had tied the surge of ghouls into a rash of recent grave robbings and kidnappings, but he had no way of knowing whether the ghouls were human or corpse. He now suspected those kidnap victims had been murdered, added to the ranks of the Living Dead.

All politicians threatened by the ghoul master had dropped out of the various local and state races. Romanero proxies ran virtually unopposed.

The opposing party had needed somebody unafraid, willing to risk life and limb for the good of the state, and had turned to Wentworth. Wentworth had indicated he might accept the nomination at the function tonight to lure the Knight into the open, though he had no real intention of ever running for office.

But he had risked Nita's lovely neck to this end. What was one life, even hers, to prevent the scourge that would occur if the Romanero family held the state in its iron grip? How many would die, then? One life against many. He was The *Spider!* Savior of the innocent, punisher of the damned. He had no other choice!

Still, panic surged like white-hot flame through his veins.

"Nita!" he cried again, his voice snapping over the screams and demonic giggling.

A shrill scream shattered his nerves and at first he thought it belonged to the woman he loved—but, no! Another woman, one dressed in a sequined emerald gown, fell beneath one of the cackling ghouls.

Good God! The thing was hideous, a monstrosity! Its dead black eyes, ravenous with the hunger for human flesh, glittered with unholy fire under the light cast from the crystal chandelier above. Its sallow sunken features looked like some sort of terrible mask from the grave. Greenish fluid snaked from either corner of its mouth and jagged brown teeth gnashed. Maggots squirmed in its matted patchy hair. Its clothing was soiled, ragged, and the stench of rotting death issued from its person, as if it truly were something extracted from a crypt.

The *Spider* stood momentarily frozen in awed horror. Then the young woman's shrieks became pitiful wailing things, shivering with agony, as the thing plunged a bony hand into her abdomen. Gouging fingers tore right through fabric, through peachy soft flesh. A gout of blood spurted and the creature drew out a snake of intestine. All the while, the woman struggled—but any resistance was hopeless. At last her head lolled back and her pitiful screams stopped, her life mercifully leaving her.

The ghoul lifted the intestines towards his lips, thick gray tongue flicking out, but never completed the move. The *Spider* unleashed a triple blast of lead that drilled into the thing's forehead. The creature flew backward, half his skull obliterated by the Master of Men's bullets. It was too late to save the young woman, but the creature would never murder another victim.

About the dining room more screams of gruesome death rang out. Men, stricken with uncontrollable panic, crushed their dates beneath their feet as they strove to find an exit. Others fell beneath the clutching zombies, who with rotting jagged teeth tore into warm living flesh!

Some with the foresight to bring weapons or who improvised with steak knives, fired and hacked wildly, madly, in some cases accidentally bringing down their compatriots.

There! Nita! The *Spider* caught a glimpse of her, dressed in a sapphire tight-fitting gown with a plunging neckline, dots of blood spattering the creamy alabaster mounds of her breasts. Her chestnut curls were in disarray and fire blazed in her violet eyes as she swept a steak knife from a table and slashed, half-severing the head from a clutching ghoul. The aberration toppled backward, crashed to the floor, but two more were closing in on her from behind.

"Nita!" The *Spider* shouted, leaping from the table. "Behind you!"

Nita Van Sloan whirled at his words. Her white-gloved hand darted between the valley of her breasts, came back out with a revolver. She fired, sending a ghoul stumbling backward into one of the open trapdoors.

The *Spider* issued an eerie mocking laugh and loosed another shot; the second ghoul was swept off its feet, nearly bifurcated.

"Nita!" he cried, reaching her side, relief washing through him. "However did you conceal such a large revolver there?" His words came half in jest but saturated with dread.

"Why, *Spider*, darling," Nita said in a rich but shaken contralto, "with this neckline I could have hidden a Tommy gun there and not a man would have noticed!"

From beyond the building, the wail of police sirens rose above the unnerving giggling and shrieks. The *Spider's* automatics thundered again and again and each time a ghoul fell beneath their lead. Nita's own gun delivered an accompanying staccato.

The ghouls, as gruesome as they were, appeared to be limited in number this time, for no more came through the trapdoor openings.

After what seemed a hellish eternity, it was over. But the Neptune Club was bathed in blood and partially devoured organs lay scattered about. In the leaden silence of death that remained, The *Spider* dove for a trapdoor, leaving behind the corpses of ghouls and innocent alike. No coward was he, but his work here was finished—though only for the moment. George Romanero, leader of the syndicate, if indeed he had directed the attack, would soon face the *Spider's* wrath.

An instant later, the remaining women began weeping, along with a number of surviving men as, the panic now quenched, they clutched to the broken bodies of their fallen companions. Then police began battering the doors…

"Oh, Dick, it was ghastly," Nita Van Sloan said, falling back against the backseat cushions of the speeding Daimler. The ivory complexion of her face and bosom were a shade paler in the moonlight that bled through the car windows. Horror had embedded itself into her violet eyes, but not fear—no, never fear. For The *Spider's* woman did not shrink from Evil!

Lovely Nita, Wentworth thought, still in the guise of The *Spider* and sitting beside her in the back seat. She risked so much for his crusade against the minions of crime. Risked and sacrificed. Her very life, and any chance at happiness with another man who could give her a stable existence, one without constant danger and threat. She deserved so much more than he could provide. Was this the sort of life for a woman of her bearing? To be placed in continuous peril in his single-minded quest for justice and the slicing of the tumor that was crime from humanity's beating heart?

But she chose this life, as she relentlessly kept informing him, chose him—chose The *Spider!*

"How many dead, *Sahib?*" came the driver's grim voice, interrupting Wentworth's thoughts.

"Fifteen, Ram Singh." Wentworth's blue-gray eyes flared with guilt behind The *Spider's* mask. "Ten women, five men. I wasn't in time…"

Nita placed a gentle white-gloved hand on his forearm. "You can't blame yourself, Dick. You couldn't save everyone. You killed all those… *things.*"

"They were already dead, Nita." Wentworth's voice came with heavy strain and dark recrimination. "I'm convinced of it, now. Had I only guessed their mode of entrance, I might have saved those innocent people."

"How did those creatures get there?" Nita asked, face tightening. "Surely those mindless things would have been seen walking the streets."

"A small submarine, if I had to guess. And inflatable boats, to carry the creatures under the docks. Only one man owns a private submersible."

"George Romanero, as you suspected?"

Wentworth nodded. "I wasn't positive until tonight. I had hoped to catch him in the act, trap him with his own creations. But it was a choice between stopping him or those monstrosities, and saving innocent lives."

"*Wah!*" Ram Singh said from the front. "If this man is suspected why does Kirkpatrick not arrest him?"

Wentworth's gash of a mouth drew thinner. "The Commissioner suspects, as did I, but has no proof."

"But this Romanero has made no secret of his political aims," Nita said. "Can't Stanley do anything?"

Wentworth shook his head. "Romanero's men have infiltrated key positions within the police force. Kirk has been blocked at every turn. He damn near pleaded with me to let The *Spider* loose on them, at once accusing me again and pardoning The *Spider's* involvement just this once."

Beyond the car windows, forest whipped by, the ribbon of road ahead glazed with moonlight. Perhaps Commissioner Stanley Kirkpatrick was powerless to act but The *Spider* could end this madness. He'd become certain after the attack catching Romanero in the act would now endanger too many innocent people. The Knight of the Living Dead had to be eliminated—tonight!

"What are those things, Dick?" Nita's contralto voice carried a hint of a tremble.

"Dead men, Nita. Dead men…" Wentworth paused, his mind sifting back through bits of memory. "Two years ago… there was a scientist from Germany named Helmut Livingstein. I remember reading about him. He made certain claims about discovering the secret to life… and the reanimation of loved ones taken by disease by the use of chemicals and electricity. But he lost the funding to carry out his final experiments after his original attempts caused backers to withdraw when his test subjects exhibited *unnatural* appetites."

"What became of this man, *Sahib?*" Ram Singh asked.

"He vanished. I've heard nothing of him since."

"Do you think Romanero abducted him, financed him?" Nita asked.

"It's a possibility. Romanero has always ruled his organization through fear. The man's a recluse, said to have suffered some sort of mental instability resulting from syphilis, but retained enough of his faculties to run his empire…"

"And crave more and more power," Nita said. "But those things… how does he control them? Surely they would turn on him when he transported them."

"If he did transport them. He might have had his men attend to that, though the question remains the same."

Nita shuddered. "How can he expect to escape federal prosecution if he comes to power in such a way?"

Wentworth shrugged as if the weight of humanity lay upon his shoulders. For indeed it did. If Romanero wasn't stopped… there would be no end to the madness that would grip the state, then, the country. A man crazed for power would not stop at mere state rule. "It wouldn't matter, Nita. Once he controlled the state, he'd be virtually untouchable. Besides, no one who might prove otherwise remains alive."

The forest thinned suddenly, waning to occasional stands of oak and pine that dotted alabaster-frosted rolling hills. Ahead, a great mansion reared from the countryside, stark and ominous in the moonlit night. A massive stone fence, rising six feet in height, surrounded the gothic structure, topped with iron spikes.

"Slow, Ram Singh," Wentworth ordered, his eyes growing grimly intense, searching every shadow. "Romanero's Mansion."

"It will be guarded, *Sahib,*" Ram Singh said as he slowed the Daimler to a crawl and doused the headlamps. "This one's blade thirsts for blood."

"Look!" Nita jutted a white-gloved finger at the iron front gate. "Two of those… *things!*"

Behind the iron gate stood two living dead men, as if oblivious to the chill of the October night and everything around them. They swayed on their feet, gaunt sunken faces more grotesque in the stark moonlight.

Ram Singh cut the engine and began to open the door.

"No!" Wentworth snapped, his demeanor changing, becoming the implacable manner of The *Spider.*

"*Sahib?*"

"You and Nita stay here. If I fail, find Kirkpatrick and tell him The *Spider* has fallen to the living dead, and that he must act with utter swiftness and strength, and without remorse. The very lives of every man, woman and child of this nation depend on it."

With that The *Spider* was out of the Daimler and drifting towards the stone fence. God knew what horrors awaited him behind that enclosure, but the two undead sentinels at the gate provided all the proof he needed to implicate George Romanero as the force behind the ghouls.

Stopping to the left at the base of the fence, The *Spider's* gloved hand went to his waist. There he extracted a small grapple attached to a silk line. He swung the grapple in a short arc then let it fly upward, to wrap with a thin clank about one of the iron spikes topping the fence. He waited to see whether the sound had attracted the attention of the dead guards. A thin giggling, eerie and incongruous in the night, reached his ears, but the zombies did not leave their post.

The *Spider* climbed, hand over hand, every fiber of his being sizzling with determination and resolve.

This lunacy ended tonight—or The *Spider's* life did.

When he reached the top, he drew up the "Web", reversed it and lowered himself to the bottom. The grounds were clotted with shifting dark shadows from ponderous oaks, their leaves burnt-orange with the fall. The scent of rotting foliage pricked at his nostrils and browned leaves, crisp with frost, crunched beneath his shoes. Jagged slices of moonlight knifed through the branches, falling in serrated patterns across the lawn.

He was well aware any number of those hideous creatures might be hiding among the shadows, but nothing moved. Somewhere, a whippoorwill uttered a haunting call. The insane low giggling from the guards kept up, but they did not turn to him.

He considered putting bullets in the backs of their skulls, ending their aberrant existence, but that would only alert Romanero to The *Spider's* presence.

The *Spider* moved towards the great mansion, two-hundred yards distant. He'd made it halfway when the front door flew open and splashed amber light across the long porch and highlighted a green-robed figure who stepped from within.

A mad cackle came from the figure, who lowered his hood. Dark eyes beneath a heavy brow glittered with an utter detachment from reality. Disheveled black hair shot through with gray streaks fell in patches over the man's lined forehead. The face was blocky, that of a man in his mid-fifties yet one that appeared older with the strain of the disease he was rumored to have suffered.

"Romanero!" The *Spider* said in a hiss.

"Welcome, *Spider!*" Romanero said, taking another step forward. "Did you think I would not have alarms concealed over every inch of this place? It is a fortress, *Spider*, protected by my Knights of the Living Dead!"

The *Spider* halted, his heart leaping into his throat, beating thickly. He whirled left, then right, a shudder of horror raking him.

From every shadow emerged men, women, all shambling pathetic semblances of the human beings they had been in life. Some dragged their limbs as they came forward, clawlike hands with fingernails grown long in the grave clutching at empty air. Eyes, on dried stalks and withered threads of tissue, dangled from sockets. Sunken features, even more ghoulishly gray in the moonlight, exhibited parchmentlike flesh from which hung torn rotting flaps. Each uttered that unearthly giggling.

"Unnerving, is it not, *Spider?*" shouted Romanero, insanity lacing his voice. "An unfortunate side effect of the good doctor's formula — along with their appetite for human flesh. But perhaps it is not so unfortunate. Perhaps it merely adds to the terror."

The *Spider* began to move towards Romanero, but the grotesque dead men converged from all angles, blocking retreat, halting advance.

"They're coming to get you, *Spider!*" Romanero shrieked. "They're coming to get you! They're hungry for your flesh!"

The *Spider's* hands darted beneath his cloak, to the brace of automatics harnessed beneath his arms. Whipping out the guns, he pulled the triggers.

"Missy *Sahib!*" Ram Singh snapped, pointing. "The guards, they retreat."

Nita's heart jumped as thunder came from beyond the walled enclosure.

"Shots!" Her hands swept to a secret drawer beneath the seat, whisking it open. She brought up The *Spider's* spare twin automatics. They felt solid and comforting in her grip and she damn well knew how to use them.

An instant later, she had flung open the door and was out of the car, running for the iron gate, Ram Singh a mere beat behind her. The Hindu loosed a dagger from the sash at his waist.

"*Wah!*" he cried.

Nita triggered two shots, aimed at the lock on the iron gate. The lock shattered and the gate lolled inward.

Dick was in danger and orders from him to remain behind would not stop her from coming to his aid. But it was not strictly her love for Richard Wentworth that drove her. The *Spider's* mission was too vital! It must go on!

The ghoulish figures drew closer to The *Spider*, their hideous cackling giggles drilling into his brain.

What madness! What twisted lunacy! These denizens of the grave, living yet not alive, mindless and driven by an insatiable hunger for living flesh by a power-crazy madman.

The *Spider* blasted away, lead punching into gray sunken torsos and hollow staring faces. One went down, then another, and another.

But more kept coming, their shambling pace inexorable, a death sentence.

The *Spider's* taunting maniacal laugh rang out, riding the chill of the night, rising above their inhuman giggling, defiant, mocking. He would die but before he perished he would send as many of these creatures back to their graves as possible.

Two more shots. Two zombies fell as if they were gruesome marionettes whose strings had been severed.

More shots crashed from the direction of the gate and more of the living dead men went down. Nita! She had disobeyed his orders, was coming to his aid.

A cry arose, damning, yet gleeful—Ram Singh! The giant Hindu slashed with his dagger; dead men lost limbs, heads, collapsed into heaps of writhing rotting flesh and aimless bone.

"Romanero, *Spider!*" Nita shouted. "Stop him! Let us battle these creatures."

The *Spider* hesitated, but only for an instant—brave Nita, he could not leave her to these creatures. Yet if he did not their mastermind would escape, and many more innocent lives would be lost. He had no choice. He triggered two shots, cutting a path before him through the converging zombies. He drove for the front porch, his own laugh growing stronger, more strident. Damn Romanero! The *Spider* would end his diabolical scheme this night.

Romanero's expression changed from triumph to anxiousness. The robed man lunged into the house.

The *Spider* gave chase, leaping over fallen dead men, losing shots to fell others. But their number was legion! They grabbed at his cloak and he revolted at their bony icy touch. *Good God!* How many crypts had been violated to satiate a lunatic's maniacal lust for power?

The creatures pulled at him, sought to bring him off his feet. Their fetid breath and the stench of corrupt tissue assailed his nostrils. Their awful giggling stabbed at his brain. No! He would not let them stay him from his goal. They would not still the heart of The *Spider*.

His arms swept out, clubbing with the heavy automatics. Rotten skulls caved under each blow, their owners dropping like the dead things they had once been, brains leaking. Arms, wrenched from sockets, dangled uselessly at the creatures' sides. Still he fought, heart drumming, breath beating out in searing gasps. He was humanity's savior! He would not fall, not like this, not until his mission to bring down Romanero was complete.

Behind him, Nita blasted away, each shot removing a living dead man from the fray. Ram Singh slashed like a madman with his knife; heads rolled, fingers and arms flew.

Strike, strike, strike! The *Spider's* guns lashed, bringing down another zombie, and another, cleaving a path through the monstrosities, opening the way.

Chest heaving, lungs burning, he broke free of the mob of corpses. With every fiber of his strength he surged forward, muscles quivering with strain, exhaustion. He was The *Spider*—the Master of Men—living and dead!

At last he reached the steps leading to the porch, took them in bounds. Heedless of caution, he threw himself inside the mansion, only to spot Romanero slamming a door at the end of the hall, disappearing behind it.

The *Spider's* taunting mirth echoed through the foyer, reverberating from the crystal chandelier and hurling itself after the fleeing Romanero. It came with the promise of justice, of death.

Whisking forward, he swept along the hall, reached the door, and triggered a shot at the lock without bothering to try the handle. The lock and part of the jamb splintered. He kicked the door inward. Steps led downward—Romanero had sought to barricade himself in the cellar.

Down The *Spider* went, gloved hands gripping his twin automatics so tightly tendons and forearm muscles throbbed. His laugh seemed still to haunt the hallway behind him, chase him down.

He halted at the base of the cellar stairs, eyes narrowing behind his mask. The cellar had been converted into a great laboratory. Rows of tables holding beakers brimming with some vile greenish fluid lined three walls. On one rested a peculiar gunlike device, thick at the nozzle. Two wooden slab tables held the corpses of recent grave robbings.

Machines along the fourth wall hummed and a heavy odor of ozone permeated the air.

Before the machines stood Romanero, his hand on a lever switch. Another man stood beside him, small, balding, terror on his blanched features.

"Dr. Livingstein, I presume," The *Spider* said, his voice a grating whisper.

"*Spider…*" the scientist said, his terror bleeding into his tone. The irony was not missed on The *Spider*. Here was a man who rose the dead, yet feared one living man—the Master of Men!

The *Spider* gestured with an automatic at the gunlike thing on the table. "You sealed the Neptune Club's doors and windows using that device, Doctor?"

The small man nodded. "A 'super' adhesive I developed… to keep the limbs on some of the more… degraded subjects."

"How do you control them?" The *Spider* asked, swinging the gun back to Livingstein.

"Im — implants," Livingstein said. "Electrical. They cause pain…"

"And I hold the controller," Romanero said, his voice unnaturally high. Sweat trickled from his brow. "They dare not turn on me or suffer the consequences. They are mindless, but heedful of pain still."

The *Spider's* gaze drilled the doctor, damning. "Why? What you have done is… against the order of things. You have played God…"

The little scientist flinched at the accusation. "I sought answers, as all scientists do."

"Some questions should not be asked," taunted The *Spider.* He moved a step forward.

"Stay where you are, *Spider,*" Romanero said. "If I pull this switch the entire room will be set ablaze. There are flame nozzles built into each wall. You cannot shoot me fast enough to prevent me from pulling the lever."

"Then pull it!" The *Spider* said. "My life is a small price to pay to stop the madness you have wrought."

A gasp came from Dr. Livingstein. He made a lunge for a table, grabbing for a beaker of liquid The *Spider* could only guess was some sort of acid. Whether Livingstein intended to hurl it at The *Spider* or Romanero was never to be determined because the Master of Men pulled the trigger and the little scientist was launched backward. He slammed into a table, went down with a bullet in his heart.

The *Spider's* laugh filled the lab, echoing as ghoulishly as the giggling of the dead men. Another shot came from his automatic and a round hole appeared in Romanero's forehead. The madman toppled forward, but jerked down the lever as he fell.

Jutting streamers of flame burst from each wall, roaring. Intense heat forced The *Spider* to leap backward, but not in time to avoid the fire licking at his cloak.

The lab became an instant inferno, many of the scientist's beakers filled with flammable liquids, exploding with resounding retorts. Flames leaped up walls, across the floor. Black smoke billowed, grew choking.

Upon the two slabs, the dead men opened their eyes! Livingstein must have given them whatever serum produced the resurrections, and the hideous things could feel pain—burning pain. They rolled off the tables, the unnerving giggling issuing from their stiff mouths. They fell, their limbs awkward, uncontrollable, after their long confinement to the grave. Terrible cries of agony began to come from the zombies as flames engulfed their struggling desiccated forms.

A wave of disgust and nausea washed through The *Spider's* being as their gray flesh bubbled and blackened. The stench of charred flesh assailed his nostrils. There was no help for those pitiful creatures. They would mercifully return to the sleep of death from whence they had come!

The *Spider*, cape aflame, flung himself up the stairs, a firebrand of movement. Out through the front door he burst, whipping off the flaming cloak and hurling it aside.

The mansion went quickly. Flames, roaring, devoured dried timber and wallpapering and windows exploded. Great beams groaned, snapped, collapsed as the massive structure fell in on itself. Tremendous clouds of black smoke billowed up and jagged fingers of fire scratched at the night sky.

The yard was littered with the again-corpses of zombies, their bodies broken, twisted, lifeless.

Pure and utter revulsion shown on the faces of Nita Van Sloan and Ram Singh. The menace was ended, but the memory of those Knights of the Living Dead would not vanish so easily.

On the horizon, dawn broke and in the distance sirens wailed. Flame cast eerie flickering light over dozens of bodies and remorse burned within the heart of The *Spider*. It had not been the pitiful beasts' fault, their rising, their gruesome hunger. And though the heart of the madman who had perpetrated the lunatic scheme had been stilled... the craving for justice and the eradication of Evil in The *Spider's* heart lived on...

Clutch of the Blue Reaper
by Will Murray

Night was falling as the passenger liner *Hypnotic* knifed through the swells and rollers of the Atlantic. A wan moon reeled through clouds resembling steel rags, casting fitful shadows along the stern deck where a man paced restlessly, restlessly....

Smoking like a demon, Richard Wentworth fought an overpowering urge to jump the rail and swim the last leg of the crossing to the Port of Manhattan, whose spires were just beginning to show their tiny lights to the gathering dusk. Under his faultless evening dress rippled the muscles of a champion swimmer.

"Damnable luck!" he muttered distractedly. "Of all the times I chose to visit the continent, it would have to be now."

From a pocket, Wentworth produced a radiogram received in Paris. It was terse:

> RETURN AT ONCE. STOP. URGENT BUSINESS
> REQUIRING YOUR ATTENTION.
>
> NITA

A wealthy man, Wentworth had no business to speak of. Only investments. But in his other self, he had dealings that might be considered business—the business of crime and retribution!

For Richard Wentworth was the man who stalked New York City in the black robes feared by the Law and the lawless alike as… The *Spider!*

A relentless foe of crime, he struck where the authorities could not, branding his kills with the scarlet seal of the dreaded Master of Men— a dreaded mark that mirrored the red scar that even now burned on Wentworth's troubled brow….

It had been madness, he knew, to go to Paris. But after his last battle with the underworld, Wentworth had sustained serious wounds. It had been his beloved, Nita van Sloan, who had convinced him to go alone.

"But you must, Dick," she had whispered. "You simply *must!*"

They had planned to voyage together. But the passing of an aunt in a faraway state had forced Nita to remain behind, promising to catch up. She would not hear of Wentworth postponing his trip. So he had gone on ahead.

Paris had been bleak without his beloved. Then came the summoning radiogram.

"If only I had stayed behind!" Wentworth muttered to himself.

But it was too late for recriminations, damn the luck. Some dire eventuality had sprung up to menace his city and to that urgent tocsin, Wentworth had responded. As he always did.

Nita would not of course specify what had transpired. To do so might have alerted prying eyes to Wentworth's true reasons for returning home.

The ship's newspaper provided the only clues. There had been a spate of grisly murders. Strangulations, the press had dubbed them. But even the spare accounts carried by the modest paper suggested something more sinister than the work of a fiend with a mania for murder.

With the illuminated spires of the city now showing off to port, Wentworth snapped his cigarette lighter alight and applied the hot bluish flame to the flimsy radiogram. The yellow onionskin flared up in his hands and he released the curling ash to the ocean breeze. Carried aloft, it dwindled to a red spark and winked out.

Turning, Wentworth called to a passing steward.

"My man, how soon do we dock?"

"Thirty minutes, sir."

Thirty minutes. An eternity. The three-day crossing had seemed like an age. And with every passing minute, another blue-faced corpse might be discovered....

At last, the *Hypnotic* docked. The gangplank was lowered and Richard Wentworth was the first to disembark. A crisp twenty dollar bill had insured that.

Ronald Jackson and Ram Singh were waiting for him, their features set and drawn. These were the trusted servants of Richard Wentworth... and his other self. Jackson wore chauffeur's grey livery with the same snap of his old sergeant's army uniform, while Ram was resplendent in tunic and turban.

"What news?" rapped out Wentworth as he stepped into the rear of his idling Daimler town car.

"Twelve dead so far," Jackson returned crisply, "All types. Men. Women. Children."

"Children!" snapped Wentworth.

"*Han,* sahib," inserted Ram Singh, dark beard bristling. "The youngest was but three years of age."

Wentworth's knuckles whitened. "Where is Nita?"

"She prowls, Sahib, in your stead."

"She has become the Black Widow?"

"When the first kid was killed," Jackson called from the driver's compartment, "she felt it was her solemn duty, sir."

"Brave Nita," murmured Wentworth.

Jackson flung the Daimler into traffic. The night was cool, but pleasant. The windows stood open. And thus they heard the screams—choking, ominous screams.

"Sounds like it's coming from the baggage claim area!" Jackson cried, slamming on the brakes.

Wentworth was out of the machine before the car body ceased rocking. Like a man possessed, he lunged into the milling throng, pushing past squirming bodies until he reached the disembarkation area.

A crowd was forming around something. No, not forming! Shrinking! They were obeying the opposite instinct that causes humanity to gather around a tragedy.

Pushing through them, Wentworth made his way to the center of all the fear-struck attention.

A woman lay in a litter of luggage—steamer trunks and hat boxes. Apparently her own. She wore a smart evening frock and a veiled hat. Stooping, Wentworth lifted the latter.

The features beneath were a cobalt blue. The woman's tongue, once so pink, had turned a livid purple. Her features were contorted with agony, the agony of a person who had been *strangled*.

But when Wentworth examined her neck, there were no signs of manual strangulation.

"The devil!" he said. Standing up, he asked, "Did anyone see what happened here? Speak up! This poor woman is dead!"

A matron volunteered, "She—she just collapsed and began clawing at her throat, making the most awful sounds you could imagine! It was horrible!"

Everyone agreed that it had been horrible. But no one had seen the person or agency that had committed the atrocity.

With steely grey-blue eyes, Wentworth scanned the milling throng. Most were turning away from the ghastly tableau. Many were already in flight.

"Ram Singh, did you see anything suspicious?" Wentworth demanded.

"Only that which lies at your feet, Sahib."

A moment later, an official limousine pulled up. Out stepped a familiar face.

"Dick!" cried Police Commissioner Stanley Kirkpatrick, his mustache points twitching in anger. "What on earth are you doing here?"

"I only just disembarked. As you know, I have been abroad."

Kirkpatrick stepped over to the body and gazed downward with eyes that were hard from too much police work.

"Do you know this woman, Dick?"

"Only by sight. I recognize her as a fellow passenger."

"I see," Kirkpatrick said thinly.

Wentworth stiffened. Long friends, he and Kirk were both upholders of the law. But it was long suspected that criminologist Richard Wentworth was in actuality the feared *Spider*.

"I suppose you suspect The *Spider* of this atrocity," Wentworth said coolly, lighting a fresh cigarette.

"He has been seen on several occasions of late. Seen, Dick, in your *absence*." Kirkpatrick's tone was pointed.

"I trust that lays to rest any lingering suspicions you might have about me, old man," Wentworth drawled.

"Tell me, Dick, why have you returned from Europe so soon?"

"A mere whim," Wentworth said carelessly. "I found Paris tedious."

Kirkpatrick said nothing. His even white teeth worried his lower lip carefully. "This poor woman is number thirteen," he said at last.

Wentworth asked, "What do you make of it?"

"In all cases thus far, police scientists have concluded that death resulted from acute asphyxiation, not strangulation, despite the evidence before your eyes."

"I myself noticed no ligature marks," Wentworth offered.

"There are none, Dick. Gases found in the blood were consistent with death by carbon monoxide poisoning."

"Carbon monoxide?" Wentworth said. "But this woman succumbed in open air. Carbon monoxide poisoning requires a confined space for the lethal gas to build up to deadly tolerances! Furthermore, such victims display a roseate complexion, not a cyanotic one."

"But there you have it, Dick. Why I and my detectives are baffled. Baffled, I tell you."

Wentworth blew out a cloud of bluish smoke. "Is there any definite pattern to these murders?"

"None. The victims do not know one another, except in a few instances that suggest common coincidence. The newspapers are calling these the Blue Reaper Murders."

"This Blue Reaper, what can his objective be?"

"If he has one," snapped Kirkpatrick harshly, "he has not yet communicated it to the police."

A lean-cheeked man stepped into the light. He looked down at the blue-faced corpse and seemed to shudder.

"Another one..."

"Dick, meet Dorsett Knowles, my new secretary."

Wentworth eyed the man appraisingly. "Curious that you should also happen along," he suggested in a cool voice. "Both of you. This unfortunate woman just met her demise moments ago."

"We planned to meet for dinner," Kirkpatrick explained, "when we noticed the commotion."

"I know a wonderful seafood restaurant on these docks," Knowles added. "Would you care to join us, Wentworth?"

"I'm sorry. I have only lately arrived from Paris. Accept my regrets." Turning to Kirkpatrick, Wentworth added, "I am at your service in this vicious matter, Kirk."

"Thank you, Dick. I will be in touch."

With that, Richard Wentworth took his leave.

Back in the Daimler, Wentworth directed Jackson to drive directly to his Sutton Place residence.

"Nita has done me a service by appearing in the *Spider's* robes," he said. "Kirkpatrick's suspicions are momentarily allayed."

"They don't stay allayed very long," Jackson reminded as he trod the accelerator.

"True, but—" Wentworth's gaze fell to his hands. He raised them to the ever-shifting light of passing street lamps.

"Curious..."

"What is it, Sahib Wentworth?" asked Ram Singh.

"My fingers... Do they not appear... *Bluish*...?"

Even as Wentworth looked at them, the blue coloring seemed to fade.

"Did Kirkpatrick notice that?" Jackson wondered.

"I failed to observe it myself."

"Perhaps it is the Major's imagination," Jackson suggested.

"Perhaps," Wentworth mused. "Perhaps not. I wonder if the police reached any of these blue-faced corpses in time to touch them while an azure residue yet lingered on their dead features....?"

"Blue faces are the result of asphyxiation," Jackson put in. "Not residue."

"In this instance," Wentworth said evenly, "it may mean more— much more. Home, Jackson. Step on it!"

But Richard Wentworth was not destined to reach home that evening. As his town car wended its way through Manhattan traffic, the keening of police sirens began filling the air, bringing the heads of passersby turning in alarm. For by now, the specter of the Blue Reaper had all of the city's populace on edge.

First one siren called out. Then another. Before a minute had passed, two more joined in.

"Jackson, follow those police sirens!" Wentworth commanded, shucking off his coat. From a door pocket, he extracted a brace of automatics in crossed shoulder holsters. This he donned. Removing his pistols, he checked both magazines and jacked a round in each chamber. Then he drew his coat over the reholstered weapons.

Presently, Jackson had maneuvered the Daimler to keep pace with a hurtling police machine. Wentworth rolled down his window.

"Murdock!" he called over. "What is the trouble?"

"They got The *Spider* cornered! Over in Little Italy!"

"We will follow."

Rolling up the glass, Wentworth said bitterly, "The police think they have snared The *Spider,* but in reality it is Nita who lies in their gun sights."

"*Wallah!*" cried Ram Singh. "Verily, we will succor her. Or die in the attempt."

"We're with you, Major," Jackson seconded.

"Thank you both. But it will take a spider to save a spider."

Pressing a button caused the seat back to revolve. Wentworth got busy. He donned the ebon habiliments of the Master of Men. A black mask went over his eyes. Canine fangs extended his front teeth. A floppy black hat completed the sinister ensemble.

Richard Wentworth was once again The *Spider!*

"Jackson, try to find a more direct way there," he said in the harsh tonality the underworld knew and feared.

The doughty aide wheeled the town car down a side street and across several busy intersections.

As they approached Little Italy, Wentworth saw that searchlights were already in place. These sent up clawing white fingers to the rooftops. They probed, crossed and moved on.

A dark figure flitted among those questing beams—a hunched thing in a fluttering black cape.

"There she is!" Jackson cried.

"Let me out here!" Wentworth urged. The door snapped open and out vaulted the dreaded silhouette instantly recognized as The *Spider*!

Wentworth dived into an alley, unseen. Scrambling over a broken fence, he worked his way toward the police cordon. All the time his grey-blue eyes raked the skyline.

This was a slum area. Scheduled to be torn down and replaced with apartment buildings. It was a rabbit warren of deserted hovels—a maze of death for any who entered.

The *Spider*—the true *Spider*—knew that the police would be hesitant to blindly barge into that death trap. But he knew also that Nita could not escape the dragnet without assistance.

As he reached the outskirts of the police cordon, The *Spider* unlimbered his automatics.

There was only one way to help Nita, trapped on those rooftops, and that was to give the officers of the Law a different target.

For some moments, Wentworth watched from the void of a side street, unnoticed.

The searchlights continued their unrelenting questing about. A minute passed and no sign of the fugitive *Spider* could be discerned.

This was the moment.

Stepping out from the alley, The *Spider* stood in the pool of a street lamp. Aiming both guns, he selected two upright standards and called out.

"Why do you seek me up there? The Spider is here among you!"

Both automatics bucked in his hands. Their lead clanged off two adjoining street standards. Hollow iron rang like struck bells.

And The *Spider* laughed!

The police turned in shocked surprise, their guns swiveling. The searchlights momentarily paused, frozen in fear.

Again The *Spider* laughed. That drew the last searching attention to the spot where he stood. Then he melted back into the alley ahead of a rain of bullets that peppered and pocketed the surroundings.

Someone bellowed, "There he goes!"

"Surround that building! He's down here. Get him!"

Like a pack of blue wolves, the police broke into a panicked run. Fearful of The *Spider*, their sheer numbers gave them courage. They descended upon the alley, choking it.

Somewhere above their heads, The *Spider* laughed again—flat, metallic and mockingly.

Bullets stormed upward, chipping brick and sending down a rain of jangling window glass.

A floppy hat floated down with it, riddled with bullets holes.

A sergeant picked it up and fingered the felt. "No blood," he said, cursing. "We have him cornered. Into that building, men! Cut off all escape!"

The building was swiftly surrounded.

But when they pounded up the staircase, they were met with no resistance.

No one noticed the cloaked form leap from the roof parapet to that of the abutting building....

Removing his cape, The *Spider* pocketed his mask and celluloid fangs.

When he emerged onto the street, he was Richard Wentworth,

unchallenged scion of wealth. His cooling automatics hung snug under his immaculate evening clothes.

Wentworth walked carefully back to his town car. Getting in, he said quietly, "Circle the block. If I know Nita—"

They all knew Nita. So they were not surprised when they discovered her walking down a street in a dark sports frock and no hat.

Wentworth drew up, calling cheerily, "Going my way, darling?"

Nita turned. A radiant smile lit up her charming features. "Why, Dick! How thoughtful of you to come pick me up."

"I understood you were in a spot of trouble. Out late without an escort and all that."

Wentworth emerged to open the door and ushered her in.

Back inside, he ordered, "Home, Jackson. Discreetly."

The Daimler lunged ahead, but at the cross street, it was blocked by a police machine. The official car of Commissioner Kirkpatrick.

"Drat!" said Nita.

"Nothing for it but to make explanations," Wentworth undertoned. Stepping out, he called, "Hi, Kirk. I see you have arrived in time to see The *Spider* brought to book."

Kirkpatrick emerged, scowling. "I thought you were on your way home."

"And I thought that you were dining on lobster and clams," Wentworth rejoined.

"Duty called me from the supper table."

"My curiosity got the better of my fatigue, Kirk," smiled Wentworth. "I had to see this with my own eyes. I imagine they have him by now."

"We shall soon see." Kirkpatrick spied Nita van Sloan in the shadows of the rear seat. "Where the deuce did you come from?"

Nita smiled bravely. "It's nice to see you too, Kirk," she managed.

"We chanced to happen upon Miss van Sloan on our way to the festivities," Wentworth supplied suavely.

The police official frowned. "Quite a coincidence, her being in this down-at-heels neighborhood."

Wentworth quirked his eyebrows up in mock humor. "Why, Commissioner Kirkpatrick. You are not accusing my fiancée of being the notorious *Spider*! Are you?"

"Of course not! Confound it, Dick. I was merely observing the oddity of the situation."

"Where The *Spider* walks, the odd follows, I imagine," Wentworth drawled. "Shall we see if your men in blue have bagged the beast yet?"

They pulled up a minute later near the cordoned-off building.

"Somehow The *Spider* got out of that tenement and appeared on this spot," a sergeant was explaining. "We chased him into this building. But all we found of him was this." He displayed the bullet-riddled black hat.

While Kirkpatrick was examining the hat for labels, Wentworth surreptitiously dropped his black mask and celluloid fangs in the gutter, then pretended to discover them.

"Kirk, here are more trophies of the bounder."

Kirkpatrick strode over and picked up the cluster of objects. He eyed the bewildered sergeant. "How did you miss this?"

"What I am wondering," said Wentworth, "is how The *Spider* managed to get past your dragnet to this spot, only to evade capture once again?"

"Just what I was thinking, too," Kirkpatrick muttered darkly. "It is almost as if there are two *Spiders*."

"I would think one was more than enough," Wentworth returned.

But Kirkpatrick's scowl only deepened.

"Well, better luck next time. We must be off."

Kirkpatrick grabbed his arm. "I would search your pockets, Dick," he said, "but I imagine you have emptied them in some matter."

Wentworth laughed carelessly. "I always travel light."

Nita joined in, asking, "Would you like me to submit to a search, Kirk?" Her eyes danced mischievously.

Kirkpatrick gave a deep harrumph and stalked off.

Wentworth rejoined his lady. "Better not to provoke Kirk, darling. By the way, what did you do with your garments?"

"I was forced to leave them in the stairwell of that dank old firetrap." Nita shuddered lightly.

"You burned them, of course..."

"There was no time, dear. When I saw that I could make my escape, I dashed for safety."

"Pity. If the police find them, they will begin to think that there are two *Spiders*, and my leaving hat, mask and fangs will look triply suspicious..."

She leaned her chestnut curls on his shoulder. "I'm sorry, Dick."

The Daimler began working through traffic, powerful motor purring.

"What did you discover, Nita?" asked Wentworth.

"Precious little. There was a report in the paper that a tramp was killed in that tenement. I thought I would search for clues. I found only... this."

From a pocket, she produced a wooden handle. It was affixed to a bit of metal and had been broken off.

"What does this suggest to you, Dick?"

"A hand-action pump. Possibly off a flit gun used for spraying insects..."

"Nasty things," Nita said. "Then it is nothing."

"It might be everything. As I disembarked, there was another Blue Reaper killing. A woman. Her face had turned blue... and some of it appeared to have come off on my fingers."

"Impossible! Cyanotic poisoning produces a change in skin color through chemical reactions in the blood. It would never rub off. Never!"

"Well, it's gone now," Wentworth said thoughtfully. "But I would like to subject my fingers to chemical tests once we are safely home."

"I can think of better ways to while away the first evening since we parted," pouted Nita.

"As can I. But tonight, our duty calls..."

Far into the night, Wentworth labored while Nita read him accounts from the file of newspaper clippings that had piled up in his absence.

"The first victim was a common streetwalker," Nita was saying.

"Chosen no doubt as a test," said Wentworth as he dipped both hands into an astringent solution, then poured the contents into a series of flasks for analysis.

"Next, a police officer was felled on his beat."

"To show that the Blue Reaper was not afraid of the authorities."

"He was not dubbed the Blue Reaper until the third and fourth victims were found in their cars on lover's lane," Nita recited.

"Victims of circumstance or opportunity," said Wentworth as he lighted various Bunsen burners and began heating up solution samples. Soon he had a precipitate, which he poured off and examined under a microscope slide.

"I do not recognize these grains," Wentworth said under his breath. "But no doubt they are significant."

"After that," continued Nita, "the pace of the murders began picking up. Sometimes three in one evening. There seems to be no pattern."

"There is always a pattern," snapped Wentworth impatiently. Catching himself, he softened his voice. "My apologies, Nita. It's just that every minute that drags by, the greater the chance that—"

Ram Singh came in with a morning paper.

"Sahib, the evil one has issued a challenge."

Ripping the paper out of the Sikh's hand, Wentworth scanned the front page with blazing eyes.

BLUE REAPER ANNOUNCES NEXT VICTIM

This newspaper has received a letter purporting to be from the mysterious Blue Reaper, scourge of Manhattan. In it, he claims that he is done with striking down persons of low station in life. That his next victim will be a man of high standing, a bulwark of the city, and by robbing him of life, he will move on to his true objective. This objective was not specified in the letter.

There was more, but it was all sensationalistic conjecture.

"As I was saying," Wentworth continued, "there is always a pattern. Now it has shifted to the Blue Reaper's true purpose. He intends to strike down Commissioner Kirkpatrick. There can be no other meant by those carefully-couched words."

"Not Kirk!" gasped Nita.

"Yes. But The *Spider* will counter that stroke with every fiber in his being." Wrenching off his lab smock, Wentworth bit out, "This experiment can wait."

"I await your command, Sahib."

"No. Ram Singh. All of you will await me here. Where The *Spider* walks, he walks alone…"

Nita cried out, "But Dick. You haven't yet slept!"

"I will sleep when I am victorious, or I am dead," he intoned bitterly.

So saying, Richard Wentworth went to a spare room where he once more donned the gloomy habiliments of the Master of Men.

A half hour found him lurking near Commissioner Kirkpatrick's suburban home, behind the wheel of a battered coupe he used when in the guise of The *Spider*. Its black-painted hood concealed a motor of tremendous power.

Hat squashed low over a lank wig, eyes glinting like knife blades, The *Spider* watched as dawn crept over the well-manicured grounds.

Wentworth knew his old friend's morning routine. Up at five. Breakfast. Then his chauffeur drove him into the city.

This time, that elegant limousine would have a shadow trailing behind it.…

At exactly 5:45, the garage door stood open and the long machine came sliding out. It eased onto the maple-lined street and Wentworth fell in behind it.

If the Blue Reaper struck, he might strike at any time, from any direction. Wentworth's eyes gleaned with eager anticipation, his slit mouth a-grin with the lust for combat.

Well did The *Spider* love battle. Great was his thirst for the blood of criminals. Perhaps this day that thirst would be slaked....

Five miles along, the limousine roared up a ramp onto the George Washington Bridge. Wentworth wheeled after it, keeping his pace brisk, but not noticeable.

On the bridge, a yellow taxicab swept out of parallel traffic and began to pace Kirkpatrick's car. Abruptly, it raced ahead and swerved to block it.

The limousine braked to a shuddery halt.

"It's come!" Wentworth gritted. He charged ahead, came around the limousine and slammed into the cab.

From out of every door billowed men in blue. Uniformed police officers! Was this a ruse? Police Positives began lifting in his direction. It lacked full light, but even in this early hour, the black mask of The *Spider* would be visible against Wentworth's tanned features.

Wentworth threw his machine into reverse. Bucking, the car came around, tires smoking hot.

Other machines surged up, surrounding him. Men in blue and plainclothes detectives known to him emerged, weapons drawn. A shot was fired into the air. A warning shot. The next would stab through his windshield, The *Spider* knew.

"Halt! Halt or I will shoot!" barked a burly detective.

Blocked, Wentworth slammed forward, throwing his front bumper into the concrete guard rail. There were curtains on every window. Hastily, he drew them all closed.

Swiftly, the battered black coupe was surrounded by men of the Law. A dozen guns—two!—bristled from white-knuckled fists. And every muzzle was trained on the blocked black machine.

Kirkpatrick levered his tall form from the limousine and took charge of the situation.

"We have him boxed tight, Commissioner," the lead detective

reported. "Shall we open fire?"

"Not yet." Kirk cupped his hands before his mouth. "*Spider*! Come out now and my men will not riddle your machine. Do you hear me, *Spider*?"

A silence lingered. Then came the flat mocking tones of the Master of Men, laughing at the Law!

"It's no use, Commissioner. He doesn't want be taken alive."

"So be it," said Kirkpatrick heavily.

Suddenly, there was a sound. A sharp report, like a gunshot.

On the side by the guard rail, through an open window, flashed an ebony apparition.

It resembled a great black bat's wing shooting out of the car and over the rail.

The pealing laughter ceased.

Police surged for the rail, bent over it. Below, they saw... *nothing!*

"I don't see him," Kirk thundered. "Did he fall?"

"He jumped."

Then a man noticed something. A stout line anchored to the inner door handle of the open window. It projected out to the rail and over it, taut as catgut.

Looking down, they could not see where it went, only that it disappeared in the morning mist.

"Jumped!" Kirkpatrick bellowed. "He anchored his *Spider's* Web and made his escape. Send men down among the girders. He's probably crawling along them like his infernal namesake!"

Officers scrambled. A police boat was summoned. The girder work was inspected and traversed as carefully as safety permitted.

But of The *Spider*, there was no living trace...

Finally, with the morning fully alive, the battered coupe was towed to the impound lot. There it was thoroughly searched for clues, but nothing was found to point to an owner. And of course, there was no sign of The *Spider* within.

An hour after the last detective had finished with the coupe, the cushions of the rear seat began to move. They fell forward, and out rolled The *Spider*, uncloaked but intact, from a concealed recess. He had, in the fashion of Houdini, gathered himself into a human ball so compact that no searcher dreamed of looking under the rear seat.

Carefully, the *Spider* climbed over the front seat and slid behind the wheel. Eyes reconnoitering the lot, the sinister figure waited until all seemed deserted. Then, after bringing the motor to muttering life, he eased the inconspicuous machine out of the lot. It was unguarded. For who would waste time watching an abandoned automobile?

Grimly, Wentworth drove to a walkup room he kept in reserve for emergencies. There he claimed the telephone and put in a call to his residence.

"Jackson, it was a police trap," he said harshly.

"Are you certain, Major?"

"Unless the Blue Reaper is one of Kirkpatrick's men, the entire charade was a ruse to flush The *Spider* out of hiding." Wentworth halted.

"Yes?" asked Jackson.

"I am beginning to wonder about the Commissioner's new secretary, Knowles."

"He has a good reputation. Comes from an upstanding family."

"Murder madness knows no class distinction," Wentworth countered. "Jackson, come pick me up. Perhaps we will change our strategy…"

Twenty minutes later, Wentworth had settled into the luxurious rear compartment of his Daimler town car.

Jackson was asking, "How did you ever escape the police?"

"By a simple stratagem. To jump into the river would be fatal, I knew. So I made the police think that I did. Affixing one end of my Web to my cloak and the other to the door handle, I fired my cape with a compressed air pistol, so that it cleared the rail. I employed dart to carry the cloak."

Jackson nodded. "The radio said they found the cloak. And assumed The *Spider* plunged to his death."

"The authorities will not suffer under that delusion for very long," vowed Wentworth. "For The *Spider* has much work to do. Where is Nita?"

"She returned to her apartment this morning."

"Take me there, Jackson."

Moments later, they were trying to calm Nita's French maid.

"Three men came," she sobbed out. "They were wearing overcoats. They took Miss Nita away. I-I could not stop them. They pushed me to the floor."

"What men?" Wentworth bit out. "Describe them!"

The frightened maid did the best she could, but from her description, they were three faceless hulking ruffians who could have emerged from any underworld dive.

"This sounds like the Blue Reaper's work, damn him!" Wentworth cried.

"That means that he has a gang," growled Jackson.

"We have much to do. Our first stop, the Commissioner's office. I must inform Kirkpatrick of my suspicions."

When Wentworth arrived at police headquarters, he was ushered into the office of the Commissioner without hindrance.

"I knew you would come," said Kirk heavily. "Dick, I had to do it. There was no other choice before me."

"What the devil are you talking about?" Wentworth asked, peeling off his white morning gloves.

"You know what. Three of my men took Nita van Sloan into custody this morning."

Wentworth reeled back as if from the force of a physical blow. "Arrest Nita? Why?"

"On suspicion of being The *Spider*!"

Wentworth almost laughed. He stifled the impulse, grew grave. "On what grounds, Kirk?"

"The *Spider's* robes and other tools were discovered on the stairwell where he had been holed up. These included a black mask and fake fangs and battered slouch hat—the very objects discovered at the location where I met you last night. Some of them found by you," Kirkpatrick added pointedly.

With studied casualness, Wentworth tapped a cigarette against his silver case, took it in his mouth and lighted the end with the platinum lighter which contained the vermilion seals with which The *Spider* branded his kills.

"Surely, Kirk, The *Spider* carried spares…"

"You were not seen near that building, but Nita was. I have an eyewitness."

"Nita—The *Spider*. You can't be serious, old top."

"Unless you are willing to confess to the crimes laid at his doorstep, Nita van Sloan will have to suffice," Kirkpatrick said gravely.

"She has an excellent alibi."

"And I have a witness."

"Who?"

"Dorsett Knowles. He spied her coming out of the cordoned-off building."

Wentworth scowled. "Knowles! What was he doing there?"

"He followed me from the restaurant, but must have gotten lost en route."

Wentworth asked sharply, "Kirk, what do you know of Knowles' background?"

"His credentials are impeccable, and you are changing the subject."

"I would like to speak to Knowles. Hear his account from his own lips."

"He has not yet arrived for work," returned Kirkpatrick.

Wentworth glanced at his watch. "Late in the morning, isn't it?"

"That is hardly your affair, Dick. Now would you care to see Nita? Provided the detectives are through questioning her?"

"Yes, I—"

The desk telephone rang peremptorily. Kirkpatrick snatched it up, spoke briefly. "What! Are you certain?" He slammed down the receiver and thumbed the desk annunciator.

"Get a squad together! Dorsett Knowles has been kidnapped!"

Wentworth started. "Kidnapped!"

"Yes, by the Blue Reaper."

"Preposterous! Why, in God's name?"

"That remains to be learned. Are you seeing Nita or not?"

"I will accompany you, if you do not mind. I am keenly interested in this kidnapping."

They rode to the scene together, Jackson following in the Daimler.

"I suspect Dorsett Knowles of being the Blue Reaper, Kirk," Wentworth said suddenly.

"Madness!" fumed Kirkpatrick. "The man is of the finest stock. A sportsman."

"Working as your confidential secretary?"

"He is dedicated to his job. Police work suits him."

They drew up before the Fifth Avenue building where Knowles had an apartment.

The door had been smashed in. There was a houseboy. Filipino. Possibly Japanese. It was difficult to say, for his features were now blue and contorted, his tongue sticking out of his mouth like a lavender viper.

The quarters were exotic and showed certain signs of a man who had roamed the world, visiting foreign lands. Trophies covered every wall. One room was given over to live specimens. Toucans and parrots paced in their cages. Serpents slithered under glass. Tropical fish swam in boxy glass aquariums.

"Knowles brought back many unusual animals from afar," Kirkpatrick explained. "Most were given to zoos. But he kept others."

Wentworth discovered a corner where insects were kept. He noted tarantulas, and other more venomous spiders under glass. They scuttled and jumped at his approach.

"Why would the Blue Reaper kidnap Knowles?" he asked suddenly.

"To follow through on this threat letter, of course!" retorted Kirkpatrick hotly. "Did you fail to read the morning papers?"

"Of course I read them!" Wentworth hurled back. "You mean to say that letter was not a police trap for The *Spider*?"

"No! It appears to be genuine."

"Then why did you have your men follow you to work?"

"Because we assumed that the Reaper intended to strike me down."

"Instead you captured The *Spider*," Wentworth sneered.

"Yes. Thank Heaven for that much."

"Kirk, you cannot possibly believe that Nita van Sloan is The *Spider*."

"We have an eyewitness who places her at the scene where The *Spider* was surrounded," Kirkpatrick reminded.

"But Nita—it's preposterous!"

"The *Spider* has often been connected to Richard Wentworth. But you assert that you are not The *Spider*. And you have an iron clad alibi for the times he has been at large these last few weeks."

"True, but—"

"The *Spider* wears a lank wig as part of his disguise. What better way to conceal the flowing hair of a woman?"

Wentworth said hotly, "Then why not accuse Jackson, or for that matter Jenkyns, my butler?" Tapping on a glass case where a cluster of spiders had spun a gauzy web, he observed, "Or Dorsett Knowles?"

Kirkpatrick frowned. "We have our man—or should I say our woman. I must return to my office to call out the dragnet. I imagine that you will want to see Nita—assuming that my detectives are through questioning her and she has not already confessed."

Wentworth winced.

At police headquarters, Richard Wentworth was taken to the dim-lit holding cell where Nita van Sloan was being held temporarily.

Her face was wan, but lit up at sight of him.

"Oh, Dick…"

"Nita, are you all right?"

"They have not broken me, if that's what you mean."

"Nita, dearest, if it comes to it, I will… tell Kirk the entire truth."

"No, Dick! You mustn't! It will mean the electric chair. So many capital crimes are laid at The *Spider's* door."

"I can't allow you to face the same fate. You know that."

"To spare you, I will walk barefoot through the coals of Hell itself," Nita breathed. "But tonight I will be transferred to... The Tombs."

"Buck up. I will find a way to free you. Count on it. But for now, *adieu.*"

They kissed in farewell. Wentworth called for a turnkey.

Minutes later, Wentworth was back in Kirkpatrick's office.

"I must warn you," he drawled. "Nita has an excellent lawyer."

"She will need him. For there will be no bail in this matter."

"Kirk, tell me what you know of Dorsett Knowles?"

"He comes from the finest stock. A world traveler in his youth. Africa. Asia. The Amazon. Cut quite a figure in his day. But he has grown older and wishes for a more sensible career. A family friend recommended him highly. He shows a talent for police work and I find him invaluable."

"Does it not seem strange to you that the Blue Reaper has suddenly turned to kidnapping?"

Kirkpatrick shook his head slowly. "He promised to strike at someone of substance, and now he has. As for the kidnapping, we don't know that Knowles is not already dead."

"It does not fit the Reaper's pattern, Kirk!" Wentworth said savagely. "Can't you see that?"

"This is no pattern!" Kirkpatrick snapped. "This Reaper is a madman bent on pointless slaughter."

"I trust you won't mind if I look into this in my own way?"

"What can you uncover that my own men cannot, Dick?" Kirkpatrick demanded.

"I do not yet know. But I have enjoyed remarkable luck in the past, as we both know."

Kirkpatrick fell silent. Wentworth took his leave.

Outside in his town car, Wentworth directed Jackson, "Home. I wish to resume my laboratory work. For I have uncovered a fresh clue."

"What about Miss Nita?"

"If necessary, The *Spider* will win her freedom by force."

"But why would The *Spider* do that? Wouldn't that implicate her in his affairs?"

Wentworth sunk into the cushions. "You have a point, Jackson. But the *Spider* will not allow Nita to languish in durance vile for long. But first I must confirm my new suspicions…"

Fortified with black coffee laced with brandy, Wentworth resumed his tests. Under the microscope, the precipitate in solution assumed startling characteristics.

He consulted books on botany, lethal poisons, exotic plants. Nowhere did he discover a chemical match.

Undaunted, Wentworth pressed on, muttering, "The secret is in this solution. I know it is. I will not rest until…"

Ram Singh entered then.

"Sahib," he said, bowing. "A report issued forth from the radio that one Dorsett Knowles was discovered blue of face and without life."

"Where?"

"Central Park. By the frog pond."

Wentworth's face darkened. "Why on earth would the Blue Reaper…"

Wentworth reached the scene in time to witness the sheeted corpse being loaded into a Black Maria.

Kirkpatrick was there, smoking furiously. "What of your suspicions now?" he said brusquely.

"Are you certain it was Knowles?" countered Wentworth.

"Do I not know my own man?" Kirkpatrick flung back bitterly.

"I wonder if I could examine the body?"

"Good God! Have you turned ghoul?"

"No, of course not."

Kirkpatrick relented. "After the medical examiner," he said at last. "For now, the Blue Reaper has fourteen dead to his reckoning."

Heavily, Commissioner Kirkpatrick turned away.

Under his breath, Wentworth muttered, "Fourteen slain and The *Spider* has yet to fire a shot…"

That night, the black robed *Spider* prowled the underworld. He went to great pains not to be seen. Nor was he. A prowler chanced to spy him on his nightly rounds. The man was in the act of burgling a modest home in Queens.

The *Spider* fell upon him, and they struggled. A knife came out. It caught the moonlight, gleaming in the pristine light, and then sought The *Spider's* vitals.

A black-gloved hand seized the wrist, captured it, and inexorably the knife wavered in between two struggling victims.

When it found lodgment in warm flesh, the prowler groaned once and expired.

The *Spider* walked free, unreported.

Burning like a red-hot brand on the dead felon's forehead was the seal of The *Spider*… proof that he walked free.

Beyond the midnight hour a black shadow flitted in the vicinity of the castle-like city jail known as the Tombs.

Slipping over a wall unseen, The *Spider* crept up to one set of barred windows, high on the third floor. Removing his Web from under his concealing robes, he cast a line up, and caught something solid. Then he began to scale the sheer stone walls.

Reaching an iron barred window, he traced a circle of glass with a diamond cutter, removed it, and began whispering words to the person on the bunk within. The exchange was soft, low, yet urgent. A small covered basket no larger than a human hand passed within…

When it was over, The *Spider* slid down his Web until his heels clicked on concrete. With a flip, he freed the Web from its anchor and coiled it back inside his cape.

The mute moon witnessed his departure. No one else did.…

As the night wore on, other victims continued to mount.

A nighthawk taxi driver found slumped at his wheel, cobalt-faced, his fare nowhere in sight. When a subway train pulled into the last stop of the IRT line, the doors opened and three passengers failed to get off. They were discovered slumped in their seats, faces blue, purple tongues lolling out like those of unslaked dogs.

The Blue Reaper had initiated a carnival of slaughter!

The next morning, Wentworth put in another appearance at police headquarters.

"I have brought flowers for Nita," he announced.

Kirkpatrick glowered. "Violets! I would have expected roses at the very least."

"Nita is partial to violets," Wentworth returned. "And blueberries. I regret that I failed to acquire the latter."

Kirkpatrick accepted the bouquet. "I will have them sent over."

"Thank you. Now about the body of Knowles…"

"The autopsy won't be held until later this afternoon. You may see the remains if you think it useful. I will write you a pass."

Inscribing something on a notepad, Kirkpatrick ripped off a sheet and handed it to Wentworth, who bowed solemnly.

"I will naturally report any findings directly," he promised.

At the City Morgue, the attendant rolled out the body and carefully folded back the sheet.

"Ghastly," said the man, who was no doubt otherwise inured to death.

"This is a rare hue of blue," Wentworth observed. He touched the cold features, then examined his fingertips. Seeing no trace of residue or dye, he stripped the sheet further.

The pale form of Dorsett Knowles was fundamentally lifeless. Of that, there was no doubt. Still Wentworth applied one ear to the motionless chest but detected no heartbeat.

"He's been dead since yesterday," the attendant pointed out.

"I prefer to be certain. Have you never heard of catalepsy?"

"This man is scheduled to be autopsied, Mr. Wentworth."

"Then let us trust that he is as dead as he seems to be," said Wentworth, lifting one blue wrist to feel for a pulse. There was none.

"You may restore the body to its former state," he concluded, walking away.

The sheet went back over the body and the drawer rolled shut with a final rumble and clang.

From a telephone booth, Wentworth called Kirkpatrick's office.

"I have found nothing," he reported, his voice tinged with bitterness.

"I trust, then, that you have absolved my late secretary of being the Blue Reaper?" Kirkpatrick returned sardonically.

Wentworth hesitated, the admission clogging in his throat. "Evidence is lacking," he allowed. "Just as there is no admissible proof that Nita van Sloan is the *Spider*!"

What Stanley Kirkpatrick would have retorted went forever unrecorded. For an interruption pulled him from the phone. Wentworth heard a low, urgent exchange. He pressed the receiver to his ear, but gained nothing by it.

The Commissioner's voice came back, charged with emotion. "Dick! Return to headquarters at once. It's Nita!"

"Nita! What?"

"I fear the Blue Reaper has struck again…."

An ambulance was parked outside the monstrous pile of masonry that was the Tombs in lower Manhattan. Two attendants were wheeling out a gurney, on which was a sheeted form.

Commissioner Kirkpatrick's official limousine trundled up, and out stepped Kirkpatrick and Richard Wentworth, faces etched in lines of deep concern.

Kirkpatrick strode up and stopped the gurney before it could be loaded in the back of the ambulance.

"What happened?" he demanded.

The warden stepped up to do the necessary explanations.

"The prisoner was found in her cell in this gruesome condition," he reported.

Wentworth yanked off the covering sheet.

Exposed were the delicate features of Nita van Sloan, dyed a disagreeable shade of blue, her tongue protruding horribly from her cyanotic lips, the organ of taste itself the color of blueberries....

"My God!" Kirkpatrick choked, turning away from the sight.

"Still breathing," Wentworth said swiftly. "Hurry, men. Get her to Mercy Hospital at once. There may yet be time to save her!"

The ambulance attendants rolled the still patient into the waiting vehicle, clapped the rear door shut and, siren caterwauling, the white machine raced away.

On the sidewalk, Richard Wentworth faced his old friend.

"Kirk, how can you still believe that Nita is The *Spider*?"

Kirkpatrick raised his haggard face. "That is the worst example of the Blue Reaper's handiwork on record..." he said dully.

"I asked you a direct question," Wentworth pressed. "Answer me please."

"What befell Nita van Sloan," Kirkpatrick said emphatically, "only compounds her unproven guilt."

"Talk sense, man!"

"Why would the Blue Reaper dare to invade the Tombs to kill Nita, if she were not truly The *Spider*—the one person the Reaper legitimately fears?"

"On that score, you are doubly wrong," Richard Wentworth snapped.

"For there is one *other* person the Blue Reaper has sound reason to fear above all men. And I am that man!"

Lifting an imperious arm, Wentworth signaled a passing taxi and left his oldest, dearest friend standing shattered on the sidewalk....

Evening was falling as Richard Wentworth paced his library of rare works, thinking, thinking...

All criminals—even the most depraved—were possessed of sound motivations for their damnable deeds. This was no less true of the indiscriminate predator the press had branded the Blue Reaper. That his victims seemed entirely random argued against that theory, true. But deep within Wentworth nagged the insistent thought that the malefactor harbored designs that went beyond mere bloodlust.

"But what?" Wentworth muttered to himself. "What?"

Ram Singh entered, salaamed, and announced, "The autopsy of the man Knowles has been completed, Sahib. He is surely dead."

"Knowles!" Wentworth bit out angrily. "With him out of picture, I have no suspect! No trail to follow! It is maddening."

"What of the dogs of the underworld whose ears hear every foul deed?" the Sikh wondered.

Wentworth broke his nervous pacing, whirled. "I had not forgotten that the Blue Reaper might have underlings, or accomplices. But where to start?"

"We are three warriors," Ram Singh intoned. "Thou, this faithful servant and Jackson. Together we will seek them in their very lairs, wring the truth from their broken necks before we slay them all."

"Summon Jackson, then we lay plans for the night's activities...."

After evening fell, a wild moon washed over the city. Throwing luminous shadows as it climbed the beclouded sky.

The *Spider* invaded underworld haunts ranging from Grogan's to the Black Crow Tavern, guns blazing, black cape billowing like wings, a laughing Nemesis that brooked no opposition.

Criminals crumpled and withered under his ferocious onslaught. Those so unfortunate as to fall into his clutches found themselves facing a terrible black-masked face whose fangs gleamed with a fierce hunger.

At the waterfront dive known as Squid's, he seized a quivering gunman after smashing his wrist bones with brutal bullets aimed perfectly.

"Who is the Blue Reaper? Tell me quick!" The *Spider* snarled.

"I don't know! You want to ask Malloy. Mike Malloy. I heard he did a snatch job for the Reaper."

"Where is Malloy to be found?" snapped The *Spider*.

"Try Grogan's! He hangs out there. Just—just don't slay me, *Spider!* I got a mother to support!"

Preparing to attend the wake of Dorsett Knowles, Commissioner Kirkpatrick received the reports of The *Spider's* latest depredations as they came in.

"The *Spider* just busted up the Black Crow! Six dead!"

"He was seen in Chinatown, at eight sharp," another detective announced.

"Eight? That's when he busted up the Black Crow. He used a sword. Beheaded Gus the Blade on the spot when Gus yanked out his Bowie knife."

Kirkpatrick bristled. "The *Spider*! Employing a sword?"

The desk sergeant burst in. "Commissioner! Precinct Thirteen just reported that The *Spider* barged into Mercy Hospital. He planted that damned seal of his on the forehead of no less than Nita van Sloan!"

"My God!" Kirkpatrick groaned. "The *Spider* has slain Nita van Sloan…"

A new voice intruded. "That means my fiancée cannot possibly have been The *Spider*!"

Opera cloak draped over one arm, Richard Wentworth entered the room briskly.

"Dick! You heard the dreadful news?"

"More to the point, I arrived at Mercy Hospital not long after The *Spider* had left. Nita lives, thank the Lord. But The *Spider* escaped."

"Strange. The *Spider* only brands his kills…"

"Perhaps," returned Wentworth, lighting a cigarette, "The *Spider* took offense at being branded a woman, and this was his way of reclaiming his good name."

"The *Spider* has been busy tonight," Kirkpatrick said dryly. "He has raided most of the underworld hangouts."

"His motives are murky at best," nodded Wentworth, blowing out a thick cloud of bluish smoke.

"In at least one instance, he was seen in two places at the same time. And not long after that, in yet a third place," Kirkpatrick added, eyes aglow. "It is beginning to sound as if there might be two, or even *three Spiders* at large tonight."

Nonchalantly, Richard Wentworth drawled, "However many there were, I suppose it is safe to assume that Nita can be none of them? Why not release her from custody, Kirk. You cannot possibly make your asinine accusation stick, now can you?"

Not taking his eyes off his friend, Kirkpatrick picked up the desk telephone and gave the order to release Nita van Sloan as soon as she was well enough to go home.

"Thank you, Kirk. Now, about the Blue Reaper…."

"He has not struck tonight," Kirkpatrick said somberly. "And I am on the way to the wake of Dorsett Knowles."

"Perhaps I may be permitted to ride with you…."

"As you wish," Kirkpatrick said stiffly. "But be advised that I don't care to hear any more of your outrageous theories as to his guilt."

"As you wish," Wentworth said, bowing gallantly.

They traveled in the Commissioner's limousine to the Powers

Funeral Home in the Upper West Side. Pedestrians were few and strode along with furtive unease, as if in fear. Fear of the Reaper....

"I have given much thought to the Blue Reaper's motivations, Kirk," Wentworth was saying.

"Confound it! I am going to the wake of a friend."

"It is a long drive," Wentworth said calmly. "This will help pass the time. Hear me out. None of the Reaper's victims seem to be connected. Nor does profit appear to motivate his slayings. Therefore, we must look to another reason for slaughter."

Kirkpatrick sat silently.

"It occurred to me tonight that perhaps the motive was to draw out an enemy, or rival."

"Such as?'

"Such as The *Spider*!"

Kirkpatrick frowned heavily. His saturnine brow furrowed.

Wentworth resumed his theorizing. "It was the specimens in your late colleague's apartment that got me to thinking along this trend. What if the Blue Reaper has the instincts of a hunter? What if his motives were identical to that of a hunter of big game?"

"Dorsett Knowles was no Frank Buck!" Kirk snapped. "He trapped exotic birds and insects."

"We are not speaking of Knowles at present," Wentworth said coolly. "I am discussing the Blue Reaper. His letter to the press hinted that he harbored an ulterior motivation. What if his purpose was to draw out The *Spider?*"

"To what end?"

"To engage in a battle of wills. Or to snare prey. In the concrete jungles of the city The *Spider* is the most wily and cunning of all prey, is he not?"

"We have never caught him!"

"Or them," Wentworth said dryly, "since they seem to be multiplying."

"Make your point, man!"

"My point is this: In the absence of the usual criminal motives, we must therefore look for the unusual. The Blue Reaper knew that The *Spider*, fancying himself an arch-criminal with a Robin Hood streak, would see in his own crimes, a fierce rival. Perhaps he sought to draw The *Spider* into a trap. The purpose: to kill him."

"It would explain his attempt on Nita's life," Kirk admitted gruffly.

"It would indeed. Fortunately, he failed. But back to my theory. Does it stand up to scrutiny?"

"It does," Kirkpatrick admitted. "Possibly."

"Once we have disposed of motive, only one question remains. Who is the Reaper?"

"Drat it! We do not know!"

"I have it on good authority that this is the very question which The *Spider* has put to the Underworld tonight. And that he may have gleaned a clue, if not a definitive answer."

The limousine pulled up into the moonlit shadow of the funeral home.

"And what is that?" Kirk asked thinly.

"Why don't we continue our conversation later? I see that we have arrived at our destination…"

The inert remains of Dorsett Knowles lay in his coffin, dressed for the occasion that all men dread. The funeral home mortician had managed to darken his lived blue face into a grim, corpsey grey. Otherwise, the man looked much as he had in life.

"It is customary on these occasions to say that the deceased looks very natural," Wentworth commented. "But in this particular case, it isn't so."

Kirkpatrick shot his old friend a withering look.

"In fact, Knowles looks much the same as he had in the morgue," added Wentworth

Features flushing, Kirkpatrick stalked off.

Wentworth scrutinized the body carefully. There were few mourners. Knowles was a confirmed bachelor, seemed to have no family and few friends.

Surreptitiously, he took the deceased's wrist in one hand, carefully feeling for a pulse. He discovered none. Wentworth frowned. Palming a pin from a coat pocket, he inserted it into the corpse's right cheek. It drew no visible response. He looked for signs of the medical examiner's autopsy scalpel in vain. But these would be artfully concealed.

Brow deeply furrowed, Richard Wentworth withdrew to the smoking room and braced his nerves with an Egyptian cigarette.

Commissioner Kirkpatrick joined him momentarily, firing up an aromatic cigar. He puffed away furiously before speaking.

"Are you quite satisfied?" he asked with repressed anger.

"I take it," Wentworth drawled, "that you observed my careful postmortem examination of Dorsett Knowles."

"Damnably indecent of you!" Kirkpatrick huffed. "The man is lying in state, dead."

"Is he? A man of Knowles' exotic background might know many secrets. Including the art of catalepsy."

"Rot. Rot and rubbish!"

"Perhaps you are correct, after all," Wentworth returned thinly. "Forgive me, Kirk, It's just that I sometimes have a sixth sense about these matters. It has haunted me that a hunter of poisonous jungle spiders might tire of that sport and turn to a greater challenge."

"Such as hunting The *Spider*?"

"Conceivably," Wentworth allowed. "I had also the notion that the criminal agency that felled so many blue-faced victims might have been gleaned from a study of jungle vermin, such as certain species of poisonous spider, one as yet unknown to science."

"That is one theory you may consign to the waste paper basket," Kirkpatrick snapped.

"I shall. But it is a shame, for all the pieces seemed to fit perfectly...."

At that moment a commotion sounded from the front of the funeral parlor.

A hearse was drawing up, but a hearse such as no one had ever beheld. For it was a dark but eerie cobalt in color.

Out of it stepped a figure in blue. He was supernaturally tall, and garbed like Medieval depictions of the Grim Reaper.

"My God!" Kirkpatrick started.

"Unless I miss my guess, it is the Blue Reaper!" Wentworth murmured, reaching for the automatics holstered beneath his faultless evening dress.

Together, the two men sought the entrance portico.

Outside, the Blue Reaper was at work. But he carried no scythe. Instead, his bony gloved hands wielded a long tube like a flit gun. This he was pumping into the faces of arriving mourners.

Dusty blue power, almost gaseous, squirted from the ominous device. And where the powder touched, faces and hands turned blue and clutching fingers grabbed at strangling throats.

Down fell victims, gasping, choking, twisting like worms affixed to pins, twisting and dying as their lungs ceased to function. They fell in heaps.

Wentworth flung the doors open. In his hands, steel automatics bucked and snapped out shells.

He aimed for the hooded and enshadowed head, which towered high over the heads of crumpling victims. Hot lead lanced and snapped at that rolling head as it turned toward its assailant. But the lead seemed to pass harmlessly through blue garments!

The Blue Reaper reeled with each impact, yes. But he failed to succumb to the leaden storm.

"What manner of man...?" Wentworth growled. Correcting his aim, he began hammering the chest area.

Two slugs bit a single hole where the heart should be. This brought results. The Blue Reaper upset, stumbled backward. All the time, his bony claws worked his diabolical flit gun, blowing blue doom in all directions.

A cloud of the lovely stuff began rolling in the direction of Wentworth and Kirkpatrick!

"Back, Kirk!"

Then a metallic laugh rang out, filling the night.

"The *Spider*!" Kirkpatrick barked. "He is here too!"

More lead began storming. And from the ornamental shrubbery popped a dread figure. All in black, felt hat crushed over his head, twin automatics barking and sniping, the *Spider* sent sizzling lead whistling at the blue-robed giant.

The Reaper turned, continued working his deadly device, aiming for his masked tormenter.

Wentworth circled around and crept closer, face set, teeth bared in a fighting snarl. The red scar on his forehead sprang into life like a blazing brand.

"Reaper!" he cried.

The Reaper whirled, crossfire lead plucking at his billowing sleeves. Bullets blasted him from all sides, and finally, the blue scourge fell, the flit gun dropping from broken and bloody arms.

Where he fell, a crimson stain spread, and showed no signs of ceasing…

His own gun smoking, Kirkpatrick hissed, "Dick. The *Spider*. We can catch him!"

With a laugh, The *Spider* ducked from sight.

They rushed to the spot. There was no sign of The *Spider*.

"Capture the *Spider*, Kirk!" laughed Wentworth. "Are you mad! The man is a black ghost. You might as well try to catch a rainbow."

Fuming, Kirk rushed to a police call box and began issuing heated orders.

Holstering his weapon, Wentworth strode over to the bleeding corpse that had been the Blue Reaper. He stripped off the hood. It came loose, bullet-riddled head and all. It had been set on a short pole to create the illusion of height.

"Just as I thought. A mannequin's head," he mused.

Digging into the costume, he discovered the true head, sheltered behind a sheet of bulletproof steel plates fitted with eyeholes. It was a face he recognized.

When Kirk came striding up, Wentworth said, "May I present Mr.

Roscoe Dillard."

Astonishment seized the commissioner. "The Bowery pickpocket? The Blue Reaper?"

"No, Kirk. This was just an elaborate subterfuge to confuse and misdirect our attention from the true Reaper."

"Who is…?"

Richard Wentworth seemed about to speak, but compressed his lips instead. "Unknown to us at present," he said carefully.

Their eyes met, gazes locking. A communication almost telepathic passed between them, but went unuttered.

Returning to the wake while they awaited the arrival of the police, the uneasy friends reassured the mourners that all was well.

"The Blue Reaper is dead," declared Kirkpatrick. "The danger has passed. The city is safe once more."

Polite applause greeted this confident declaration.

A vague rustle brought heads turning around. Eyes grew wide.

The corpse lifted from his coffin! The dead man sat up and looked around with a studied and dazed expression.

Women fainted. Men screamed. Even Commissioner Kirkpatrick looked thunderstruck.

Nonchalantly, Richard Wentworth said, "Welcome back to the world of the living, Knowles." And proffered a monogrammed cigarette from his jeweled case.

"What-what happened," mumbled Dorsett Knowles.

Wentworth smiled. "Your timing is exquisite. The Blue Reaper was just gunned down outside this very establishment. Strange that he should materialize at the wake of one of his victims…"

"Is he dead?"

"Quite dead, yes. I had the honor of blasting him down. Although I must confess that I had a little help from an old acquaintance of yours… The *Spider*."

Kirkpatrick shook himself out of his stunned trance. "Dorsett, please. Climb out of that wretched thing. Tell us what happened, man."

"I remember being ambushed by a tall specter in blue. Then I blacked out, choking."

Wentworth said, "Odd that you are the only victim of the Reaper to recover. In his coffin, no less."

Kirkpatrick whirled on his friend. "Stop this! Stop it this instant. Have you no respect!"

Arching an eyebrow, Wentworth inquired, "For the... dead?"

Kirkpatrick seemed ready to explode.

"Tell me, Knowles," continued Wentworth. "How is it you were not embalmed?

"Embalmed? Why—er—I gave explicit instructions not to be embalmed."

"Really? Were you expecting to die?"

"I mean," Knowles said, flustered, "my next of kin knew of my wishes."

"Oh? Kindly point them out to me. I am not acquainted with your esteemed relatives."

Dorsett Knowles surveyed the assembled mourners. He saw only co-workers. And the curious.

"Could it be that this entire charade was staged?" Wentworth challenged. "Staged to throw suspicion off the only person who could be the Reaper. The one man who possessed the knowledge of exotic poisons necessary to slay innocents. I seem to recall that you were on the scene when I encountered that first blue-faced corpse upon docking..."

"Ridiculous!" Knowles snapped. "Kirkpatrick, must I stand for this?"

"You must. For I have a question: How is it you stand before us... *after being autopsied?*"

"No doubt, Kirk," said Wentworth, "a body was substituted at the last moment, or a bribe paid."

"Speak up, Knowles," Kirkpatrick urged. "We are all waiting."

Explanations died on dry lips. Suddenly, Knowles whirled, grasped something long and dark from under the plush lining of his coffin. He pointed it at Richard Wentworth.

"Damn you! Everyone knows that you are The *Spider*!" he screamed.

As if to give the lie to that denunciation, from the entryway came a wild hilarity. Eyes swiveled. Gasps issued forth.

The *Spider* burst in, guns blazing. Knowles whirled. Too late!

At his very wake, the "deceased" was blasted into eternity, his implement of sudden death falling from his nerveless grasp.

With a final flurry of warning shots, The *Spider* vanished! No one dared follow. Kirkpatrick stood stunned by the suddenness of it all.

Wentworth knelt at the body of Dorsett Knowles and lifted a flit gun into view. "Planned to carry the evidence to his grave, I imagine." He glanced in the direction of the empty coffin. "Someone kindly assist Mr. Knowles back onto his last pillow. The funeral is back on."

The police poured in moments later. No trace of The *Spider* could be found... or was ever found. Only a hastily dropped mask.

"Clever fellow," Wentworth said dryly. "He blew Knowles to his just reward before I could even draw my own pistol."

"Peculiar," Kirkpatrick muttered suspiciously.

"What is?"

"That The *Spider* should have followed the same trail of suspicion that you privately declaimed."

Wentworth smiled. "I *did* say that he was clever... By the way, I neglected to inform you that Nita will fully recover. It was only a case of acute blueberry poisoning, after all."

"Blueberry?"

"Yes. Somehow a small basket of spoiled blueberries were smuggled into her cell and she ate them, discoloring her tongue. Ptomaine set in. In her agony, Nita rubbed her face with the violets I sent her, smearing it an ungodly azure. She was not a victim of the Blue Reaper after all." Wentworth smiled again.

Commissioner Kirkpatrick eyed his friend for a very long time before speaking. "I wonder," he muttered.

"Wonder what, old boy?"

"I wonder if Nita van Sloan has an alibi for the period corresponding to The *Spider's* rather timely appearance tonight."

"If that is an official request, I will ask her for you.... And include my entire staff, since more than one *Spider* appears to be at large..."

"Mark me, Dick," Kirkpatrick said gravely. "One day someone will sit in the electric chair for The *Spider's* crimes. And on that day there will be nothing I—or any other man—will have to say about it."

Coolly and calmly, Richard Wentworth fired a cigarette with the platinum lighter that concealed the scarlet symbol of The *Spider*... No one noticed as the coffin lid snapped shut, this very sign lay bright as a drop of blood on the forehead of the murderer who had been the Blue Reaper....

The Screaming Death

Featuring The Spider and The Green Ghost
by Eric Fein

D eath came to Coney Island on a hot lazy Sunday afternoon in late August. It arrived in the form of an armored van. Few people took notice of the van as it made its way through the streets to Steeplechase Park. And even if they did, they would be dumbfounded to know that it carried the means of their death.

The armored van made its way along West 12th Street until it reached the corner of Surf Avenue. There it pulled over to the curb. Four men, dressed in guard uniforms, exited from the rear of the van. Each one carried a large black satchel. The lead guard was a tall muscular man with cold black eyes. He led his men through the crowd like a general leading his troops to war.

One block away, a tall handsome man in a dark suit made his way through the crowds, searching for the van.

The man was Richard Wentworth. The public knew him as a millionaire and an amateur criminologist who sometimes worked with the police. But there was another side to Wentworth – one that was driven by the need for justice. And when the law could not deliver said justice, he took it upon himself to do so as the menacing figure of darkness and violence… the Master of Men known as… The *Spider*!

The *Spider* was on a desperate mission, knew he had only minutes, if that, to get to the death dealing thugs before they turned Coney Island

into an orgy of death and destruction. The impending attack on the
boardwalk amusement park was only just the latest in a series of
unexplained attacks over the last couple of weeks in and around New
York City.

It was only through his tireless investigations that The *Spider* had
managed to shake loose information about this attack. Those he elicited
information from were now either dead or in police custody.

Steeplechase Park was made up of several rides and attractions.
The centerpiece of the park was the Steeplechase ride. It consisted of
mechanical horses, sitting side by side, that people rode down a track
that was more than 1,000 feet long.

The supposed guards made their way to the top of the Steeplechase
ride. The leader looked around. Satisfied, he nodded to his cohorts.
They snapped into action.

One of the guards pulled his revolver and shot the ride operator in
the head. The others pulled machineguns from their satchels. Panic
ensued as people screamed and ran for cover. The guards were
unmoved by the chaos they had caused.

Instead, they set about their task. Each man extracted a piece of
equipment from their satchels and handed it to their leader. He took
them and assembled a device that resembled a futuristic cannon –
something straight out of a Flash Gordon serial – that sat on a tripod.

Being at the top of the Steeplechase ride gave them a good view of
a large chunk of the park that lay below and led out to the beach. The
leader again nodded to his men and they immediately pulled out heavy
plastic dome shaped ear protectors and slid them on, covering their
ears. The leader flipped a switch on the device and it began to emit a
low whine. Within seconds, it grew into what sounded like a prolonged
scream.

The leader flipped another switch on the device and then swiveled
its muzzle to the left and began firing. Blasts of intense sound shot
from the device, emitting a thunderous boom that froze almost

everyone in fear.

He repeated this act, blasting every area of the park before him. The sound waves bore into people's skulls, penetrating their brains – boiling them from within the gray matter. As soon as they were hit by the sound waves, people shrieked. They clawed at their faces, ripped the flesh in a vain attempt to tear out their own brains to make the pain – the agony and madness that engulf them – stop.

What had been a fun day at the beach had become a day of horror – hell on earth – as people ripped chunks of hair and scalp from themselves. Others clawed at their faces so deeply that their cheeks hung loose from their skulls.

Two blocks away, the effects of the screaming blast were also being felt. Some people banged their heads against lampposts or walls or on the street. Others gouged out their own eyes. Still others were compelled by the madness that engulfed them to chew off their own fingers.

This is the horror that greeted Wentworth when he entered Steeplechase Park. These horrific sights would stay with him for the rest of his life.

Before he could act, he found himself victim to the sound beam. It felt as though a giant fist had slammed into his head. Waves of panic and anxiety washed over him. He dropped to his knees. This is not right he thought. I'm so scared. The pain is beyond comprehension. He feared that his brain was boiling. His breathing became labored. The pressure in his skull increased by the second. His vision was going red.

He had to get out of the area. He had to make his fear stop so he could save the others. At first, he could barely walk, but the further he got from Steeplechase Park, the easier it became for him to move. The terror subsided.

Whatever had gripped him had a specific radius. If he could figure out what that was, he could figure out a way to get close enough to destroy whatever was causing it. Over the next fifteen minutes, Wentworth made his way along Surf Avenue, near the area known as The Bowery. By this time, the fear and ensuing panic that had gripped the area was beginning to quiet.

He entered Steeplechase Park. He spotted dark figures at the top of the Steeplechase ride. They were disassembling something. His eyes narrowed, a barely controlled rage filled him. It was only his steel will harden due to years of facing down the worse horrors imaginable that The *Spider* was even slightly able to over come the effects of the sound waves. He girded himself for battle with a guttural roar, straightened up. These men would pay with their lives. He ducked behind an exhibit and with a few quick changes to his attire Richard Wentworth ceased to exist. In his place stood a grim and ghoulish sentinel of justice, The *Spider*!

A black slouch hat pulled down over a fright wig, a domino mask, fanged teeth, and a billowing black cloak gave The *Spider* an unholy appearance. He was vengeance incarnate.

The guards, the job finished, had just started making their way down the Steeplechase ride when The *Spider* reached the top. They were too busy joking to notice him at first. But when the leader heard the flapping of The *Spider's* cloak in the breeze he swung around and opened fire. The other men followed his lead.

The *Spider* laughed a laugh filled with dread and loathing for his targets. The men were halfway down the ride. The *Spider* kicked the lever to start the ride and hopped onto one of the mechanical horses. Standing perfectly balanced upon it as it zoomed down the track, he fired his twin .45s at the men.

His bullets found their marks on the first two, exploding their skulls like rancid melons. Again he laughed as his black cloak bellowed out behind him, giant and bat-like in appearance. His guns spat more lead death as he neared the others.

His lips snarled back, baring his fangs. And his eyes… they burned with vengeance – dark pools of barely contained rage. They locked in on the fleeing thugs and wherever his gaze fell, it was followed by gunfire from his twin .45s.

The leader and one remaining cohort ran for the park's exit. Carrying the weapon in its satchel slung over his shoulder, the leader managed to escape.

His companion was not so lucky. He slid in a puddle of blood, from the body of a man who had ripped out his own throat, and fell to his knees. Cursed. Spun around to see –

The *Spider* leaping off of the mechanical horse into the air above him.

The *Spider* laughed. The gunman opened fire on The *Spider* but his aim was off. The bullets tore holes into the black cape as it fluttered in the air above The *Spider's* head as he landed.

Though his gun was out of bullets, the gunman continued to pull the trigger. The *Spider's* long dark shadow fell across the now cowering gunman. The gunman cursed and threw his empty automatic at The *Spider*, who didn't flinched as the useless weapon bounced off of his right shoulder.

The gunman tried to flee but again slipped in the mess of blood. Seeing that escape was no longer an option, the gunman spun back to The *Spider* and lunged at him, letting out a guttural growl as he did.

The *Spider* laughed again and opened fire. The bullets tore off the top of the gunman's head. Blood spurted from it like a gruesome fountain. The *Spider* paused long enough to kneel and put his mark, with his cigarette lighter, on what was left of the gunman's forehead and then continued on.

He had kept the leader in his sight the whole time. The man was one block ahead of him. The *Spider* quickened his pace. The leader was now in striking distance. The *Spider* raised his guns, taking aim. He pulled the triggers.

But just as the bullets let loose, the armored car came screeching around the corner and slammed to a stop in front of the leader so that the bullets hit it and not him. The back door swung open, the leader tossed in the death-dealing device and jumped in after it.

The *Spider* running now closed the gap between himself and the van. It wasn't enough. The van took off, wheels burning rubber, just as The *Spider* reached it. The driver swerved, slinging the rear of the van violently against The *Spider*. The impact sent The *Spider* crashing into the pavement.

Though winded, he got to his feet, fired at the fleeing truck. The *Spider* grimaced, blood trickled from the corner of his mouth. It was pointless now. The bullets bounced off of its armor as though they were jellybeans.

The *Spider* stood and watched the armored vehicle disappear in the distance. He looked around to survey the bloody carnage that surrounded him. The dead and the dying littered the streets for as far as the eye could see.

Waves of nausea and dizziness washed over him. His vision began to spin. The next thing he knew, he was lying in the middle of the street. He had blacked out, that was obvious. What caused it? He was not sure. He felt around his midsection and head searching for any signs of gunshot wounds but found none.

He stood, took two steps. Another whirlwind of dizziness and vertigo consumed him. Again, he drew deep down, tapped his iron will to continue on. He made his way to his car and headed home. As he did, he could hear sirens from police cars and fire engines closing in fast. He was long gone by the time the horrified responders arrived on the scene.

Back home, Wentworth gave his assistant Ram Singh orders that he was not to be disturbed for two hours so he could overcome the lingering effects of the sound waves. He went to bed, hoping sleep would restore him to full strength, calm his mind.

Though Richard Wentworth slept, there was nothing healing about it. His dreams were filled with fear and horror and pain. Images of what he had seen that day burned his brain – a woman pulling out long locks of her golden blonde hair, a man using a switchblade to cut off his own face, a pretzel vendor shoving his head into the flames of his pretzel cart. The horrors assailed him one after the other in a never-ending line of macabre mutilation.

He woke to find Ram Singh standing at the foot of the bed, face lined with worry.

"Sahib, you shouted. You're drenched in sweat," Ram Singh said.

"Bad dreams," Wentworth replied, his throat as dry as sandpaper.

"The only way to stop such dreams is to destroy the source of them," Ram said. "I know your mission is not over, let me join you so I can whet my blade with the blood of the guilty."

"No," Wentworth said. "Not yet. Has Nita called?"

"Missie sahib is in the living room," Ram said. "She came over despite the fact that I told her you were sleeping and left instructions that you didn't want to be disturbed."

Wentworth smiled. No matter what, he could always count on his lovely Nita to be there for him. His mood lightened just thinking of her.

"Okay, tell her I'll be out in ten minutes and we'll have lunch together."

"Very good, Sahib," Ram said.

Fifteen minutes later, Wentworth, showered and shaved, sat in his pajamas and dressing gown at the dining room table digging into a blood rare steak with French Fries, and a cup of coffee. Nita had tried to hide her shock at his appearance. Even cleaned up, the events of the day still wore heavily upon him.

While he ate his hearty meal, she opted for a light salad. Their great behemoth of a dog, Apollo, a harlequin Great Dane, lay at their feet. Though he appeared to be asleep, the mammoth pooch, kept one eye open, alert for Nita's safety and hoping that Wentworth would have need of him in his latest adventure.

It wasn't until he was done eating that Nita asked him about the day before. Wentworth took a deep breath and described what happened. Nita listened, containing her emotions, as he described the horrors he had witnessed.

When he was done, she put a hand on his. "You did everything within your power, Richard. You can't hold yourself responsible for the deaths of those innocent people. You know that."

He gave her a sad smile. "Of course I do," he said. "That doesn't mean I still don't feel responsible. I've been tracking these criminals for weeks and I always seem to get there too late. I should have been able to stop it by now."

"You will," Nita said.

"That's very sweet," he said, patting her hand.

"Don't patronize me, Richard Wentworth," she said. "I won't stand for it. Now, tonight, you and I will stay home and have a romantic evening in front of the fire. After all, even Spiders need time to spin their webs."

He smiled at her, leaned over and kissed her on the lips. "Ah, what would I do without you?" he said. "I'd love to do nothing more than to do as you suggest –"

"Richard—"

"But… I can't. I'm sure that these criminals are ramping up their attacks for a reason. I think they could strike again tonight and I think I know where."

Nita sighed. "You win, where?"

Wentworth smiled, "Oh, I think you'll like it. There's a charity event on Broadway tonight to benefit the city's orphans. It's a magic show and the magician is George Chance."

"Isn't he the protégé of Harry Houdini?" Nita observed.

"Yes," Wentworth said. "He's supposed to be quite good. In fact, tonight the main attraction of the evening is going to be him performing the straightjacket escape while suspended from the theater's ceiling."

"And you expect that during the show your "friends" with the scream machine will make an appearance?" Nita asked.

The good humor left Wentworth's countenance. "Yes, if I am not mistaken, what better place to sow more fear than to attack at the city's high society and civic leaders. Police Commissioner Kirkpatrick as well as the mayor will be there.

"And now, so will The *Spider*," Nita said.

"Yes," Wentworth said, returning her smile.

The leader of the guards, Jack Wallace, and the armored van driver, Edgar Moore, sat in the office of Dr. William Kane, owner and chief administrator of the Institute of Mental Health and Rejuvenation in Scarsdale, New York.

They sat there, on two hardwood chairs, like two children called to the principal's office for misbehaving in class.

Dr. Kane, was a tall, grimfaced man of fifty-two. His graying black hair was combed back into a widow's peak and his black eyes glared through wire-rimmed glasses that sat low on his aquiline nose.

"So, gentlemen," Kane said. "Based on the late evening editions and radio broadcasts, your little mission today at the amusement park seems to have gotten out of hand."

Though he said it with a calm voice, there was no disguising the rage burning in his eyes.

"I know, sir," Jack said. "I'm sorry."

"You had very strict and very simple orders," Kane said. "You were to transport the device to the specified location and activate it, let it run for the prescribed time, make note of any flaws in its performance, shut it down, and return here.

"The whole point was to show prospective bidders how unobtrusive the device is, how effective it is under all types of circumstances, and how low key and professional I am to deal with. Instead, you turned it into a boardwalk sideshow."

"I know, sir," Jack pleaded. "I made an error in judgment. I allowed myself to be talked into doing more than was required. But we were doing it for you. Honest."

Kane's eyebrows rose. "Really?" Kane said. He leaned back in his chair, pulled open the top drawer of his desk, and from it pulled out a lacquered black box. It was a little bigger than a cigar box. Without looking down, he flipped the lid and reached inside. "Today's debacle was for my benefit? Explain."

Jack and Edgar looked at each other. Neither one wanted to talk first. Finally, Jack said, "It's like this, Edgar here and a couple of the other fellows thought that we could get a better overall effect with the device by placing it at a higher point than street level—"

"And we did," Edgar said. "You should have seen the way them suckers did themselves in. The were squirming like worms in a frying pan."

Kane sneered. Jack put a hand on Edgar's arm in the hopes of shutting him up. It didn't work.

"Yeah, you've got a great invention there, Doc," Edgar said. "We're going be as rich as kings with it."

"We?" Kane said.

"I mean, you, Sir," Edgar said. He looked from Kane to Jack and seeing the grim expressions, realized he had misplaced his hand. "I promise... next time, I'll follow your orders to the letter – and we'll be sure to kill The *Spider*. Won't we, Jack?"

Jack didn't look at him. Instead, he was looking at Kane who was now holding something that resembled a ray gun in his right hand. The device emitted an unnerving hum that started low but grew louder by the second.

"I'm so glad you have such faith in my project, Mr. Moore," Kane said to Edgar. "And because of that, I think you should be the first person to see my latest invention in use for the first time."

"I'm honored, Dr. Kane," Edgar said. "But it's late and I'm tired. I really should be going." Edgar got up and started for the door.

"Mr. Moore," Kane snapped.

Edgar forced himself to look back at the doctor. Kane was standing now, aiming the gun at him.

"Please, Sir," Edgar said. "I'm sorry."

"I know," Kane said. "In actuality, it really is my fault. After all, I hired Mr. Wallace, here, to assemble the team and he chose you and the others."

Jack went white.

"It all falls on me," Kane said. "Being a manager means one has to make unpleasant choices. And as much as I would like to punish Mr. Wallace for his lack of judgment, I still have need for him. Your usefulness is limited to being my first test subject for the miniature version of my device."

"Screw that," Edgar said and made a break for the door.

Kane pulled the trigger. There was a shrill sound, the tip of the device glowed a bright hot white and then an invisible concentrated blast of energy shot from the weapon and hit Edgar in the back. The impact slammed him into the door and he fell to his knees. He tried to get up but couldn't.

The weapon's high-pitched scream drowned out Edgar's own agonized screams. He rolled around on the floor scratching at his face one second, pulling out his hair the next.

Jack sat transfixed in horror watching his sometime friend and cohort mutilate himself.

Kane smiled, pleased with the results. "Now, let's see what happens when I turn the power level up to full blast."

Using his thumb, he flipped a lever on the side of the gun. The screaming of the weapon grew to a near deafening pitch. Edgar's head began to swell and throb. He grabbed at his temples and slammed his head into the floor. Once. Twice. Three times. "Make it stop! Please!" The words were barely discernable above the sound of the weapon.

A series of convulsions shook Edgar. He lurched forward, then back. He coughed up blood. More blood seeped from his ears, eyes, and nose.

Jack's heart raced. His breathing grew labored. He was trapped, crouched in his chair, hands over his ears in a vain attempt to protect his hearing. As long as a person wasn't in the direct path of the sound wave they were safe from deadly frenzy the wave evoked.

Kane stood silent, undisturbed by the sound of his weapon or the screams of his victim. He looked from Edgar to Jack and said, "I think this has gone on long enough, don't you?"

Jack nodded, relief coming back into his face.

It was short-lived.

Kane flipped another switch on the weapon and the decibel level jumped up to the point that the windows were trembling in their frames.

"Watch this, Jack," Kane said.

Though he didn't want to, he looked at Edgar who was slumped in a corner of the study, covered in blood. His head swelling to the size of a balloon made him look like a grotesque carnival prize. Jack heard a sickening crack and crackle and suddenly, Edgar's head exploded in a wave of brain, bone, and blood.

Jack felt his lunch surge up his throat. He forced himself to keep it down. If he got ill, showed any more signs of weakness, he knew he would be next.

The room went silent, save for the ringing in Jack's ears. He glanced at Kane, who was once again seated at his desk, the weapon back in its case. Kane looked up at Jack and gave him an almost fatherly smile. He closed the lid and stuck the box under his arm.

"Well," Kane said. "After all the testing of the various components over the last month, I am satisfied that we are ready to begin phase two of the project. It's time to assemble the battle suit. Once that is field tested, I will be able to offer bidders an array of options – the cannon for large-scale attacks and the smaller device and the suit for more precise targeting. Nations and even independent factions will throw millions of dollars at my feet in hopes of buying the exclusive rights to them."

Kane stood. Jack started to speak but thought better of it. Kane walked over to Jack. "Jack, I have an important task that needs doing."

"Yes, Sir?" Jack said.

Kane's smile brightened. Jack felt a small sense of relief.

"Yes," Kane said. His voice was little more than a whisper. "It's something only you can do, Jack."

"Tell me, Sir," Jack said. "I'll make sure it gets done."

"Oh, I'm sure you will," Kane said. "It's the janitor's night off so I need you to clean up in here. If the blood isn't washed off before it dries, it'll be hell to clean in the morning. After that, take Mr. Moore down to the furnace and dispose of him."

"Sir?" Jack said. The sick feeling washed over him again like a waterfall of sludge.

"Are you questioning my orders, Mr. Wallace?" Kane said.

"No, sir. I'll take care of it," Jack assured him.

"Good," Kane said. "I have to go into the city this evening to tie up some loose ends on the project. See to it that you are done by the time I get back."

"Yes, sir," Jack said.

Kane nodded and walked out of the office humming a tune.

"We've got a packed house tonight, boss," Tiny Tim Terry said. Dressed in a tuxedo tailored to his small frame – he stood at no more than four foot eight – Terry was a striking figure. His brown hair slicked down and parted on the side. His brown eyes glimmered with a touch of mischief – a hold over from his days as a circus performer. He stood behind the curtains that hid the stage from the audience.

His boss was George Chance, the famed illusionist, escape artist, debunker of phony spiritualists, and amateur criminologist. Chance stood behind him directing last minute adjustments to the set and props for the evening's show. "I expected nothing less, Tim," Chance said, a tall man, six-two, with a lean yet muscular build. He cut a dashing figure in his finely tailored tuxedo. His black hair neatly combed and his dark eyes jovial but ever alert for danger.

"George, given what happened at Coney Island yesterday, are you sure this is a good idea?" Meriem White said. The petite brunette had entered the stage from the dressing room. Her beautiful figure showcased in a tight silver satin dress. Her green eyes sparkled like emeralds as she smiled, took in the sight of Chance. Her dark hair glimmered in the light as it fell over her shoulders, giving a sensual mystery to her face. She stood in the doorframe. Her hand rested on her outthrust hip.

Chance looked at her as she approached, a smile growing on his lips and in his eyes. "Meriem, when was the last time I told you that you were breathtakingly beautiful?"

"This morning at breakfast," she said.

"Morning seems like another lifetime ago," Chance said. "I know we agreed that you wear something slinky tonight to keep the audience distracted but I may need to get blinders myself if I want to survive."

"Don't joke, George," Meriem said. "Just because Harry Houdini taught you the trick doesn't mean things can't go wrong."

Chance took Meriem in his arms and kissed her gently. He whispered, "Nothing can go wrong with you at my side."

Meriem stepped back and gave him a hard look. "Enough of the Romeo routine. You're trying to change the subject and I won't let you. Are you sure that this is a wise decision? What if there is an attack of this Screaming Death mob that have been attacking the city?"

Chance dropped the happy playboy façade and looked at her. In a calm, serious voice he said, "I'm sorry, Meriem. I think it will be highly unlikely an attack will happen here tonight. The police are covering all the exits and entrances. Tiny and Joe Harper are also keeping an eye out for trouble.

"Besides, all of the previous attacks have happened in outdoor venues. That tells me that whatever is causing these horrible attacks is too big to be smuggled into this theater in a lady's handbag or a gentleman's cigarette case."

"I hope you're right," Meriem replied.

"Aren't I always," Chance said with a big smile.

"No, my beloved, not hardly," Meriem said. "I better finish putting on my make up."

"Ouch, that's got to hurt the old confidence," Tiny said.

Chance smirked. "Don't you have to meet Joe and make your rounds before the show?

"Right, boss," Tiny said and left. Chance stood looking at the pulley system that was rigged to the stage and the ceiling above it that would soon hoist him into the air while he was encased in a straight jacket.

He would never openly admit it to Meriem or anyone else for that matter, but every time he had to perform an escape he got nervous. For all the precautions he took, it was still a very dangerous trick.

But, George Chance was driven to succeed, driven to challenge death and come away victorious. The day that challenge became too much was the day that George Chance would hang up his tuxedo and find another line of work.

As he predicted, Chance had a great show. He wowed the crowd with his stories and sleight of hand illusions and knocked them out of their seats with the straightjacket trick.

He had improved upon it since Houdini had done it. He added a fiery element. Once he was hanging upside down over the stage, the rope that threaded through the pulley system and held him aloft was set on fire. He had mere seconds to free himself and swing to the safety line that hung next to him before the rope holding him burned through and sent him plummeting to a certain death.

Wentworth and Nita also enjoyed the show, even though, given Wentworth's experiences, he was able to decipher how each illusion was done.

Wentworth studied George Chance. Behind the showman's smile were the eyes of a hunter – the gaze of an intense, driven man. Even though Chance managed to convey an air of lightness and frivolity to the audience through his outward body language and demeanor, there was something about the slight tensions in his facial muscles that Wentworth recognized. That told him there was more to Chance than he was showing his adoring fans.

It was also in the way Chance stood, casual yet ready for action. In fact, Wentworth suspected that George Chance – the celebrity magician – was just another of his illusions. He wanted to know more about Chance. He was looking forward to meeting him at the reception after the show.

"George Chance meet Richard Wentworth," Police Commissioner Stanley Kirkpatrick said as he steered Wentworth and Nita over to where Chance was standing with Meriem. Kirkpatrick had known Wentworth for many years and had called upon his help, unofficially, many times.

Despite all of that, he suspected that Wentworth was The *Spider* and had told Wentworth that the day he had proof of it would be the day he arrested him. However, until that day came, the men maintained a delicate alliance.

"Wentworth?" Chance asked. "I've heard a lot about you. You've lived quite an exciting life."

"I'm sure it couldn't be more exciting than yours," Wentworth said. "After all, you seem to like pulling the wool over people's eyes."

"True," Chance said. "But mostly for fun."

"Mostly…" Wentworth said.

"Hey, Commissioner, don't you want to introduce us girls or are we just for show," Nita said.

Kirkpatrick blushed. "Sorry. This is Nita Van Sloan."

Meriem smiled and extended a hand. Nita took it. "Hello, I'm Meriem White. It's lovely to meet you."

"You too," Nita said.

"And it is a pleasure to meet you, Ms. White," Wentworth said.

Chance took Nita's hand, bowed and kissed it. "Enchanted, Ms. Van Sloan. I do hope you enjoyed the show."

"Very much so," Nita said.

"I enjoyed the show, too." It came from behind the group. They all turned to see Dr. Kane. He was a compelling sight. His tall lanky figure dressed in a well-tailored tuxedo. He had forgone his glasses so his black eyes held an intense, unsettling stare for those he gazed upon. He was sipping a martini. "Forgive me, I'm sorry to interrupt a private conversation but I truly wanted to meet you Mr. Chance. I am Dr. William Kane. I specialize in treating fear and anxiety. I found your show quite illuminating."

"Really," Chance said. "How so?"

"Your act is centered on surviving death," Kane said. "That is a concern of all living things. The audience identifies with you. When you escape, you've conquered death and so have they by way of you as their proxy."

"That's an interesting theory, Doctor," Chance said. "But, I like to keep things simple. People like a good scare. It's cathartic. And they like a happy ending. It reassures them that the world is a safe place."

"Not these days, not with war brewing in Europe and not in New York City," Kane said. "The city itself is gripped in fear. If these mysterious attacks keep up, it could be the first steps back into anarchy."

"Not on my watch," Kirkpatrick stated.

"But it's already happening," Kane said. "Or don't you read the papers, Commissioner?"

"What?" Kirkpatrick said, face red as a beet.

"Easy, Kirk, Wentworth said. "I think what the doctor is saying is that whoever is causing these outbursts of violence that have plagued New York seems to be trying to upend the city's law and order."

"Yes, that's close to what I meant," Kane said. "Perhaps, I was just clumsy with my words."

He looked around, glanced at his watch, and said, "Well, I must be going. It was so nice to meet you all. Good night."

They watched him move through the crowd until he exited the room.

"That is one strange man," Nita said.

"You ain't kidding, Sister," Meriem said. "He gives me the creeps."

"He does seem a little too excited by the recent bloodshed, doesn't he?" Chance said.

"Excuse me, Mr. Chance."

Chance turned to where the voice came from to see a plain but pretty blonde young woman. She was dressed in a dark blue dress and still wore her evening coat.

"I'm sorry to interrupt," she said. "I'm Nora Thorne and it is urgent I speak with you in private."

Chance looked at her and could tell from her eyes that she was serious. This wasn't an obsessed fan or someone wanting an autograph. This was someone troubled by something.

"Certainly, Miss Thorne," Chance said. "This way."

Chance excused himself from the others and led the girl to an empty prep area adjoining the reception room. He closed the door behind them and indicated a chair for her to take. She did. He leaned against the counter, folded his arms across his chest, and said: "Go ahead. You have my undivided attention."

"I need your help, desperately," Nora said. "My father is C. W. Thorne."

"The millionaire industrialist?" Chance said.

"Yes," Nora said. "My father's missing and I need your help finding him."

"Why me? I'm just a magician." Chance said.

"I've read about you in the papers," Nora said. "You sometimes solve crimes when the police can't or won't. And in my father's case, they won't. Dr. Kane – that man you were just speaking to – has seen to that."

"What? I think you need to start from the beginning," Chance said.

"Two months ago my father checked into Dr. Kane's sanitarium to cope with the crippling depression he was experiencing after my mother's death last year. She was killed in a hit and run accident. They never caught the driver."

As she spoke, she absentmindedly pulled at and twisted the fingers of the gloves she clutched in her left hand.

"The first two weeks," she continued. "Everything seemed normal. I spoke with him on the phone every day and visited once a week. We would have lunch on the grounds.

"Then, he stopped taking my calls. When I spoke to the doctor, he said my father wanted to be left alone – that talking to me was too painful because I look and sound so much like my mother. He said that I would be contacted when my father was strong enough to speak with me again.

"I went to the clinic myself to demand to see my father and they wouldn't let me in. I went to the police up there. They said unless there was a crime committed they couldn't do anything. I tried to file a missing persons report but they said because I knew where my father was he wasn't missing.

"I went to the executives at my father's company but they weren't concerned. They said that they were in contact with him and his doctor. They patted me on the head and told me to go home and bake cookies.

"Finally, I decided to take matters in my own hands. I've been staking out the sanitarium for the last week, hoping that I would catch a glimpse of my father walking the grounds. But I haven't seen any trace of him there.

"Tonight, I saw Dr. Kane leave and I decided to follow him. I figured I could confront him in person."

She trailed off for a moment, looked at the floor, chewed her bottom lip. Chance watched her. He sensed that she was struggling with something very big. She took a deep breath, looked into Chance's eyes.

"Then when I saw him come in here and saw your name on the marquee, I decided to speak to you," she said. The words rushed together. "I thought you would help me. I want you to break into the sanitarium and find my father. Please."

"Ms. Thorne," Chance said. "You're asking me to commit a felony by breaking into the sanitarium and kidnapping your father."

She was on the verge of tears now. Her face congested with emotion, eyes watery. She reached out and gripped his hands in hers.

"I'm lost. If my father doesn't return soon, some of the executives are going to make moves to wrest control of the company from my family. If my father loses his company, he'll have nothing left to live for."

"No, he'll have you," Chance said. "Okay, Nora, I'll look into the matter."

She jumped up and hugged him. "Oh, thank you, Mr. Chance."

"If you followed Kane here, there is a chance that he might have spotted you tonight. Do you have a safe place to stay for a few days?"

"Yes," Nora said. "I have a girlfriend who lives with her parents on the Upper East Side. I can sleep on their couch."

"Good," he said. He took a scrap of paper from the counter and removed a pen from the inside of his tuxedo jacket and handed them both to her. "Write down the name and address of the sanitarium as well as where you'll be staying."

When she was done he pocketed the information and his pen. They went back into the reception room to find that the crowd had thinned out. Chance spotted Meriem sitting at a table with Nita Van Sloan. The two women were talking and laughing. Wentworth was standing to the side talking with Commissioner Kirkpatrick.

"Good night, Mr. Chance," Nora said.

"Good night," Chance said. "Perhaps, you will allow me to have one of my associates drive you to your friend's apartment?"

"That won't be necessary," Nora said. "My car is parked in a garage around the corner."

As soon as she left, Chance went to Joe Harper, one of his trusted assistants. Harper was a gambler and Broadway booking agent and had contacts all over the city. Harper stood an inch shorter than Chance. His brown eyes, though world weary, were vigilant. His light brown hair slicked back.

"What's up, boss," Harper said.

Chance spoke so that only Harper would hear him. The man listened, nodded, and exited the room. With Harper now assigned to watch over Nora Thorne, Chance joined Meriem who had just finished wishing Nita and Wentworth a good night.

"What was that all about?" Meriem said.

"I'm not sure yet," Chance said. "But, if what I think is true, tonight won't be the last time we see Dr. Kane."

"Huh?" Meriem said.

"I see you and Nita have become fast friends," Chance said as he slipped his arm through hers.

"Yes, she's a real pip," Meriem replied. "We've scheduled a lunch tomorrow. But if you need my help, I'll cancel."

"No, I wouldn't dream of it," Chance said.

Nora walked to her car feeling calm and hopeful for the first time in weeks. George Chance would take care of everything. Father would be back home soon.

So engrossed in these thoughts was she that she never saw the navy blue sedan charge down the street, its headlights off, until it was too late. Then, she had just enough time to scream but it died in her throat as she was thrown up in the air, smashed into the car's windshield, and then rolled off into the gutter.

There were screams of horror and for help, but when the police and ambulance arrived, it was too late for Nora Thorne.

Harper stood on the street, stunned. He had been too far away to save her. He was looking for signs of a tail, not a murderer lying in wait.

"It's not your fault, Joe," Chance said. "It's mine. I should've been more cautious and insisted on arranging her transportation."

They were in Chance's dressing room in the theater. Meriem and Tiny sat on the couch. Chance and Harper stood in the middle of the room.

"You're being too hard on yourself, George," Meriem said.

"Am I, Meriem?" he said. "I should've known better."

"What do we do now?" Harper said.

"You and Tiny find out what the police know – that's a busy street. See if any of the regulars on the block or merchants saw the driver or caught the license plate number. When you're done, report to me as soon as you can."

"Right," Harper said and he and Tiny left.

"Terrible accident tonight," Police Commissioner Kirkpatrick said. He was sitting in the study of Richard Wentworth as the millionaire mixed drinks for the two of them.

"Was it really an accident?" Wentworth asked.

"Probably not," Kirkpatrick said. "It happened so fast, few people were paying attention."

"You have to admit that it is highly suspicious that it happened to that young woman just after she had a private meeting with George Chance," Wentworth said. "And that it turns out that she is the daughter of C. W. Thorne."

"Who by the way, we have been unable to track down," Kirkpatrick said.

"What about Dr. William Kane," Wentworth said. "At the reception, you had started to tell me you knew of him."

"Yes, he's a slippery eel," Kirkpatrick said. "We have a file on him at headquarters. About ten years ago, he was arrested for performing experimental brain surgeries on human subjects. The D.A.'s office brought him up on charges but couldn't make them stick because none of the patients would testify against the good doctor.

"However, the medical board did suspend his license for a year. After that, he opened up shop out of our jurisdiction. Somewhere up in Scarsdale in Westchester County. Haven't heard a peep about him since."

"Something tells me that that is going to change," Wentworth said. He handed Kirkpatrick a drink.

They clinked their glasses, "To better days," Kirkpatrick said.

"Yes, here's hoping they come sooner rather than later," Wentworth replied.

"What did you find out?" Chance said. He was in his inner sanctum – an abandoned church rectory on East 55th Street. The rectory was linked to his brownstone on East 54th Street thanks to an abandoned subway shaft. He, Tiny Tim, and Joe Harper were sitting in the rectory's well-furnished basement.

"The murder car was stolen about five minutes before it ran down Nora," Harper said. "It was found a couple of hours later on the Bronx/Yonkers border."

"Yeah," Tiny Tim said. "The plates had been stripped from it but blood matching Nora's blood type was found on the bumper and grill."

"Yonkers is not that far away from Scarsdale," Chance said.

"It's spitting distance," Harper said.

"Me and Joe asked around, no one saw the driver clearly," Tiny Tim said. "One newsie thought the guy could have been bald but he wasn't betting his life on it."

"Kane has a receding hairline and he combs it back, that could look like he's bald from certain angles in a dark car at night," Chance said.

"It's a bit circumstantial," Harper said.

"True, but my gut tells me that we are on the right track," Chance said. "After speaking with Kane, I can tell you that there is something off with his affectation. He should be a patient in his clinic, not the person in charge."

"What's our next move?" Tiny Tim said.

"I'm going to pay a visit to the clinic and have a look around," Chance said.

"You or ..." Harper said.

"The Green Ghost?" Chance said, smiled. "Yes, it's time that The Green Ghost once again haunts the night."

C. W. Thorne, strapped into a wheelchair, was pushed into the treatment room. He was cold and tired. His wispy gray hair was mussed and he shivered in his flimsy hospital scrubs. The orderly who had transported him to the room was a big, ugly man named Boyle.

He unstrapped Thorne and yanked him out of the chair and pushed him up against the tile wall. "Stay," Boyle said. His voice was flat and uninterested. He went over to the phone, picked up the receiver, dialed a two digit number, waited for the person on the other end to answer, then said, "He's ready, Doctor. Yes, very good."

A few moments later, Dr. Kane arrived along with Jack Wallace. Jack was haggard and pale. He stood behind Kane holding the lacquered box.

"Now, Mr. Thorne," Kane said. "We have business to conclude. During our last session, I asked you to consider signing your company over to me. You were hesitant to do that. I hope the special room I provided you allowed you the solitude to think things through."

"I'll never sign, you conniving son of a bitch," Thorne said.

Kane shook his head sadly.

Boyle took a step toward Thorne. "Do you want me to give him another physical therapy session, Doc? It might loosen him up – get the blood flowing."

Thorne flinched.

Kane waved off Boyle. Disappointed, the larger man stepped back.

"I didn't want to have to tell you this but perhaps having all of the facts before you will help you with the decision making process," Kane said. "Up to this point, Mr. Boyle aside, I've tried to deal with you gentleman to gentleman. That doesn't seem to be working.

"So, please consider the following. If you don't do as I ask, I will send Mr. Boyle out to kidnap your daughter and I will allow him to use her for his amusement. Let me assure you, what he finds amusing is anything but normal. I wouldn't wish it on my worst enemy."

"Bastard," Thorne said.

"Nonetheless, harm befalling your beloved daughter is a very real possibility if you do not do as I request."

"I don't understand any of this," Thorne said. "I came here for therapy. You were highly recommended to me by my doctor."

"Ah, Doctor Gregson," Kane said. "Yes, an associate of mine from many years ago. He, too, fears Mr. Boyle and was quite willing to push you into my open arms."

"What?" Thorne said. "But how could you know that I would have a nervous breakdown when my wife died?"

Kane smiled. "My dear Mr. Thorne, who do you think is responsible for your wife's death?"

"What?" Thorne said.

"Nothing that has befallen you or your family over the last year has been by chance," Kane said. "I targeted you. You see, your company's factories are equipped with the tools I need to mass produce my device. Not to mention your wonderfully well stocked bank account."

Kane snapped his fingers and Jack Wallace sprang forward, holding out the box. Kane opened the lid and pulled out the weapon.

"What do you think?" Kane said, marveling at the device as the light in the room bounced off of it. "The newspapers have dubbed its bigger brother the Screaming Death – melodramatic for certain but it does speak to its truth. Let me show you."

Kane adjusted the setting on the weapon, aimed it at Thorne, and pressed the trigger. The hum of the gun echoed off the walls. The sound grew louder, more intense. Thorne's face flushed deep red and his hands covered his ears. He screamed in pain and slid down the wall to the floor.

"It hurts. Stop! Please, stop," he said.

"Not just yet," Kane said.

The weapon's scream grew louder. Thorne was gripped by a series of spasms that had him rolling all over the floor. Boyle laughed.

"I think I've made my point," Kane said. He switched off the weapon, placed it back in its box. "I'll give you a minute to collect yourself and then we'll have you sign the paperwork necessary to make me the administrator of your estate and company."

He turned to Boyle and Jack. "Gentlemen, a moment of your time outside."

The three men went into the hallway and stood a few feet from the treatment room.

"When are you going to tell him that you killed his daughter?" Boyle said.

"My dear, Karl," Kane said. "That information is not to be shared with our patient. Certainly not until I've gotten what I need from him. Should either of you slip and mention that to him, I'll have to punish you severely. Do I make myself clear?"

Both men nodded.

"Good," Kane said. "Now, I have a task for the two of you. Before I could stop her, Nora Thorne had a private conversation with George Chance. I'm concerned that she hired him to snoop around here.

"But if we kill Chance so soon after Nora's death, that could raise all sorts of red flags with the authorities since the two were seen speaking in public.

"To keep him occupied and out of my hair, I want you two to kidnap his girlfriend, Meriem White. That will give me the leverage I need to keep him in his place long enough for me to complete my plans for mass-producing the Screaming Death.

"And Karl, nothing untoward is to happen to her until I give the word. Do I make myself clear?"

"Yes, sir," Boyle said.

"Good," Kane said. "Now, go get Mr. Thorne so he can sign the papers."

"This was fun. We'll have to do it again, Nita," Meriem said.

The two women were leaving the Plaza Hotel where they had just had lunch.

"Yes, it's wonderful to have another woman who understands my unique circumstances," Nita agreed.

"That's our burden for loving such complex men," Meriem said.

"Are you sure I can't give you a lift?" Nita asked.

"No, it's such a beautiful day, I think I'll walk," Meriem said.

Meriem was no more than halfway down the block from Nita when Boyle and Jack pulled up in a flower delivery van, jumped out, grabbed her by the arms. Meriem resisted. A mix of terror and anger flashed in her eyes. She kicked at both men but the contact did not slow them down. Boyle slapped her hard across the face. It left her dazed, knees weak, with a dark red handprint across her cheek. Jack had the van's rear door van open. Boyle shoved her in.

"Let her go," Nita screamed as she ran at them.

"What?" Jack grunted. He stood next to Boyle at the rear of the truck. Its doors still open.

Boyle looked up, smiled. "Jackpot. She's mine."

Nita went to strike him, but he was too fast. He moved out of the path of her fist and slammed his own into the back of her neck. Her head snapped forward, smashed into the side of the van. She groaned. It took all of her might not to pass out. Boyle's gorilla-like arms wrapped around her body, pinned her arms against her sides. Her back was tight against his stomach. His rancid breath assailed her nostrils.

"You've got spirit," Boyle laughed. "I like that. I'm going to enjoy beating the spirit out of you."

He had dragged her to the rear of the van.

"Come on," Jack said. "Get her in and let's go."

Nita stopped struggling. She allowed her body to go limp. Her head lolled forward.

Boyle laughed, made a crude remark about his plans for her, and dragged her to the rear of the van.

Nita snapped her head back, rammed it into Boyle's mouth. The impact caused them both pain. But it was worth it. The head bunt made him release his grip on her as his hands went up to his busted lips.

Nita staggered forward but didn't get far. Jack grabbed her by the arm, spun her around and punched her in the jaw. She crumpled to the street. He yanked her up and tossed her into the van like a sack of dirty laundry. She landed on top of Meriem, knocking her out, too.

Jack slammed the van's rear door shut, locked it.

He grabbed Boyle by the arm, guided him to the front passenger door. Boyle cursed, shrugged him off, and got in. Jack ran around the front of the van and took his seat behind the wheel.

The van was in gear and running lights all the way to the highway before anyone could figure out what had happened.

Chance answered the phone on the first ring, expecting it to be Meriem. Instead, he got: "Mr. Chance, please listen carefully. The life of your beloved Meriem White depends on it."

"Go ahead," Chance said. He didn't ask who it was because he recognized Kane's voice from the other night.

"Ms. White is unharmed and will remain that way as long as you take no action. She will be released in a week. If you go to the police or try to find her yourself, she will be killed."

"I understand," Chance said. "I want to speak with her."

"That's not possible," Kane said. "She's a bit tied up at the moment. Remember, cross me and she's dead."

The connection was broken. Chance hung up.

"What was that all about, Boss?" Harper said. He stood next to Tiny Tim in the hallway.

Chance told them. "We've got to find her," Tiny said. "This guy will never let her go."

"I know," Chance said. "But I gave my word. George Chance won't act. Of course, I said nothing about acting as The Green Ghost."

The two men smiled at their boss.

"I'm sorry to be the bearer of such bad news, Richard," Kirkpatrick said. "But I wanted you to hear it from me and not some newshound or on the radio. I promise you we're doing everything we can to track down Nita and Meriem White."

They were standing in the living room of Wentworth's home. Kirkpatrick glanced at his watch. "I have to get going. I've got a press conference in thirty minutes. I'll be in touch if there are any developments."

"Thanks," Wentworth said.

As soon as Kirkpatrick was gone, Ram Singh appeared.

"We must do something, yes?" Singh said.

"Yes," Wentworth said. "We need to investigate George Chance since it seems that it was his girlfriend who was the target and Nita was at the wrong place at the wrong time."

"We're being followed, Boss," Tiny Tim said. He was in the back seat. Chance was behind the wheel and Harper sat in the front passenger seat. Their car was making its way up the Bronx River

Parkway North to Scarsdale.

"Yes, I noticed," Chance said.

"Kane's men?" Harper said.

"Maybe," Chance said. "Or it could be Richard Wentworth trying to get a line on Nita. If the situations were reversed, that's what I'd do. That's why I chose to leave through the brownstone and not the rectory. I wanted to draw out anyone who might have been watching us."

"He could be trouble," Harper said.

"He could also be a valuable ally," Chance said. "I sense there's more to him than he seems. When I spoke with him at the reception I had the strange feeling I was almost looking at myself in a mirror. Friend or Foe, we'll find out soon enough."

Ram Singh drove while Wentworth sat in the back seat, gazing out the window.

"Sahib, why did we not confront the magician before he left?" Singh said. "My blade would have drawn the truth from him."

"Because there is more to all of this than I can put my finger on," Wentworth said.

"We have just entered Scarsdale," Singh said.

"That's it," Wentworth said. "We're headed to Kane's clinic. I'm sure of it."

"Sahib, do you think Chance is working for him?" Singh said.

"I doubt it, but you never know," Wentworth said. "He could also be delivering a ransom or going to bust the women out on his own. If it's the latter, he'll need help. If it's the first one, we'll take him and Kane down. Either way, this, whatever all of this is, ends tonight. The *Spider* will see to it."

Meriem White and Nita Van Sloan awoke within minutes of each other to find that they were both standing chained spread eagle against a bare brick wall in an underground cell.

"This was not exactly what I was expecting when you said we should meet for a lazy lunch," Nita said.

"Me? I thought you arranged this detour to spice up the day," Meriem said.

The women looked at each other and laughed.

"You're as cool as a cucumber," Meriem said. "I take it this is not the first time you've been in an "awkward" situation such as this one?"

Nita smiled. "Are you kidding me? When you bounce around the country with Richard Wentworth things tend to happen to you. One time, a mad scientist vacuumed out part of my brain. So being chained to the wall in some slimy cell isn't so intimidating."

"How about being kidnapped by an irate spiritualist who decided the best way to get back at George for exposing his fraudulent ways was to subject me to a real life pit and pendulum?" Meriem said.

"I'm impressed," Nita said.

"Yes, George Chance really has a flair for showing a woman a good time," Meriem said. "Of course, he's also shown me how to escape from almost any type of restraining device. These handcuffs are child's play. Give me a second and I'll have us out of them and we can figure out what is going on and why we were kidnapped."

"Great," Nita said. "But, actually, they kidnapped you specifically. I just came along for the ride – to keep you company."

"Thanks," Meriem said.

For the next minute there was only the sound of Meriem breathing and the clinking of the handcuffs as she dislocated her wrists the way Chance had taught her years before and freed herself. A minute later, she was able to free Nita by using a hairpin to pick the lock on the cuffs.

They were discussing their options for escaping the cell when they heard heavy footsteps in the hallway outside.

The voices of Boyle and Jack could be heard.

"Remember, Karl," Jack said. "Dr. Kane said to check on them to make sure they were okay, give them some food and water, and leave. No touching."

"Shut up," Boyle said. "Kane said that the White broad had to be pristine. He didn't say nothing about the other one."

From the sound of their voices they were now in front of the door to the chamber.

During this time, Nita had been carefully arranging the chains that had previously held her. She positioned herself on the side of the door that would shield her from view when it was opened. Meriem had gone back to her place against the wall, making it look like she was still chained to it.

The door opened with a rusty groan.

"Wake up ladies," Boyle said. "It's room service."

He was laughing at his lame joke when Nita swung the knotted end of the chain, smashing him square in the nose and breaking it. Blood spurted out like jelly from a squashed donut. Boyle dropped to his knees, clutching his face.

"Thanks, but we prefer to eat out," Nita said.

Jack cursed, dropped the food tray and grabbed for his gun. He never reached it. Nita stepped into him, jamming the heel of her hand under his jaw causing his head to snap back into the open door. He was unconscious before he hit the ground.

Pleased with her handiwork, she turned back to Meriem only to be confronted by a very angry Boyle.

"I'm going to kill you," he said through the blood and snot that covered his face.

"Not today," Meriem said.

Boyle turned to look at her, thinking she was still chained to the wall. Instead, he got whacked in the face again with a section of chain swung by Meriem. Boyle crumpled to the ground and stayed there.

"Nice work," Nita said.

"Thanks. Let's get out of here," Meriem said.

They were stopped by the sounds of screams and gunfire coming from upstairs.

A few moments earlier…

Chance parked his car off the side of the road behind some brush. When he emerged, it was as The Green Ghost. He was clad in black, wearing a fedora, trench coat, and gloves. His face was hidden behind a skull-like mask that glowed green.

He disappeared into the night, followed by Harper and Tiny Tim. Wentworth, watching from the backseat of his car that was now parked on the other side of the road, thought they were one of the most bizarre sights he had ever witnessed.

"What are they doing?" Singh said.

"Looks to me like they are on a reconnaissance mission," Wentworth said. "I think we all may be on the same side of this fight. Did you notice the mask?"

"The green glow makes it quite visible, Sahib," Singh said.

"There's only one mysterious figure I've heard of who wears such a mask – The Green Ghost," Wentworth said. "It seems Chance is one of my brethren. Come, my friend. It's time for The Green Ghost to meet The *Spider*.

Two minutes later, The *Spider* and Ram Singh intercepted The Green Ghost and his aides as they were scouting the sanitarium.

"Keep your weapons holstered," The *Spider* said as he came up behind them like a shadow in the night. "We are here on a common mission. I suggest we pool our resources."

The men turned to find themselves face to face with The *Spider*, armed with his .45s, and the ever-loyal Ram Singh brandishing his blades. Chance, viewing The *Spider* through the green shaded lenses of his mask marveled at Wentworth's physical transformation from millionaire society scion to dark avenger of the night.

Anyone else would never have identified The *Spider* as Wentworth. But for Chance, not even The *Spider's* horrific disguise could camouflage the burning rage he had spotted in Wentworth's eyes the first time they had met.

"What did you have in mind?" The Green Ghost said.

"We play to both of our strengths," The *Spider* said. "Since you have a way with locks you can sneak into the sanitarium without tripping the alarm. Then the rest of us can enter unseen. You rescue Meriem and Nita and I'll take care of Kane."

"We'll also need to find C. W. Thorne," The Green Ghost said. "Kane is holding him hostage. That's why his daughter, Nora, came to me. She wanted my help in saving him."

"Okay, my man and your men can handle that task," The *Spider* said.

Within seconds, The Green Ghost had disabled the alarm system and picked the lock to a side entrance. The small group entered the building and split up to fulfill their individual missions. Then, all hell broke loose.

"Intruders!" an orderly shouted. The man had just come out of a men's room when he happened upon Ram Singh, Harper, and Tiny Tim. Ram ran him through with his blade. But it was too late. Several other orderlies came running down the hallway. They carried machineguns.

Soon, the hallway was filled with gunfire. Singh, Harper, and Tim returned fire while seeking cover behind a row of filing cabinets they knocked over to form a shield.

With gunfire now echoing throughout the building, The Green Ghost knew that the plan he had just agreed to with The *Spider* for a stealth attack was out the window. He moved fast and silent through the halls of the sanitarium. Though The *Spider* was supposed to handle Kane, The Green Ghost knew he had to get to him first to make the crazed doctor tell him where the women were being held.

The Green Ghost moved fast and silent through the halls of the sanitarium. He needed to locate someone who knew where the women were being held. The only person he knew for sure who would have that information was Kane himself. He had to find him and make him talk.

Light shone from under a door at the end of the hall. He moved to it. He heard voices and then footsteps coming close on the other side of the door. He braced himself to attack, standing on the side of the door, and waited. The door opened and…

…Out stepped Meriem followed by Nita.

"You're okay," The Green Ghost said.

"Of course, we are," Meriem said.

"Good, stay out of sight and get out of here," The Green Ghost said. "Things are heating up. I'm not here alone. The *Spider* is also around. The car is down the road. We'll meet you both there. Now, move."

The women took off down the hall. The Green Ghost headed off to find Kane.

The Green Ghost ran down the hall, kicking in any door that was locked. He found C. W. Thorne strapped to a vertical operating table. The man was semi-conscious, his face bruised and bloodied, and his clothes shredded and caked in dried blood and filth.

"Who are you?" Thorne gasped.

"A friend," The Green Ghost said. "Your daughter sent me to find you."

"Nora, my Nora," Thorne said. "Is she safe?"

The Ghost, not wanting to tell the old man the truth at that moment, changed the subject.

"Where is Dr. Kane?" The Green Ghost said.

"Right behind you," Kane said.

The Green Ghost turned to see Kane, garbed in an armored suit that had a power pack on the back and power cables going from the pack to the arms and legs of the suit. A helmet with a visor that ended just below the nose protected Kane's head.

"Cute costume," The Green Ghost said. "But Halloween isn't for another couple of months.

Kane smiled. "Good. You're not afraid. That will only make your defeat – your pleading for a merciful death – all the more enjoyable."

Kane raised his arms. The Green Ghost saw that there was what looked like miniature radio amplifiers attached to each of Kane's palms.

"It's time you experienced the power of the Screaming Death first hand," Kane growled.

Before The Green Ghost could react he was blasted by the sound waves that surged from Kane's hands. His head snapped back. It felt like he was being worked over with a sledgehammer. The Green Ghost could feel his bones shake and his emotions begin to roil. Fear. Pure unadulterated fear was racing through him. Suddenly, it was hard to breath. He didn't want to be here. He wanted to be home with Meriem. So scared. These thoughts raced through his mind in seconds.

He dived for cover behind a cot, flipping it onto its side to act as a shield. It didn't work. Kane laughed, spittle and foam flecked his chin, and blasted the cot with his sound waves. The waves shattered the bed. The shrapnel from it exploded in every direction.

The Green Ghost grunted in pain. Several of the fragments had cut through his clothes and protective body armor he wore, embedded in his chest and abdomen. He could feel the liquid heat of his blood pour forth, drench him. The room spun. He was going to blackout. If he did, he was dead. He only had one chance left. With his last remaining ounce of strength, The Green Ghost raised his hands as though to surrender but instead he snapped his fingers. From them the special flash powder that coated his gloves ignited creating blinding white green light that filled the room.

The pyrotechnic display lasted only a few seconds but it was enough to startle Kane causing him to stumble back and deactivate his palm blasters.

"Magic tricks?" Kane said. "Do you really think that will stop me?"

"No, but I will," The *Spider* said as he ran into the laboratory, guns ablaze. His maniacal laugh that cowered the most hardened of criminals echoed through the room.

Kane cursed and raised his hands at The *Spider*. The memory of his last run-in with the device sent a slight shiver down The *Spider's* spine but he steeled himself and charged right at the mad scientist.

Kane blasted him with both hands. The force of the beams caught The *Spider* dead center in the chest and slammed him into the far wall.

His head bounced off the wall, stars exploded before his eyes. He could feel a trickle of blood run down the back of his skull into his collar.

The *Spider* staggered to his feet. He still clutched his guns.

Kane smiled. "Stubborn to the end. I'm going to enjoy killing you slowly. I think I'll start by having you rip out your own eyes."

The *Spider* tried to raise his guns but couldn't. The Screaming Death seemed to turn his muscles into jelly. The incessant droning the device gave off felt like worms boring through his brain. "I'm not giving this bastard the satisfaction of killing me," The *Spider* thought.

He shuddered as the Screaming Death set his nerve endings afire. But he was The *Spider* and he would not yield. He took an agonizing step forward. Kane laughed again. "Pathetic hero in a fright mask. You are no match for me."

"Oh, yeah? How about now?" The Green Ghost said from behind them. Then he let fly his throwing knives. They found their target – the power pack on Kane's back. There was an instant crackle of electricity as the tips of the knives pierced the protective housing.

Kane cursed, spun around and blasted The Green Ghost. "Fun time is over. You two are too dangerous to keep alive any longer."

Convulsions wracked The Green Ghost.

The *Spider* took the opening and tackled Kane, driving him to his knees. The *Spider* was a blur of manic rage as he slammed Kane's helmeted head into the floor over and over. He stopped once he was satisfied Kane was stunned. Then, removed Kane's belt and used it to tie his hands to the sides of his helmet so that the amplifiers were aligned against the man's ears.

The Green Ghost was now standing, just barely. The *Spider* pointed to Thorne. The Green Ghost nodded. He freed Thorne from his restraints, took him outside.

The *Spider* drew a deep breath, exhaled. At his feet, Kane struggled to break free.

"Now, Doctor," The *Spider* said. "It's time that you get to experience your evil first hand."

The *Spider* bent down and twisted a dial on the power pack. It hummed and sparked. The Green Ghost's knife attack on it had left the device unstable. Now, with its power turned up, it was volatile.

Through the growing hum of the machine, Kane pleaded: "Wait. Turn it off, please. Please!"

Kane's voice rose to a shriek as the Screaming Death sound waves washed over him.

The *Spider* stood in the doorway to the lab and watched as Kane shuddered and convulsed like a snake in boiling oil. The scientist soiled his pants as he flopped around. His eyes bulged. Blood spurted from his ears, mouth, and nose. So much blood, it drowned his shouts into gurgles of agony. There was a series of popping and cracking noises from deep within his body. He lurched up, seemed suspended in time and space. Then his skull exploded. Blood and brain and fingers splattered the walls like a demented finger-painting done by Satan.

His now handless arms flapped at his sides and then the corpse keeled over on its side. A final burble of blood and entrails plopped out of the opening that had been Kane's neck.

When the dust settled, The *Spider* destroyed every piece of the Screaming Death in the building and set the laboratory on fire. No one else would ever benefit from Kane's work.

Two nights later, Wentworth and Nita had Commissioner Kirkpatrick, George Chance, and Meriem White over for drinks.

"Here's to the silencing of the Screaming Death," Wentworth said.

"Yes, and to Dr. Kane spending eternity in Hell with a bad case of tinnitus," Chance said.

They all laughed.

"Not to bring everyone down, but I feel so bad for Mr. Thorne," Meriem said.

"Yes, the poor man's life was destroyed by Kane," Nita said.

"C. W. Thorne is a tough man, he'll pull through," Kirkpatrick said. "I'm sure of it."

"It's a good thing that The *Spider* and The Green Ghost appeared to save the day," Meriem said. "Isn't that right, Commissioner?"

"Oh, don't get him started," Nita said.

"I don't understand?" Meriem said.

"They're vigilantes, Ms. White," Kirkpatrick said. "Yes, they may do more good than harm but they still work outside the law."

"Sometimes, that seems to be necessary," Chance said. "After all, had the police in Scarsdale been more helpful to Nora Thorne, she still might be alive today and Kane never would have gotten the chance to subject the city to his perverse machine."

"The law does not recognize vigilantes," Kirkpatrick said.

"So you would arrest them the first chance you had," Wentworth said.

"Yes," Kirkpatrick said. "If I could find them, I'd slap the cuffs on them myself."

Wentworth, Chance, Meriem, and Nita all exchanged glances and laughed.

Kirkpatrick, ruffled by the joke he seemed to miss, said, "What's so funny?"

"Nothing, it's just good to have everything back to normal," Wentworth said.

The Steel Tsars

by James Chambers

A jet of flame forced The *Spider* to his knees. Heat seared his face and a cloud of choking, black smoke rolled toward him from the smoldering guts of a burned-out taxi. The trapped cabbie had stopped shrieking minutes ago, but a riot of screams still filled the air. It came from people lying partly crushed under falling debris, from people caught inside the fire-engulfed lobby of Madison Square Garden. Nearly a quarter of the great arena was being consumed in a red-hot blaze, and all around burned smaller fires, too numerous to count. Gray and black pillars of smoke blotted out the night sky and dimmed the glow of streetlamps and building lights. Eighth Avenue between 49th and 50th was a scene from Hell and at its center stood the scene's own Lucifer: a man in steel armor with a flamethrower bolted to his back.

The armored man traced The *Spider's* scrambling progression along the sidewalk and then sent another lance of fire at him. It hit low and flooded the area with an expanding cloud of flame. The *Spider* leapt into the air to avoid it, but for the panicked crowd rushing all around him, there was little chance of escape. The flame torched a police officer, a woman, and two young men fleeing the block, all of whom ran unknowingly into the fireball's path.

The *Spider* howled in rage and anguish. He was no stranger to the death of innocents, but had the flames met their true target—*him*—those people might have escaped. In the *Spider's* mind, the horror translated to fury and hatred. Not only had this armored madman brought death and destruction to New York, but now he had forced the blood of innocents onto The *Spider's* hands. It would have been almost more than he could bear had he not used his outrage to further fuel his will to destroy the armored man before too many more perished.

Already the conflagration had claimed the lives of hundreds of boxing fans that had come to attend the night's prizefight. Some of the dead were unlucky enough to have been sitting where the blaze began when the madman attacked. Others had been too slow to escape being trampled by the crowd or tumbling chunks of the collapsing building. And now the surrounding intersections were closed by debris and walls of flame, keeping ambulances and firefighters from reaching the Garden and the worst of the blaze. Yet nothing The *Spider* did so much as slowed the man with the flamethrower.

"What's the matter, little arachnid man?" the firebug said. He spoke with a thick Russian accent, and the resonator in his helmet gave his voice a metallic quality. "How is it you Americans say? Can't stand the heat then go leave the kitchen!"

The man laughed. The sound of it cut through The *Spider's* last reserves of self-control. Bringing his twin .45s to bear, the masked crimefighter unleashed a fusillade of lead at his enemy, firing round after round, until his clips ran empty—every shot simply pinging off his opponent's steel shell.

The man laughed again. "Not so easy to stop one of the Steel Tsars. I am Ivan! Strong and powerful, not like your weak American gangsters with their fedora hats and cheap talking. You have never met anyone like me and my brothers."

"I've met plenty of men like you—men with cheap ambitions and power and not the intelligence to use it wisely," The *Spider* said. "Get you out of that tin can and I'll blow you away as easily as all the rest."

"Bah!" Ivan raised the muzzle of his flamethrower for another blast.

Holding his breath and draping his black cloak over his head, The *Spider* vanished into a cloud of dense smoke. Ivan held his fire. The *Spider* ran blind along the sidewalk, relying on his incredible memory to help him avoid obstacles and burning debris. Confronting Ivan head on would only get him killed. He needed to find the killer's weak spot. If he could get behind the Steel Cossack, there was a scaffolding he had seen earlier where repair work was underway on the Garden's exterior lights. If it was not yet burning, he could use it. He counted his running steps to track his position. His lungs ached for a breath of air, but to inhale the oily smoke would be like swallowing poison. The *Spider* forced himself faster, further, until a darkness apart from the smoke closed in around the edges of his vision. Then he broke free of the cloud and found his destination.

Swallowing a gasp of hot air, The *Spider* leapt onto the scaffolding and clambered to the top. He whirled, reloaded his .45s, and then planted his feet and spied his target.

Ivan searched the sidewalk for him, spitting out threads of flame at anyone or anything that moved. A running usher caught fire, fell, and rolled screaming in the street. From atop the scaffolding, The *Spider* surveyed the full scope of death and destruction Ivan had rendered. Although he had killed many men during his war against crime, The *Spider* had never done so for the pure joy of murder as Ivan did. All the men who had died at his hands had deserved it and few more so than Ivan. He studied the madman's armor, his sharp eyes zeroing in on the tubes, valves, and tanks that fueled the flamethrower.

The *Spider* opened fire.

His impeccable aim sent slug after slug beating against the flamethrower's valves and hoses, seeking a weak point, but they proved as solid and well protected as Ivan himself. Bullets dinged them then glanced away, wasted.

Ivan circled and faced The *Spider*.

"There you are, my friend," Ivan said. "I was worried the fire had burned you up. I am happy it did not. I would like that honor for myself."

The *Spider* leapt free as Ivan doused the scaffolding in flame. The wood planks caught with a flare and paint blistered on the structure's steel frame.

The *Spider* hit the ground and tumbled.

Ivan surged after him.

A steel boot slammed down on the edge of The *Spider's* cape, halting his rolling escape. The *Spider* gagged as Ivan grabbed a handful of the black cloth clasped around his neck and dragged him back. The Russian's mocking laughter grated in The *Spider's* ears. The crimefighter snarled, then released the clasp of his cape and scrambled away, but Ivan's steel fist crashed against his shoulder and neck, slamming him to the ground. Shaking off the blow, The *Spider* flipped onto his back and fired on his attacker. He concentrated on the armor's joints, hoping at least one shot might penetrate, but the steel plates held. Ivan crouched over The *Spider*. The black gape of the flamethrower's muzzle was only inches from The *Spider's* head.

"You are too easy," Ivan said. "You scramble and climb and spit bullets as useless against me as a *Spider's* web. Now I will turn you to ash. The Americans' greatest crimefighter, the killer of more criminals than can be counted, the so-called Master of Men—but you are no match for good Russian steel and the fire that will never go out. I will enjoy very much my new home here in New York when you are gone."

This time Ivan's laughter chilled The *Spider*. He was trapped. There would be no dodging the flamethrower's next blast. Determined to face his fate head on, The *Spider* stared up into the eyes of the man who would kill him—*the eyes!* The *Spider's* almost superhuman reflexes transformed the thought into immediate action. He snapped one of his .45s to bear and fired. It was an almost impossible shot; the open eye slits in the Steel Tsar's faceplate were barely as wide across as silver dollars, but The *Spider's* single shot found its mark. The slug bit into Ivan's left eye and entered his skull. It clanged twice as it ricocheted inside the helmet, shattering through Ivan's head; the bullet never emerged.

The *Spider* scurried to his right.

Ivan collapsed, missing him by inches. His armored body cracked the paving stones where he fell.

The *Spider* shoved Ivan onto his back. To eliminate any doubt, he placed his weapons against the fallen Russian's eyes and fired. Both guns clicked dry. Tonight, The *Spider's* life had hinged on a single bullet, but The *Spider* did not dwell on how close Ivan had come to ending his war. He had survived and that was all that mattered. He had no time to unlock the dead man's helmet, so he left his ghastly red mark stamped upon its shining surface and then reclaimed his cape.

Racing to the street, The *Spider* dashed uptown. Firemen finally had cleared the roads of fire and debris, opening the way for the caravan of fire trucks now rushing past with sirens wailing to save what remained of the Garden. An ambulance followed. Many more would be needed. It appeared the city's entire resources of emergency personnel were on the scene.

Parked at the curb beyond the firefighters' perimeter waited a familiar black limousine. A powerful, turbaned man, Ram Singh, sat inside it, waiting and ready at the wheel. The *Spider* bolted across the road, ignoring the startled shouts of the firefighters and paramedics who noticed him, and slipped into the limousine's back seat. He slammed the door shut after him, and in moments the car was bumping over sidewalks and rolling through near-impossible squeezes between stopped vehicles to find a path into the city.

"When I said we had a hot date tonight, this isn't what I had in mind," Nita Van Sloan said. The beautiful socialite, dressed in an elegant evening gown and fur stole, sat across from The *Spider*. A leather overnight case rested on the seat beside her. "But I suppose if you weren't a man of extremes, I might not love you as much as I do."

The *Spider* removed his domino mask, revealing the handsome, cultured face of Richard Wentworth. He wiped soot from his face with a handkerchief then smiled at Nita.

"No extreme would be too great to attain to please you, my dear," he said. "And I do apologize that our evening out was interrupted. Madmen have no respect for romance."

A grave expression came over Nita. "But, Richard, are you all right? Are you hurt?"

"Nothing that will slow me down," he said. "I'm afraid The *Spider's* work for tonight isn't over yet."

"You're correct." Nita handed Wentworth a newspaper. "It's the late edition."

Wentworth read the headline: Russians Challenge The *Spider*! The article described a letter and phone call the paper had received only hours ago, announcing a plot by a criminal group from Russia that intended to conquer New York and from there, claim the entire United States for their criminal empire. They planned to launch their war by killing The *Spider* and promised to come at him until they succeeded.

"Damn the bastards," Wentworth said. "They'll turn the city into a battlefield. I'm the only one who has a chance of standing against them."

"Do you have any idea who they are?"

"That one was called Ivan and he has brothers. I don't know how many. They call themselves the Steel Tsars."

"What's your next move?"

"First, back home to get properly armed," Wentworth said. "I wasn't exactly dressed for duty when we left for the Ritz-Carlton tonight. Then I track down these fiends before they kill anyone else."

Nita handed him the overnight case stashed next to her.

"I can save you a trip, at least," she said. "After you ran out on our beef Wellington, Singh and I stopped by your house to collect a few things."

The *Spider* opened the case. It was stuffed with ammunition, guns, even a few hand grenades, and other explosive devices.

"Thank you, Nita," Wentworth said. "As always, your help is invaluable to The *Spider's* mission."

"You're welcome," Nita said. "A few things that didn't fit in the case are in the trunk."

Wentworth plucked two clips from the case and reloaded his .45s. Then he gathered more ammunition, extra guns, grenades, and explosives and concealed them in his clothing and cape. He reached past Nita and rolled down the window between the driver and the passenger compartment.

"Ram," he said. "8th and 14th, northwest corner."

Ram nodded.

Wentworth settled back into his seat. He stared at Nita, admiring her beauty, and she smiled at him, taking pride in the way he looked at her. Between them passed a silent recognition of the sacrifices each made for The *Spider's* war on crime, the seemingly endless battle that kept Nita and Wentworth from being truly together. But then the moment passed and Wentworth once again donned the mask of The *Spider*. When the car stopped at its destination, he threw the door open and jumped out.

Nita called, "Be careful," as he left her.

His only reply was a deep, crackling laugh that echoed along the city street. Then The *Spider* disappeared down an alley. He ran to the end and clambered over a chain-link fence, landed, and crossed a small courtyard to reach the back door of a bakery that fronted onto 13th Street. In the bakery's cellar, The *Spider* knew, was an illegal betting parlor, one of the few criminal enterprises around the city that he tolerated because it served his purposes to do so. He pounded on the back door. When he heard the click of locks being opened, he withdrew and melded into the shadows. The betting parlor's proprietor, a wiry, gray-haired man in a dark suit, appeared in the doorway.

"Who's there?" he said.

"You haven't forgotten our deal, have you, Henry?" The *Spider* said. "There's nowhere you can escape the cold shadow of my justice."

The man turned pale and scanned the darkness, unable to locate The *Spider*. "No, no, *Spider*, I ain't forgot nothing. How could I? If I forget, you'll put your mark on my head. What do you want?"

"Information," The *Spider* said. "About the Steel Tsars."

"All's I know is what I read in the papers, same as everyone else."

"Men like that don't come into town on the 5:15 out of Philly. There must have been talk on the street and the street is where rats like you live."

"I heard nothing. They came out of thin air," Henry said.

"An armored man with a flamethrower? Did he purchase his gear at Woolworth's?"

"No, no, course not, but what makes you think I know anything?"

"Because you are only useful to me when you do," The *Spider* said. "And when you cease being useful, you cease giving me a reason to allow you to live."

"Okay, okay," Henry said. "Listen, maybe I got something, maybe not. Couple of things I heard came to mind when I saw tonight's paper. Grandinetti Steel Works out in Queens got hit about two weeks ago. Five or six guys killed. Three men took them all down, made off with a couple of truckloads of steel, welding torches, and other gear. Could maybe be they used it all for the armor, right? And there's a new name been making the rounds, supposed to be a real tough monkey, killed a guy with one bare hand over... well, over a financial dispute. It's a Russian name."

"Which is?"

"Yuri Olgachenski."

"Olgachenski? You're sure?"

"Course, I'm sure. That's what I said, ain't it? That's all I got, all right? Don't put this on me. I don't want to see the city burn anymore than you do," Henry said. "It's bad for business."

The *Spider* left without a word.

Yuri Olgachenski.

The name echoed in his thoughts. He wondered if it was possible, if the man he had known by that name had—against all odds—survived the War to End All Wars despite rumors he had been killed in battle. The *Spider* had never met Olgachenski in person, though he had come close a few times. But the reputation of the war's greatest tank engineer had been the stuff of legend. A brilliant man, Olgachenski had insisted on supervising the construction of every single tank he designed and then taking them himself into combat for the first time. Not even his own people could have said for sure if he was a genius or a lunatic.

Richard Wentworth had fought alongside one of Olgachenski's armored vehicles and he had no doubt that had Olgachenski allowed them to be mass produced, World War I would have ended much earlier than it had. If Olgachenski had indeed survived the conflict and now turned his efforts toward conquering New York, no one but The *Spider* could hope to stop him.

The *Spider* returned to his waiting limousine, but as he gripped the door handle, an explosion roared through the night. The ground shook, and less than two blocks away, a fireball rose into the sky like a miniature sun. Without hesitation, The *Spider* whirled and ran toward the source, hoping it was not where it appeared to be, praying that even the Steel Tsars would not be so cruel and callous. But in less than two minutes, he covered the ground between only to face the very nightmare he feared.

A blaze engulfed the front entrance of St. Vincent's Hospital. A horrified crowd was gathered on the street. A second explosion embraced them with smoke and flame, erasing any doubt in The *Spider's* mind that he was about to meet the second Steel Tsar. The powerful shockwave staggered The *Spider*. There was nothing he could do to help those caught in the blast. Even worse, he knew, with so many of the city's firefighters and equipment concentrated uptown to fight the Garden blaze, it would be a long time before any of them responded here.

A third explosion rose from the far side of the hospital. The *Spider* dashed around the corner and found the emergency entrance now burning too, but at least the firebug was in sight. Down the block, a man in armor similar to Ivan's knelt outside another entrance to the hospital, setting what appeared to be a fourth bomb. In a heartbeat, The *Spider's* .45s were in his grip and raining bullets on the armored man's hands, driving him clear of the bomb. Startled, the man jerked back too fast, succumbed to the weight of his armor, and fell onto his back. He grappled around for the torch of his flamethrower, but The *Spider* gave him no respite.

The masked crimefighter reloaded his guns as he closed the

distance between them. He leapt onto the fallen man, intending to deal with him as he had Ivan, and let loose a barrage of shots against his enemy's eyes. Realizing The *Spider's* target, the armored man raised an arm to deflect the bullets. With his other arm, he swept The *Spider's* feet from under him and then began the process of picking himself up off the ground.

"I will crush you!" the man shouted. His voice echoed from inside his helmet. "How did you kill my brother? How did you do it? If you are here then Ivan must be dead. But I will send you to join him soon."

"Stay down," The *Spider* said. "You're only standing up to greet your death."

"I will not let you taunt me." The man had one foot planted, kneeling like a crude knight, and was shifting his weight to bring his other foot into position. "I am Alexei the brave and the powerful. I will crush you and make your people my slaves."

The *Spider* did not answer. He drew a grenade from inside his cape, pulled the pin, and rolled it beneath Alexei. The Russian swung the muzzle of his flamethrower and batted the grenade back toward the retreating *Spider*. It exploded en route and the impact drove both men to the ground, but erupting midway between them, it was not enough to finish either one. The *Spider* shook off the blast and scrambled to his feet. A spray of flame singed the edges of his cape. He tumbled out of range of Alexei's flamethrower and then tossed a fresh grenade. Slowed by his armor, unable to reach the explosive, the Russian caught the brunt of the blast this time. It jolted him into the side of a parked ambulance, crumpling it.

The *Spider* tossed a third grenade.

It lodged in the ambulance's dented fender and, when it exploded, the impact lifted Alexei into the air and dropped him down amidst the debris of the destroyed emergency vehicle. A nearby streetlamp cracked and fell onto the wreckage, hinging precariously on the cracked roof and pinning Alexei in place. The muzzle of the flamethrower landed beyond the Russian's reach. Guns ready, The *Spider* approached his enemy. He glimpsed Ram Singh, down the block, helping people to avoid the flames as they fled the hospital.

"I sent your brother to the hell he deserves the same way I'll send you—with a single bullet," The *Spider* said.

"Stop!" Alexei shouted. "Or I'll blow the entire hospital into an inferno. You think I was unprepared for you? No, little man. While you battled Ivan, I planted half a dozen explosives around this building. They are positioned to seal the exits while the building burns. Their detonators may be triggered by a radio transmitter in my armor. Now, lay down your guns and die or I will kill all inside."

The *Spider* halted. "I don't believe you."

"Yet my flames will cook them all alive whether or not you believe," Alexei said. "Look at my shoulder, beside my fuel tanks. There is a silver antenna. You see it?"

The *Spider* had not noticed it earlier, but a slender wire poked up beside Alexei's head. It was coiled at the top and shielded by the same steel guard that protected the flamethrower's fuel lines.

"Yes," The *Spider* said.

"It will be the means of their deaths."

"You and your brothers made this between you and me. Leave these people out of it. They're nothing to you."

"Nyet. They are mine to do with as I please," Alexei said. "Do you not yet understand? My brothers and I are taking this city away from you. This city belongs to the Steel Tsars to keep or destroy as we like. And tonight, I feel like breaking things."

"I won't allow the innocent to die for my sake."

The *Spider* pointed his guns away from Alexei.

"You are soft, *Spider*. That is why you hide behind a mask and try to frighten spineless American gangsters. Perhaps I will not kill you right away. It might amuse me to play with you first. Throw down your guns."

"Throw down my guns?" The *Spider* crouched as if to place his guns on the ground but feinted and instead opened fire on the base of the broken streetlamp. "I don't think I will."

The *Spider's* bullets ripped the wires and last scraps of iron holding it in place. Before Alexei could react, the top edge of the lamp shifted with a metallic shriek and plunged down on top of him. The weight of it clamped him more tightly to the wreckage of the ambulance.

"Liar! Now they die," Alexei shouted.

He activated his transmitter, but no explosions came.

The *Spider* approached him.

"Did you think I would ever surrender to a coward who hides behind steel and shields himself with the lives of women and children?"

"I don't understand. Why does it not work?"

Gesturing with a .45, The *Spider* pointed at Alexei's antenna and the fuel line beside it, both of which had been severed by a sharp edge of the collapsed streetlamp. Alexei's helmet kept him from looking over his shoulder to see, but The *Spider* explained.

"I cut your line and your antenna," he said.

Alexei grunted. He twisted and thrust against the wreckage pinning him. It shifted but he could not gain the leverage to rise. The *Spider* bent down to pluck a scrap of burning debris from the sidewalk. He held it up for the struggling Russian to see.

"Your fuel line is open," The *Spider* said. "I won't kill you like Ivan after all."

Alexei snarled and then shouted, "You will die tonight, *Spider*!"

The *Spider* ignored him and shoved the burning scrap into the open fuel line, then raced away toward a low brick wall along the hospital walkway. He leapt over it and pressed his body against its base for cover. A moment later Alexei's fuel tanks erupted and The *Spider* imagined he heard Alexei's final screams among the roar of fire. He rose and watched the body burn for several seconds, wondering if somehow Alexei might have survived, but it was impossible. He was completely bathed in fire, and even if his armor somehow protected his body, he would still have to breathe in the flames and super-heated air. The *Spider* felt a twinge of disappointment that he could not leave his mark on the dead man's forehead.

Ram Singh approached him. "Many have been evacuated from the hospital," he said. "Where will the next strike come? I am eager to wash my blades in the blood of evil men."

"I don't know, but I'm sure we won't wait long to find out," The *Spider* said. "Right now we need to reach Police Commissioner Kirkpatrick. There are half a dozen bombs left here to be defused. And I know who's leading the Steel Tsars."

The two men returned to the limousine, and as Ram drove, The *Spider* told Nita what he had learned.

"If any man could do what the Steel Tsars plan, it's Yuri Olgachenski." He paused then added, "Although I guess it's only the Steel Tsar now that I've killed Ivan and Alexei."

"What will the third attack be?" Nita asked.

"Whatever it is will be deadlier and more spectacular than what we've seen so far," The *Spider* said. "Olgachenski isn't the type to share power or wealth. I half wonder if my killing his brothers wasn't part of his plan. If it was, he's quite confident he can handle me on his own."

"Then he's underestimated you."

"Let's hope so." The *Spider* took Nita's hand. "Now, you know what to do when we get to police HQ? I would do it myself if I could."

"The *Spider* can't exactly waltz into Commissioner Kirkpatrick's office," Nita said. "Don't worry, I'll tell him everything you've told me and attribute it all to Richard Wentworth's criminological astuteness. He'll know enough to listen."

The limousine stopped at the curb across from the police station. Nita wrapped her stole around her and then got out when Ram opened the door. She glanced back for a farewell smile at The *Spider* and then she crossed the street, her heels clicking on the pavement. Ram closed the door and returned to the driver's seat.

The glass partition behind his head was down. He asked The *Spider*, "Your instructions, Sahib?"

"Drive downtown," The *Spider* said. "I need to think."

The car rolled through the sparkling night of lower Manhattan. So many blocks away from the fire attacks farther uptown, it was as if nothing had happened. Cabs clogged the roads and people moved along the sidewalks. It was New York after dark and the only sign of trouble was the bright hellish glow visible against the low clouds where the blazes still burned. The *Spider* wondered where Olgachenski might hit next. The man was a master tactician who understood the value of bold maneuvers and the need to break his enemy's hope. Whatever the next attack was, it would be not only devastating but symbolic. The *Spider* considered the city's many famous landmarks: the Brooklyn Bridge, the Empire State Building, the Statue of Liberty, Times Square. The destruction of any one of them would strike a powerful blow against the city, but once the initial shock passed, New York would rally back stronger to resist and rebuild. Olgachenski needed an attack that would crack the hearts of its populace, something aimed at the very core of their security—and then it came to him.

"My God! I've sent Nita into a deathtrap!" The *Spider* shouted. "Turn around, Ram! Go back! Olgachenski will strike at police headquarters."

The limousine tires squealed as Ram obeyed. For all the city's faults, crime, and corruption and despite the inevitable few cops who turned bad, New Yorkers still looked to their police force to keep order. Many of the men who wore the uniform and the badge were among the bravest and most honorable The *Spider* knew. Every day they set an example to all New Yorkers about the best of what lived in the city's unseen, beating heart. It was the unbreakable will to hold the line against the darkness and terror of crime no matter how long or how hard the fight. A fatal blow to the police would be a death-strike against that heart, one that could end all resistance to the Steel Tsar's conquest in a single night.

Minutes later, Ram barreled the limousine over the curb outside police headquarters and the car lurched to a stop. He twisted around in his seat, but even before he spoke, The *Spider* knew by the look in Ram's eyes that the attack had begun.

"There are many armored men with flamethrowers charging the building," Ram said. "Many foolish men who wish to meet my blade."

"Then let's go introduce them."

With a harsh laugh, The *Spider* kicked the door open and burst from the car. His .45s spit death at the men in shining metal who were taking up positions outside the police station. Their armor covered only their torsos, parts of their arms and legs, and the back and top of their heads. The sight of so many weak points brought a smile to The *Spider's* face. He celebrated by shooting two of the attackers between the eyes. They went down without having so much as ignited their torches. Several others noticed The *Spider* and leveled their flamethrowers at him. Two crumpled to the ground as a bloody flash of metal ripped through their throats. Ram had already insinuated himself among the men and put his blade to work. At close quarters, the men's flamethrowers were useless, and their incomplete armor insufficient to turn back the edge of Ram's weapon. A spray of blood painted Ram's cheek. He grinned and stalked another target. The *Spider* used the time Ram bought to retrieve a coil of rope and grappling hook from the trunk. He thought he might need it to rescue Nita.

The battle raged.

Gunfire and hand grenades clashed against armor and flame. The street lit up with fire. Men encased in silver steel poured from the alleys and side streets like strange, burning insects. From police headquarters flowed a steady stream of officers, armed and eager for the chance to hit back for what had been done to their city. The *Spider* and Ram waded into the thick of the conflict. The *Spider* sent the Steel Tsar's men to the ground with expert shots, and Ram opened throat after throat with his blood-slicked blade. The *Spider* put three bullets into one man, two in his legs, and the third in his forehead as he fell to the ground. Ram whirled and feinted, licking out with the tip of his blade to blind the man nearest him with a single swipe before he sliced the man's hands from his wrists. The *Spider* fired a round up the muzzle of a flamethrower; the backlash ignited its fuel and turned the man and five others into pillars of fire. Ram cut off a man's leg then stabbed the two who tripped over him in the back of their necks, severing their spines. The dead and the maimed piled up, and still the armored men came.

The *Spider* and Ram fought their way toward headquarters, The

Spider hoping to get Nita out before the fighting closed off all avenues of escape. He did not get the chance.

Ten feet from the entrance, The *Spider* and Ram found themselves cut off by a wall of flame that erupted out of the air. Behind them, a motor growled and metal clanked and from an alley emerged a sleek silver tank mounted on wide, high treads. Fixed to its turret was a fire-cannon with incredible range. It was this weapon that had set the entrance to headquarters ablaze. Now its deadly flame sliced into the ranks of the police officers, cutting down men six at a time. It showed no preference for the Steel Tsar's thugs. If they were in its line of fire, they burned.

The *Spider* grabbed Ram by the arm. "I need to get inside that hellish machine," he said. "Take the car. Use it to distract the operator."

Ram nodded and sprinted across the burning battlefield. His blade danced to the left and right as he went, finding the exposed places on the armored men he passed, spilling their blood in a macabre breadcrumb trail. Pulling his cloak across him, The *Spider* shifted into the shadows and edged away from the melee. Once clear, he rushed down the nearest block until he found an alleyway that allowed him to come up behind the silver tank. He watched the armored vehicle crawl into the street outside police headquarters. The *Spider's* black limousine was on the move, weaving to dodge fire-blasts from the cannon and avoid running over police officers. The brakes squealed and the big car skidded and spun to face the side of the tank. The motor revved and the limo rocketed forward, racing beneath the range of the fire-cannon. A heartbeat before impact, the driver's side door flew open and Ram shot out. He rolled into the street, cracking his head against the curb. The limousine collided with the front end of the tank, jarring the armored machine and wedging metal from a flattened fender in the treads. The tank slowed then stopped.

The *Spider* raced to the vehicle's rear, leapt atop it, and then worked the latches of the upper hatch. The tank's motor grinded and shuddered until the limousine debris gave way and then the vehicle lurched forward again. The sudden motion jolted The *Spider* off-balance. He hung on and found the last release clamp, but it was locked. He jammed a grenade against it, pulled the pin, and then dropped to the rear of the tank for cover. The tank vibrated with the explosion, and then The *Spider* knocked aside the broken clamp and kicked the hatch open. He did not look inside before he fired several shots into the cockpit. Then he dropped a grenade down the hole and jumped away from the tank.

The explosion sent a column of fire into the air.

The concussion rattled The *Spider's* bones.

The tank halted again; The *Spider* watched and waited.

A hand appeared through the smoking hatch.

A steel-gloved hand, a steel-clad arm.

An armored figure emerged amidst a gray and white cloud. Its silver shell was marred by dents and scorch marks, but it was seemingly unharmed. Its face was a solid steel blank except for two shimmering eyes of what The *Spider* took to be bulletproof glass. A gun was mounted on one shoulder. Three tanks fixed to the man's back made him look like an enormous beetle with an oversized carapace. The *Spider* could not fathom the engineering feat of building such a thing, of fashioning it so that a single man could bear its weight and become a living tank. Yuri Olgachenski had saved his masterpiece for himself. The *Spider* lamented what marvels might have come from the man's mind had he not chosen a life of crime.

The Steel Tsar spotted The *Spider* standing in the street, reloading. The Russian leapt down from the tank, his weight crumbling pavement underfoot, and then he charged toward his target. His shoulder gun fired shot after shot, ripping up the street all around The *Spider*. There were no taunts, no bravado like there had been with Ivan and Alexei. The last Steel Tsar battled in silence. The *Spider* tossed a grenade into his path. The explosion forced Olgachenski to slow and change direction, buying time for The *Spider* to dart back down the alley from which he had come. Only the shadows could protect him now.

In seconds, Olgachenski appeared at the mouth of the alley, backlit by stray firelight.

He sprayed flame into the narrow passage.

On a fire escape high above, The *Spider* pressed himself against a window to avoid the sudden rush of rising heat.

His body ached and his mind reeled. He had been on the move nonstop, fighting, sweating among the flames, inhaling smoke that strained his lungs, and Olgachenski had sacrificed his brothers to soften him up. He could not face the Steel Tsar head-to-head. The *Spider* studied the Russian's armor as he clanked down the smoking alley, but he saw no chink in it. The shell was as seamless and perfect as those of Ivan and Alexei, as hard and impenetrable as a true tank. Inside it Olgachenski could fight without risk, as if he were not even on the same battlefield. The mad engineer had thought of everything.

Or had he?

A vague notion rose from the back of The *Spider's* weary mind. Olgachenski's armor was superior to that of his brothers in many ways, but it was different too, in some crucial way that made it inferior.

What is it? I can feel it's there. I know it is.

A line of bullets ripped up the brick wall to The *Spider's* left. Olgachenski had spotted him and opened fire. The *Spider* stared down at the black mouth of the flamethrower. He was trapped. He had used his last grenade to make it this far. In seconds, Olgachenski would burn him alive. The *Spider* dug the small explosives packages from his pockets and placed them along the braces of the fire escape. Then he tossed the grappling hook onto the roof of the building across the alley. It clunked out of sight and held fast.

Olgachenski fired.

The alley brightened orange and white like a flash sunrise.

The *Spider* threw himself into the air, swinging over a rising cloud of flame. He angled to miss it, but when the flames ignited the explosives he had left, the blast slammed him through a window into the next-door building. The fire escape he had left behind and a massive section of wall broke loose and avalanched into the alley, burying the Steel Tsar.

The *Spider* tumbled to a stop inside an unoccupied office. Struggling to clear his head, he poked through the broken window and surveyed the damage. The falling bricks and metal had driven Olgachenski to the ground. The shining tanks on his back prodded up through the rubble. The *Spider* seized his opportunity. He clambered down the dangling rope and hit the ground running. He readied his last explosive pack, already certain how he would use it.

He thought of Alexei trapped in his armor inside a fireball that left him no air to breathe.

That had to be why Olgachenski had three tanks: two for fuel—and one for oxygen to supply air inside the sealed casing of his helmet.

That was his weakness.

The *Spider* shoved the explosives among the valves and hoses of Olgachenski's air supply and then fled. The sudden explosion dogged after him, buffeting him along the sidewalk, and when the dust settled, he returned to the alley to look for Olgachenski's corpse. Instead, he found himself face-to-face yet again with the living tank. There was nowhere for The *Spider* to flee. Olgachenski leveled his flamethrower and fired. Only a drizzle of flame came and then fizzled out. The gun on his shoulder was empty. The explosion had damaged the gear but not the man, and again The *Spider* marveled at Olgachenski's creation. The armored Russian grabbed a length of broken metal from the fire escape, raised it like a pole axe, and swiped at The *Spider*. The crimefighter leapt clear. Olgachenski staggered after him for another try, but there was something wrong with the way he moved, as if he were dizzy. He managed one more failed swing and then he dropped to his knees.

The *Spider* trained his .45s on the Russian.

Olgachenski removed his headpiece. He wiped sweat from his beard and black hair, then sucked in a long, deep breath of air and gasped to recover his wind.

"You are a most troublesome opponent," Olgachenski said. The deep, noble tone of his voice chilled The *Spider*. This was no simple criminal he faced. "A clever and determined one. The kind of man who loses an arm or a leg on the battlefield yet fights on out of hatred and honor. The air was my only weakness, but you found it. A man who leaves his tank in combat is a dead man—and you have driven me from mine."

"You never should have come here," The *Spider* said.

"There were no more satisfactory battlefields left in Europe," Olgachenski said. "I missed the war. I wanted to fight an army with metal shaped by my hands, but the armies are all gone. So I chose you."

"Bastard," The *Spider* said. "There was no need for so many to die."

Olgachenski's eyes narrowed. A hard, fatalistic expression filled his face. "Was there any reason for them to live?"

The *Spider's* .45s pointed at Olgachenski's exposed head. At the same time, Olgachenski lifted one arm. Three gunshots snapped in the night, somehow sounding like thunder despite the clamor of the nearby battle. The *Spider's* two shots entered Olgachenski's face and painted the Russian's death across the pavement behind him. His armor, solid to the last, kept him from falling. The *Spider* glanced at the patch of blood spreading above his abdomen.

Pain radiated from his wound.

The ground rushed up to meet him.

Blackness came.

Later he opened his eyes to Nita's face. His heart leapt to see her safe and unharmed. He tried to sit up, but agony lanced through him, keeping him down.

"Don't try to move," Nita said.

Ram appeared behind her, a bandage visible beneath his turban. He handed The *Spider* a drink from a tray in his hand. "Drink this, Sahib," he said.

The *Spider* sipped the warm liquid, a painkiller, Ram's own recipe akin to laudanum. He felt better in seconds. He dropped back against his pillow. "Tell me there were no more brothers in the Olgachenski crime family," he said.

"You killed them all," Nita said. "Commissioner Kirkpatrick oversaw the bomb removal at St. Vincent's. I was on my way there with him when the attack came."

"You weren't even in the building," The *Spider* said.

Nita shook her head. "But be glad we came back when we did. I gave Kirk the slip and found Ram trying to carry you home. I got us a car so we could high-tail it out of there, and left the police to mop up the rest of Olgachenski's thugs. But you're going to need a new limousine."

A grim frown creased The *Spider's* lips. "I didn't get to leave my mark on Yuri's or Alexei's forehead. Do you think people will know it was The *Spider* who killed them?"

Bemused, Nita said, "Is there any other man in this city who could kill three armored men with flamethrowers in one night and live to tell the tale?"

Demon Slaves of the Red Claw

A Spider and Operator 5 story

by Gary Phillips

W obbly from a bullet in him, the hoodlum stumbled to a knee. The *Spider* shoved his remaining .45 into the crook's mouth, breaking some of his front teeth. The fanged vigilante blew out the back of the man's head. Blood and brain matter stained the rust colored leaves on the ground a dark crimson. The *Spider* briefly surveyed the six dead bodies laying about him, an incongruous array among the expanse of the mansion's garden and greenery. Various topiary loomed around the crouching figure – shrubbery in the shape of elephants, antelopes and deer presented in larger-than-life scale.

His now exposed right arm and hand festered from where one of the gunsel's flame rifles had spewed its dragon's breath and seared his flesh and muscle. The third degree burns were painful and he couldn't close that hand nor move his arm much. This had caused him to drop one of his .45s. Emotionally detached, he watched as some charred bits of him dropped away as he walked toward his goal. The *Spider* stepped past a gut shot hood lying on the ground, holding his destroyed stomach.

"You're through, you freak bastard," the thug promised. "The Claw will see to that."

The *Spider* didn't waste a bullet on the dying man. He turned at the sound of two preternatural growls. Trampling over the foliage and sculpted animals were two beasts Darwin hadn't foreseen. Each had the head and upper body of a crocodile of prehistoric proportions. Powerful front legs propelled these creatures toward their prey, muscled jaws opening and closing, displaying numerous large jagged teeth. Their rear sections were that of a massive serpent's body and tail. Each circled to either side of The *Spider*, seemingly plotting in their reptilian reactive brains on how best to attack him. But the one to his left smelled fresh blood and set its red slit eyes on the wounded man.

"Keep it away from me, *Spider*," the hood pleaded. "Please." He tried to crawl backwards but in a bound the thing was on him. The man screamed as the creature began eating his legs.

"Oh, God," he managed, gurgling blood.

The *Spider* took pity on the gunman's plight and killed him with a single shot to his temple. The black avenger then shot at the beast to his right, intending to put rounds through its eye and into its brain. But the thing had turned its head down and his twin blasts sunk into rough, scaled hide, though not penetrating its skull. The second abomination struck and wrapped its massive tail around The *Spider's* torso, squeezing him like an anaconda. The masked vigilante grimaced and made to let his automatic do the talking again.

Then the second mutant lashed out and wrapped its coils around his gun hand and wrenched, cracking his wrist. The gun fell. The two deformed beasts had a hold of The *Spider*. Each wanted to feast on him and each tugged on him, lusting to devour the struggling Master of Men. From a marble and stone balcony of the mansion overlooking the grounds, a figure in a silk Mandarin coat and hood of the same material watched the battle of man and creatures with subdued anticipation.

Initially neither creature would let The *Spider* loose. But as they both snarled and snapped at each other, the tail around the *Spider's* body loosened as the mutated reptiles were now biting at one another. He compressed his body in a maneuver learned years ago among yoga adepts on distant travels with his friend Ram Singh. He wrenched himself around and dropped free. The masked man knew he would only be loose for a few seconds but maybe that would do. Where he'd been dragged was near a flame rifle on the ground. He picked it up and triggered it to life as one of the mutations ran at him with its jaws wide open. A spray of sizzling flame set its head on fire and the thing wailed in pain, staggering about blindly. It brushed against a bush in the shape of an elephant and the greenery burned. The *Spider* showed no mercy for the second abomination either as he torched it too. As a foul order arose from their burning scaly bodies, The *Spider* stalked toward the mansion.

It was the beginning of autumn in New York City. The official search for pilot Amelia Earhart and her navigator Fred Noonan had been over for months, but private efforts were still underway. The aviatrix in her Lockheed Electra Model 10 had been attempting a circumnavigational flight around the globe. Somewhere over the Pacific Ocean on their approach to Howland Island, they'd radioed to the *Itasca*, the Coast Guard ship tracking them that they were running low on fuel. That was their last communication. So far, neither bodies nor pieces of the airplane had been recovered.

Sitting in her modest third story law office near the city university, Constance "Nan" Christopher read about a growing rent strike among tenants in Harlem in the bulldog edition of the *Herald*. The strike had been organized by a grouping of painters and writers who'd come out of the Harlem Renaissance period, and members of the Brotherhood of Sleeping Car Porters and Maids, the largest labor union of black workers in America.

The striking woman, dressed modernly in tweed, cuffed slacks and a silk-rayon blouse, displayed a thin smile on her face. She'd had a call late yesterday from the Brotherhood. They wanted to retain her services as they knew sooner than later, the landlords would be hauling them into court – before or after possibly getting their heads cracked by the police, she reflected archly.

"Yes, come in," the lawyer said at a knock on the frosted glass of her door. She couldn't afford a secretary.

In stepped an older man in a worn tan suit and bow tie, sweat-stained hat in hand. His complexion was sallow, his silver hair receding but longish at the sides and back. His alert watery blue eyes scanned the room. He came over to her desk, extending a hand.

"You're Miss Christopher, aren't you?"

She was standing and shook his hand. "I am. Have a seat."

They both sat on opposite sides of her heavy oak desk, a present from the woman's brother, Jimmy Christopher.

"I know about you through Stan Bisson," the man said. "He and I go back a ways."

Nan Christopher nodded. Stanislaw Bisson was a mathematics professor at the nearby City University of New York. He'd once been accused of stealing a colleague's research, as well as assaulting his fellow professor to intimidate him. But the victim admitted he hadn't seen his assailant clearly on the night of the incident. Through legwork and interviews, Nan Christopher had proven it wasn't Bisson, but an ambitious teaching aide who was the culprit.

"What can I do for you, Mister...?"

"Aubry, Aubry Ashcroft. Please call me Aubry."

"Fine, call me Nan. Cigarette?" She offered him one in a silver dish of them from her desk.

"No, no thank you." He cleared his throat. "I'll get right to it or I'll burst. I've invented a water engine and I want to patent it."

Her eyebrow went up. "Really. Like for a car?"

"It'll have many applications," Ashcroft said gravely.

She started to smile then caught herself. Well, it was a slow morning so why not humor him for a few minutes. "You have a background as an engineer, Aubry?"

"Oh no, my field is physics," he stated matter-of-factly. "You see, my engine essentially releases the molecules in water and uses that reaction, under pressure you see, as a combustible force."

"Okay," she drawled. "Go on."

"It has taken me many years, much trial and effort, but here I am before you today." He clasped his hands together as if hearing imaginary applause. He looked off momentarily, then back at her.

"So you are," she began but didn't finish as the window overlooking the street below burst inward. Glass flew everywhere, several shards cutting Nan Christopher's forearm, which she'd raised defensively.

A man came through the broken window feet first, rappelling on a cable from the roof. He was dressed in dark clothes, gloves and a bandana-type mask tied around the top portion of his head. The intruder got his footing, his back against the window sill. He reached for a gun in a shoulder holster strapped over his torso. The lady lawyer was in motion and used both hands and threw her Underwood typewriter at the goon, smacking him loudly in his upper chest. Dazed, he was momentarily unable to unholster his weapon.

"I didn't think they'd be on me this damned soon," Ashcroft said, out of his chair fast for a man his age.

Without hesitation, Christopher launched herself at the hood. He back-handed her and she went down.

"Crazy skirt," he said. His automatic now in hand, he growled, "Stay put and you won't get hurt. We only came for the egghead."

Christopher feigned being frightened. As the man stepped past her, she socked him between his legs. He doubled over, cursing.

"You get drilled for that, girlie," he wheezed, leveling the gun on her as she charged him.

Nan Christopher was a blur. She kicked the gun from his hand and karate chopped the side of his neck. The man collapsed onto the floor. Her brother had trained her in the martial arts and strike points on the body. The masked thug was temporarily paralyzed.

As Nan Christopher bent and gripped the immobile man's gun, the front door crashed open, knocked lopsided off its hinges. Bulling in was another man dressed as his companion. He brandished a revolver. Crouching, the lawyer shot at him.

Her shot went off and nicked the doorframe next to his head as he ducked back into the corridor. He shot back, a bullet passing through the fleshy part of the woman's leg as she pushed the older man behind a double set of filing cabinets. Bullets singed into the room and Christopher returned fire from behind her heavy desk. She struck the second intruder in his side while he also let his gun blaze again. Stumbling back from impact, he spun and ran off, dripping crimson.

Christopher went to the doorway and peered along the hallway. The gunman was gone. From the dance school down the hall, Nya Vindavova stuck her head into the corridor. As usual, she wore a colorful scarf tied around her dyed black hair.

"What is going on, darling?" she said in her accented English. "Sounds like the Rockettes are parading through here."

"Bill collectors," Nan Christopher joked. Her leg was starting to ache as the excitement wore off. She turned back into the room. Ashcroft was unsteady, but seemingly unhurt.

"You alright?" she asked, limping toward him.

"Yes, yes," the older man said. He was sweating hard and wiped at his face with his shaking hand. "I didn't think they knew. I'd been so careful."

"Who?" she asked.

"Off hand I'd say those men were sent by Lasher Petroleum or maybe even Global Motors." He hunched a shoulder. "Or any of the ones who sell gasoline or make cars." He sat heavily in the other chair. "You can own a well but no one owns the oceans," he said, looking off.

"Representatives of Lasher and Global have approached you?" Christopher asked as she stooped to pull the mask off the hoodlum. It was a face she didn't recognize.

"Yes," Ashcroft said. "Separately they made threats to tie me up in endless lawsuits if I tried to get my engine mass produced."

"Is there a prototype?"

He grinned knowingly at her. "Yes, only one. And only I know where it's hidden and all its parts." He tapped his temple with his forefinger. "And the only complete blueprint is up here."

She sat partially on her desk. Using her foot to drag a hard-backed chair over, she put her foot on it and tied the mask as a tourniquet around her thigh. She regarded her visitor, the man on the floor, then back to Ashcroft.

"I liked to see this miracle motor," Nan Christopher said.

Her visitor smiled knowingly. "Draw up a contract, counselor."

"Okay," she agreed but then heard the sound of an approaching siren coming through the broken window. She jabbed a finger at him. "Clam up about why you came to see me. You and I were meeting on the matter of a will when these yeggs rolled in here, blasting. Got that? Put it on me, see?"

"Yes ma'am," he said, impressed by her toughness. She was something; he reflected. Ashcroft knew from his friend Bisson she'd studied at Oxford and got her law degree from Harvard.

Christopher asked, "When can I see the water engine?" She slipped the automatic into her waistband like a gun moll.

"Today," he said. "My lab is out a ways, but safe and secure."

"And hidden?" she asked.

"Disguised," he answered.

She got off the desk and went to one of the shot up file cabinets to retrieve a standard contract she intended to modify. Christopher looked regretfully at her broken typewriter on the floor. "I'll have to borrow a friend's typewriter to make some changes to this." She shook the sheaf of papers, starting for the dance school.

Before Ashcroft could respond there were footfalls on the stairs. Two uniformed police officers braced the office. One of them had his nightstick out.

"Gentlemen," the attorney said. "Seems we've had a bit of a dust up." Something caused her to frown at the cops.

"Yeah, we got a shots fired call," one of the cops said. He reached for his holstered gun.

A wary Nan Christopher got her hand on the butt of the automatic. But the cop with the nightstick was faster and clubbed the brunette over the head, twice, dropping her to the floor.

"I think you killed her," the other one observed dispassionately.

"So what? We got what we came for." This one had his gun aimed at a blinking Ashcroft.

They left, pushing through Madam Vindavova and some of her young students who crowded the landing at the renewed sounds of the commotion.

"How many fingers?"

"A regular Jack Benny you are."

Her brother touched her shoulder. "How'd you know those two were fake cops?" He'd talked to the dance instructor and she'd told him she saw the two supposed officers getting in a Lincoln that wasn't a patrol car with an older man.

Nan Christopher winced, a throb bolting through her bandaged head. Her leg was bandaged too.

"Docs say your skull has been cracked in two places," Jimmy Christopher said. "Good thing you got the family's hard head."

"Their badges," she answered. They wore city police uniforms but had on transit cop badges – who as we both know, aren't armed."

"You got the brains and beauty, didn't you, dear?" Her father John Christopher said as he entered his daughter's hospital room. He kissed her on the forehead and added his flowers to the gardenias his son had brought on the nightstand. The World War One veteran was in a tweed jacket and black tie, his youthful face belying his age. He looked more like a professor of philosophy rather than the retired spy once known as Q-6.

Father and son nodded at each other. Jimmy Christopher asked, "So what was all this about, Nan?" The son had taken up the family trade and was known as Operator 5 of the secretive Intelligence Service Command.

"Aubry Ashcroft. Claims to be some sort of physicist who's invented a water engine. You see," she added cheerily, "it's all about breaking down the molecules, darlings." She told them about Ashcroft seeking a patent.

"Sounds like hooey except for those torpedoes who shot up your office and grabbed your would-be client," her brother stated. In addition to talking with Madam Vindavova, he also found out the real patrolmen responding to the scene had been distracted so as to allow time for the fakes to get to her office.

"Someone had planned thoroughly to snatch Ashcroft," Operator 5 said.

"There indeed might be something to it," her father added in a low voice. "I know Ashcroft has done work for us in the past. Though he wouldn't know me."

By 'us' his son wondered if his father meant the government or the Hidden Hundred. The latter was a grouping of former men and women of the intelligence service. For various reasons had been pushed out of active duty, yet weren't going to go quietly into the night. In his father's case, he'd been retired due to a bullet fragment near his heart.

"So spill it, Dad," his son said. "What do you know?"

Their father smiled thinly, looking a lot like his twin son and daughter at that moment.

"I appreciate you seeing me on short notice, Mr. Wentworth," Jimmy Christopher said as the turbaned Ram Singh ushered him into the millionaire's study and home office of his penthouse.

"Not at all," Richard Wentworth said. He came from around his desk and offered his hand which was bandaged. He was two inches taller than Christopher's even six feet.

Christopher returned the gesture. He noted the unadorned left hand had heavy veins on the back of it and two of the knuckles misshapen. He considered they'd gotten that way not from hitting the heavy bag in a gym workout, but from striking faces.

"Shukriya, Ram Singh," Wentworth said, Hindi for thank you, Christopher knew. His accent was good he also noted.

Ram Singh nodded and departed, closing the double doors to the room. There were built-in shelves of books and masks on the wall from

Africa, the Amazon and the Pacific Islands.

"Please," Wentworth said, retaking his seat behind the Italian Rococo desk. There was a picture of a striking looking woman in a black frame on the desk. At one of the windows was an upholstered chair and reading stand. Open on the stand was a first edition of Rousseau's *Reveries of a Solitary Walker.*

Christopher sat, noting these items. There was also a tray with a coffee pot and two china cups and saucers to one side but Wentworth didn't offer any. It was as if they'd been put out, expected for someone like him to do so, but ignored by his host as useless props.

"I understand you've financed the research and experiments of Aubry Ashcroft over the years, Mr. Wentworth."

Wentworth laughed briefly, lightly. "I'm guilty as charged. Has ol' Aubry approached you in some way about some wild idea of his?"

"Can I ask how you two met?"

"He's a friend of the family. A kind of eccentric uncle really. Why?"

Christopher told him what happened this morning. He left out the detail about Ashcroft having done work for the War Department and other data he'd gotten from his father. Because Ashcroft was considered odd but had delivered in the past, Operator 5 had been ordered by his chief in the ISC's Washington headquarters, a taciturn sort known only as Z-7, to find the kidnapped scientist.

Something dark came and went behind Wentworth's face. His blue-grey eyes going black then back again.

It was quick, but Christopher observed the change. He betrayed no acknowledgement of this. "Does Ashcroft have a wife, children?" he asked.

"No, none that I know of. Life-long bachelor it seems. His work was all-consuming I guess." Wentworth then asked pleasantly, "What is it you do, Mr. Christopher?"

"A dabbler I guess you'd say. Done a bit of exploring now and then. Chasing this or that."

"That right?"

"Um-hm."

"That why you carry a gun? Your coat is well-tailored to hide it though." Wentworth wondered what else his visitor might be concealing on his person.

"Sometimes my… exploring gets me in places I shouldn't be. I'm sure you know how that goes."

"Oh, really, I couldn't imagine. The hardest thing I work on is trying to tell Moet from Dom Perignon."

"Yes, well, would you know where Ashcroft kept his lab?"

"It's probably been cleaned out by now. These fellows you described I imagine play pretty rough."

"I'm sure they're worked the old boy over, still, it's a place to start."

"Agreed," the millionaire playboy said. He took a Waterman fountain pen from its desk set and, uncapping it, wrote out an address and directions on a notepad. It was to a building in Brooklyn, not far from Ebbets Field. After blotting the paper, he handed the sheet across to Jimmy Christopher.

The secret agent rose, folding the note in half after glancing at it. "Like I said, I appreciate you seeing me, Mr. Wentworth."

Wentworth had risen too, fixing the other man with a look. "I hope your exploring yields results, Mr. Christopher."

"So do I."

Wentworth didn't say anything, but he had some exploring to do too which eventually would take him to the fights that night.

Charley Burley landed a hard right on Achilles "Decimator" Smith's jaw. He fell slack against the ropes, momentarily dazed. But Burley was frustrated in finding his target who adeptly slipped and dodged blows as he worked himself off the ropes and back into the center of the ring. The crowd in the Velodrome on Coney Island yelled unsolicited instructions at the respective middleweight they had money on down in the ring.

"I didn't know you were a boxing fan, Wentworth," Chester

McKeaver joked, a black cigar dangling from his mouth, and a blonde not his wife sitting next to him. McKeaver was an active stock holder in Global Motors.

"There might be some blood flowing up there tonight 'cause that colored boy, Smith, knows how to dish it out, brother. And I know how delicate you are." He guffawed and squeezed the knee of the blonde who giggled and put her bedroom eyes on him.

The two men sat ringside. They knew each other from this or that night club, from Greenwich Village's Cobalt Room to Small's Paradise in Harlem. "You know me, Chet, I get my excitement through others' labors."

McKeaver wasn't listening. He was nuzzling his companion.

Wentworth knew how to get his attention. "After the fight, I want to talk to you about possibly investing in Global stock."

"Sure thing, we'll get a drink afterward and talk." McKeaver whispered something dirty to his girlfriend and she giggled, slapping him playfully on the shoulder.

Wentworth looked from him and nodded at two other men in his tax bracket, Ferris Driscoll and Garrison Hayden. They too were sitting close to the action. A knockout redhead was with Driscoll, and not for the first time.

"A small wager, Richard?" Driscoll challenged. He was a row back and to the left of where the other man sat. A matching patterned tie and handkerchief accented his blue serge suit. "I've got five hundred on Burley." Driscoll, unlike Wentworth, came from inherited wealth.

Wentworth turned some to glance up at Driscoll. From the sounds of the exertions, he felt confident that Smith was pressing his attack. "Make it a thousand on Decimator Smith." He wagged his finger. "But if I win, you donate the money to a soup kitchen of my choosing."

"You damn Roosevelt softie. It's a bet."

"Light me, baby," the redhead asked Driscoll in a husky voice.

"Sure thing, doll." He lit her cigarette with a gold lighter and had one himself, a custom blend he got from a gold cigarette case.

Both men grinned wolfishly at each other.

When Jimmy Christopher left Wentworth's home earlier that day he'd driven to the laboratory of Dr. Aubry Ashcroft. The place, a two-story converted structure, had been searched and stripped as expected. Being thorough, Christopher scouted the neighborhood. He found a talkative newsie named Sammy.

"A sawbuck," the kid stared transfixed at the bill. "That's more than I make in two weeks, mister."

"It can be all yours," Christopher said. "See anybody coming out of that building lately?" He pointed at Ashcroft's lab as a well-dressed pudgy man walked past him and the newsie..

"Yeah," Sammy said. "I seen a couple of lugs taking machines out of there and loadin' 'em into a truck. Looked like stuff from one of those mad scientist Karloff pictures," the youngster added. "They was taking orders from that Eddie Silver Fingers."

"Who's that?'

"He's a louse. Thinks he's a big man with his silver buttons on his vest. Huh." Sammy took his eyes off the money and regarded Christopher. "Say, you dress too swell for a cop. You some kind of G-Man?"

Operator 5 handed him the ten. "About this Eddie?"

Christopher learned Sammy had it in for the local muscle as he often took the daily paper from the news hawker, not bothering to pay him. This meant the kid had to fork over the difference to the unforgiving Hearst Corporation. Christopher followed the trail of the so-called Mr. Silver Fingers which eventually led him two days later to where he was now, a supposed abandoned rail car roundhouse near the Brooklyn docks.

"You might as well show yourself," Operator 5 announced, after entering a slightly ajar side door into the roundhouse. In his fist was his modified Colt .38 automatic. Somebody was there ahead of him.

A hard, metallic laugh echoed in the gloomy area. A stooped figure in black suit, black shirt and tie, matching cape and a slouch hat appeared on an overhead catwalk. He had on an eye mask and long, wild black hair cascaded below the hat. He held a .45 automatic in his right hand.

"The *Spider*," Christopher said. "Those fangs are a nice touch," he added dryly. "It was you as the hunchbacked fiddler in Bedford-Stuyvesant, wasn't it?"

The figure slid down from the catwalk on a slender line. "The villain calling himself the Red Claw is not here," he declared.

"Who?"

"The one behind this evil business."

"I know about you," Christopher said sourly. "You're a self-appointed avenging angel, that it, *Spider*?"

"And you?" The *Spider* grinned and it wasn't pleasant. Each still held their gun on the other.

As Christopher traced the steps of Eddie Silver Fingers, more than once he'd had the impression he was being hunted as well. There had been the gregarious hunchback, laughing and playing his violin on the street corner, an upturned hat on the sidewalk where the entertained left money. Then there had been that old arthritic lady, her bony hands like the feet of birds, selling apples and peaches from a cart near the waterfront bar at dusk. Her hair not dissimilar to the *Spider's* untamed mane, Christopher reflected.

"I'm a sanctioned --" Christopher began but didn't finish as a grenade went off, blowing the two off their feet. Fortunately, only small amounts of shrapnel tore into them due to the protection of the railroad cars in the roundhouse.

His ears ringing, Christopher shook his head and speculated aloud. "Why throw the grenade beyond us?"

"I believe our attackers aren't quite used to their newly acquired strength." The *Spider* was looking into the shadows between some rail cars as what had been men emerged toward them. For these were no longer ordinary henchmen. Like the creatures The *Spider* battled on the estate, they'd been transformed. The changed hoodlums were now some seven feet tall, their muscles enlarged and their faces monstrously distorted. A few had weapons, most not. Their torn clothes barely contained their enlarged forms and their feet, like that of Neanderthals, burst the seams of their shoes.

"Huh," Christopher said, eyeing their attackers, assessing weak points.

The *Spider* appreciated the other man's calm as he unlimbered another automatic in his other hand.

"Let's get to it," Operator 5 said grimly.

A machine gun opened up from one of the monster men and the two sought cover in separate locations among the train cars. The mutants spread out after them, grunting and growling.

"Their speech seems impeded," Christopher said to his temporary ally. "Possibly their higher thinking is as well."

"Watch out," The *Spider* warned, suddenly appearing near the secret agent as a large fist swung at Jimmy Christopher.

Operator 5 ducked. Simultaneously he spun, his leg sweep bringing his attacker to the ground. He then launched himself into the air and as he descended, smashed his heel into the transformed hoodlum's neck, breaking bone. He landed in a crouching position.

The *Spider* put two bullets into one of the enlarged men in the chest. This as the man rattled rounds out of a drum-fed Thompson machine gun at the masked predator. But so charged was his attacker that the bullets didn't slow him down. He continued firing the Tommy gun. The *Spider* was behind a single partially dissembled rail car. Bullets sparked and ricocheted off the train tracks near him.

The mutated thug with the machine gun was in work pants, the cuffs mid-way up on his heavily muscled calf. He wore no shoes on his suddenly size twenty feet and no shirt. Small, conical-shaped spikes protruded from his tawny, leathery skin. His eyes bulged and his body shook as he advanced. He screamed and, getting closer to the rail car, he crouched and effortlessly leapt onto its roof. He then emptied the drum of his weapon on The *Spider* below.

But his target was no longer where he'd been. The monster man looked confused. At a sound he turned to his left. There before him was his black clad nemesis atop the rail car as well.

"The *Spider* should feel sorry for you," he rasped as if detached from his own psyche. "Almost." The transformed gunsel rushed at him and dispassionately the fanged vigilante drilled two bullets into the monster's face. The corpse went over like a felled tree, cracking its head open as it struck the rail line below.

In another part of the roundhouse, Operator 5's flying kick didn't have the effect he hoped as his target reared back but was still able to grab the spy's leg. He whirled about in a circle and let go, sending Jimmy Christopher into tools and metal parts. A rattled Christopher was on all fours. Big hands clamped on him and jerked him up. This one was at least eight feet tall, his torso almost as wide as the front end of a DeSoto, the battered spy noted. His face was misshapen, the forehead protruding. Spikes the consistency of calluses in various sizes studded his sweating body. The muscles of the mutated man's bare arms were like sculpted granite. Each hand under Christopher's armpit, the giant squeezed, cutting off his breath, his rib cage starting to give as he tried not to black out.

Christopher reached a hand into his vest pocket and removed a fountain pen. It wasn't fancy like the one on Richard Wentworth's desk. But then, he wasn't worried about writing a love note to his sweetheart, reporter Diane Elliot. The giant bellowed and threw him into a wall and Christopher bounced off, landing hard, upsetting some equipment. The big man rushed forward and the secret agent, bleeding from the forehead, rolled over, aiming the nib of the fountain pen at him. There was a tiny puff and the nib flew off the pen at the berserker. The nib exploded on contact and blew a hole in that massive chest.

The changeling dropped heavily to his knees, hands to his ragged fatal wound. He smiled crookedly. Operator 5 wondered if the hood was relieved he didn't have to live his life as a monster. He took a last look at Operator 5 as his failing heart pumped a final spurt of blood through the hole in him and his eyes closed for good. The dead man fell face first to the grease coated floor. Christopher glanced up at a sound and saw The *Spider* was back on the catwalk. He'd just shot one of the altered hoods, but there was a second one who knocked the automatic from The *Spider's* hand. Before the fanged avenger could reach his other gun, the beast man was on him, swiping at his ebon form with elongated nails.

Christopher refocused as a duo of transfigured thugs loped at him, growling and snarling. One had a handgun down at his side but he didn't bring it level to fire at Christopher. This confirmed his guess they were rapidly losing reasoning. But he better save his bacon first, he reminded himself, diving for his Colt which he'd lost possession of in the previous fight. One of the gibbering hoods leapt at him at the same moment.

On the catwalk, the railing was giving way due to the increased weight of the transformed brigand The *Spider* grappled with who pressed against him, the masked vigilante's back on the railing. The changed thing was even more animalistic now. The man-creature snapped its jaws at The *Spider*, seeking to bite his face off as it continued to claw at him as well. Its humanity was growing dimmer and dimmer in those enraged eyes. The *Spider* slugged at the mutated hood but he latched his crooked, blunt teeth into the black clad avenger's shoulder. The *Spider* gasped but didn't cry out though the pain was tremendous.

The *Spider's* silken web line was still dangling from where he'd secured it to the catwalk's railing. He'd finally reached it and pulled the line up and looped it around and around the neck of the man-creature. The mutant's jaw went slack on his flesh as The *Spider* tightened his grip on the line. A hand with its long nails grabbed his arm but The *Spider* was determined. The two went over but the line remained around the mutant's neck and it snapped taut. The *Spider* let go of where he'd been hanging onto the enlarged man, and dropped to the ground in a roll.

His dangling foe sought to break the line cutting into his neck, strangling him. But the stuff was of enhanced tensile strength developed by Professor Ezra Brownlee. The animal man did tear one of the loops loose, but by then his legs began to buck as air was cut off from his brain. He spread his arms out and there was a loud, hoarse roar of defeat. The wild eyes lost their savage sheen and rolled up in his head as he expired, his head and body going limp, swinging slightly from the makeshift hangman's cord.

Jimmy Christopher was hit in the face with a big fist. His bestial attacker latched his large hands around the woozy Christopher's wind pipe. He was crushing Operator 5's neck as he held his body aloft, barking and howling and drooling. The other mutated man looked on as the secret agent was choked.

Doing his best not to black out, Operator 5 retrieved what looked like an over-sized marble made of thin Bakelite from a padded inner pocket of his vest. As blackness crowded the edges of his vision, he crushed the ball between thumb and forefinger. He held his breath and shoved his hand and the emerald gas released from the ball into the mutated man's misshapen face. The beast man quickly succumbed, letting a weakened Christopher go who hacked and coughed. The other attacker moved in on him.

Operator 5 held up a hand for The *Spider* not to shoot. He and the seven-footer circled one another in the style of bare knuckle fighters. The giant's clothes ill fit him now and his large feet burst out of his formerly fancy two-toned shoes. His once tailor-made vest was ripped in two in the back. Its silver buttons were polished and shiny. Jimmy Christopher figured the transformed Eddie Silver Fingers must have been one of the last of the gang to be changed by the Red Claw. The mutated torpedo seemed to retain some of his normal sense, though like the others, the change had robbed him of speech.

He rushed Christopher, but a quick round house kick caused him to move sideways. Given he didn't go into a rage and merely come at Christopher again, this confirmed that the transformed being was still able to think. The longer they were changed, the more zombie-like they became, Operator 5 concluded. The two combatants circled each other briefly again and this time Christopher went into motion.

Eddie Silver Fingers lunged but Jimmy Christopher was also in motion, side-stepped to avoid contact, and a double hammer strike to Silver Fingers' back caused him to stumble. He turned back, growling and showing nasty teeth. Quickly pivoting, his leg lashing up then sweeping across, Christopher struck the bestial man in his jaw, staggering him. Silver Fingers threw a powerful overhand right but Christopher was not there as he ducked under the swing. The spy came up, unleashing a series of elbows and using the flats of his hands against the larger man's chest and head. Eddie Silver Fingers reeled. Operator 5 finished the morphed hoodlum off with a standing flying kick that took him off his feet as if he'd been blasted with both barrels from a shotgun.

"A blend of Japanese and Chinese styles," The *Spider* observed as Jimmy Christopher joined him. "A smattering of ju-jitsu but mostly wing chun, I believe."

Operator 5 said, "You've studied in the East?"

"We must search." The *Spider* turned away.

There was a thin smile on Christopher's face as he retrieved his Colt and followed the mysterious man. Soon they discovered the Claw's laboratory beneath the roundhouse, and his prisoner, Aubry Ahscroft. He was shackled by proscribed length of chain and clamp around his ankle. This gave him movement in the lab and to a toilet in a separate room. His only mark of torture was a missing little finger on his right hand.

"He's a devil and perniciously brilliant," the old man said. There were three bodies in the room that had once been human. But now the three were deformed masses as if their bones had been partially dissolved and disconnected. The trio were laid out on autopsy tables side by side. One of the disfigured lumps had been recently dissected.

"He changed their molecular structure," The *Spider* observed. "These are his failures."

Operator 5 said, "That's why he wanted your expertise, isn't it? He didn't care about your water engine but wanted to advance his research into mutating humans."

"And other life forms," The *Spider* added. Investigating underworld rumors of the Red Claw's gruesome mutation experiments, he'd discovered the mansion and laboratory on Long Island. That was where he'd fought the metamorphosed reptiles, but the Claw had escaped.

Operator 5 bent and using a lockpick, freed the scientist. The *Spider* doused his bite wound with rubbing alcohol to prevent infection.

"I don't know exactly what he's planning," Ashcroft began, "but it involves Times Square. I overheard one of his hoods joking about that."

Jimmy Christopher had stepped into a makeshift operating room through a set of swing doors.

Over his shoulder, Ashcroft explained. "His process involves injections and then radically affecting the molecular structure if you will, of the growth hormones in the pituitary gland." In the makeshift operator room was an inclined table where the Red Claw strapped his subjects for the transmutation. Near the tables was a conical-like device on casters with a blunt nodule with three glass rings pointing out of its center. This in turn was wired with heavy cables to a bank of several machines the size of file cabinets with dials, switches and gauges on them.

"When you two showed up, he'd just finished his transformations," Ashcroft went on. "He left with a flatbed of his monster men and a few transformed smaller animals on leashes.

"He means to unleash terror in the city," The *Spider* said. He'd been looking in a small room also off the lab that he surmised was used by the Claw as an office of sorts when he wasn't masked. There was a cathedral-style Philco radio on a table, ashtray with cigarette butts and even a liquor cabinet. Forced to abandon this location when he and Christopher had arrived, he'd hurriedly set fire to identifying papers and other items in a metal wastebasket. The *Spider* handed Jimmy Christopher a chrome rifle of advanced design that had also been in the room.

"What is this Buck Rogers gewgaw?"

"A flame thrower essentially. A small tank with the incendiary chemical is built into the stock."

"Handy," Christopher said. He leaned the flame rifle against a desk and extracted a Zippo lighter from his trouser's pocket. He opened it and part of the inner works slid up from the casing. The lighter was in reality a two-way radio. Christopher spoke into this.

"This is Operator 5 calling Division Zeta." This referred to the Intelligence Service Command's secretly located Manhattan bureau. "I repeat, this is Operator 5. I need all available operatives in the area to converge on Times Square. Bring armaments. Your mission will be clear when you arrive." He provided more details then signed off.

"Time to put a stop to this wickedness," The *Spider* declared, starting away.

"You'll be okay for a few minutes?" Christopher asked Ashcroft. "I've got agents coming to retrieve you."

"You two go on."

The pair exited the roundhouse and walked to a large dark car parked nearby, though hidden from the front entrance. The vehicle was a new Light Straight Eight Daimler and the *Spider* got behind the wheel as Operator 5 got in on the passenger side.

"Must be nice to afford a car like this," the secret agent commented wryly.

The *Spider* stared straight ahead. The car went away quietly and a smallish man, pudgy but in a well-tailored suit, emerged from the shadows of a lone caboose on a siding. He carried a leather attaché case like a banker's and he entered the roundhouse the two had left.

It didn't take him long to find the stairs leading down to the laboratory and other rooms.

"Yes?" The smallish man didn't strike him as a threat. "Who are you and how did you find me here?"

"Being generous with money loosens many a tongue," he answered flatly. "Well, sir, I represent certain industrial interests who have become aware of your efforts regarding your water engine."

Suddenly his impression of the unobtrusive man changed. "Big oil's sent you, haven't they? You've come to silence me."

His visitor shook his head reproachfully and walked closer. He opened the attaché case and held it so the other man could see inside.

Ashcroft looked shocked.

"I can assure you that cashier's check is real, sir," the smallish man said, smiling pleasantly.

The frenzied mutated goon grabbed the pretty woman's head and twisted, breaking her neck easily. He then wrenched it in the other direction and ripped her head from the neck. Blood spurted on him but he was gleeful as he danced with his prize. He didn't cavort for long as John Christopher shot him once through the eye with his Mauser machine pistol. Bounding for him was a slavering dog – or rather it had been a dog, a Greyhound in fact. But its head was far too large for its body and the teeth looked like they belonged to a shark and not a canine.

"I got him, old timer," the teenaged Tim Donovan said. He put two rounds from his revolver in the thing's head, stilling the dog-construct instantly. "Sure hated to do that," he grumbled, "I like pooches."

"Right now we have to save human lives, Tim," the older man reminded him.

"I understand, Mr. Christopher."

Like a drunken sailor, a mutated hoodlum crashed through a plate glass window attacking a mannequin in a Seedman discount store.

Tim Donovan pointed up at the news ticker display that went around the *New York Times* building. Atop the array on a ledge was a maddened mutant. He'd grabbed a child and somehow clambered up there, and was about to throw the crying girl down into the street.

"We'll never reach him in time." Donovan grabbed the ex-spy's arm. The former bootblack and newsie worked as a mechanic in a garage owned by one of the Hidden Hundred. After Jimmy Christopher had broadcast his message, in the Daimler with The *Spider*, he'd resent the message to the Hundred using the Morse code feature of the lighter. His father was their leader.

One of the mutants was running, screaming and on fire. He'd forgotten how to use the flame rifle he was holding. The weapon was shot by a policeman and the tank burst. He ran right into a wall with a Federal Theater Project poster on it announcing an all-black version of Richard III. As the transformation process invariably robbed the transformed of their reasoning, the burning man would retreat a few steps then run back into the wall, banging into it, trying to climb. He did this a few times until the flames devoured his brain.

"Come on," the man once known as Q-7 said. The two waded through policeman beating at mutated men with their nightsticks, agents of the ICS, some breaking their covers as a baker or a hobo, saving lives, and at the edges, Hidden Hundred members making sure no changelings got into the other parts of the city. But they had to reach that girl. He quickly explained his plan to the young man.

Fortunately the transmuted gunsel had been distracted as a biplane soared close to the area, a news cameraman strapped to the wing, cranking his camera, filming the events.

"Ready?" John Christopher said as the two got in position. He was sweating.

"No," Donovan said, rubbing his dry hands together.

Suddenly a policeman, a captain in fact, was there and the teenager assumed he was going to interfere. But the officer merely nodded curtly at the elder Christopher. Clearly there was a history between the two. The cop had a net with him. The fire department had also responded to the scene as several small fires had erupted.

John Christopher evidenced the same ghost smile as his children. He looked up and shouted, "Hey, ugly, down here. Down here you stupid ape."

The berserker at first didn't respond, but continued to hold the child aloft, shaking her. Christopher repeated himself and finally got his attention. He glared down at the two and screamed like a bear in a trap. The child fainted from fright.

"Now," the retired spy said and steadying his hand with his other, rapidly shot one then the other shoulder of the man-creature.

Reflexively the brute's hands spasmed and he released the child. She fell right into the fireman's net Donovan and the policeman held. John Christopher then shot the berserker in his open mouth as he bellowed, enraged. The mutant's body broke at various angles as he struck the sidewalk.

"That was close," Donavan said.

A relieved John Christopher finally exhaled.

Jimmy Christopher barely breathed hard as he contended with two unchanged hoods in the darkened lobby of the Brackett building. The first crook he took out with a stiff finger underhand strike to the man's heart, causing it to seize momentarily and the man wilted to the polished floor. The other muscle ran toward the back.

Meanwhile upstairs in a plush office, The *Spider* confronted his quarry. "You're reign as the Red Claw is over, Ferris Driscoll."

The lanky millionaire playboy held a gun and smiled at his accuser. There were two large satchels at his feet. "You don't scare me with your theatrics, *Spider*. Beneath the false fangs and fright wig, you're a man like any other and can bleed and die."

The *Spider* also had one of his .45s in his fist. He'd looked into ownership of the mansion on Long Island, but it was veiled through various false names and companies. When Christopher had come to him about Ashcroft being kidnapped, he'd gone to the fights that night to question McKeaver who he knew was a fan of the boxer, Smith – and who had expressed interest at a dinner party several months ago about Aubry's work.

"You let your monsters loose in Times Square as a diversion. I'm sure you have there bearer bonds and cash you've stolen from the various companies on whose boards you sit." The *Spider* paused, a silence settling like that of a tarantula savoring the trapped fly it was about to devour. "Your evil will not go unpunished,"

The *Spider* had confirmed it was Driscoll in the little private room he'd seen beneath the roundhouse. When he lit his papers in the wastebasket, he'd used a handkerchief to handle the hot metal. Driscoll had thrown the handkerchief into the fire too, but it was only partially burned. There was enough left that The *Spider* recognized it as the kind Driscoll favored, custom made by a tailor Wentworth also frequented.

Driscoll said proudly, "My experiments have interested a certain former house painter with a funny little mustache. He's very interested in me helping his scientists create their over men, their über soldiers." Driscoll leaned forward. "The Red Claw will bring this diseased nation of race mixers and Marxist politicians to its knees. I am not alone in this goal." Briefly his eyes flitted left then back.

"Your man hidden behind the trick panel in the wall is dead, Driscoll. There are no avenues of escape for you. Your death is foretold. The *Spider* has spoken."

They were less than twenty feet apart and fired their weapons simultaneously. The bullets aimed at The *Spider* missed as he became a blur, seemingly moving with inhuman speed. Conversely, his rounds aimed at Driscoll struck home, chest and head. He went over, dead, sprawled across his ill gotten gains.

By the time Operator 5 dealt with the fleeing thug and got upstairs, The *Spider* was gone. But he'd left his vermillion *Spider's* mark on the forehead of the corpse of Ferris Driscoll.

"That chap might not have all his marbles," Christopher observed coolly. "But he's damn efficient.

Aubry Ashcroft sent flowers to a recuperating Nan Christopher. In his attached note, he mentioned he'd been premature, that indeed he needed to do more work on his water engine. He never did patent the motor.

The search for Amelia Earhart continued.

Death Ghost from the Future War

by Rik Hoskin

March 1941.

The sounds of clinking wine glasses and convivial conversation filled the evening air over Hudson Bay as the steamer beat a languorous path around Bedloe's Island. On board, eighty of the richest and most influential men in New York were discussing the stock market, the unseasonably warm spring and the terrible news that filtered daily over the Atlantic from faraway Europe, all in that same tone of studied nonchalance the rich affect at such functions. The function itself was a fundraiser held in honor of their European brethren who were even now struggling under the grim plans of the German madman calling himself the *Fuhrer*.

The men were accompanied either by their wives, their girlfriends or fiancées and a few of the widowers had brought their glamorous daughters if they were of age, showing them off like trophies to their assembled peers. Without exception, each woman sported an exclusive gown and the most exquisite jewelry to better augment her perfect skin and flawless teeth.

Yet among the group on the raised forecastle of the refitted steamer, two of the party's attendees seemed to consistently stand at arm's length from the others, their shared *joie de vivre* strained and somehow artificial. The man's name was Richard Wentworth and he habitually swirled the ice in his glass of Florida orange juice as he spoke with his delightful companion, the noted beauty Nita van Sloan whose face had appeared time and again on the society pages of New York's newspapers. With his broad shoulders, Wentworth cut an impressive figure dressed in a dinner jacket with a cornflower resting in its buttonhole, while his attractive companion's violet dress seemed to offset that flower to perfection, matching her pretty eyes. To many, Wentworth and van Sloan made a picture perfect couple and it was a source of hushed discussion why the pair had taken so long to announce their engagement, despite several years of courting. However, were one to listen in on their conversation one might have some inkling as to why the two remained perennially engaged without ever committing themselves to a wedding date, for their concerns were anything but normal.

"I can't remember the last time we were together like this," Nita said, her melodious voice like music over the sluicing sounds of the waves. "It's been so very long since we last enjoyed something so... well, ordinary."

"One day, my love," Wentworth replied wistfully, "when the fires of evil finally burn themselves out..."

His words trailed off, the rest left unsaid, for a moment the two of them stood in companionable silence on the forecastle, watching the waves lap against the hull as the steamship maneuvered closer to Bedloe's Island, nudging across the rolling waters in the shadow of Manhattan. They were haunted, this pair; the weight of great responsibilities resting uncomfortably on their youthful shoulders.

"Lady Liberty looks ever so beautiful tonight," Nita observed as the boat approached the towering statue, "standing over us like some watchful guardian. If only she could witness the horrors that are occurring even now across the Atlantic, I wonder what she would say."

Wentworth shook his head in despair. "Barely two decades ago the world was in the grip of that so-called 'war to end all wars'. And yet mankind seems ever inclined to fight. Now it is hard to envision an end to the calamity that shakes Europe to its core, we can only pray that it never reaches America's shores."

Nita nodded, knowing full well why her companion was so troubled. Richard Wentworth had been a major in that so-called Great War; and he had seen such terrible things, things which still caused him to wake up sweating in the middle of the night, the sheets wrapped about his taut body like a lunatic's strait jacket. It was ironic since Wentworth himself was an expert in fear, for in secret he donned the guise of The *Spider*, Master of Men, to battle with the criminal underworld in its many terrible forms. Fear was The *Spider's* weapon, and Wentworth had employed it time and again against the most frightful foes.

As they stood at the railings that surrounded the cruiser, Nita placed her slender hand over Wentworth's and gently squeezed his fingers. "My father never dreamt that we would be raising funds like this for another war," she lamented.

Wentworth's blue eyes narrowed for a moment as he gazed at Lady Liberty where she towered above them on her star-shaped plinth, her torch thrust high in the air above her. "The Statue of Liberty was funded by charitable donations," Wentworth recalled, "to send out a beacon of hope from this great land. It seems fitting that we find ourselves here raising funds for that same belief, all these years on."

Waves lapped against its hull as the steamer nosed towards the shores of Bedloe's Island while the last of the sun's rays painted the waters a glistening gold. Out there, a second steamer was cutting its own languorous path through the water without a care in the world. For a moment, Richard Wentworth and Nita van Sloan admired that statue, that beacon of hope in a world turning ever madder, their hands touching just barely as the ship edged closer towards it.

"Wentworth," a man's voice called from behind the handsome couple, breaking their reverie. "Wentworth, old man — I didn't see you there."

As he turned, Wentworth recognized his old banking colleague, Miles Hankerson, waddling towards him in a rather too-tight tuxedo and tails. The rotund fellow held a cigar in one pudgy hand and had his other arm around a beautiful blonde haired young maiden of no more than sixteen years of age.

"Miles, how are you?" Richard said, proffering his hand to the older man.

"I can't complain," Hankerson admitted with a laugh as he grasped Wentworth's palm with a firm two-handed shake. After acknowledging Nita, the pudgy old banker gestured to the young woman who stood self-consciously beside him, biting at her lip as she stared at a spot on the deck. "Nita, Dick — I'd like you to meet my daughter Misty."

"A pleasure," Richard assured the young lady, taking her hand and gently brushing his lips across her knuckles. Delighted, the girl giggled a little too loudly as the handsome millionaire let her hand drop away from his.

"My father has told me ever so much about you, Mister Wentworth," Misty said, her words tumbling forth in an excited rush.

Wentworth looked from Misty to her father and winked. "Don't believe half the stories he tells you," he said with mock seriousness. "This old scallywag has a memory like a gin-soaked fish."

"Except when it comes to your accounts," Hankerson justified, puffing out his chest.

It was at that moment, as the steamer sidled up to the westernmost shore of Bedloe's Island, that gunshots rang out and a hail of bullets blurred across the darkening sky. Richard Wentworth, whose reflexes would put even a striking cobra's to shame, reacted with astonishing swiftness, his hand reaching back to swipe Nita aside even as he shoved Miles Hankerson to the deck.

But he was too late!

Two bullets cut cruelly into Hankerson's broad chest, ripping through the breast of his shirt and carving great red trenches through his flesh as they burrowed between his ribs.

A further volley of bullets struck the wooden decking like cruel raindrops of death as Wentworth powered forward like a leaping jungle predator. Several feet away, more of the party's attendees were dropping before that savage hail of bullets from above, and cries of terror came from all about the deck of the old steamer. Misty Hankerson stood amid it all like an actor in the spotlight, staring at her father's bloody corpse.

"Everyone below decks!" Wentworth ordered loudly with a cadence and authority that anyone from his old military unit would have recognized in an instant.

Wentworth leapt for cover as a third burst of bullets struck the deck, urging the party guests down the stairwell that led to the ship's saloon. Behind him, Nita van Sloan was ushering partygoers down another stairwell that led to the galley. She crouched behind the housing of a lifesaver for cover as bullets peppered the deck all about her.

Up ahead, to her horror, Nita saw a vision that would stay with her until the grave. In her hurry to escape that vicious hail of death, Misty Hankerson tripped over her father's wounded body, not used as she was to wearing heels. As she did so, a large bore bullet struck the back of the young woman's head, painting her fine blonde hair with a red mist as it tore through her skull. Nita gasped as the girl slumped to the floor, her eyes losing focus, never to see her seventeenth birthday.

Richard Wentworth saw Misty fall too and he felt the indignation rising in his breast. As Nita hurried the other guests to cover, Wentworth stepped boldly out onto the bow, his pale eyes searching the horizon for the source of this deadly assault. For a moment the air was silent, just the swishing sounds of water as the waves brushed the ship's hull. Then a loud crack cut the air as the gunman took another shot at the retreating guests hurrying to safety, felling another in a shower of blood and bone. There were two weapons then, Wentworth concluded — an automatic rifle and a sniper shot — and maybe two gunmen.

There! Wentworth spotted the distinctive gun flash high up in the crown of Lady Liberty herself. The telltale burst of light came from between the window struts that made up the sunburst-like circlet of that magnificent statue. No longer a Statue of Liberty then, Wentworth realized, but now a colossal avatar of the Grim Reaper himself; a Statue of Death!

A dozen soldiers hurried from the open doors of Fort Wood, at the base of the Statue of Liberty, as the sun sunk behind Bedloe's Island. Each GI carried a Garand M1 rifle as he hurried towards the towering form of Lady Liberty, determined to put a stop to the madman who was picking off passengers from the passing boats. The familiar star-shape of Fort Wood had formed the base of the statue since its erection in 1886 and, though the military stronghold had stood largely disused since then, it had recently been brought back into active service with the growing threat that Germany and the Axis Powers posed.

From the nearby steamer, Richard Wentworth watched with hope rising in his breast as those brave young men charged across the open ground to the recessed entrance of the statue itself. Behind Wentworth, the last few party guests were scampering below deck even as the captain began turning the wheel, steering the nautical behemoth out of the danger zone. Across the sound, its sister vessel was doing likewise, desperately pulling out of the line of fire.

Nita van Sloan was helping an elderly stockbroker along the gangway and down into the darkness below while Wentworth continued to scan the island. For a moment it seemed that those brave soldiers might have a chance, using weight of numbers to storm the statue and overwhelm the sniper lodged at its summit. Then the sniper turned his rifle on them, picking off two men as they charged towards the statue's entrance, and Wentworth felt an empty helplessness grip him as those young men were brought down the remaining members of the platoon reached the door and stopped — it was locked, Wentworth realized. They struggled with the locked doors and as they did so Wentworth saw a tiny black shape fall from a window in the crown. The item was no bigger than a child's ball, but Wentworth's heart sank for he immediately guessed what it was — an MK 2, military-issue fragmentation grenade.

"No, get back," Wentworth muttered as he helplessly watched the grenade plummet to its inevitable destination followed swiftly by two more.

Then there came the flash of light as the first grenade hit, followed a half second later by the muffled sound of the explosion as it carried across the bay to the deck of the retreating ship, two further explosions following in quick succession. Wentworth watched grimly as the squadron of soldiers was turned into so much butcher's offal. In that second, ten brave men were turned into a bloody mush of broken bodies in the heart of that fearsome conflagration.

Nita van Sloan came charging up the stairs, her *House of Gucci* heels clattering against the wooden staircase as she hurried to retrieve Wentworth. Nita stopped at the top of the stairs, watching as Wentworth's hands tightened on the railing of the steamer and his lips pulled back to reveal a terrible sneer of rage. She knew from years of experience what must be going through her lover's mind, knew without a shadow of a doubt that Wentworth — ever impatient for action — was even now contemplating how he might stop that crazed gunman taking pot shots from the Statue of Liberty's copper skull.

Another bullet struck the deck just two inches from Wentworth's Saville Row loafer, and then a second a few feet further back, but still Wentworth stood his ground, unfazed, watching those now familiar muzzle flashes light up Lady Liberty's crown like caged lightning.

"Richard," Nita urged, not daring to step out from behind cover, "it's all right. Everyone else is safely below decks."

"Not everyone," Wentworth grumbled as he continued to watch those far off muzzle flares. Then, Wentworth's haunted figure turned to Nita. "I'm sorry, my love," he said quietly, "but I have to go."

"Richard, you mustn't," Nita begged, hoping against hope that he would not put himself in danger once again. As Nita watched, Wentworth turned once more, ducking down as another vicious hail of lead peppered the deck all about him.

While the other guests were cowering below decks, there remained several other figures on the forecastle where he stood. One was the ruined shape of Misty Hankerson, the gooey sludge of her spilled brains oozing from a massive rent in her skull; beside her, the girl's father Miles, runnels of red ruining his crisp white shirt. Justice demanded vengeance on the killer; justice demanded The *Spider*.

"Death," Wentworth muttered through tight lips. "Death to the bringers of death."

Then, with one hand on the steel rail of the ship, Wentworth leapt, propelling his agile form over the balcony and down into the cool waters of the Hudson as more shots rang out. Nita mouthed a silent prayer as she watched her companion disappear from view amid a hail of bullets. He was Richard Wentworth no more, she knew — now, Wentworth's place had been taken by that of The *Spider*.

Bullets slapped at the water about him as Wentworth's muscular figure disappeared below the surface. Wentworth held his breath as the bullets cut through the water, leaving spiraling trails of bubbles in their wake as they sunk into the river. Wentworth powered through the water like a shark scenting blood, mighty shoulders driving his arms onward, scooping great handfuls of water behind him as he torpedoed beneath the surface, out of sight of that mad gunman. Bullets continued to spatter the dark waters behind him as they sought their courageous target. Wentworth dismissed them, reaching into a hidden pocket within his dinner jacket and pulling free several items he had concealed there. His hands went to his face for a moment, smearing a waterproof sealant there that altered his features beyond recognition. When he pulled his hands away, false teeth shone in place of his grim smile, long canines protruding past the edges of his lips like some vampire of yore, while his skin was obscured behind a terrifying fright mask. His whole demeanor had changed too, his body language taking on the fearsome movements of something strong... powerful... dangerous! He was no longer Richard Wentworth — now, he was The *Spider*.

Ahead, The *Spider* saw the shadow of the great statue marking the river like the reaper's scythe, its black lines cutting through the shimmering waters with surety. Behind, bullets continued to slap into the Hudson and echo across the bay, the noise of their passing faint and eerie to Wentworth now, submerged as he was, like something from a dream.

The *Spider* could not possibly guess what was happening while he hurled himself beneath the dark waters, had no inkling that a second platoon of brave soldiers had emerged from Fort Wood to halt the gunman, only to be picked off in turn by the man hiding in Liberty's crown. How many would die today? How many must before this madness was at an end?

Wentworth drove himself on, moving with uncanny swiftness as a burning sensation began to press at his lungs. He would need to breathe soon, which meant revealing himself to his would-be executioner. Wentworth ignored the pain, his face set with determination as he cleaved the water. Above him, the setting sun painted the churning waves with amber, then red as their hidden interloper continued on towards the towering Statue of Liberty. The gunman in Liberty's crown had stopped firing as the steamer drifted out of range.

For a moment, Hudson Bay was quiet; the far off sound of the retreating steamer chugging across the waves the only intrusion on the tranquility. Then, a desperate splash as something burst from the water, a man's figure emerging in the lee of the statue, all but hidden by the shadow cast over the red painted waves as he pulled himself up onto the shore. That that figure had been socialite Richard Wentworth just minutes ago seemed now to be a fabrication. For instead, stepping from the bloodlike waters, came a figure from nightmare — a man dressed in swirling black cloak and slouch hat, his face replaced with a hideous visage as if he had emerged from the very depths of Hades itself. This was The *Spider*, Gotham's grim avenger, the Master of Men.

For a moment, The *Spider* let loose a hideous laugh, its mocking sound echoing across Bedloe's Island. Beneath his mask, The *Spider's* pale eyes darted this way and that, searching for other possible assailants who might even now be waiting to assist the gunman in the statue. Whoever the madman was, he had cut down over a dozen of Uncle Sam's best men in cold blood, the evidence of his evil delivery all around the base of the towering statue that dominated the isle. But no, the man appeared to be alone.

Keeping to the shadows, The *Spider* made his careful way towards the stretch of open ground that led to the foot of the statue, pulling the dark cloak around him to better disguise him in the twilight. It was a ways to the statue. How was he to pass that open area without being spotted? He could not yet guess, but he knew that he must, that men's lives were at stake.

Just then Wentworth heard a noise behind him, glanced that way and saw more soldiers scrambling from the entrance to Fort Wood, making their way towards the Statue of Liberty. There must have been fifteen men at least, each one sprinting the sixty yards that marked the space between them and the entrance to the statue. Although not far, those sixty yards were open ground, a no man's land - they didn't stand a chance, and the *Spider* had to warn them. But even as he cried out, the first shot rang across the harbor. The *Spider* watched helplessly as a dozen men were systematically cut down, a bullet drilling into him from high up in the statue. He ran, but he was too late, they were dying with every urgent step he took.

The *Spider* cursed the time it had taken to get here, cursed that his bellowed warning had not been heard over the cruel sound of the rifle.

Two of the soldiers ran for the cover of the light shrubbery that sprouted close to the statue. Then, from their hiding positions, both soldiers aimed their rifles high, targeting the head of Lady Liberty and shooting round upon round at the window-like partitions between the struts of her crown.

"I got him," one of the soldiers cheered, and for a moment, the sniper's fire stopped.

Wentworth prayed that the man had been killed, his brief reign of terror ended. Then it started again and a continuous stream of 9 mm bullets from a machine gun sliced the night air like lethal wasp stings. It was the automatic again, blasting its stream of hot death. The *Spider* hunkered down in the shadow of the statue as those bullets drilled into the limited cover that the two soldiers hid behind. Wentworth felt the bile rise at the back of his throat as those two men screamed in agony, suffering a handful of shots before they finally slumped to the ground.

Whoever this maniac was, he had to be stopped. Yet, The *Spider* could not possibly know how well armed he was, what armaments this sniper might possibly turn against him. No matter — Wentworth felt no fear, not now. He was The *Spider* now and the sounds of blazing gunfire only made him feel alive.

The *Spider* hurried across the short space of open ground to the foot of the statue, his dark clothes hiding him in the poor light of dusk. Whoever the gunman was, he had exceptional eyes however, for The *Spider* had to leap aside as a swarm of bullets burst forth and struck the ground where he ran. Then The *Spider* was at the statue's base, amid the remains of ten dead soldiers, victims of the madman's grenades. The *Spider* trudged through the human debris, feeling his loafers sink into the ground with a squelch of spilled blood.

Another bullet struck the ground by The *Spider's* foot, and Wentworth hurried onwards until he was flush against the wall of the statue's plinth. He was hidden from the gunman now, the lip of the plinth screening him from the man's bullets. But if he followed his previous pattern, it wouldn't take long for the gunman to switch to using grenades, wiping out anything living in the vicinity of the statue's base. The *Spider* needed to hurry.

Wentworth glanced around, searching for the door that led into the statue. Ahead of him, he could see the dark line where the locked door had been forced open — at least those brave soldiers had not died in vain. The *Spider* hurried over, pressing his hand against the heavy door to shove his way inside. But the door did not give. While the soldiers had unlocked it, something within still blocked the way, some barricade placed by the senseless gunman.

The *Spider* shoved at the door again, this time harder. As he did so, Wentworth became aware of a whistling noise coming from overhead. He glanced up in time to see the familiar pineapple-shaped outline of a grenade as it dropped towards him from Lady Liberty's crown.

With fierce determination, Wentworth shoved at the door with all his might, using his shoulder to slam against it like a charging bull as the frag grenade dropped towards him. The *Spider* knew the power of those grenades, had already calculated that there was no time for him to run, to seek cover — the radius of the blast would be enough to seriously injure if not kill him.

With maximum effort, The *Spider* forced the heavy door back. He heard something scrape against the tiled floor beyond as the table that had wedged it there was shoved aside. The door gave and Wentworth followed, crashing into the lobby as the grenade hit the ground where he had stood an instant before. As The *Spider* went sprawling across the floor, his left foot kicked out at the door, slamming it shut even as he lost his balance. At the same instant, the grenade exploded outside.

The door shook in place as that lethal blast went off, dust billowing from all about its edges accompanied by a cacophonous clap like thunder.

In the moments after, the lobby went graveyard silent as the echoes of that explosion petered out. Unmoving, The *Spider* lay face down on the darkly tiled floor, his black-clad form sprinkled with dust, his hat thrown fully ten feet ahead of him with the force of the blast. Then, slowly, warily, Wentworth began to move, rolling his shoulders and pulling himself up to a sitting position, glancing about him instinctively for any signs of his attacker. Understated lighting emanated from wall-mounted lamps that dotted the circular room, but the lobby appeared empty.

Wentworth's ears were ringing as he retrieved his slouch brimmed hat from the floor, brushing plaster dust away. Then, The *Spider's* lips pulled back in a taunting sneer and he let loose his hideous, mocking laugh once more. He had survived!

With determined strides, the frightening form of The *Spider* made his way across the lobby to a doorway, shoving at it with the heel of his hand. The door opened to the stairwell that led high into the body of the statue and, once inside, Wentworth glanced up the tightly coiling flight of stairs that led up over one hundred feet to the statue's observation crown. This was the obvious route to take to reach the gunman. But it was too obvious — the sinister sniper had come prepared, there could be little doubt he would either have booby-trapped the door or have it covered for any eventuality.

Wentworth spun, peering around the stairwell with the urgency of a bug caught in a jar. There had to be another way up into the statue, some way to reach its crown that the gunman wouldn't expect. The *Spider's* eyes fixed on a low door located several steps down from where he stood, hidden in the wall and abutting the staircase itself. The door was barely four feet in height and was marked with an unobtrusive sign reading:

Private access only

Perfect.

The *Spider* tried the door handle and found it locked. He stepped back and kicked, his heel crashing against the lock once... twice... until on the third time the door burst open, the lock just a ruin of twisted metal. Without a backwards glance, The *Spider* stepped inside.

The access door opened into a hollow chamber that Wentworth guessed was roughly thirty feet across and climbed up the height of the statue. The area was unlit, with only the light from the open doorway providing any illumination. It was something like a grand hall, with metal scaffolding running up its entire height, tightly-placed struts running at regular intervals up the statue's interior and a caged cylinder to one side where the visitors' staircase stood. Once more, The *Spider* opened his mouth and let loose that eerie laugh, listening with satisfaction as it doubled and redoubled up and down the length of that great statue. Outside the statue itself, that sound echoed like a haunting, ethereal howl, like the devil's snickering on the wind, alerting the gunman to The *Spider's* presence. Let the gunman know he was coming; let the gunman know his short reign of terror was coming to an end, courtesy of The *Spider*.

The struts that made up the internal structure were constructed from four-inch thick metal bars, triangular arrangements running in parallel rows that soared upwards like a series of otherworldly ladders. The nearest of these was a little over two feet above The *Spider's* head as he reached up, grabbing it and hoisting himself up with both hands. Swiftly, Wentworth's agile form clambered up to the peak of the first triangular arrangement, heels teetering on the thin rungs of the lower strut.

The spacing between the struts had not been designed for the job at hand and as such it was awkward for The *Spider* to climb up easily. A gap of roughly four feet spanned between each triangle's base and its apex, forcing Wentworth to move in a semi-crouch, unable to stretch out to his full height. Worse yet, the next line of struts was four feet above its predecessor and Wentworth found he could only just reach it as he balanced on the lower level of the beam he stood upon, barely brushing the one above with his fingertips. Wentworth was in the prime of physical fitness and his determination was boundless, but clambering up the inside in this manner, he realized, would prove far too limiting. Every noise he made in the echoing chamber threatened to draw the unwanted attention of the crazed gunman, exposing his position in the half-light.

For a moment, The *Spider's* grotesque figure crouched back down on the lowest strut of the scaffold, frantically searching inside his cloak for the trick pocket hidden in its folds. It was a supreme feat of balance for The *Spider* to remain there like that, and yet his nightmarish figure made it look easy. When Wentworth's hands reappeared they pulled a thin line from the masking folds of his cloak. This was The *Spider's* web; thin as fishing wire, but with the strength of tensile steel. With a flurry of movement, Wentworth reeled the wire out as he whipped it around and around, faster and faster. Then he let go as the web swooped to its pinnacle and the end of the wire arrowed upwards, weaving through the struts until it found purchase three-fourths of the way up the statue's body. The *Spider* tested the strength with a swift tug before swinging free of the scaffold and clambering hand-over-hand up his web.

In less than a minute, the black-garbed man of mystery had climbed eighty feet in silence and secured himself on the second highest of those triangular structures that crisscrossed the statue's innards. Up above, just nine feet from where he now stood, Wentworth could see another small access door and he knew this one must lead into the hollow skull of the statue itself. There were other access doors throughout the inside, Wentworth noticed, but with time at a premium he wanted to get to the statue's head as swiftly as possible — every second he wasted gave the madman another chance to take a shot at an innocent ship passing the island.

Leaving his web hanging from the I-bar, The *Spider* pulled himself up to the topmost bar of his current strut. Then he heaved himself up, straightening his arms until he was balanced like a circus acrobat on a trapeze. A moment later, Wentworth began swinging his body like a pendulum, gathering momentum before throwing himself up in the air. His hands let go of the strut he was clutching and for a moment The *Spider* flew free, darting through the air towards the highest of the struts that crisscrossed the structure.

Then his arms grasped the uppermost beam, flipping over it to discharge his momentum. As he did so, the small door opened to the side of the strut and a man's face poked through, alerted by the noise of The *Spider's* passage.

"Death!" the man yelled, brandishing a service revolver. "Death to the enemies of liberty!"

The *Spider* leapt back as the man's revolver spat lead fury at him.

The revolver's report was deafening in the confines of that echoing chamber inside the statue, its muzzle flash lightning-bright in the gloom. The *Spider* leapt backwards from his tentative position on the uppermost beam, diving away as the gunman's first bullet cleaved the air. The bullet raced past Wentworth, cutting a smoking hole through his swirling cloak before pinging off the wall behind him as he fought to retain his balance.

Already the mysterious gunman was firing again, his pistol discharging staccato bursts of fire. With each muzzle flash, Wentworth saw his opponent's face — a hideous, scarred thing, utterly hairless and with the intense eyes of the drug addled.

The *Spider* dropped down, assuming a crouch on the narrow metal scaffold as more bullets flew overhead. Then, with a mocking laugh he reached beneath his black dinner jacket, pulling loose twin .45s from their hidden holsters located beneath his arms. The automatics glinted silver as they caught the flashes of light from his opponent's pistol, and The *Spider* simply laughed. It was a terrible braying laugh and it seemed to mock the gunman as his revolver missed its target again and again. One final blast and the madman's revolver clicked on empty.

The *Spider* turned his twin automatics on the figure who stood framed in the open access doorway leading inside the statue's head. Both pistols fired as one, the sound of their fury loud in the enclosed space of the statue's core. Wentworth watched as those twin bullets rushed at their target, drilling into the sniper who stood perfectly framed before him; one bullet hit the man's head, the other struck lower, cutting him in his chest beside the breastbone.

The *Spider* laughed once more, the hideous sound reverberating through the Statue of Liberty as his bullets found their target.

But, as The *Spider* watched, the man in the access door just stood there — incredibly his bullets had had no discernible effect. The *Spider's* weapons spat again and again, blasting bullets at the figure who stood unmoving before him. The *Spider* watched incredulously as the man efficiently reloaded his gun before raising it to target the cloaked man once again — The *Spider's* bullets had had no effect!

Poised on the narrow strut, The *Spider* ran as bullets knifed through the air towards him. He felt the slugs cut into his billowing cloak, inches from his torso, but on he ran, determined to stop this demented madman once and for all.

As he fired from the access door, the maniac shouted, his hollered words echoing through the hollow structure: "Death to the enemies of America. Death to the enemies of liberty!" It sounded almost — but not quite — like The *Spider's* familiar refrain.

Still running the thirty-foot length of that thin I-beam, The *Spider* flipped one of his own weapons in his hand, tossing it ahead of him in a rotating arc. The chromium sheen of the gun blazed like a camera flashbulb as it reflected the muzzle flashes and for a fraction of a second the gunman was distracted, aiming high as The *Spider* powered toward him.

And then The *Spider* was upon him, leaping through the air as bullets screamed all around him, his right fist connecting with the gunman's arm and battling his assailant's revolver away. The two combatants tumbled through the access doorway and rolled across the floor of the room beyond.

They were in the observation deck of the Statue of Liberty now, Wentworth saw, a tidy stack of military weaponry resting against one of the curving exterior walls beside a doorway that led to the stairwell. Outside, the sun had set and a silvery moon lit the sky, its milky beams bathing the observation deck in a ghostly wash.

Beneath that alabaster glow, The *Spider* saw his foe properly for the first time. The man's scalp was shaven and he had no eyebrows, no hair of any kind on his head, in fact. The man was huge, over six feet in height with shoulders as broad as the front door of Wentworth's townhouse apartment. He was so wide, in fact, that Wentworth guessed he would have trouble getting into a normal automobile or taxicab. He was a monster. The man was dressed in a drab olive undershirt and loose pants — army fatigues. There was blood on his top lip and his blue eyes had an intensity that The *Spider* recognized as that of the paranoid drug abuser. There was something else in those eyes too, something Wentworth knew all too well — fear.

"You're the enemy," the gunman howled as he glared at The *Spider's* frightening visage, "every last one of you!"

The maniac moved with such speed that The *Spider* had no time to dodge in the confined space. His hands were upon The *Spider* in a second, then The *Spider* was tossed up into the air as the hulking madman threw him aside. The air rushed from The *Spider's* lungs as his back slammed against the roof of the observation room and then he was dropping back down towards the floor, his remaining automatic tumbling from his hand. The *Spider* tasted blood in his mouth then — not the blood of the *Spider*, that unstoppable scourge of evil, but the blood of Richard Wentworth, a man who could be hurt, a man who could die.

The madman in the army fatigues tossed aside his own empty revolver as Wentworth crashed against the floor. But The *Spider* had no time to react as his opponent charged at him, unleashing a brutal kick to his side. A pained gasp burst from The *Spider's* bloodied lips — this enemy was incredibly powerful, it was more like being kicked by a mule than by a man.

The *Spider* rolled as the madman kicked out a second time, but he was too slow, and he felt the blow shake his body like an ax blow to a mighty oak. The *Spider* tried to make space, to get away from his fast-moving foe, but he was caught by a third kick, and Wentworth heard something in his chest crack as he rolled across the decking. His vision swam as he tumbled about the confines of Lady Liberty's crown. "America shall survive," the maniac was shouting. "You'll never get her daughters, you evil goose-steppers."

Then the madman was charging again, head down as he rushed at The *Spider* like some runaway freight train. The *Spider* rolled aside, groaning at the unexpected pressure on his cracked rib, and the lunatic ran past him, stopping just shy of the curving external wall, palms slapping against it to slow himself.

With a tremendous force of will, The *Spider* stood, using the nearest wall as a prop to steady himself. "I'm not your enemy," The *Spider* muttered, his words spat through bloodied teeth.

But the madman was upon him again, swiping at him with a bearlike fist. The *Spider* blocked with his forearm, but it was like being hit by a sledgehammer. The *Spider* struck out, seizing the opening and driving his fist into his foe's gut. The maniac did not even seem to feel it; he just stood there taking it as The *Spider* threw another punch at his face. It was like striking a wall.

Then the lunatic was moving again, brutally smashing The *Spider* across his masked face.

Wentworth fell once more, tumbling over and over as his cloak wrapped around him. He had landed by the access door, he realized. Even as that thought struck him, the madman's shadow loomed over his reeling vision, and Wentworth felt two strong hands reach down and grasp him, lifting him from the decking.

The *Spider's* legs kicked helplessly as the hulking lunatic shoved him effortlessly through the low door, driving him back onto the narrow strut that was just below it. Wentworth's vision blurred and blotted and his head rang with the pain of the blows he had sustained.

In the distance, The *Spider* became aware of voices echoing up through the hollow structure of the statue; army men shouting orders, commanding a thorough search. They must have followed The *Spider* in, no longer stalled by the madman's bullets while he was instead engaged with the Master of Men. The brute's hands were on Wentworth's chest now, hoisting him high overhead, preparing to toss him one hundred feet to the base of the statue and certain death. Wentworth's mind focused, those shouted army orders echoing like something from his past. And with a flash of inspiration, he knew exactly what he must do.

"At ease, soldier," Wentworth commanded, his voice suddenly hard with authority. "Stand down."

For a moment, The *Spider* hung there, poised helplessly above the hulking brute's head, about to be thrown to his doom. And then, magically, the madman relented, gently — almost delicately — placing his opponent on the narrow I-beam of the internal scaffold.

Wentworth gazed at the brute with incredulity. Used to commanding men, Wentworth had drawn upon all the authority he had employed when he had been a major in the army, turning every single word he spoke into an unquestionable order for the enlisted man. Remarkably, his command had stopped the brute — a soldier to his core — in his tracks.

"What is your mission, private?" The *Spider* asked as he balanced on that narrow beam opposite the monstrously scarred soldier. He guessed the man's rank, felt sure that an enlisted would react to the term.

"To protect these shores, sir," the grotesque soldier barked back, snapping off a brisk salute. "To defend liberty."

As the man spoke, Wentworth saw a dark stain beside his ear. Then another line appeared from his left nostril. It was blood. The man was bleeding inside, a brain hemorrhage, Wentworth recognized. Something was destroying him from within, driving him mad and killing him all at the same time.

The soldier sank to his knees then, clutching at his skull as the blood began to rush from his mouth and nose and ears.

"It hurts, sir," the soldier howled. "It hurts so much. Tell my mom I did my duty. Tell her..."

"You did your duty, soldier," Wentworth said, placing one hand on the man's shoulder. "Your mother can be proud."

The brute was weeping now and the tears mingled with his own blood. And then he swayed, tumbling over the edge of the narrow beam.

"No! The *Spider* cried, leaping forward and grabbing the soldier by his undershirt. The soldier rocked in place, dangling over infinity.

"It's okay, son," The *Spider* assured him, pulling him back. "I've got you."

But then there was a tear, and suddenly the tragic figure was falling — and so was the *Spider*. Wentworth's arm reached back, snagging the narrow beam as he started his descent. The soldier was not so lucky. Wentworth watched as he fell down into the depths of the Statue of Liberty. The soldier made no noise as he fell — he was already brain dead.

The clattering of footsteps came from the open access door and The *Spider* knew it was time he disappeared. Wentworth was capable of many incredible feats, but he would sooner not face a platoon of soldiers who had watched twenty of their brothers get shot down just minutes before.

The *Spider* stepped back into the shadows and dropped down to where his web line waited. He watched as, up above, silhouettes crossed the open access door, soldiers searching for the dead sniper.

Wentworth hung there in silence, modulating his breathing as his cracked rib pressed painfully against his right lung. A voice above demanded a flashlight and after a moment one appeared in the access door, motioning left and right as its holder searched for the missing man.

"Hand it here," an irritated voice called, and The *Spider* saw someone being shoved rudely aside. He recognized that voice and the thick-jowled silhouette in the doorway confirmed his assumption. The man was called William Augustyn and he had served with Wentworth once many years ago, back when they had both been fresh-faced recruits. While Richard Wentworth had left the army at the end of the Great War, Augustyn had stayed on, reaching the rank of General. The two still socialized now and again, members of the same gentleman's club just off Broadway.

The *Spider* dangled in the shadows, his black cloak wrapped around him as the General played that flashlight over the dark interior of the statue.

"Subject Alpha is down there," Augustyn cried. "He must have fallen. Quickly, go get him. On the double."

The access door slammed shut and Wentworth heard the clatter of army-issue boots trek past on the other side of the spiral cage by his head as the soldiers hurried back down the three-hundred-and-fifty-four steps to the statue's base.

It was early evening in the club. Rain slicked the windows; the clouds darkening the streets below. Richard Wentworth sat in his usual chair in one of the club's intimate corners, the leather upholstery smelling faintly of one-hundred years worth of fine cigars smoked in this very spot. For once, Wentworth had declined the offer of a cigar himself; the kick he had taken had left a hairline fracture in his third rib on the right side and inhaling the heavy smoke made it burn like the devil.

As he sat there, his pale eyes scanning the club's comings and goings, Wentworth spied General William Augustyn roll in, battling to close his umbrella as the maitre d' hurried to take it from him.

"Bill," Wentworth called jovially, two fingers casually extended as he held aloft his hand to get the man's attention.

Augustyn smiled as he saw his old friend, and made his way to greet him. "Wentworth old man, it's been — what? — five months."

"More like a year," Wentworth said, calling the house butler over and ordering a scotch for the General as well as a top off for his own.

"What brings you here?" Augustyn asked, his voice sounding — as ever — like it was barking orders rather than asking questions.

"Things on my mind," Wentworth explained as he lit the man's cigar with his silver lighter. Then he shrugged. "I hear things are going well for you over at Fort Wood."

"Hah," Augustyn laughed, a mean sound reminiscent of an old man's cough. "Then you heard wrong. We had a disaster yesterday and I've been in meetings all day. Emergency conference tomorrow out in Washington — blasted mess if you ask me. No good ever comes of getting politicians involved in Army business."

Wentworth raised an eyebrow in polite interest. "What's the problem?" he asked lightly. "Perhaps I can help."

Augustyn laughed again. "You were a good man when you were in the service, Richard, but this one's a little out of your league." Augustyn peered over both shoulders, checking that they weren't overheard. "Negotiations for the funding of a project I've been heading up trying to create a superior soldier, something we might deploy against the Nazis if the need arises. Strictly hush-hush, you understand."

Wentworth nodded. "A superior solider, you say? Sounds promising."

"It was," Augustyn enthused. "We'd hit on a mixture of steroids that can bulk up our boys, turn them into human tanks. You wouldn't believe the things they can do, lift a man like he was a child's doll. Just a few teething problems to sort out."

Wentworth remained silent, but he was thinking back to the way the hulking soldier he had encountered had behaved, intense paranoia giving way to the brain hemorrhage that killed him. Steroid misuse, clearly.

"There's a black cloud sweeping across Europe," the General was continuing. "We must do everything we can to defeat the enemies of freedom and liberty, and my *Superior Soldier Program* may just provide the advantage we need."

"Everything?" Wentworth spat, anger welling within him now. "Once we surrender our humanity, we're no longer fighting a war worth winning, Bill."

Astonishment was etched across General Augustyn's features as Wentworth stood up and left him to his scotch and his fine cigar— alone, with nothing but his thoughts. Alone and entangled in the web of… The *Spider*.

Fear the Dark
by Bobby Nash

Marianne Nelson was afraid of the dark. It was no mystery to her where this fear originated. There were dangers lurking in the shadows. They were there. She had seen them. In the darkness, evil waited, it plotted, it planned, and it thrived.

She wanted to scream, but couldn't. Once again she had been betrayed by her own voice as it deserted her in a time of great need. Such a thing was not unusual in this place. She didn't really know where this place was on a map, but she recognized her surroundings when she visited.

The images came at her quickly, each one more frightening than the last. She saw a man, or at least she thought it was a man. He had two arms, two legs, and the general proportions of a well-built man, sturdy and strong. He would have been the perfect male specimen, she reflected, if not for that face, that horrible, horrible face that sat atop those finely chiseled shoulders. Sharp teeth glinted in the light. She couldn't tell if it was a reflection from moonbeams or produced by an electric bulb, but the sun had already dipped below the horizon, plunging the world into darkness. His hair was wild and unruly, much like the man himself.

The monster sneered at her with his misshapen face and spoke, but she couldn't make out what he was saying as her ears worked only slightly better than her voice at times like this. He reached out toward her from the darkness, his fingers threatening to close around her like a vice.

Marianne ran.

That's when she realized that she was not alone. Another woman ran at her side, their hands clasped tightly together. The woman was a stranger, but she stood taller than Marianne's petite frame. They were in a forest or some other type of wooded area with a lake nearby. Even though everything moved in slow motion, she could tell that they were in a hurry.

Something was chasing them through the dark.

Was it him?

Or was it something worse?

The woman at her side was pretty, thin, and fit. She had chestnut colored hair that bounced playfully around her shoulders as she ran. She appeared dressed for a night out on the town, or a black tie gala of some kind based on the skintight slinky black dress and high heels she wore. How she was able to run in them, especially over the soft earth of the forest floor, Marianne couldn't even begin to guess.

If not for the monster pursuing them, she might have considered this fun. It had been so long since a visit to this place made of smoke and whispers had been enjoyable. All she saw these days was death and destruction. No one should have to witness the images Marianne Nelson had been forced to endure. Not for the first time, she wondered what cruel quirk of fate had chosen her to see these horrific visions. In her nightmares she watched helpless as raging rivers ran red with the blood of the innocent. She saw the sky blacken and burn as maniacal laughter covered the Earth. And even worse was that she had to watch a good man die over and over and over again, each time in a different manner, and each time more gruesome than the last.

It was that last vision that seized her heart again and again.

A clawed hand slashed at them and the mystery woman pushed Marianne to safety. Marianne had not noticed that the mystery woman had been carrying a gun in her free hand. The stranger opened fire at whatever was after them, but all Marianne could see were bright flashes that punctuated the darkness. The thunderous echoes of each shot reverberated in her brain.

She heard an inhuman howl.

Then all was silent.

The woman was gone.

The monster man was gone.

She sat on the cold, damp dirt.

All alone in the dark.

She wasn't sure how long she sat there shaking from the cold and the fear. It could have been minutes or even days. She really couldn't say. Just as the trembling in her hands started to subside, she heard a new sound. It was faint at first, but ever so slowly it grew louder and louder until the thunderous droning hurt her ears. It was the tell-tale beating of a human heart. But whose heart?

Was it hers?

Was it the man monster's heart?

She clamped her hands over her ears in a futile attempt to shut out the noise, but to no avail. The sound grew louder and louder, so deep and booming that Marianne feared the rhythmic thump, thump, thump might well drive her mad.

Then an inhuman growl joined the chorus in concert with the steady thrum, thrum, thrum of a powerful heartbeat. For a moment she felt as if she were inside a bear or some other great beast. There was nothing but blackness punctuated by strange distorted flashes of light.

Then there was a slashing of claws from out of the inky blackness followed by deep searing pain.

Blood splattered across a wall.

— and Marianne Nelson found her voice at last.

Marianne Nelson screamed.

She sat straight up in her very own bed, drenched from head to toe in a cold sweat, her short-cropped black hair matted to her face. At first she was disoriented, not an uncommon sensation after a vision as intense as the one she had just experienced. She was certain it wasn't just a nightmare. She never remembered her dreams, but visions always stayed with her clear and plain as if they contained information she needed to recall during the waking day. This was not her first either, although she prayed it might be her last.

She looked over to the empty side of the bed and ran a hand over the crisp cool bedspread that lay there unwrinkled by the weight of a human body.

Even after all these years she still slept on her side of the bed. James, her husband of ten years had been dead and buried almost twice as long as they had been married. Even though the pain of his death, and the uncertainty of how he spent his final moments, haunted her as if it was only yesterday that she had watched his empty casket lowered into the cold hard ground.

Marianne had been having visions all her life, but they were more like quick flashes of insight. Nothing like the intense sensory overload that they became that lonely December evening almost ten years earlier.

It had felt so real. She had watched James die over and over as if on a loop, shot in one, stabbed in another, and falling to his death in yet another. She told him what she had seen, tried to warn him away from the business trip that was to take him out of the country for a week's time. James was not the type of man to put stock in her foolish dreams so he smiled at her and insisted that there was nothing to worry about. He promised her that he would be all right and that he would return in a week and that they would celebrate Christmas and New Years together.

Marianne relented even though every fiber of her being screamed at her not to let him go.

The plane carrying her husband crashed into the ocean en route to London. The authorities had not been able to recover his body so she had been forced to bury an empty box under the grave marker bearing her husband's name. No one could explain why the plane had crashed. All she knew was that James was gone.

That was the first Christmas she had spent alone.

It would not be the last.

It was, however, the last time she ignored one of her premonitions.

The woman in her vision was unknown to her. All she knew was that this woman would be somewhere where she was wearing a slinky black party dress and high heels. That wasn't much to go on. In a place like New York City, there was an almost infinite number of parties, galas, fundraisers, and other such events. There was no way she could cover them all until she found this woman.

But she had to try.

Nita Van Sloan loved a good party.

Because of her high profile socialite status, Nita attended quite a number of fancy galas and black tie events. Some would say she attended more than her fair share, but she chose to ignore this comment because... well, because she could. Nita loved a good party. There was something exciting and glamorous about getting all dolled up for a night out on the town.

Her date, Richard Wentworth, on the other hand, was a different matter.

Wentworth hated parties, especially these social functions with a secondary agenda beyond simple enjoyment. He saw these large to-dos as little more than pompous fat cats talking about their latest business conquests while showing off their trophy wives and trying to one up each other. Politicians hiding behind false smiles as they made promises to campaign contributors, many of which they knew could not be kept no matter their intention. There were many powerful men in this room and he suspected that many of them would one day cross paths with The *Spider*. On that day there would surely come a reckoning.

These were generalizations, of course. Wentworth suspected that there were some in attendance, men and women of influence who were truly happy to help out the cause of the moment. He held no ill will toward those select few, but that didn't mean he enjoyed hanging out with them either. In his mind, it was as if everyone at the party wore their wealth and prosperity like a mask to disguise their true natures. That was something that Wentworth did understand because he too wore a mask.

Only his mask was far more frightening.

Unbeknownst to everyone except the lovely lady on his arm, Richard Wentworth was also the masked vigilante known to newspapers and law enforcement as The *Spider*. There were many in this room who had no doubt lost money on some shady back door deal that The *Spider* had derailed. Although he would never admit it to her out loud, Nita knew that he would rather be out there in some dingy alley fighting with some crook or other bad guy, than standing inside the stunningly beautiful hall at the Plaza Hotel wearing his "monkey suit" as he called it. Personally, Nita thought Richard looked great in a tuxedo and wished he would wear one more often, but she would take what she could get. She counted his appearance as a hard won battle. It took all of her wiles to convince him that even The Master of Men needed to take the night off every once in awhile.

He wanted to argue the point, but surrendered to Nita's inevitable charms. He was just glad the lovely Miss Van Sloan was on his side. With her formidable strength of will he would hate to oppose her in battle.

Tonight's festivities were part of a fundraising effort organized by the Ravenwood Foundation, a charity that had been recently set up as a way to provide aid to orphans of war. Victoria Aldridge, the charity event's organizer, explained the foundation's mission statement during her lengthy speech.

"The continuous escalation of war and fighting around the world has left a long line of victims in its wake," she told the assembled crowd. "The Ravenwood Foundation's goal is to provide aid, both social and economic to those children devastated by war. And we need your help to do it."

After the speech ended to thunderous applause, Aldridge made the rounds. She made it a point to shake everyone's hands. Of course, she also spent a few extra minutes with the big spenders. It was her job to grease the wheels in the hope of increasing their donation to such a worthy cause. After the meet and greet there was an assortment of performers lined up, from jugglers to psychics to comedians. An exhibition containing a unique collection of priceless ancient artifacts from around the world was on display in the hotel lobby directly below them. The exhibit was part of a traveling museum collection and included pieces from the foundation's personal collection, as well as those of other private donors. It was billed as one of the most eclectic displays of the abstract and the unexplained, popular topics these days. Everywhere Nita traveled lately, it seemed like the supernatural was the main topic of conversation. The exhibit played up the mysterious past of the artifacts on display and it worked. It was popular wherever it stopped.

The house band was in full swing, playing a medley of smooth jazz classics. Nita had been informed that jazz was a favorite of the foundation's founder, even though he was not on hand for tonight's gathering. Victoria Aldridge apologized for Mr. Ravenwood's absence most of the evening.

"Would you care to dance, Mr. Wentworth?" Nita said, trying to prompt Richard to loosen up a bit for the evening. He had been preoccupied for the past few days. She knew he hadn't been sleeping well either.

"It would be my pleasure, Miss Van Sloan," he replied, smiling for the first time since they arrived.

They took to the dance floor and enjoyed themselves.

Unfortunately, for both of them it was only a brief respite from their normally turbulent lives.

This wasn't the normal type of gig that Marianne Nelson accepted.

She hated to see her gift touted as if it were some sort of carnival act, but she hated the thought of losing her apartment or starving to death even more. So when the lady from the Ravenwood Foundation approached her about doing a reading at their gala event, she couldn't rightly say no because her landlord was only days away from putting her out on the sidewalk.

She arrived early and helped herself to a plate of hors d'oeuvres and the most exquisitely tender cut of roast beef she had ever put in her mouth. Those Ravenwood folks had spared no expense to wine and dine their supporters.

She watched the couples on the dance floor with envy. Marianne had always loved to dance, but the last time she had stepped foot on a dance floor was when her husband was still alive. She had yet to meet another man whom she could see herself dancing with.

Marianne was about to head backstage to get ready for her performance, which was scheduled to start after the band finished their set. It didn't take much preparation for her gift to work. All she needed was focus.

Ironically enough, she was so focused on finding her focus that she didn't see the couple step off the dance floor right in front of her until it was too late. She felt the collision more than saw it. Startled back to reality, she lost her balance and fell in a most undignified manner, on her rear.

The man she had bumped into reached out a hand and helped her back to her feet. He was tall and handsome with a smile that lit up the room. Just as her husband's had.

"Are you all right, Miss?" he asked.

"I'm terribly sorry," Marianne said, feeling her cheeks blush with embarrassment, her eyes scanning the floor for anything of interest.

"It's okay," the man's companion said politely.

"My mind must have been else…" Marianne's voice trailed off as she looked up and saw a very familiar face, one she was beginning to think she would never see in the waking world. " — where."

"Are you sure you're okay?" the woman with chestnut colored curls asked. Genuine concern was etched on her face.

Marianne Nelson couldn't help herself. "It's you!" she blurted.

Then promptly fainted.

The first thing Marianne Nelson saw when she opened her eyes was her husband James' handsome face. James smiled down at her, but when he spoke it was not with his own voice, but rather a deep timbre she had never heard. That was when she realized that the man standing over her was not, in fact, her husband.

"I'm sorry," she said. "What?"

"I said, everything's okay," the handsome man she had bumped into earlier repeated. He knelt next to the outdoor lounge chair where she was sitting. For a moment she wasn't sure where she was. Stars loomed high over her head and for the life of her she couldn't figure out how she had gotten outside.

"What happened?"

"You fainted," he said.

"I'm so embarrassed," Marianne said, a hand to her cheek before she blushed again.

"No need to be, I assure you. It happens."

"How did we get…"

"Oh. We figured you needed a little air so I carried you out onto the balcony. Nita went to fetch a cold wet washcloth."

"We?" Marianne asked while looking around. The balcony was empty, save for the two of them. Across the street she could see the trees of Central Park and the lake just beyond.

"Where are my manners," he chuckled. "I'm Richard Wentworth. And this — " He pointed at the woman walking toward them with the wet washcloth. "This is Nita Van Sloan."

"A pleasure to meet you," Nita said as she touched the cool cloth to Marianne's head.

"Marianne Nelson," she said by way of introduction as her eyes locked onto Nita's face.

"The psychic?"

"Yes, Miss Van Sloan," she stuttered. "You've heard of me?"

Nita smiled and took the seat next to her. "Only by reputation. I saw your name on tonight's schedule. I was looking forward to seeing you in action."

Marianne noticed the forced smile on the handsome man's face. "I'm guessing Mr. Wentworth doesn't share your enthusiasm on this subject," she said.

"She's good," Richard said sarcastically. He smiled to let her know he was only fooling, but the comment stung nonetheless. After all the years of scrutiny and outright mockery, she still hadn't gotten used to not being taken seriously.

"I'm afraid Richard is a skeptic by nature, Mrs. Nelson," Nita said. She knew that Richard viewed everything with a skeptic's eye, despite some of the unexplainable things they had seen over the years. Of course, she could tell none of that to Mrs. Nelson.

"It's okay. He's not the first I've run into. I doubt he will be the last," Marianne said. "At least Mr. Wentworth was more polite than most."

He smiled at that.

"I do have one question," Nita asked. "Before you passed out you looked at me as though I'd grown an extra head or something.

"Oh. That."

"I admit, it's not the type of reaction I'm used to getting whenever I meet someone for the first time," Nita said. This time it was her cheeks that reddened slightly.

"It might have been the first time you met me, Miss Van Sloan," Marianne said, her tone suddenly serious. "But I've been seeing visions of you for over two weeks."

Richard Wentworth, Nita Van Sloan, and Marianne Nelson sat together on the balcony. They were alone. Nita had taken a few moments to explain to Victoria Aldridge that Mrs. Nelson wasn't feeling well and that she would have to shuffle the schedule a bit to cover. This, of course, sent the already fussy Miss Aldridge running off backstage like a chicken who had lost her head.

Marianne laid out the entire story. She told them what she had seen in her vision. The first one featuring Nita had come to her two weeks earlier. From the description she gave, Richard was fairly certain his masked alter ego had also made an appearance, which grabbed his attention. If this woman had somehow deduced The *Spider's* connection to Nita then he needed to know what she knew and how. He also had to determine whether or not she was a threat. If she was, then he would have to take steps to minimize that threat.

Nita led the conversation, asking questions where they seemed relevant. Richard was more of an iron fist and had he been asking the questions, he would have hammered them at her furiously fast. Nita had correctly informed him that a softer touch would be required with Mrs. Nelson. As he so often did, Richard took her advice.

Marianne told them in as much detail as she could what she had seen in her visions. The fact that Nita was wearing the exact same dress and shoes as she had in the vision only strengthened the young psychic's resolve that whatever her visions had shown her, it was happening tonight.

"What do you think?" he asked Nita after they stepped out of earshot from the psychic.

"I believe her," Nita said.

"You can't be serious," Richard said, looking at her as if she had sprouted a third eye. "Do you honestly think that you and she will be attacked by The *Spider*?"

Nita smiled reassuringly. "No."

"Then what?"

"She obviously saw something, but it's just as clearly disjointed. She sees things in flashes, not in any linear fashion. What if there was something chasing us in the woods? Are you telling me The *Spider* wouldn't rush to our rescue?"

"Of course I would," Richard said sternly. "No question."

"And that's why I believe her. And let's not forget that she said this was what I was wearing. I just bought this dress this morning. There's no way she could have known about it."

"It's all still conjecture."

"Yes it is," Nita said. "Did you happen to look across the street?"

"Yes."

"What's over there?"

He knew where she was going with this. "The park."

"Woods. A lake. It's dark. This dress. The *Spider*. Can we afford to discount her story outright?"

Richard relented. "So what do we do now?" he asked.

Nita glanced back at the woman. Marianne was visibly shaken by their encounter. Her hands trembled slightly, which she tried to hide by keeping them in the pockets of her unassuming dress. "Let's start by making sure Mrs. Nelson gets home all right."

"We should leave now," he said.

Nita smiled. "Yes. We should leave now." Richard had wanted to leave ever since he got to the party. He was finally getting his wish.

"I'll get the car," he said.

"This really isn't necessary," Marianne Nelson said.

"Nonsense," Nita Van Sloan told her. "We're happy to give you a ride. Isn't that right, Richard?"

"Hmm...? Richard said, his attention drawn back to the here and now. He was focused on their surroundings, which told Nita he was taking Marianne's vision more seriously than he let on. "Oh, yes. It's our pleasure," he added once he realized what Nita had asked.

The three of them were waiting just outside the Plaza Hotel's lobby with a few of the others who left the party early. Word had been sent for Ronald Jackson, Richard's trusty driver, to bring their car around from the garage at the back of the hotel where tonight's partygoers were told to park.

Nita leaned in close to Wentworth. "What's wrong?" she whispered.

"I'm not sure," he muttered back without looking at her.

"Something is… off. I just can't figure out what."

Nita followed his gaze.

Richard was staring at the entrance to Central Park across the street. There was also a good bit of traffic on the road between the hotel and the wooded area that lay beyond. Nothing looked out of place to Nita, but she knew better than to second-guess his instincts. If Richard Wentworth suspected there was trouble afoot then you could bet your bottom dollar that he was right.

He was about to tell Nita to take their new friend back inside when he noticed a car pull to a stop in front of the hotel door. The car itself was fairly nondescript. Wentworth probably would not have given it a second look under normal circumstances, but tonight The *Spider's* senses were on high alert. As a result, he recognized the car from the two passes it had made since they stepped outside. Whoever was behind the wheel, they were waiting for someone. And that someone was—

—Inside the hotel.

Wentworth spun around and positioned himself between the lobby doors and the women, a hand on each of their shoulders as he moved them away from the door.

Unfortunately, he wasn't fast enough.

An explosion ripped through the hotel lobby, launching shards of wood, concrete, and glass into the night like thousands of tiny missiles. Had they not already been on the move, Richard Wentworth and his companions would have been cut to shreds by the flying shrapnel.

The force of the blast pushed them forward and they were slammed down onto the concrete sidewalk. On instinct, Wentworth used his body to protect Nita and Marianne from flaming debris. Small pieces of concrete bounced off the sidewalk around them and a couple of pieces off Richard's body.

"Everyone okay?" he asked as soon as it was safe to sit up.

"What happened?" Nita asked as Richard helped her to her feet.

"Explosion. We need to get out of here before — "

He didn't have time to complete the thought before a roar like that of a wild animal filled his ears. Wentworth spun to face the sound just as the massive beast burst forth from what remained of the lobby entrance. It was huge, easily ten feet tall, if not more, and covered in fur. Long claws were at the tips of thick fingers the size of a man's foot. The beast looked inhuman, but at the same time still roughly humanoid with two arms, two legs, and a head.

The creature reared back and howled at the crescent moon high overhead, partially shrouded by thick clouds that threatened rain. It had a snout like a wolf along with the sharp teeth to match. Its' eyes were a sickly yellow that all but glowed against the deep black hair that covered the beast's body.

But there was something else that stood out.

Wentworth noticed the strips of dark cloth hanging from the beast's body. He recognized them because he was wearing the same thing. They were the remains of a tuxedo ripped apart from the inside. It was a realization that stunned him. Whatever this creature was, it had been a man just minutes earlier. Tucked carefully into the tattered remnants of his clothing was a cylindrical golden object about three feet long with a round globe at one end. It looked like one of the items from the museum display.

Whatever the object was supposed to do, it was possible it was responsible for transforming man into beast. Wentworth did not know how such a thing was possible, but he would worry about that later. His first priority was protecting Nita, Marianne, and the others around, who were beginning to scatter.

Panic was the enemy and it seized the crowd. Someone screamed at the sight of the creature emerging from the ruined hotel entrance. Others pushed their fellow New Yorkers out of the way as they tried to get away from whatever chaos was happening. Suddenly, it was every man for himself. Above, the partygoers from the foundation gala had poured out onto the balcony to get a glimpse of whatever was going on.

Just then Jackson appeared with the car.

"Go!" Wentworth shouted to the women, pointing toward the car.

Nita grabbed Marianne by the hand and they ran to the car. Jackson had the door open for them and pushed it closed behind them.

Jackson tossed a briefcase to Wentworth as he approached.

"Get them out of here," he told the driver.

"Yes, Major," Jackson said as he dropped back behind the wheel. "Hold on, ladies," he said and gunned the accelerator.

"But what about Mr. Wentworth?" Marianne shouted.

"Don't worry," Nita assured her. "He's going for help."

Richard Wentworth ducked into a deserted alley.

He stepped behind a dumpster and opened the briefcase. Inside were the tools of his trade. Hat, wig, mask, cape, false pointed teeth, and most importantly, his trusty .45s and plenty of ammo. The transformation happened quickly, perfected due to the frequency with which he found himself in predicaments much like this one.

Although it had been playboy Richard Wentworth who had entered the alley, it was The Master of Men who emerged.

The *Spider* quickly summed up the situation. The beast was no longer in the hotel entrance. It had moved into the street and was swatting away cars as if they were children's toys being swept aside by an angry toddler.

One of those cars was his.

The sidewalk was impassible, filled to capacity with scared, screaming people. The *Spider* leapt onto the hood of a car parked near the alley, then leapt to another then another until he was close to where his limousine lay at an odd angle against a two foot tall stone wall on the side of the road.

"Nita! Jackson!" he shouted as he approached, his voice distorted thanks to the prosthetic teeth he wore.

"Major?"

"Jackson!" The *Spider* knelt next to his old friend, still inside the car. A quick inspection told him that neither Nita nor Marianne was inside. "Are you injured?"

"I'll live," he grunted painfully. The driver was visibly shaken, but alert. His freshly broken left arm hanging uselessly at his side, but otherwise he suffered no permanent injury.

"Where's Nita?"

Jackson pointed weakly in a direction.

The *Spider* followed his gaze, but saw only the monster and a crowd of frightened people next to the park entrance. It was pandemonium. It wasn't until he heard the gunshots that he knew precisely where Nita Van Sloan had gone.

As usual, she was right in the thick of things.

The *Spider* ran toward the sound of gunfire.

Nita Van Sloan slapped a new clip into her gun.

Unlike Richard, Nita preferred something a little smaller than a .45, but her .38 was still powerful enough to make any villain stand up and take notice (at least human villains). She had unloaded a full clip into the howling monster, which should have put it down like any other rabid beast.

All it did was make it mad.

The beast lumbered forward, howling in anger.

Nita stayed between Marianne and the monster, not that she could do much to protect her at the moment. If that thing hit either of them with its massive clawed hands that would be the end for them.

A wave of black passed in front of her and suddenly they were not alone.

Nita sighed. "What kept you?" she muttered.

The *Spider* turned and looked at the women.

And Marianne Nelson felt the world fall away beneath her feet.

"GO!" The *Spider* shouted to Nita, but it was good advice for anyone listening, which, thanks to The *Spider's* deep commanding voice, was everyone. "Get clear! Now!"

Without another word, Nita grabbed Marianne's hand and they ran.

Directly into Central Park.

The *Spider* had gone up against powerful foes before.

Despite evidence to the contrary and everything he had seen before, in spite of all of the werewolves, chemically changed madmen, giant robots, and vile villains intent on conquering the world, it still came as a surprise to him that the supernatural existed. There was still a small part of his brain that couldn't grasp the reality of dark magic in the world.

The *Spider* was a realist. Whether this beast was a product of nature, sorcery, or some super science gone mad, one thing was for certain. It was dangerous and needed to be stopped.

The *Spider* opened up with both guns as the creature approached. An expert marksman, he made sure every shot hit the mark. Despite the amount of hot lead both he and his beloved had poured into the beast, it kept coming.

If the creature expected The *Spider* to simply step aside for it, then he had another think coming. The *Spider* held his ground, slapped in two fresh new clips, and raised his guns.

He didn't have a chance to fire.

The big black beast hit him at full speed, knocking him aside like an insect against a windshield. An apt analogy as The *Spider* landed on the windshield of a nearby automobile. The glass cracked beneath his weight, but did not shatter.

The *Spider* watched as the beast headed into the park in hot pursuit of Nita and Marianne. He couldn't let it catch them.

Every muscle in his body ached, but The *Spider* slid off the hood of the car that had broken his fall and followed them into the woods. As he ran into the darkness, the only thing The *Spider* could think was that Marianne Nelson had been right after all.

Her vision was coming true.

That meant she and Nita were in big trouble.

Marianne Nelson had never run so hard in her life.

Just as she had been in her visions over the past two weeks, Nita Van Sloan ran at her side, grasping Marianne's hand as she propelled them forward through the darkness of the park. All around them the trees served to block out the moonlight. All she could see were quick splashes of light in those bare spots where the moonbeams managed to push through the leaves. As near as she could tell, they were on the path leading to the lake.

She was scared. Everything else in her vision had come to pass just as she saw it, although she would be the first to admit that she had misread some of the images. She would never have assumed the scary man with the teeth was there to help, or that he would put himself between her and harm's way, but that was exactly what he had done. She wasn't sure why, but she wanted to find out. At the moment, however, she was too terrified to think clearly.

She heard the roar behind them. It sounded so close, as if the beast that had made the sound trailed them by mere inches. She wanted to turn and look, but fear propelled her forward instead. They crested a hill and made their way down the slick grass, still damp from an early evening shower.

Reality seemed to blur around her, which is probably why she did not notice the rock until she had already tripped over it. She hit the ground hard, knocking the wind out of her.

Nita Van Sloan was at her side, shouting that she needed to keep going while pulling her back to her feet.

It was too late.

The fall had given the creature all the time it needed to catch up with them.

Nita aimed and fired again, unloading her entire clip into the creature, each shot hitting it center mass. It reared back and screamed toward the heavens. Nita couldn't tell if it was a scream of pain or one of rage. Honestly, she didn't care which. Her only thought was wondering what had happened to her fiancé.

She didn't have to wait long for an answer.

The *Spider* came out of nowhere. Dressed all in black, save for the red lining of his cape and the businessman's tie that now replaced the bow tie of the tuxedo, he was all but invisible in the darkness of the woods. He slammed into the beast, knocking it off balance with a flying tackle, but he did not have enough force to topple it completely so he grabbed a fistful of fur and held on tight to the monster's back.

The *Spider* fired at the head of the creature. At point blank range he hoped that the .45 slugs would do more than sting as they had back on the street.

The beast grabbed furiously at the mosquito on his back, trying to pry it off, but The *Spider* held tight for as long as he could. It only took a couple of attempts before the creature got lucky and snatched The Master of Men's cloak. With a mighty thrust he pulled The *Spider* from his perch and tossed him several feet away.

The *Spider* landed in the grass before sliding to a stop. He was thankful he hadn't hit a tree, which he was certain would have been a far more painful landing. The *Spider* watched as the beast roared again, its hands clutching his wounded head. In the darkness the monster all but melted into the shadows. If not for those sharp teeth, enflamed eyes, and something metal on its hip, The *Spider* might have lost sight of it. He pushed himself back to his feet just as Nita and Marianne reached his side.

"Tell me you have a plan," Nita said.

"I do now," The *Spider* replied. In the struggle he had forgotten about the cylindrical golden piece from the museum, but now he noticed that it was still tucked in the cloth that dangled from the beast's body.

The *Spider* slapped a fresh clip into his gun, his last, and chambered a round. "Go! Find cover!" he commanded.

Nita and Marianne headed toward the lake where several large boulders had been placed as benches. They would offer them some cover.

The *Spider* lifted the gun, steadied his aim, and fired three shots directly at the artifact. The first shot ricocheted off the globe casing. The second cracked it. The third shattered the globe.

An explosion of white-blue light filled the forest, illuminating the area like the midday sun. The *Spider* dropped to a knee to ride out the blast and shielded his eyes with his cloak.

As quickly as it appeared, the light vanished and darkness surrounded him once again. The beast was no longer anywhere to be seen. In its place lay a crumpled body lying in a heap. The *Spider* stepped close to the body, cautious in case it was a trick or trap. It was no longer a ten foot tall monster with ink black fur. Instead, it was a man, in his twenties from the look of him. He lay naked in a pool of blood, save for a few scraps of shredded cloth stuck to him. His lifeless body was riddled with bullet wounds that The *Spider* could only conclude had come from his and Nita's guns.

The globe was gone, destroyed, but the golden cylinder remained. It lay inches away from the dead man's body, blood pooling around it as well. Whatever strange magic had been contained within the globe had somehow transformed the man into that creature he had fought. He wouldn't cry over the dead man. Whether intentional or not, he had become that creature by his own actions or by accident, The *Spider* could not say.

He couldn't explain what had happened or how, but he knew someone who could. As soon as he got Nita and Mrs. Nelson safely to their respective homes, The *Spider* was going to find and have a few words with Mr. Ravenwood.

Richard Wentworth was troubled.

He hadn't been sleeping well of late and this night was no exception. He stood on the balcony of his penthouse suite and stared out at the city. It had been days since the incident in the park. Life had returned to what passed for normal. He had accompanied Nita to yet another social engagement where they danced, ate, and sipped champagne while boring people spoke of boring things. Exhausted from her day, Nita had dropped off as soon as her head hit the pillow, yet for some reason sleep eluded him. Somewhere out there an act of evil was being perpetrated or planned. The *Spider* itched inside his brain to leap once more into the fray. There would be time enough for that soon, he knew. The *Spider* would be needed again sooner or later.

"Richard?"

So lost in thought was he that he hadn't even heard Nita step out onto the balcony. She was wrapped in a blanket, her hair tangled from lying on it. "Did I wake you?" he asked.

"No," she lied. "Still can't sleep?"

"No."

"Are you worried about Marianne?" Nita knew it was still a concern with Richard that Marianne Nelson had seen them both in her visions. Nita was fairly certain that Marianne had not deduced that Richard Wentworth and The *Spider* were one and the same. She had kept in contact with her in the days since the incident at the Plaza Hotel. If Marianne had put the pieces together, then she was keeping that secret to herself.

Nita knew that Richard wouldn't be so quick to let it lie though. It was bad enough that his friend, Stanley Kirkpatrick already suspected that he was the masked vigilante his department sought. She would make sure to keep an eye on Marianne Nelson. There was nothing as important to her as her fiancé.

And keeping his secret.

"Come back to bed," Nita told him and took his hand.

As usual, he decided it was best not to argue with her.

Marianne Nelson closed her eyes.

In the weeks before that night, her dreams had been anything but terrifying. Since her encounter with Nita Van Sloan and her friend in the park, however, Marianne had slept soundly. Evil still existed in the world. Of this she was certain. She had seen it with her own eyes. The danger that lurked in the shadows was still there. In the darkness, evil still waited, still plotted, still planned, and still thrived.

But she now understood that there was something else out there in the dark.

And evil feared it.

Evil feared The *Spider*.

Marianne Nelson smiled as she drifted off to peaceful sleep.

She was no longer afraid of the dark.

Spider Trap
by Ron Fortier

G orban Jemers watched his men gather around the long dining hall table and felt a fleeting sense of foreboding. Although there was no rational reason why he should be worried; the building renovation job he and his crew of Hungarian carpenters had finished two days earlier had met with their employer's approval. In fact this celebration in the hall their brotherhood rented from the Brooklyn Carpenter's Union, was being hosted by that very same employer, a tall, silver haired fellow named Edwin Regent.

Upon arrival, he and the others had found Regent's personal aide and chauffeur, Porter Lyle awaiting them. Lyle was a giant of a man with a cruel hard face, small beady eyes and close cropped brown hair. Lyle always wore gray suits. He reminded Jemers of the ogres in his mother's fairy tales told to him in the old country.

Lyle had pointed to the long covered table and two wooden boxes at its center. "A gift from Mr. Regent for a job well done," the big man said obviously having rehearsed the words. In the four months the Hungarian builder had known him, the brute had barely uttered two words to him or his men.

Before he could thank the man, his foreman, Josef Tantu, ripped open one of the boxes and jubilantly announced, "It is champagne!" He pulled out an elegant green bottle and waved it over his head to the delight of his mates.

"Tell Mr. Regent that was most…" Jemers stopped as Lyle was already pushing the exit door open and disappearing without a backward glance. "Hmm, such a cordial fellow."

Watching his men pass the bottles around and uncork them merrily, the tired crew chief sat back in one of the folding chairs and rubbed his temples. He really should be home with Marla and the children. Still, the job had been a long and difficult one and it would have been wrong for him to deny his men this little party before they began looking for any new work commissions. With the depression in full sway, locating enough good jobs was an almost impossible task, especially for immigrants who were seen by most American craftsmen as a threat to their livelihood as well.

Which is why Jemer had ignored the peculiarities of Mr. Regent's unique demands. Somehow the rich American businessman, or so he identified himself on their first meeting, had learned of his crew's expertise in constructing complex carnival fun houses; most of these skills having been acquired from their gypsy ancestors over the centuries and incorporated into their building trades.

"Here you go, Gorban," Josef laughed, interrupting Jemers' reverie by handing him an overfilled glass of champagne. "Tonight we drink like the bourgeoisie, no?"

Jemers took the glass, spilling a bit on the table cloth, and chuckled. "Yes, my friend, we do." He took a long swallow and felt the bubbly liquid rush up his nasal canal. He coughed, feeling foolish. It had been a long time since he had tasted expensive champagne.

Watching Tantu rejoin the others he chided himself for his gloomy mood. He was being ridiculous. Yet knowing the death traps they had installed in that old brownstone, Jemers couldn't help but be concerned. Regent had merely explained the house would ultimately contain a valuable treasure and thus the required elaborate security. But what if some innocent soul were to enter unannounced? He had voiced that thought to his mysterious employer only to have him retort, "Then they will die."

There was a cry from across the room and the construction boss looked up to see one of his men double over and collapse to the floor.

He started to rise from the table when suddenly his lower abdomen was lanced with pain. He gasped, grabbing his middle. It felt as if every nerve in his body was afire and his lungs suddenly couldn't take in air. Bile arose in his esophagus at the same time as his bulging eyes watched several other men vomiting uncontrollably.

Jemers tried to push away from the table, gulping air, his heart racing, as more of his carpenters fell, throwing up all around him.

Poison! Now he understood the true price for what he had built Regent.

He had made a deal with the devil and the bill was due.

Gorban Jemers vomited as he fell to his side, his body convulsing like a beached fish and then he was still… forever.

The cigar in Police Commissioner Stanley Kirkpatrick's mouth seemed to be alive as he moved it from one corner of his mouth to the other: a sign of his inner agitation. It had started raining by the time he and his officers arrived at the scene of the horrendous crime, and his brown topcoat and fedora were dripping as he paced around the union hall. Smoke spiraled from the stogie's red tip, obscuring the hard look in his blue eyes. A seasoned veteran, the Commissioner had witnessed more than his share of dead men, but through an iron will of character, he would not allow his soul to be hardened. There were still good men in the world; men who would look upon the grotesque shapes of these poor immigrant workers and demand justice. Kirkpatrick was one of those men as were the uniformed officers he commanded.

Someone had murdered fifteen good, honest men and in one heinous act deprived their families of their love, strength and leadership. Fifteen women had become widows on this cold, miserable night and who knew how many boys and girls now were left without a father. The thought tore at Kirkpatrick's heart as he bit down on the chewed end of his cigar.

Someone would pay, he mentally swore to himself. Someone would be held accountable and justice meted out.

While the coroner finished his examination of all fifteen bodies, a police photographer moved about the corpses taking photos while another copper was busy drawing white chalk outlines around each victim doing his best to avoid the dried, putrid smelling vomit.

Over by the far wall, standing near the windows, two nervous old women stood with Detective Reese giving him their accounts as he scribbled into his small, dog-eared notebook. Reese, one of the best homicide dicks on the force, had briefed the Commissioner upon his arrival. The women were cleaners hired to pick up the place after the party was over by the now deceased Gorban Jemers. When they arrived shortly after eleven thirty, they had discovered the gruesome tableau and one of them had raced down the stairs to use the phone in the main lobby to call the station house.

"It was poison alright," the coroner grumbled, surprising the Commissioner from behind.

"Geez, Doc, don't do that!" Kirkpatrick snapped.

"Jumpy tonight are we?"

"Aw, it's this rain and all. It puts me in a foul mood without having to add mass murder to the evening." Kirkpatrick took hold of his cigar stub and dropped it to the floor, then crushed it out with the toe of his shoe.

"No argument there," agreed the white haired coroner, his eyebrows looking like tufts of cotton balls. "Anyway, my best guess is cyanide in the champagne. Won't be conclusive till we get them back to the morgue and run some tests, but I'd bet my next pay check on it."

"Cyanide, huh?" Kirkpatrick tilted his wet fedora back on his head and scratched his chin. "Now why on earth would somebody want to poison a bunch of harmless Hungarian carpenters?"

"That's your job, Commissioner. Mine's to determine cause of death, then bag and tag them."

"Getting callous in your old age, Doc?"

"Like you said, it's a foul night. For all of us."

"That it is." Kirkpatrick looked back over his shoulder. "Especially for them."

Seeing that Detective Reese had things in control and the ambulance attendants were busy carting the bodies off, the Commissioner exited the hall and made his way down the stairs to the front entrance. The rain had picked up and he squished his damp hat down tight as he dashed across the street to his parked sedan doing his best to avoid any puddles.

Once inside, he shook himself like a mangy dog and then started the engine. He would be glad to get home. As he turned on the headlamps and pulled away from the curb, he hoped his wife, Lona, would have some warm milk and cinnamon ready. It always helped him sleep.

The streets were fairly deserted at this hour and the streetlamps on the block corners did very little to thwart the encircling darkness. New York could be a fearsome place, he thought, when such a night descended and the good decent folks secured themselves in their homes.

He was turning a corner down a quiet residential block when he spotted the harsh glare of headlights in his rearview mirror. They were moving up on him rapidly and the closer they came he was able to see that he was being followed by a commercial truck of some kind. He twisted the mirror to the right as the glaring reflection was having a blinding effect on him.

Suddenly the following vehicle slammed into his rear without warning. Kirkpatrick was shoved forward, then back into his seat, his hands leaving the steering wheel. His car veered right, hit the curb and plowed into a rigid lamppost, which bent at the impact. The Commissioner's head slammed into the steering wheel as his sedan came to an immediate crashing stop.

Pain erupted in his head; his vision becoming blurred. His hat was gone. He felt along his forehead gingerly, still dizzy from the blow. There was blood on his fingertips.

Hurried footsteps and voices sounded around him. His mind, confused, tried to rationalize what was happening. He'd been deliberately run off the road.

Someone yanked his door open just as he began to fumble in his jacket for his police revolver. Massive hands grabbed his coat front and pulled him from the ruined car and hurled him to the wet pavement. His body was bruised badly; painful spasms radiated from his lower back while his throbbing headache intensified. He shielded his eyes from the rain to look up at his assailant, a brutish giant of a man in a fancy looking gray suit.

Then the fellow reached down and punched Kirkpatrick into welcome oblivion.

It was shortly after ten a.m. when the doorbell of Richard Wentworth's penthouse suite began to chime repeatedly. Jenkyns, the white haired butler, hurried at the best speed his old legs would carry him, all the while retaining a proper dignified grace. Unexpected, anxious visitors were nothing new to the family retainer.

The second he had pulled opened the front door, the beautiful Nita Van Sloan came swooping in like a fiery and vivacious comet out of the heavens. Even though it was evident she was extremely flustered, it did nothing to dampen her elegant charm. Dressed to the nines in the latest dress fashion, a pearl white form hugging affair topped of by a saucy green beret over her auburn hair, the ex-debutante was a living, breathing, gorgeous cyclone in motion.

"Good day, Miss Nita…"

"Where's Dick?" she interrupted, her head turning to and fro.

"Master Richard is in the kitchen having …" She marched off in a flash, her expensive high heels beating a tattoo across the carpeted floor. "… brunch." Jenkyns shook his head wondering at what was becoming of good manners and closed the door.

Millionaire philanthropist Richard Wentworth was enjoying his Eggs Benedict with his personal servant and bodyguard, the massive Indian Sikh Ram Singh, when Nita burst into the spotlessly clean and modern kitchen.

"Nita, darling," Wentworth's face beamed at the sight of his lover. "Ram and I were about to have our second cup of coffee. Would you care to join…"

Nita stopped at the table and grabbed the morning papers she carried tucked under her arm. "Kirkpatrick has been kidnapped!" she announced, handing Wentworth the newspaper. "It's all over the front page."

"What?" He put down his cup and took the paper, hastily unfolding it. The headlines in bold three inch type proclaimed, POLICE COMMISSIONER MISSING! Quickly he began to read the lead feature, which also displayed a grainy black and white photo of Kirkpatrick's car smashed into a city streetlamp where, according to the story, it had been discovered by a beat cop shortly after sunrise.

His mind awhirl with what he had just read, the handsome Wentworth pushed back his chair, tossing his napkin beside his empty plate. "I have to make a quick call. Nita, please, sit down and have some coffee. I'll be right back." With that he disappeared into the den.

Removing her beret and cotton gloves, Nita moved aside as the tall, bearded Sikh jumped up and pulled a chair out for her.

"Would you care for some coffee?"

"Very much, Ram, thank you."

Before the helpful, turban wearing Ram Singh could act, a bemused Jenkyns materialized with a new cup and saucer and placed them before the lovely brunette.

"Allow me, Miss Nita." As he picked up the carafe and began to fill the cup with steaming black java, Ram Singh reached over and grabbed the discarded newspaper, sat and began perusing it for himself.

Like Richard Wentworth, both Nita and Ram Singh considered the pugnacious, tough minded Police Commissioner a friend and ally, and had fought beside him against criminal villainy many times. It was a delicate association, as Kirkpatrick only suspected what these two knew for a fact; that Richard Wentworth was the mysterious crime fighting vigilante known as The *Spider*, Master of Men. The Commissioner was no fool and suspected Wentworth was The *Spider* but had never been able to gather enough solid proof to confirm his suspicions. Thus the two maintained a tenuous unspoken agreement totally dependent on Wentworth's cunning. But should he ever slip and provide the veteran copper with such damning evidence, then Stanley Kirkpatrick would have no choice but to hunt him down like any other lawbreaker and bring him to justice.

Nita stirred a teaspoon of sugar into her coffee and was taking her first sip when Wentworth reappeared from the den.

"I got a hold of Detective Reese," he explained, moving around Nita towards Ram Singh. "Seems fifteen immigrant carpenters were murdered last night at a local union hall. Kirkpatrick was on the scene and supposedly was grabbed on his way home from there. Ram, may I have the paper please."

As the servant complied, he tugged on his brown beard. "Could it be possible the Commissioner was injured in the automobile crash and a passing motorist took him to a hospital for treatment?"

"Reese had the same idea, but calls to all the downtown hospitals came up empty handed."

Now it was Nita's turn. "You think there's some connection between those deaths and his disappearance?"

"I don't know, Nita. They may be two totally unrelated affairs." He was holding up the paper and the fingers of his left hand turned the pages, his eyes scanning each as he did so. "Then again, if there is a connection, we need to explore it.

"Ah, here it is. On page three." He folded the page and read the report of the macabre deaths. "It's as Reese said, they were all poisoned with cyanide."

"Why would anyone wish to murder a group of foreign carpenters?' Singh mused aloud, stating what each of them was thinking.

Wentworth refolded the paper and handed it back to his loyal friend. "I don't know, yet, but that's what you and Nita are going to investigate."

The brunette sat up straight sensing adventure at once. "What do you want us to do, Dick?"

"Visit the city morgue and see if you can learn their identities, then, without arousing undue attention, visit some of their families. See if you can discover what their last construction project was. I want to know everything these men were involved in over the past few weeks. Somewhere in their activities may be a clue as to why they were targeted for death."

"Gotcha," Nita Van Sloan rose to her feet, her cheeks rosy with excitement. She loved nothing better than assisting Richard Wentworth in his crusade against crime. "But what will you be up to?"

Wentworth smiled. "I think its time our old safecracker pal, Blinky McQuade made the rounds of his favorite gin joints to see what's brewing in the underworld."

Commissioner Stanley Kirkpatrick's headache had miraculously dissipated by the time he regained consciousness. For that one small fact, he was extremely grateful even though his current predicament seemed bleak indeed.

His senses were all functioning properly and thus he knew the street attack and his abduction hadn't critically injured him despite the many body aches he was left with. As his eyes opened, he took in his surroundings at the same time feeling the tight ropes that bound him. He was tied to a hard, wooden chair in the middle of what appeared to be an empty studio loft. Overhead, a glass skylight allowed him a glimpse of the gray, cloudy day outside. Still it was enough light to survey his immediate surroundings. The long, rectangular room appeared bare save for his chair. The far corners were hidden in shadows and he couldn't see beyond them.

There was one door located in the wall approximately ten feet to his right. A life long resident of New York City, Kirkpatrick had visited many such lofts in his lifetime. Most were ideal settings for bohemian artists seeking the natural light provided by the glass ceiling portal.

He tried to shift his position only to discover the chair had somehow been bolted to the hard wood floor so that it could not be moved.

"Don't bother," a soft, cultured voice said. "The legs have been nailed to the floor."

Emerging from the corner shadows to Kirkpatrick's front was a dapper looking man with silver hair, neatly cut, wearing a fancy three piece suit and carrying an ornately carved walking stick.

"Then you'll forgive me if I don't stand and shake your hand," Kirkpatrick sneered.

"Ah, most likely you would employ those hands to throttle me were they unbound."

"The thought crossed my mind," the veteran copper admitted. "You got a name, buster?"

"I am Colonel Edwin Regent, formerly of the United States Army."

"Really? Can I ask why you've gone to all this trouble to kidnap me like this?"

"Not at all, Sir," Regent tapped his cane lightly, happy to play the gracious host. "You were taken to act as bait for our true quarry."

"Oh, and just who might that be?"

"Why The *Spider* of course."

"What? The *Spider*! What on earth makes you think you can use me to catch that cape wearing freak?"

"Ah, don't be modest, Commissioner. You see, I was in military intelligence during the Great War. I am a master of strategy and have researched this character in great depth. According to dozens of documented newspaper accounts, The *Spider* actually values your continued well being."

"Huh, that's pure bull-feathers! Besides, what's your stake in this? You planning on starting your own crime syndicate or something?"

"Nothing so pedestrian, I assure you. I am a private contractor and have made my services available to a certain mob figure who will pay me an obscene amount of money to eliminate The *Spider* once and for all."

"And you think you can succeed where everyone else has failed?"

Regent touched his forehead and smiled. "The *Spider* has never dealt with an opponent of my intellect before. I will defeat him by outthinking him."

"I know a lot of dead men who had the same idea, Regent. None of them ever came close."

Regent might have argued the point but at that moment the door opened and in walked the big bruiser in the gray colored suit. Kirkpatrick recognized him immediately.

"I see you're not above using a little muscle as well."

Regent ignored the remark, giving his attention to Porter Lyle. "Is everything in place?"

"Yes, sir. All the charges have been primed and the telegram sent."

"Excellent, then our work here is finished." He turned to the bound Kirkpatrick.   "I'm afraid we must bid you good evening, Commissioner."

"Don't stay on my account."

The two men started for the open doorway when Regent stopped and looked back at their captive. "If you are a praying man, I would suggest you use what time is left to do so. Farewell, Commissioner."

As the door closed behind them, Kirkpatrick tried to free himself from the heavy ropes wrapped around his wrists, arms and legs; all to no avail. He was no Houdini. Regent's last words came back to him ominously and he looked up through the skylight at the thick clouds overhead.

He wondered if God could see through them.

The shady denizens of the city's Lower East Side were all familiar with the small time safe-cracker, Blinky McQuade. Stoop shouldered and needing thick spectacles to see, the half-blind McQuade was considered more a barfly than active criminal these days. The sight of him nursing a drink in some seedy bar had become so routine, most underworld figures considered him a harmless old man. In reality he was a well crafted character disguise created by Richard Wentworth; one of several invented to allow him access to the underworld of the city. As McQuade he could walk amongst the grifters, pick-pockets, and other assorted mobsters as one of their own. Thus he was often able to gather invaluable information as was his goal on this particular day.

As he shambled along the dirty sidewalk in his hunched over gait, McQuade was surprised to witness several police paddy wagons parked along the street in front of several bars and dozens of uniformed officers escorting various men and women out of the drinking spots and up into the big oversized trucks.

"Hey, Blinky," a harsh voice called out from a darkened alley.

The old man turned and tried to peer into the gloom of the narrow space. A tall, ugly figure emerged, cautiously peering down the street and McQuaade recognized Bruno Pertelli, a one time heavyweight boxer and now leg-breaker for Jack Spinolli's crew.

"Don't go down there," the big man cautioned, indicating the scene of activity.

"What the hell's going on?" McQuade asked cocking his head, his eyes barely visible through their think lenses.

"It's a neighborhood roundup," Pertelli explained. "The coppers have been emptying up all the joints from here to Carnarcy all morning."

Hurriedly McQuade moved into the alley's shadow as a black and white patrol car went speeding by. "I don't understand, Bruno. What's got them coppers so riled up?"

"Ain'cha heard? Someone snatched the Police Commissioner."

"Kirkpatrick?"

"Yeah, that's the guy. Flatfoots are really up in arms about it."

"No foolin', you don't say." McQuade tugged at his unshaven chin. "Who would be so stupid as to pull off a stunt like that?"

"Who the hell cares," the ex-boxer growled. "Ain't no skin off my nose what happens to that guy."

"Oh, I'm with you, Bruno. Still, gonna make it tough to get a drink with all this going on, ain't it?"

"I heard tell it's some kind of set up."

"Huh, what is?"

"This grabbing the commish. A few of the boys been saying it's part of something bigger."

"What could be bigger than snatching the Police Commissioner? That don't make no sense."

Pertelli took a step into the light and leaned in close to McQuade, his voice dropping to a lower whisper. "Keep this to yourself, Blinky, but they're saying it's some kind of trap to catch The *Spider*."

It was shortly after sunset when Richard Wentworth returned to his penthouse headquarters. Accompanying him was Ronald Jackson, a ruggedly handsome and resourceful fellow employed as Wentworth's chauffeur. Sergeant Jackson had been Major Wentworth's aid-de-camp during the Great War and eagerly accepted his new position upon their return to civilian life. There was no one better behind the wheel of an automobile than the dark haired Jackson, nor anyone his equal as a weapons expert. He had proven to be a valuable asset to The *Spider's* war against crime.

Both men came out of the hotel's elevator in time to see Nita Van Sloan and Ram Singh about to enter the penthouse. As Wentworth still wore the shabby clothing of his Blinky McQuade disguise, the quartet hastily entered the suite without verbal greetings. Once inside, they made their way to the spacious den where Jenkyns awaited them with coffee and sandwiches, easily presuming his employer's needs.

Normally Wentworth would go to a shabby apartment he rented as Blinky to remove his disguise thus avoiding the threat of someone seeing the snitch enter his home. But on this day time was of the essence and he could not afford to waste a second of it. With Kirkpatrick's life hanging in the balance, he was forced to take such extraordinary risks.

Ever the gentleman, Wentworth deferred to Nita. "What did you learn?"

For her reply, the lovely socialite took a cardboard tube being held by Ram Singh and held it up. "We lucked out, Dick. The wife of the deceased carpenters' foreman, Gorban Jemers, was just leaving the morgue after having identified his remains. Ram and I convinced her we wanted to help find her husband's killer and she was most cooperative."

"Did she know what his last job had been?"

"Yes, a strange renovation of an old four story brownstone in the Bronx. She said he had been uncomfortable about the project, confiding in her that what he and his men were doing seemed eccentric and dangerous."

Wentworth peeled off his ratty jacket and flop hat, handing them to Jenkyns, whose nose wrinkled at the garments alcoholic odor before exiting the room. "Were you able to get the exact address?"

"You bet. Then we raced over to City Hall and the City Engineer's office where I was able to get copies of the building's blueprints," she beamed, handing Wentworth the cardboard tube.

"Nita, you're an angel." He removed the cap end and, tipping the tube, began tugging out the long, rolled up document. Ram Singh and Jackson cleared the polished coffee table of the coffee and sandwich tray so their boss would have room to display the architectural schematics.

"How about you, Dick? Were you able to learn anything new?"

Wentworth, having knelt down by the short table, looked up and nodded. "Yes and if it's true, Kirkpatrick is being used as a pawn."

"To what end, Sahib?" Singh said, setting an empty mug on the far end of the blueprint.

"To trap The *Spider*. It seems a former military tactician hired by mobsters has devised a scheme using the Commissioner as bait and this house may be the setting for that action."

Before any of the others could respond to Wentworth's claim, old Jenkyns came hustling back into the room appearing very agitated.

"Forgive me for interrupting, Sir, but there is something on the radio you must hear immediately!" He moved past the group to the new Philco cabinet model standing to the left of the fireplace and turned on the switch. There was a slight static crackle as he toyed with the tuning knob and then a crisp, clear voice sounded through the speakers.

"Allow me to repeat this message," the announcer declared, "recently delivered to this station. It reads as follows; 'For The *Spider*, we are holding Police Commissioner Kirkpatrick a prisoner in a house located at 128th Lexington Avenue in the Bronx. The house has been rigged with explosives which we will detonate at precisely eight o'clock this evening. We dare you to save him.' This station has notified the authorities and will assist them in any way possible. As we have been reporting throughout the day, there has been a city wide manhunt for the missing…"

"Shut it off," Richard Wentworth ordered and Jenkyns complied immediately.

"Dick," Nita exclaimed, turning her gaze from him to the blueprints. "Those blueprints are of that exact location."

"I know, Nita. Things are starting to make sense now. Whoever is behind this has planned well and if your report from Jemers' widow is accurate, then what we have here is a very well thought out death trap."

Jackson peeled back his coat sleeve to look at his wristwatch. "It's almost seven now, Major. What are you going to do?"

Wentworth ran a hand over his hair, his eyes focusing on the lines and angles drawn on the sheet before him. "Our opponent is a strategist. Meaning he's laid out his scheme like a game of chess, believing he can outmaneuver my response to his challenge."

"What other choice do we have?" Nita asked, biting her lower lip.

"Only one, my dear. We outguess him in return." He pointed to the blueprints. "I need to study these meticulously. Once I've committed them to memory, it will be time for The *Spider* to make his appearance."

The British built Daimler Lanchester touring car sped through the narrow streets, its six headlamps ripping away the darkness before it. Ronald Jackson gripped the wheel of the heavy twelve cylinder vehicle, his eyes glued to the road ahead, as the semi-automatic engine purred. The expensive automobile had been customized with bullet proof one way mirrors and steel armor plating beneath its rich Windovers

Coachwork. Jackson often kidded that she was the first sports model tank on wheels.

"Get ready," Nita Van Sloan advised, seated beside him in the passenger seat. "We're only a block away now after the next corner."

"The police will have the road blocked," a raspy, guttural voice added from the backseat.

"Right, Major." The driver glanced quickly at the rearview mirror and caught a glimpse of the hideous figure now giving orders. Although he had fought alongside the dark avenger many times, the ex-soldier was still unnerved by the hook nose, the lipless gash of a mouth and the protruding fangs all surrounded by a wig of coal black hair over which was a wide-brimmed slouch hat. The face of The *Spider* remained a frightening mask of terror behind the domino mask covering his eyes.

The Daimler took the sharp corner and suddenly they were barreling towards a three ring circus made up of dozens of police cars gathered at both ends of the avenue. There where three huge spotlights set up directly across from the targeted building, bathing it from top to bottom in a harsh white light. A crowd of curious citizens had gathered to either side of both roadblocks which were merely four carpenter's sawhorses set end to end with two heavily armed coppers stationed behind them.

"Hit the horn and move them," The *Spider* commanded. "You both know the plan."

Jackson slammed his hand down on the horn and held it there. The loud hooting noise reached the assembled crowd and upon turning to find its source, they scattered like a herd of stampeding cattle thus clearing the lane. The two officers, each armed with a shotgun, leveled their weapons at the oncoming car, yelling for it to stop, their voices drowned out by the unceasing blast of the horn.

At the last second, Jackson let off the horn to grip the steering wheel and breathed a silent prayer of thanks as both coppers, after firing their weapons, scrambled out of the Daimler's path. As expected, the shotgun pellets had pinged off the car harmlessly and then the front end was smashing the sawhorses to kindling as it plowed on through to the center of the deserted street.

Jackson stomped on the brake pedal, downshifted and caused the car to spin around in a half circle stopping with the back door on the passenger's side facing the cement stoop of the old Brownstone. The back door opened and The *Spider* jumped from it, barely maintaining his balance with three quick steps. In a heartbeat, the Daimler roared away back through the open lane, leaving the crouched cloaked figure standing exposed to the glaring Klieg lights.

"Holy crap," a copper invisible behind the lights cried out, "it's The *Spider*!"

The grotesque looking figure in the opera style cape and slouch hat turned his back on the astonished officers and looked up at the front door to 128. He made a quick motion with his arms and suddenly, as if by magic, two silver plated .45 automatics appeared in his hands. Without waiting, he aimed them for the doorknob and fired off two shots, both hitting the brass ball at the same time.

A powerful explosion vaporized the thick door, sending shards and broken glass flying in every direction. The *Spider* spun about, shielding himself with his cloak woven of special fibers that even a pistol slug could not penetrate. As the rain of shrapnel diminished he started back up the stairs and the gaping, smoking portal before him. Every single officer on the site was too stunned to do anything but watch and then wonder what the hell was in that house. For his part, The *Spider* was grateful to have arrived before they could make an attempt to enter the premises. That certainly would have spelled doom for all involved.

Inside the still smoky vestibule, The *Spider* faced a staircase going to the second floor and a corridor moving further into the house's interior. Although there were no lights on, the powerful glare from the spotlights behind him reached into the building to battle the cloying darkness. To his immediate right, its front destroyed by the booby-trap blast, was an old mahogany grandfather clock. The hands had stopped at 7:40. He had twenty minutes to find Kirkpatrick and get out.

Logic dictated his foe would have put the Commissioner in the furthest spot from the front entrance, forcing The *Spider* to climb through various floors. He ignored the corridor and started to put his foot down on the bottom stair step. Then he stopped. If the stairs themselves were gimmicked, he would have little time to react and need both his gloved hands free. Reluctantly he holstered his guns and began to climb. His long, ghoulish shadow preceded him.

He was lowering his left leg on the eighth step when the entire frame of the stairwell dropped from beneath him in two halves. With almost inhuman speed, The *Spider's* hands grabbed a rung of the stair banister as his body fell. It jerked to a stop, slamming his chest against the railing support. He hung there, slowly catching his breath. A careful glance down revealed the entire cellar floor had been covered with pointed two foot spikes. Had he fallen, he would have been impaled like a prize butterfly.

Hand over hand, The *Spider* pulled himself along the banister until he was able to climb onto the second floor proper. Looking down at the pit one last time, he began to understand the ingenious cruelty of his opponent. He had barely avoided one death trap, he was sure there were still others awaiting him. Fearlessly he moved down the corridor, once more with guns drawn.

He was moving to the next flight of stairs when suddenly the wall to his left louvered back into the ceiling to reveal a Remington 12 gauge shotgun affixed to a four-foot metal stand bolted to the floor, its twin barrels pointing directly at him. As it began to fire, The *Spider* pivoted around and pulled his cloak over his head as dozens of bullets smashed into his back. The painful impact drove him into the wall, where he snarled at the damaging impact which shredded the black cape. Yet not a single pellet penetrated his remarkable mesh weave and when the gunsmoke cleared he was still alive. His body had crumbled in on itself. As he strengthened up, pin pricks of agony lanced across his back where the slugs had hit. They may not have ripped into his body, but their stings were nonetheless savage and a lesser man would have collapsed under the barrage.

More determined than ever, The *Spider* kept moving.

He reached the next set of stairs and once again opted to climb them with his hands empty, this time hugging the railing. He moved cautiously, though doubted his enemy would duplicate himself with the same trap. The stairs were solid and upon reaching the third floor landing he armed himself again and cautiously started down the hallway, his keen senses ever alert to whatever new threat awaited him.

The last thing The *Spider* expected to find was a pungent animal smell. Then there was a tiny clicking noise under his shoe and he knew he had tripped another mechanism. Down from the ceiling behind him, a heavy steel plate descended blocking that end of the corridor. At the same time a door to his front opened and his ears were assaulted by a deafening roar.

A lion! The *Spider* could barely see the massive shape hurling towards him, moving in a graceful charge, powerful clawed pads carrying his doom. He turned to his right, fired two shots shattering the door lock, then using his shoulder, rammed through the ruined portal into an empty room eerily illuminated by the police spotlights outside.

The giant cat hit him from behind and he was thrown to the floor, one of his pistols knocked from his grasp. The lion's claws had ripped through the clothing over his right shoulder, tearing four slashes into his flesh before he was flung away.

He could sense it moving behind him and he kept rolling across the floor, coming to a halt against the wall beneath the windows. He sat up, careful to maintain his hold on the remaining automatic in his right hand. The other had to be on the floor somewhere and was not of immediate concern; the lion was.

It growled and came into view opposite him, its long, tawny shape moving regally as its golden eyes, squinting under the white glare, tried to find him. Known for their nocturnal activities, The *Spider* realized the blinding beams were to his advantage and he pushed himself to his feet, keeping himself in the black zone between the two windows. The lion could hear his movements and he had only seconds before it would leap.

Purposely, The *Spider* moved to stand before one of the windows, his body becoming outlined with a harsh white corona. The powerful beast roared and threw itself at him like a living missile of fangs and

claws. The *Spider* fired three shots into it and dropped to the floor.
Mortally wounded, unable to stop its forward momentum, the mighty
creature crashed through the fragile glass falling to the hard, unyielding
pavement below.

The *Spider* could hear screams from the street as he half moved in
a crouch to where his second pistol had landed. The pain racing through
his right shoulder was excruciating. He reclaimed his gun and bolted
out of the room heading for the third and final stairwell that would bring
him to the top floor.

He had been mentally timing his progress and estimated his twenty
minutes were nearly over. His time to find and extract Kirkpatrick was
dwindling and so he threw caution to the wind and raced up the final
flight of steps. There simply was no turning back now.

"Kirkpatrick!" he called out, reaching the top floor. "Can you hear
me?"

"Here!" came the muffled reply from behind a door at the end of the
short corridor. The *Spider* raced to it and kicked it open, guns ready.
Inside was a long, bare studio with a rising skylight at its center beneath
which was the trussed up Commissioner.

"The *Spider*!" gasped Stanley Kirkpatrick. "What the hell are you
doing here?"

"I was invited," the gruesome midnight avenger answered.

He surveyed the tight horsehair rope wrapped around the top cop,
then looked at the four chair legs, each nailed tightly into the floor.
Minutes were ticking away and he simply didn't have enough of them
remaining.

"Well, don't just stand there," Kirkpatrick barked. "Cut me loose."

The *Spider* shook his head. "Not enough time. Look down."

"What?"

The *Spider* stood next to the tied Commissioner and, pointing his
guns upward, blasted the skylight into millions of pieces. He leaned
over Kirkpatrick, shielding them both with his cloak as the glass rain fell
over them.

Wasting no time, The *Spider* then holstered one gun and from inside his jacket pulled out another pistol, this one stubby with a large barrel. Kirkpatrick, raising his head, recognized it as a flare gun and he watched in puzzlement as The *Spider* held up his right arm and fired it. The magnesium projectile shot through the open skylight into the heavens above and burst into a powerful fireball.

"What the hell are you doing? Just cut me loose."

"Pull your legs together."

"Huh…?"

"NOW!" The *Spider* dropped to one knee and carefully blasted away at each of the chair's four legs, tearing them free from the floor. Slivers of wood dug into the Commissioner's calves and he screamed.

"You bloody idiot!" Kirkpatrick bellowed with pain.

Then he heard a powerful airplane motor approaching from above. He tried to cock his head up as a gust of night air suddenly blew over him. He shook his head from the swirling dust and bits of debris and was shocked to see a rope ladder dropped down through the ruined skylight.

The *Spider* put away his gun and clutched the rope desperately. He put his two legs on the bottom steel rung and slipped his right arm through the closest at chest height. .

An explosion rocked the building.

No more time.

The *Spider* grabbed the back of the chair firmly and felt himself yanked upward. The pain in his right shoulder flared and he gritted his teeth. Kirkpatrick watched the floor vanish beneath him as they rose up through the skylight as the entire Brownstone blew up.

Edwin Regent watched 128 Lexington vanish in an ear walloping boom as the hundreds of pounds of dynamite his men had planted ignited simultaneously. He and his aide, Porter Lyle, witnessed it all from the flat rooftop of a neighboring house. Regent was not the least surprised when a weird looking aircraft materialized from the top of the concussion cloud.

"What the hell is that thing?" Porter Lyle asked.

"It's an autogiro, Mr. Lyle," Regent smugly explained. "A winged aircraft with the rotors of a helicopter thus allowing it to move both vertically and horizontally."

Porter looked at his boss while clutching a Thompson submachine gun in his hands. "You knew he had one of those?"

They could see the small craft moving towards them with its rope ladder trailing beneath it; a cloaked figure hanging from it while at the same time carrying the weight of a man tied to a chair. The pilot wore a white turban, was bearded and had flight goggles on. He was doing his best to maneuver the machine as the explosion's final buffeting pushed at it from below.

"Not really," Regent confessed. "But I correctly assumed The *Spider* would use the skylight to make his egress. It was the only option open to him."

The big man lifted the Tommygun to his shoulders and began to sight along the barrel at the quickly approaching targets. "Gonna be like shooting fish in a barrel," he laughed, ratcheting a round into the firing chamber.

Lyle squeezed the trigger and sent a stream of hot lead towards the dangling figures. The kickback and the swaying motion of the rope ladder caused his salvo to go wide, missing his targets by several yards.

He tightened his hold on the front grip and started to fire a second round. There was a single bang and the back of Porter Lyle's head ruptured like a ripe melon, sending bits of skull, gore and brains splattering over Regent. Startled, he jumped back as his aide toppled over dead.

A block away, Ronald Jackson, dressed in a one piece gray coverall, chambered another round in his sniper's rifle.

"Bullseye!" Nita Van Sloan applauded, putting down the binoculars in her hands. Crouched beside Jackson, she was dressed similarly in a one piece jumpsuit.

"The other one has dropped down," Jackson said, still sighting through his telescopic sight affixed to the top of the slim Army rifle. "I can't get a bead on him."

"Leave him to The *Spider*," Nita said confidently. "Our job here is done."

Together the two moved from the edge of the roof and disappeared down the building's fire escape.

The *Spider* thought his arm was going to be torn from its socket as he fought through the relentless pain to keep his grip on Kirkpatrick's chair. Seeing their attacker fall, he mentally thanked the fates that had brought Ronald Jackson into his service. Once again the loyal marksman had saved him.

They were almost over the roof where their enemies had stationed themselves and he knew Ram Singh would lower them just enough. A gust of wind pulled his hat off as he looked down at the top of Kirkpatrick's head.

"Get ready for a rough landing," he called out.

They passed over the ledge and The *Spider* released his hold on the chair. Relief surged through his cramped muscles as his bound cargo fell approximately four feet onto the roof. Fortunately Kirkpatrick's weight had shifted him and he fell onto his side rather than face first.

Meanwhile Edwin Regent had looked back to see the whirling autogiro and its passengers descend on his position. Seeing Kirkpatrick come crashing down only a few feet from the dead Lyle Porter, an overwhelming fear gripped his heart. Still clinging to the rope ladder was the cloaked demon, its mop of black hair whipped by the wind, its hideous face laughing.

Regent jumped to his feet and ran, his stomach turned to jelly.

Seeing his route, Ram Singh pushed forward on his control stick, sending the autogiro after the fleeing criminal. Below, The *Spider* leaned down, his empty hand reaching out to snare his prey.

Edwin Regent felt his jacket gripped by its collar and suddenly he was airborne. Above him The *Spider* continued his mad laughter. Then they were over alleys and other roofs and the former strategist realized they had come around and were flying back towards the still burning Brownstone, or what was left of it.

"Fifteen souls cry out for you," The *Spider's* cold voice pronounced judgment from above. "Fifteen innocent men demanding justice."

Swiftly they flew toward the conflagration that had once been a home. The house Edwin Regent had cleverly turned into a death trap.

As they moved over it, the heat of the scorching flames reaching up, Regent knew it would become his grave. Then The *Spider* let go.

Prey of the Mask Reaper
A Spider and Black Bat story
By I.A. Watson

The foul Eastern gale washed high waves right over the rotting wharves of the old pier. Heavy rain hosed blood off the dead man who'd been nailed to the door of the Carson Fish Warehouse. The tortured corpse's ragged remains stared sightlessly at the angry tide.

Early morning longshoremen found the murder victim not long after the gulls did. The harbor cops took one look at the grisly remains and called Police Commissioner Kirkpatrick.

There were two reasons to bring New York's senior cop down to the crime scene. The first was the ragged remains of a mask and costume that revealed the crucified victim as the vigilante crimefighter called the Sportsman. The rookie adventurer had just made headlines taking down Major Corcoran's opium ring in Chicago. Now he was gull-meat.

The second reason was that the vicious sea and churning rain hadn't yet washed away the livid red mark on the Sportsman's forehead - the outline of a spider!

The *Spider* dropped his web-line from the roof of the Anderton building and rappelled eighty feet down to the eighth story window. The driving rain made the ledge slick but it only took the dexterous crimefighter a moment to defeat the catch and slip inside apartment 804.

The silent chambers were even darker than the foul New York night, but the *Spider* halted, realizing that he was not alone. He swung round, brining his twin .45s to bear on the unseen intruder.

Another pair of handguns pointed straight back at him.

"Don't move," a half-whispered voice warned him from the shadow behind the Smith & Wessons.

The *Spider's* half-masked face twisted into a savage grin. "I've heard that line before," he chuckled; it wasn't a reassuring noise.

"Not from me, *Spider*." His opponent shifted position. A pale slat of watery light from the rain-slick window picked out a skull-like fright-mask under a deep cowl. Heavy robes rustled. Still concealed behind were bulky shapes that could have been wings.

The *Spider* stood silhouetted by the window, a dark outline with wild ragged hair and a cape that might be tattered or might be cobwebbed. He had not moved, but he already knew who the intruder was and how the apartment had been breached.

"You're a long way from home, Black Bat. If that's who you really are."

"Justice knows no boundaries." The vigilante shifted his head slightly. "You are a known murderer," he warned The *Spider*. "Yet you have often brought the guilty to book. You may serve a higher law." Each sentence was pitched differently, as if the Bat debated with himself.

"You're wanted yourself," The *Spider* pointed out. "Criminals are my prey." He eyed the guns that covered him as closely as his weapons oriented on the Bat. He licked his lips in anticipation.

The Black Bat shifted again and reached a decision. "You're not my target today, *Spider*. Depart, and leave me to my work."

"Murder in this city is my concern. Pack up your cowl and begone while I allow it."

"You know nothing of this case. Do not seek to interfere in the investigations."

The *Spider* glanced around the unlit room. "I know this was the temporary digs of Gary Stockbridge, the pro football star, while he visited New York. And I know he was murdered because of his secret identity as the crimefighter the papers called the Sportsman."

"So he was. I observed him in action recently. He was young but earnest, a talent to be cultivated."

"Breaking the Chicago opium ring was not for the weak. It required experience. I should have guessed he had assistance."

"I met him but briefly and pointed him to the lead he needed. It was long enough for me to discern who he was behind his mask."

The *Spider* knew that the Black Bat was a skilled investigator "What was the clue?"

"He used a custom baseball bat from Lanning & Garvey and he wore designer sports boots from Tyrells of Chicago. A little research easily turned up the one man who'd ordered both such items."

The *Spider* frowned. "If you could work that out then a clever criminal might."

"A very clever criminal has," agreed the Bat. "Stockbridge's family went missing three weeks ago. He vanished two days later. His parents tortured bodies were found in a Fulton River landfill last Friday. His seventeen-year-old sister remains unaccounted for."

"Somebody cracked the Sportsmen's identity and used his family to lure him into a trap. He was captured and tortured to death."

"And probably made to watch his loved ones die too," growled the Black Bat. His deepest voice was like Death himself.

The *Spider's* own tones became cold and measured. "Stockbridge was dumped at the very warehouse where the Chicago connection sent their drugs into this city before you and he broke the gang. He was branded with my mark."

"Yes. Whoever killed the Sportsman wants you to know that he's coming after you next."

"Obvious.

The Black Bat gestured with one revolver to the table in the centre of the room. A stiletto knife was stabbed through the top. "When the police searched this place earlier that was not present."

The *Spider* ignored the guns on him and inspected the dagger. It transfixed a greenbottle blue tarantula. Under the dead arachnid was an ichor-stained numbered ticket, similar to those given out in any waiting room. It read: "13".

The Master of Men did not comment on the find. He knew that when he turned around the Bat would have vanished. It was what the *Spider* would do.

Behind him, the Black Bat was no longer there.

The man with the white cane and dark glasses arrived at Richard Wentworth's fifth avenue penthouse exactly on time. The sightless visitor was guided by his well-tailored mid-twenties blonde secretary and accompanied by a small shifty-eyed man dressed as a butler.

Wentworth's own man, the impeccable Jenkyns, received the visitors at the elevator and led them to his master's chambers. "Mister Quinn and Miss Baldwin," he announced as he let them into the library. He didn't bother to identify 'Silk' Kirby, but he kept an eye on the little man. Jenkyns had already spotted a rogue.

Wentworth rose from the table where he'd been poring over documents with a chestnut-haired lady. "This is Miss Van Sloan," he introduced the society beauty. "She helps me keep my files in order sometimes."

"I try to keep him in order," Nita Van Sloan corrected him. She moved from the desk, shimmering in Paris silk, and held out her hand to greet Carol Baldwin. "They need keeping in order now and then, don't they?" She hoped the visitors wouldn't construe that as a remark about Tony Quinn's blindness.

"I like to think they'd be lost without us," Carol smiled back. They looked quite different, these two young women, the one Grace Kelly slim and brunette with striking violet eyes, the other Lana Turner blonde with a Mansfield hourglass figure. The women sensed in each other kindred spirits, both independent and adventurous, yet both tied by their hearts to impossible men.

"Thanks for agreeing to see me," Quinn told Wentworth as Kirby guided him to a wing-backed chair. "I'm pleased to meet the author of those monographs in *The Criminologist's Review* at last. The one on linguistic choices in witness statements was particularly fine."

"And I'm glad of a chance to talk to the man who wrote 'Legal Precedents for Spontaneous Confessions Obtained After Near-Death Trauma' for the *Law Review*. Fine piece of work. Of course, my door would be open to you anyhow with a recommendation from my old buddy Commissioner Kirkpatrick."

"The Commissioner was very helpful," Quinn admitted. "He said he'd send over some files I asked for to your address."

Wentworth nodded. "You're here on behalf of your own Commissioner Warner, I understand?"

"Yes." Quinn touched the scars under his dark glasses. "Before my... injury I was a D.A. Now I help out a little on a consultancy basis when there's something out of the ordinary that a blind man can handle."

Richard Wentworth already knew that Quinn had lost his sight to acid thrown in his face by a man he'd helped convict – the same man who'd murdered Carol Baldwin's father.

"You're investigating the Sportsman murder."

"Well, more exactly, I'm looking into any connection that might help the police locate young Lizzie Stockbridge. Given what happened to her brother and parents, her fate cannot be a pleasant one."

"And Kirkpatrick suggested I could help?"

"He said I should ask you about that vigilante criminal-killer called the *Spider*. The Commissioner said that you know all about him."

Kirk suspects that I am the Spider, Wentworth thought to himself.

"I've got some files on him," he told Quinn. "Nita can give copies to Miss Baldwin if you like. But the cops have got files of their own."

"That's what they're sending over to us," Carol informed Wentworth. "Commissioner Kirkpatrick said you'd find them of real interest."

"I bet he did," sighed Nita.

"On the subject of mystery men," Wentworth pressed on, "what can you tell me about one that you've apparently encountered a couple of times, Quinn? A strange monster called the Black Bat?"

"Is he tangled up in this? Then my advice is stay away from him. He's decided that he's called to deliver justice where conventional law fails. Prosecutor, defense, judge, jury and executioner all wrapped up in one lethal angel-winged bundle."

"There's a lot of nut-jobs in the world, isn't there?"

The telephone tinkled. Jenkyns glided over and answered it. "It is the Police Department, sir, with an apology for Mr. Quinn. It seems as though the file on this *Spider* person that was requested has gone missing from its locked cabinet. Their conclusion is that it has somehow been stolen, a very professional job."

"By somebody who wants to try and crack The *Spider's* real identity," suggested Quinn with a frown.

"That would be very dangerous," noted Richard Wentworth. He didn't say for whom.

Beneath Wentworth's fifth avenue building was the *Spider's* lair. "We need to work this fast," he told Nita and Ram Singh. The big East Indian had already been told about the Sportsman's slow and cruel death and the murdered vigilante's missing sister. "From what the Black Bat said this rookie Stockbridge could have been smarter hiding his secret ID, but somebody was clever enough to crack who he was and everyone he loved suffered for it."

Nita shuddered. "You're much smarter than him, Richard, and much more careful. And when you put on that mask and fright wig and those awful fangs you... well, it's as if you're not you anymore. You're... something else. Something terrible."

And you're starting to like it. Whenever you let yourself go to that place, some small part of you doesn't come back, she worried.

"There's a couple of lines of enquiry I want to try," Wentworth said.

"First off, Ram, I need you to head to Chicago. The Black Bat was able to track down Stockbridge by his bat and boots. Check that trail for yourself. Find out who was asking about them. I don't suppose the Bat will have been careless enough to leave tracks back to himself, but you might just find out if some other person's been coming round with the same questions – and that would be the killer."

"I shall go," agreed Ram Singh.

"I could go too," Nita offered.

"You stay here," Wentworth ordered. "And you keep Apollo close." He gestured to the big dog sitting at the girl's side. The protective Great Dane looked up as he heard his name.

"I'm not hiding out!" Nita objected.

"But think how much you object to doing the hostage thing," the criminologist countered with a smirk. His smile faded. "And think what's probably become of that little Stockbridge girl."

Ram Singh broke the sober mood. "You said two lines of enquiry, Sahib?"

"Yes. We know that the Sportsman made a big splash when he took down Major Corcoran's Opium Ring. That was a pretty big operation, with some pretty high-up customers. It branched out into blackmail and white slaving and all kinds of nastiness. So maybe Stockbridge's death was in revenge for taking Corcoran down." Wentworth reached for The *Spider's* straggly wig. "The Major's defense argued he couldn't get a fair trial in Chicago. He's incarcerated in New York right now, waiting to face a grand jury."

The wig went on, and the mask, and the vampire fangs. Civilized, urbane, compassionate Richard Wentworth sank beneath the countenance of the inhuman vigilante. "I believe that I shall invite Corcoran to discuss the Sportsman with… the *Spider*!" he cackled.

The laugh that strangled from his throat after was like nothing that should come from a human.

'Silk' Kirby slipped back into Quinn's hotel room and dropped a folded bundle of lockpicks on a side-table. "I went to Police headquarters," the ex-second-storyman reported. "Got inside despite their improved security. It was tough, but not too tough for someone in my class. Made it to the file room, took a look at the lock on the cabinet where the *Spider* folders had been."

"And?" Quinn prompted. Away from the public he was able to move freely. The pretense of still being blinded by an enemy's vengeance was just another burden in the ex-D.A.'s war against crime. The secret retinal transplants from Carol's dead father worked perfectly, though now he saw with a murdered man's eyes.

"The thief probably slipped in disguised. And left no marks. Either the guy who cracked it was as good as I am, or he'd bribed someone for a key."

"Either is possible," Quinn mused.

Carol Baldwin shifted from the desk where she'd been collating papers and brought them over to the not-blind ex-D.A. "Here's the whole file," she announced.

"File?" Silk asked. His boss and Carol had clearly been working while he'd been crawling around police HQ void spaces.

Quinn spread the papers out to examine them. "We've been going back over some old reports," he explained to Kirby. "At the Sportsman's lodgings where the dead spider was skewered there was also a waiting-room ticket. That's not the only time such a thing's been found associated with a disappearance or murder case."

Carol swept her blonde curls away from her face and pointed a perfectly-manicured finger at a succession of papers. "Nearly two years ago, the burned remains of mysterious detective Dr Eureka were found outside the Washington police headquarters with such a docket pinned to his chest. That was ticket number one. Eighteen months ago, ex-Navy diver Bill Harrow vanished off a boat near Bermuda. A number three ticket was pinned to the ship's wheel – and nobody saw the hero called Piratebuster again. Number 5 turned up in the same railway locker as some random body parts that were never identified. Number 6 was stapled to the forehead of jet-setter Susan DeBrough when her corpse was rescued out of the lion pit at the San Francisco zoo. Tony thinks she must have been Lady Hood, that mystery woman who broke open the California vice ring. Number 9 was found on the door of the Conway house in New Orleans, where the whole family just upped and vanished about the time the vigilante Brother Zambo was last known to patrol there. And 11 was almost ignored by the investigators examining that terrible Philadelphia orphanage massacre where they found the shattered remains of the masked crimefighter the papers called White Lamp."

"We should have put this together long before now," Quinn snarled. "There's a mask-killer out there. Someone who's methodically targeting mystery men and women and destroying them in the vilest ways possible – them and their loved ones!"

Silk whistled softly. "So this goon's killed twelve heroes so far, and now he's gunning for the *Spider*?"

"So it seems. He is hunting The *Spider*, which means he will seek to unmask him. Only one course remains to us. We must discover The *Spider* first!"

He reached for the case that contained his Black Bat paraphernalia.

Carol watched him change, biting her lip, but remained silent.

He is not putting on a mask, she recognized. *He is taking one off. Whatever that acid exposed, whatever he saw while he was blind, that is what he is now.*

The Black Bat folded shadow round him like a lover and vanished into the night.

The Mask Reaper sat alone in his echoing brick basement. The bulbs above him cast uneasy shadows over the cluttered desks that ringed his high-back swiveled chair. The naked lights failed to reach to the cages against the walls or the trapped areas further up the tunnel, but were sufficient to illuminate the stacks of spiked papers filed on the tables.

"By now The *Spider* will have taken up the hunt," the Reaper noted. His voice was cultured, scholarly; in other circumstances he would have been taken for a quiet academic. "He will begin by chasing up Major Corcoran in his cell. It helps that I was able to convince the defense to petition for the trial to be moved to New York. An interview with Corcoran should be sufficient to set the so-called Master of Men upon my trail."

The Reaper paused to nibble a strip of meat from the dish next to him before continuing. "My profile of The *Spider* suggests he makes use of lieutenants. I expect he will deploy some minion to follow up the Chicago connection. Make arrangements to inconvenience the fellow. A little blood may provoke the savage side of The *Spider's* nature and make him careless."

He shifted to the next desk. "The Black Bat? Another fractured psyche, I fear. His mind runs along different courses to the *Spider*. The Master of Men prefers to draw his clues from interview, to deduce from the weaknesses of the lesser intellects he encounters. The Bat oft-times pursues material evidence, relying on his analytical observations to follow intellectual bread-crumbs. I expect he will obsess over the ticket and arachnid I left as a trail of bread-crumbs for him."

The Reaper had another thought and scribbled it down in tight neat script for later action. "The Bat is not yet aware that The *Spider* is bait for him. Why add one masked mystery to my collection when I can have two? And such specimens! There will be nothing to match them. I must be particularly diligent in ensuring they have slow, awful deaths. Mere torture is not enough. I must crush every spark of hope, convince them that justice is a cruel illusion, show them the uttermost depths of degradation and despair before they perish. A challenge, my friends. A real challenge, such as I have not had since the destruction of Dr Eureka."

He swiveled round and pointed. "*You* will see to things at the spider dealer's. And *you* will acquire the bait for our own *Spider* trap."

He glared at his reflections in the mirrors that surrounded the desks until he was sure they understood and would obey. Then he went back to nibbling at the last portions of Lizzie Stockbridge.

The grey penitentiary walls were darkened and slick with rain. They were no barrier to The *Spider's* web and grapple.

Major Corcoran couldn't sleep. He sat in his cell, reading by the dim light of the flickering bulb. He looked out-of-place in prison grays rather than his usual immaculate suits, stripped of his gold watch and diamond cufflinks. He did not relish his coming trial; the evidence that damned Sportsman had passed to the police was overwhelming.

A tiny smirk flickered across the drug-lord's face regardless. At least he had got his revenge. The Mask Reaper was expensive, but the accounts of the destruction of the Sportsman and his family had been graphic and gratifying. Corcoran treasured them.

It should have been impossible to enter the room without being heard. The cell door usually creaked. The bolts always clanged. The lock clacked when it turned.

And yet - the weird insane chuckle came right in Corcoran's ear.

The felon twisted round. He lost his balance and toppled from his chair. A fright-faced monster leaned over him, fanged and wild-eyed under a gruesome mask. Somehow Corcoran felt thankful for the mask; he feared that worse was concealed beneath it.

"Major Corcoran…" It knew his name! It *owned* him!

An identification clawed its way to Corcoran's throat. He'd faced a mystery man before, had actually fought with the Sportsman before that baseball bat had caught him in the gut. This was different – the Sportsman had been human!

"Tell me about Stockbridge," The *Spider* hissed. "Tell me before the pain starts."

"You can't do this to me here. There are guards. I'll call out…"

That echoing laugh again. A jab to the throat. A noiseless shriek. A devil's grin.

Pain.

Lennie 'the Zoo' Cassidy occupied a special niche at the fringes of the New York underworld. He never committed crimes, except perhaps in relation to border regulations regarding the transportation of exotic and dangerous species. If he procured rare animals for rich clients who had uses for shark tanks or scorpion pits, it was not his responsibility to ask the purpose of such installations. 'Zoo' simply provided the required fauna and asked no questions.

If someone shady wanted a specimen of *Chromatopelma cyaneopubescens* to transfix with a stiletto as a challenge to a crimefighter, Lennie Cassidy was the go-to guy. If someone wanted to trace such a purchaser, Lennie Cassidy was the man who might get an unpleasant midnight visit.

The Black Bat disarmed the crude alarms on Lennie's shop with the contempt that they deserved. He moved silently and swiftly for an intruder garbed in dark robes and angel wings. Had anyone but the caged animals seen him pass they might have thought him the wrath of God incarnate, or perhaps Death come to pass judgment on the world.

The Zoo had one last defense. His favorite personal pets were a pair of Indonesian reticulated pythons that he had raised from hatching and shared his bedroom with him. These fierce killers ensured that the purveyor of lethal animals had an uninterrupted sleep.

Until now. Lennie awoke as a cold sharp nail pricked at his throat.

"Leonard Antony Cassidy, also known as The Zoo, awaken and face your judgment."

The man jerked to consciousness, suddenly aware of a looming black figure crouching above him.

"Wha…? Icha! Lita!"

The Black Bat gestured to the serpentine heads pinned to the bed-end.

"My… my snakes!"

"You have supplied animals knowing they would be used for murder," the Bat accused him. Rough hands slammed Cassidy down hard and pinned him as ruthlessly as a serpent squeezed his prey. "That makes you an accessory to first-degree homicide."

"No! No, I just… oh C_____!"

The Bat's tones changed, became a little more conciliatory. "There might be a chance for plea bargaining if you confess. Tell the police everything you know. Everything. And tell us now who purchased a Greenbottle Blue Tarantula from you recently. It's your only chance."

The Zoo tore his gaze away from his skewered pets to meet the skull-glare of the horror who held him down.

A different tone again: "Last chance, Cassidy."

The Zoo believed it. He stuttered out a name, a delivery address. He described a thin academic who knew all about him, who paid in cash. "That's all! Please, you have to believe me! That's all…!"

"Silence," growled the Black Bat. "The jury is reaching its verdict."

Commissioner Kirkpatrick was still at police headquarters. He'd pretty much worked out how the files had been extracted – nobody could identify the well-spoken plain-clothes detective who'd signed in to examine an entirely different fraud case and had wandered away into the records section – but New York's senior policeman didn't like people breaking into his files. Especially not *those* files.

"This has to be linked to the Stockbridge murder," he muttered to himself. "The spider-mark on the forehead usually means the victim was a criminal. Either the Sportsman was double-dealing, only pretending to be on the side of the angels, or else the thing's a set-up aimed at The *Spider*. But The *Spider* doesn't torture men to death like that – not unless he's gone completely off the edge now."

He reviewed what he'd written in those documents that had been taken. There had been accounts of all The *Spider's* public appearances; of the times the Commissioner had actually encountered the fright-faced vigilante; and statements from those lucky criminals who had survived their meetings with the Master of Men long enough to confess their misdeeds.

"Someone wants to know The *Spider* inside-out," Kirkpatrick concluded. "Maybe someone who wants to do to him what he did to Stockbridge."

The idea of The *Spider* being slowly carved up, screaming and bleeding, did not please the Commissioner as much as he might have expected. The *Spider* was as much a criminal as the men he hunted, and a bigger murderer than most of them, but he was… more than that. Arresting The *Spider* to face his crimes was one thing. Allowing him to be slaughtered in the meanest, cruelest of ways was something else entirely.

"Not on my watch," decided Kirkpatrick.

This was a case he'd have to take a special interest in.

Nita Van Sloan checked the peep-hole carefully before admitting Carol Baldwin into her boyfriend's fifth avenue penthouse. It was quite late into the evening and she'd been warned to stay on her guard. When the caller was made welcome, the massive Great Dane Apollo greeted the visitor with a friendly tail-wag.

"Pardon me for bothering you at this late hour, Miss Van Sloan," Carol apologized. She peeled off a rain-soaked coat and shook out her sleek fair locks. "Mr. Quinn asked me to make some additional enquiries of Mr. Wentworth, if it's not too much trouble."

"I'm sure Richard will be glad to help when he returns. He's at some tedious charity fundraiser, and I expect he'll be out half the night jawing with boring old men in dinner jackets. Will you come in and have a brandy? Maybe I can help."

"You didn't go with Mr. Wentworth?" Nita Van Sloan had a reputation as a socialite.

"Some of the more conservative and religious-minded of the charity trustees take a dim view of my relationship with Richard. They view it as… irregular. We didn't see any reason to provoke an upset at some gala that's not about us."

Carol wondered why the attractive young woman wasn't lawfully wedded to her lover. Perhaps one of them had some dark and scandalous secret in their past? Well, it was none of her business. Carol Baldwin could hardly point fingers at others when she ran around with both Tony

Quinn and the Black Bat!

Nita led Carol to Wentworth's drawing room. In the lamp-lit evening the women felt more informal with each other. The socialite had exchanged her fashionable gown for as comfortable check shirt and slacks; it made her seem less like a goddess and more like a girl awaiting adventure. The court reporter had swapped her severe business suit for a dark green casual dress; it turned the bombshell into a fellow conspirator.

Carol accepted the brandy glass, surrendered her coat to Jenkyns, and explained the purpose of her visit. "Tony's got an idea that the Sportsman murder might be linked to quite a few other deaths of folks who might be described as… mystery men. Some of these killings have been notable for the presence of a small ticket, like that given for a cloakroom or raffle, at the scene of the crime."

Nita masked her reaction. Carol must not learn that The *Spider* had found just such an item at Stockbridge's rooms or she would realize the link between the Master of Men and Richard Wentworth.

"The first such ticket, numbered 1, was discovered on the body of a Washington-based vigilante detective who used the soubriquet Dr Eureka. He was subsequently found to be a Justice Department special investigator named William Liddell. In his Eureka guise he had acted to undertake such investigations as the rules of his department prevented him from tackling."

"That's the sort of thing that could happen, I suppose," Nita admitted. "I imagine all these strange shadowy crimefighters one hears about have such a rationale."

"I suppose so. Anyway, Dr Eureka had a number of successful cases before his burned and mangled body turned up, dumped outside police headquarters. Tony was hoping Commissioner Kirkpatrick, with his interest in colorful crimefighters and their bizarre cases, might have some files about what Eureka had been working on just prior to his demise. The Police Commissioner remembered that your Mr. Wentworth has worked with the Justice Department and keeps detailed files. Maybe he even corresponded with Liddell?"

"Richard would have recognized the name if he had. But he does hoard away little news snippets for use in future publications. I can check the index."

Carol pushed back a bob of platinum hair from her left eye. "Anything that gives some insight into Eureka or his passing," she pleaded.

"Something that might trigger off the first of these mask-killings," Nita summarized. "Yes, that makes sense. We'd better go to Richard's study and check his records. Although I warn you he just keeps notes on whatever events catch his interest at the time, anything that might make a good paper later. And he's got the most appalling scrawly handwriting, like a... schoolboy."

Wentworth's dossiers were in good order. There was a file of newspaper clippings from the relevant period, detailing the discovery of the charred corpse and the subsequent investigation that revealed Liddell's secret life.

"These masked men don't last long, do they?" said Carol, almost in a whisper.

"No," answered Nita tightly. "One wonders... what about the people who care for them? What becomes of them when...?"

"Liddell had a wife," Carol noted. "She vanished without trace the day after the funeral."

"Just like Lizzie Stockbridge." Nita flicked over more pages and found a yellow legal pad where Wentworth had scribbled some tentative conclusions. "It looks like Dr Eureka had just exposed a blackmail scandal run by a rogue calling himself the Truth Reaper. This villain was some kind of genius at ferreting out secrets and using them against people. A games player, and as nasty as they came. Look at some of the disgusting things he made his victims do once he had evidence against them."

Carol looked down the sheet and shuddered. "That kind of mind... it's the best argument for vigilante mystery men there can be!"

Nita began to get excited. "But look! Don't you see? This Truth Reaper has exactly the sort of skills that whoever is behind Eureka's downfall might possess! Or the Sportsman's exposure and destruction!"

"I agree. But see this report. Eureka's own testimony to the chief of police that the Truth Reaper died resisting capture. Fell into a printing press – or was tossed there by Dr Eureka? Either way, it's clear that this Truth Reaper perished."

Carol frowned. "Tony's prosecuted quite a few cases against men who were thought already dead," she noted. "I think it would be a good idea to…"

The conference was interrupted when Jenkyns reappeared. "My apologies for the intrusion, madams, but there is an urgent trunk call from Chicago. It appears there has been an explosion…"

When the Black Bat first flew into the nightmares of the underworld it had been common for him to rely upon the additional brawn of the good-hearted pugilist Butch O'Leary. As Tony Quinn's crusade had taken him on darker and darker paths, O'Leary had become a more infrequent companion. But when the Bat needed to be in New York and required questions asked in the Windy City, O'Leary was more than happy to hammer on a few doors.

"Who else asked about these here boots?" the huge fighter demanded, looming over the counter of Tyrell's shop. The exclusive store offered a fine selection of hand-made sporting footwear, all stitched and cobbled by the very proprietor who now cowered behind his cash-desk.

It was a question that Vincent Tyrell was becoming familiar with. "F-first a thin-faced man in his late thirties, with a cultured voice and well-made Italian shoes. Then three weeks later a young lady with silver Chanel slingbacks."

The girl had been Carol Baldwin, on behalf of Quinn, chasing up Stockbridge's murder. The original enquirer was presumably the man who'd captured the Sportsman and tortured him to death after making him watch the destruction of his loved ones.

"Anyone else? Anyone since?"

O'Leary managed to menace even without meaning to. Tyrell's pale face nodded frantically. "One more," he agreed.

This would be The *Spider's* agent then, one tiny possible lead that might help the Black Bat to trace the Master of Men before the mask-killer hunted him down. "Who? Describe him."

The bootmaker pointed a trembling finger. "H-him!"

O'Leary turned in time to see Ram Singh lunging for him. The Indian was fast and skilled at combat. His first stomach-blow hammered the wind from the big fighter. A palm slap snapped O'Leary's head back and set him up for a knockout.

Except that O'Leary was tougher than that. He caught Ram's haymaker in a crushing grip and returned a killer left hook. The Indian dodged so it only caught him a glancing box on the ear, then hooked out a leg to sweep O'Leary's feet from the ground.

"Speak!" Ram Singh demanded. "Who is your master? Why did he send you here?"

O'Leary growled and tossed his attacker away from him. "You're going down, buster!" he snarled, gaining his feet and thundering forward.

Ram caught the charge, tripped the giant, and tumbled him into a wall. The shelving splintered, cascading the combatants with expensive footwear.

The terrified shop-keeper fumbled for his telephone. "Hello? Hello? Connect me with the police! Quickly!"

That was enough for the gunsels watching the shop and tapping the wire. Four men with machine-guns emerged from a black sedan and took station outside the plate-glass window.

O'Leary managed to land a solid punch on Ram Singh at last. The Indian took the blow with a grunt and jabbed his fingers at the fighter's shoulder; O'Leary's left arm became heavy and unresponsive. The big man grappled Ram and pulled him to the floor.

The window shattered as bullets sprayed across the shop. Tyrell shuddered as he was riddled. He was dead before he hit the floor. O'Leary and Ram Singh, already on the ground and partially shielded by the counter, avoided the first lethal rounds.

The two men rolled apart and crawled for better cover.

"Four of them," Ram Singh judged, peering out into the darkened street where the gunmen stood.

"Local goons-fer-hire," O'Leary recognized.

"They'll have to stop to reload," Ram noted.

"You take the two guys on the left."

The East Indian's scimitar left his sash with a silk and steel whisper. Ram Singh almost smiled. "Agreed," he told the huge Irishman. "My blade thirsts."

"Yeah. An' my fists… wanna hit something. So…"

The gunfire ceased. Ram and O'Leary made ready to spring.

The grenades came through the shattered window.

"They survived," the Mask Reaper summarized. "There was a hatch down to a cellar workshop. The two men managed to scramble in before the fuses burned out. They were buried when the shop floor gave way on them, but I have no doubt that they dug their way out despite their injuries." He shrugged. "No matter. The object was to prick their masters by harming them. By now The *Spider* and the Bat will be aware of the ambush. Each will be seeking me out to deliver his unique brands of justice."

The cellar was better lit now, with two arc-light lamps shining into the further parts of the underground space. The area was revealed as an unfinished subway tunnel. Beyond the ring of desks and mirrors that served as the Mask Reaper's New York base, the arched passage was filled with scaffolding, a maze of bars and wires extending all the way to the distant entrance.

"The *Spider* will have learned from Major Corcoran the name of the man he employed to destroy the Sportsman. The Black Bat will have forced similar information from Zoo Cassidy. Both will be combing the city's underworld seeking traces of my location."

The Mask Reaper turned to the captives he'd hung in chains at the inner end of his iron maze. "They'll find me, of course. The *Spider* because I have you, the Black Bat because I have the *Spider*. Two commissions in one. The Mask Reaper has quite a reputation now for bringing rich felons' mystery-man adversaries to unpleasant and humiliating deaths. It is a fortunate man who can combine his natural inclinations and hobbies with his work."

The prisoners were hooded blind and gagged so they couldn't speak. It didn't stop the killer from supplying both sides of the dialogue. "What then? Well, if I haven't been able to discern the actual identities of my subjects – The *Spider* and the Black Bat are both very good at concealing their secrets – then I'll learn whom they are when I capture and unmask them. Then I make sure they cannot escape – cutting the main tendons in their limbs tends to do it – and leave them in fear while I go collect their loved ones. There is always someone. A wife or sweetheart, parents, siblings, children sometimes. Children are especially good. And these shadowy vigilantes almost always have fanatical followers. All must be collected so that they can die in front of the hero's eyes."

The prisoners tugged at the chains. The iron links were too strong.

"Then comes the interesting part, stripping the subject of all their illusions of justice and right, showing them that the world is cruel and meaningless. Do you know how long it took me to break the Sportsman enough that he would eat his sister's flesh? Of course, by the end he would do anything at all – and he did!"

The Mask Reaper checked the dials on his control panel. The steel floor segments could in turn electrify various bars in the scaffolding maze. The pacification gas cylinders were full and ready for the endgame.

"Of course, the imminent arrival of the heroes in no way excuses you from revealing what you know or suspect of them. We can occupy the time it takes for those beacons of righteousness to beat this location out of the scum of New York by torturing the pair of you for what you know. Who would like to go first?"

The Mask Reaper pulled the hood and gag from Police

Commissioner Kirkpatrick. "You're a madman," the prisoner spat. "And you'll get nothing from me!"

"And I think so highly of you, 'Kirk'. May I call you 'Kirk'? Your notes on The *Spider* that I extracted from police headquarters were tremendously useful in understanding that particular quarry. So detailed and meticulous. I can see why you've risen to your present rank."

"The *Spider's* police business. When you're in jail awaiting the Chair, I'll be going after him."

The Mask Reaper chuckled. "The so-called Master of Men has done a good job concealing himself and his operatives, but he could hardly obscure the name of the policeman with whom he had most often associated."

"I haven't worked with him by choice."

"But you have spent a lot of time trying to determine who he is. Your notes were clear on that. And yet I couldn't help feel that you'd failed to commit to paper your innermost thoughts. I suspect you have a secret inkling about the true identity of The *Spider*. You might not have proof that would stand in court, but *I* am perfectly happy to test your theory through practical experiment."

"Go to hell."

"Oh, I believe I already am, Commissioner. I was shown, once, that hell is right here with us. Since then I have simply made sure that I am the devil rather than the damned. Hence my pastime." He reached for a pair of electrodes and twisted a dial half-way to its limit. "Would you prefer I used these on you or your fellow captive?"

"On me, damn it," hissed Kirkpatrick. "I'll tell you this much – you'd better pray I get loose to arrest you before The *Spider* gets to you! I'll – aaagh!"

The Commissioner spasmed in his chains and slumped. The Mask Reaper gave a dissatisfied sigh. "No, this won't do at all." He sneered at the unconscious police officer who hung limply in his fetters. "My judgment, 'Kirk', is that another's screams will motivate you more than your own pain. I shall revive you and begin again – on your young friend. If either of you feels you want to tell me something about The

Spider then, by all means, shriek it out."

The Mask Reaper reached for a hose to douse Kirkpatrick back to wakefulness, so the captive could watch Wentworth endure the electrodes; but then a warning buzzer and flashing console light diverted his attention.

He checked the outputs on his panel. "Ah, it seems as though we have a visitor. A cautious one, clever enough to find and disable my monitors as he comes. He's entering via the drainage tunnels and using a lateral approach pattern. That makes him more likely to be the Black Bat. He should be encountering my hired thugs about now. He'll be with us in less than ten minutes."

The Mask Reaper hurried to find his own cowl and faceplate. He wanted this one to be perfect.

The Black Bat dropped the last of the mercenaries into the sewer. The man floated there, face down, and gradually drifted off towards the outlet grate. The Bat ignored the obvious ledge with its inlaid traps and made his way forward using grapples and wires of his own.

It was clear that his enemy had left a trail into a trap. Since the Mask Reaper had also kidnapped hostages the Bat had no choice but to walk into it.

But the Black Bat set traps of his own!

He unhooked the last of the tunnels' concealed electrical sensor gadgets. Ahead were big flood doors to a sealed section of the abandoned underground railway. The absence of all records for this construction betrayed its re-use for something nefarious. The doors were unlocked. One creaked open at his touch.

The Black Bat could see again because of the donated eyes of Carol's murdered father, but a side-effect of his original injury and the procedure that had restored his vision had left his other senses heightened. As he stepped into the vast darkness of the tunnel section those other senses flared up, recording the height, construction and layout of the space he entered. The vastness crackled with electricity and smelled of old blood.

"Black Bat. Welcome!"

The Mask Reaper's mocking greeting was the last thing the intruder heard. Furious white noise crackled from gramophone speakers around the chamber. Scent bombs exploded, filling the space with pungent odors that rendered his nose useless. Radiators began to pump out sweltering heat. In a mere instant, the Bat was left truly blind in his enemy's labyrinth.

The metal shutter behind him slammed down. There was no retreat.

The Black Bat groped forward. His hand brushed one of the metal poles that criss-crossed the tunnel. An electrical flash lit the darkness as the live metal discharged into the studs on his glove. His costume's interior insulation protected him from harm; only leather charred. This time.

He moved forward cautiously, but not slowly enough to avoid the next moving pole, which slashed down with razor edges to slice through his outfit's arm. This time the shock charge did penetrate, staggering him to his knees.

"Did you think I would not have studied you?" the Mask Reaper challenged. "I know all your strengths – and weaknesses. I have designed my trap especially with you in mind."

"Then you've not done your homework properly," the Bat called back.

"Really? Are you not now cornered, caught in a live-metal labyrinth that I control? Are you not now but one more subject for… the Mask Reaper?"

Quinn gasped as other electrified threads dropped on him from above at his enemy's command.

"Mask Reaper? Is that what you're calling yourself these days? Catchy." The Bat's voice changed pitch. "It will look well upon your tombstone."

"What else should I call myself, subject thirteen? Or do you believe you know me better?"

"The Truth Reaper? Dr Eureka's old enemy that got tossed into a press? Is that who I'm supposed to think you are?" The Bat laughed hollowly. "Justice is not so easily blinded."

The Mask Reaper jabbed another control savagely. The Black Bat was forced to climb onto the electrified metal rails to avoid the heated floor-panels. "What do you mean?" the villain demanded of his prey.

"Dr Eureka's body was charred beyond recognition. I don't know what 'truth' that Truth Reaper showed to Bill Liddell that caused a hero like Dr Eureka to snap, to torture his own family to death and become the Mask Reaper, but it must have been something pretty nasty to shatter your sanity like that."

Even through the speakers' blare the Bat could hear the Mask Reaper's intake of breath. "*Very* clever. Quite the detective. Full marks, Black Bat. What a shame you are utterly trapped with no escape and no rescue."

The Black Bat's deep voice came back like a death sentence. "What a shame you turned the lights out so you couldn't see what was happening behind you."

The Mask Reaper swung round. He lifted a hand torch to his prisoners. Kirkpatrick still hung insensible in his chains. The second set of shackles was open and empty.

The Mask Reaper had taken the Commissioner because of his expert knowledge of The *Spider* – the Commissioner and the man he most often discussed The *Spider* with: Richard Wentworth.

An unearthly hollow laugh echoed round the abandoned tunnel.

Something slippery and rubbery slid under William Liddell's feet. It was a flimsy facemask with the contours of Wentworth's features.

"One last mask for your collection," hissed The *Spider*, right in the villain's ear.

The Mask Reaper brought up his off-hand, clutching a knife. The slash tore through the *Spider's* cloak but the Reaper's hand snagged in the shifting fabric. He had to abandon the blade as The *Spider* pummeled into him with rock-hard fists. Captured Wentworth had been frisked for weapons, of course, but The *Spider* was deadly with nothing but his knuckles.

"You forget, *Spider*. I'm a fighting hero too!" mocked the Mask Reaper, hammering back at his foe.

A shattering uppercut cracked the Reaper's rib. "You are scum, murderer," declared The *Spider*. He kicked Liddell back into his control console, collapsing the desk. The white noise fuzzed out. Electrical sparks painted the room as a flickering blue hell.

The Mask Reaper seized up the electrodes he'd used before. This time the dial was twisted to maximum – to lethal. He held the naked ends of the wire close to Commissioner Kirkpatrick.

The *Spider* froze.

"There's no justice," spat the Mask Reaper. "I was shown that. The Truth Reaper worked out who I was. He showed me what my wife really was too, and all those around me. I killed him for it – and then my work began!"

Kirkpatrick stirred back to wakefulness as he realized he was a hostage. "*Spider*!" he called out. "Never mind me. Get him!"

"Oh, he won't," the Mask Reaper mocked. "The great hero will sacrifice himself rather than let an innocent come to harm. He'll let me take him and bind him for torment and destruction rather than allow you, his hunter who despises him, to come to any harm. Isn't that right, 'Master of Men'?"

The *Spider* stepped away from the Mask Reaper.

Liddell laughed.

The *Spider* stepped away from the Mask Reaper so that the Black Bat could get a clear shot.

"William Liddell, I find you guilty," thundered the Black Bat. "The sentence is execution." His '45s thundered in the darkness.

The Mask Reaper was blown back through his shattered mirrors. Whatever bleak last words he might have uttered went unsaid.

The Black Bat picked his way over the now-inert maze of scaffolding. "Well done," he said to The *Spider*. "You anticipated the Wentworth kidnap and took his place?"

"Yes. I expected you would recognize my plan and supply the distraction. Well played."

"Justice must be seen to be done."

"Your Chicago man is going to be all right?"

"Just some burns and bruises. Yours?"

"He'll be fine." The *Spider* shook the Bat's hand. "Now get out of my city."

The Black Bat swept his wings around him and faded into the darkness.

The *Spider* dropped the commissioner from his chains. "You get the clean-up, Kirkpatrick. Farewell."

"You're under arrest," the policeman replied; but he was speaking to an empty room. He pulled the shackles from his wrists, sighed, and went over to inspect the Mask Reaper's corpse. There was going to be paperwork.

Nita and Carol hugged as they said good-bye to each other. "Have a great journey. Sorry your trip was wasted." said Nita.

"I wouldn't call it wasted. Sure, Tony's investigation for the D.A.'s office became pointless once the Mask Reaper came across a pair of vigilantes he couldn't torture to death, but ridding the world of a mad killer's a good thing. And it was nice to meet you."

"We should keep in touch," Nita offered. "Us girls who have to put with obsessed brooding men that have impossible social consciences need to stick together."

"We sure do," agreed Carol.

The two women paused for a moment as they each considered, then dismissed, a wild improbable theory.

Then they went their separate ways.

Terror of the Rangoon Raiders
by Don Roff

T he young Marine lay dead. Once a guard at the gate of the
Brooklyn Navy Shipyard, now a corpse sprawled face down in
a pool of blood. The *Spider* turned the body over. The guard's
throat was slit from ear to ear. The wound looked like a macabre scarlet
mouth smiling at him.

Ambushed from behind, The *Spider* thought. *Kid didn't know what
hit 'em.*

He left the Marine's corpse and slipped inside the now unattended
gate. His cloak blended with the cold December shadows. The *Spider*
possessed information that a saboteur would plant a bomb tonight. A
bomb to blow up the USS Saratoga.

The Master of Men would not allow that to happen.

He stalked along the dock that collared the shipyard, avoiding the
pools of white electric light from arc lamps. The frigid wind whipping
off the water bit at his masked face. He saw the 880-foot Navy aircraft
carrier in port. The lights from the deck illuminated the dark waters of
the harbor.

Something moved.

The *Spider* halted and watched. A shadowy figure climbed out of the
water away from the USS Sarasota and onto the dock. He slunk across

the wooden boards, water seeping from his skintight black body suit. Most likely the murderer of the Marine. And a high probability of having just planted a bomb.

He wouldn't get far.

The *Spider* reached for his twin .45 caliber pistols. He would fill that fleeing saboteur with so much lead, his corpse would be too heavy to float.

Then he felt something sharp in his ribs, a swift roundhouse kick.

With lightning reflexes, he rolled into the blow, tumbled, and grabbed his pistols, ready to come up firing at the unseen aggressor.

Another blow struck him in the back of the head.

Black.

The shock of cold water awakened The *Spider* from unconsciousness.

The chill of the East River paralyzed all the muscles of his body and his lungs screamed for oxygen. The *Spider* fought his way to the surface of the frigid, murky water.

He broke through, struggling to maintain his head above the icy water.

The stringy, dark wig that The *Spider* wore under his soggy fedora hung limp on his head like the tendrils of a dead octopus against his domino mask. The chill of the water struck like arctic lightning through his dark tweed suit, into his goose-pimpled skin, and down into his aching bones.

The bomb.

The *Spider* ignored the freezing water and swam for the aircraft carrier. After five minutes of feeling around, he found the time bomb attached to the side of the ship, just below the water line. A clock piece with 10 bound sticks of dynamite, all neatly water-proofed.

With a precise yank of the proper wires, he deactivated the bomb.

This was evidence he would show Police Commissioner Stanley Kirkpatrick, "Kirk," back at police headquarters. Of course, as the dapper-dressed playboy Wentworth, and not as The *Spider*. Kirk already suspected that Wentworth and The *Spider* were one in the same. Often it was a dangerous game that he played with Kirk, despite the fact that they were good friends. But justice needed to be served; there were cretins who needed to pay in full—the would-be saboteurs who attempted to blow up the USS Saratoga. Before their next sabotage attempt, he vowed to himself that the one responsible would wear the vermillion insignia of The *Spider* on the skull of his corpse. He would see to that.

The *Spider* swam back to the dock. He placed the disarmed bomb onto the wooden dock. He then grabbed the edge of the splintery wood and hoisted himself up, straining the waterlogged muscles of his back and arms.

He flopped onto the deck like a heap of netted fish, feeling colder in the wintry air than he did in the water, and the frosty wind whispered through his soaked clothing. He could still feel the roundhouse kick that had exploded across his ribs; he hoped that none were broken. The back of his neck still ached where it felt like something hard and heavy— like iron—had landed there with a dull thud. That was the last thing he remembered until he was 10 feet under the greasy East River water. His beloved dual chrome .45s that usually rested in their holsters under his cloak were both gone, probably beginning to rust at the bottom of the dark river.

Yes, those bastard saboteurs will pay.

After a few frigid moments, the soggy *Spider* scooped up the bomb and that's when more trouble began.

"Put your hands in the air," a voice commanded.

The *Spider* turned. Two Marines, two more guards at the Naval yard, aimed their M-1 rifles at him. One of the stern-looking soldiers asked: "What's that in your hands?"

The *Spider* knew not to make any sudden moves with the bomb or he'd be breathing through the extra ventilation in his chest provided by the trigger-itchy Marines.

Damn, The *Spider* thought. *Hard to believe that 24 hours ago, things were better…*

"What are you thinking about?" was the question that had attempted to shake Wentworth from his daze as he stared across the room at his smiling friend Fred Rasool, the host of the party. Wentworth didn't answer. The question had originated from Nina Van Sloan, Wentworth's fiancée, who slow danced with him to Cole Porter's "Begin the Beguine," provided by the 10-piece band on the stage. "So who am I dancing with," the blue-eyed woman in the swayed-back sequin dress asked. "Is it my beloved or is it The *Spider*?"

On that last word, she seized his complete attention. "We're one in the same. Synonymous, my dear." He smiled. The couple moved in time to the punchy tune amid a sea of other huddled dancers. But in her sequins and his tailed tuxedo, not to mention their Hollywood matinee idol looks, they outshined the other festive partygoers.

"You seem more interested in our host than in me," Nita said. "Maybe I'll ask him to dance instead." She nudged her head toward the short, wiry man adorned in a white tuxedo, Fred Rasool, who smiled and chatted with his party guests. The black moustache on his face seemed to dance and curl on its own as he broke into a grin. "What's the story with Mr. Rasool anyway?" she asked. "He mentioned that you were old friends when we were introduced, but I've never heard you talk about him before."

"We were in the war together," Wentworth said. "He was a corporal in the company I commanded. He followed his father into airplane production afterward. He's now built an empire that rivals my own in terms of net worth."

"Hmm," Nina said with a joking tone. "You're probably lucky that you're a shade more handsome, or I might have to let you go and discover the mystery behind the mysterious Fred N. Rasool."

"There's nothing mysterious about him," Wentworth said. "And if you want mystery, I'm all yours in spades." The song ended and the band announced that they were going to take a 20-minute break.

"There's a couple of martinis with our names on them, darling," Nina said, swishing her way across the dance floor in her glittery sequins. She took two V-shaped glasses filled with gin and a green olive from one of the waiters hefting a silver platter.

"Ah, Richie Rich," Fred said as Wentworth and Nina joined their host with their icy cocktails. Fred had always called him Richie Rich. Something Wentworth would *never* let anyone else get away with. But Fred wasn't like other people; there was something that immediately made you like him, either from his always smiling face or his incredibly warm generosity. Fred, more than once, had attempted to supply Wentworth with a free plane. But Wentworth didn't accept the generous offer. He'd just smile and say, "Another time, Freddy, another time." Fred was known for these lavish parties at his Park Avenue house, not far away from Wentworth's 5th Avenue, fifteen-room penthouse. "You two are the loveliest couple on the dance floor. Your fiancée, Richie Rich, is a ravishing beauty."

"She came with me and she goes with me," Wentworth said. "So don't get any ideas." Fred laughed with his trademark laugh that sounded like a chortling summer breeze across red velvet. "My own fiancée, who is at a spa in Paris, would be quite jealous," Fred said. Fred gestured to Nina. "Do you mind if I take aside your handsome date to speak in private? We won't be but a moment."

"Go ahead," Nina said. "But you owe me a dance Mr. Fasool when you return."

"You drive a hard bargain, Miss," Fred said, chortling again. "But I will take you up on it."

After the two men excused themselves and headed down the hall, Fred's gregarious tone immediately changed to grave. "I think there are some foreigners who are attempting to sabotage my plane factory."

I knew it, Wentworth thought. *Between all the smiles and laughs, I could see something was troubling him.* That's why he had been staring at him from across the dance floor. Wentworth sometimes wished he wasn't so keen when it came to understanding the unspoken subtext of people. It could be distracting. "Why do you think so?"

"One of my supervisors saw three men who looked Asian, definitely not employees on the payroll, enter my plant and survey it. When a guard asked them what they were doing they incapacitated him—and nearly killed him. Except when they left, there was a scrap of paper. I had to have the writing translated—it was written in Burmese. My plant was on the list, along with a ship in the Naval shipyard. And one item on the list was crossed off, that munitions factory in Westchester County that went up last week."

"That was judged an accident," Wentworth said.

"I don't believe it was," Fred said.

"Have you gone to the authorities yet?" Wentworth asked. "This is serious."

"I wanted to tell you first, Richie. I know that you and the Police Commissioner are friends. I want this thing handled quietly. No press. These guys have to be caught under the radar, if you know what I mean. People would go into a stark-ravin' panic if they knew there were some fifth column saboteurs running around American shores."

"I'll get into it," Wentworth said. "Can you give me that list?"

Back on the dock, The *Spider* clutched the diffused time bomb in his gloved hands.

"He looks like that *Spider* guy the cops are after," one of the armed Marines, who couldn't have been older than 19, said. "Bet he's the son of a bitch that killed Tomlinson."

"Well he ain't going to be bombing ships *or* killing anymore," the other Marine holding an M-1 said. "Move forward real slow and easy, weirdy. And keep that bomb out in front of you. Any deviation, and I'll put you down."

It will go down my *way,* The *Spider* thought.

Then he smiled, revealing his faux fanged teeth that made both of the young Marines' eyes widen with quiet terror. With that, the masked figure arched backward off the dock and back into the frigid water that hit him like a snowdrift.

He could hear the dull crack of rifles and the *vip-vip-vip* of bullets as the Marines fired. Their bullets cut past him in the oily water. He held his breath as long as his aching lungs could and swam, still clutching the explosive parcel. Then he surfaced 25 yards away under another dock. He watched the two Marines. One had a flashlight, combing the black rippling water like a searchlight while the other followed the beam with the M-1, hoping to spot the "weirdy" surface.

Moving like a tarantula, albeit a near frozen one, The *Spider* crawled through the water with silent grace until the Marines were out of sight.

A short time later, he was lounging in the back of the Lancia limousine. His chauffeur, Ronald Jackson, drove. Pulling the curtain closed across the limousine windows, Wentworth slipped out of the sopping wet dark tweed suit of The *Spider* and into the dry clothing of Richard Wentworth. No more action for The *Spider* tonight until he could refit back at the penthouse.

"I was worried for you, Major, when you didn't show up at the designated time," Jackson said from the tube, a handheld microphone.

"Thanks for waiting, Jackson," Wentworth replied via the tube. "Let's go home."

Wentworth, of course, didn't have to thank Ronald Jackson for waiting. His chauffeur, who served with him during World War I, would have waited until hell froze over if need be.

A shot of brandy warmed his insides like a liquid fire, the warmth seeping through his icy body and out his extremities. He looked at the dripping bomb that sat at his feet. The night wasn't a total loss.

Wentworth had met with Kirk earlier that day to show him the note. Kirk said he would have trouble supplying the police work force that it would take to cover the city for any potential saboteurs, and suggested that Wentworth get assistance from the military. That proved to be a dead end, too. Other than adding some extra guards at the aircraft plant and Naval shipyard, there was little those agencies could do—the military was already spread thin in an effort to avert other rumored sabotage attempts. That's when it was time for The *Spider* to swing into action. There is no red-tape bureaucracy when it comes to brandishing swift justice with two blazing, chrome-plated .45s.

Still, it seemed strange to The *Spider* that saboteurs, as careful as they were to enter Fred Rasool's aircraft factory, left a note behind upon being discovered. Did they *want* to be discovered? Was it some kind of smoke screen for other heinous activity?

No, something was not adding up, something fishy was going on. And it was not the stench of his river-soaked clothing discarded on the limo floor.

"Seems that The *Spider* is behind the attempted sabotage," Police Commissioner Stanley Kirkpatrick said the next day. "That's an act of treason that could get him executed when he's caught." Kirk eyed Wentworth with a suspicious gaze as he inspected the damp, dismantled time bomb.

"When we find the men who made that bomb and attempted to use it, they will no doubt be executed," Wentworth said.

"Curious that you brought the bomb here. It was last seen in the hands of that… criminal."

"And it made its way to me," Wentworth said. "The *Spider* couldn't very well waltz into the precinct and lay this down. He's not stupid. He'd be arrested in a New York minute."

"Yes, we do work fast here," Kirk said, smirking under his pencil-thin black moustache.

"Not fast enough—those dangerous men are still out there," Wentworth said.

"The responsible party will be brought to justice," Kirk said, looking into Wentworth's gray eyes. "Have no doubts about that."

"No doubts," Wentworth said with an almost inaudible tone. He gazed at the upright calendar on Kirk's desk. FRIDAY, DECEMBER 5, 1941.

"Something you want to say, Wentworth?" Kirk said, now turning the small bomb over in his hands.

"Bagging these bastards will make for an early Christmas present is what I was thinking, that's all," Wentworth lied.

As Wentworth departed the police station and headed toward his Hispano Suiza roadster, he almost lost his life. If it were not for the screech of tires right before the *ratatata* report of the Thompson submachine gun, he would have been a dead man. As the hunter green '39 Packard turned the corner onto the midtown avenue, dark figures moved inside.

From a glance, Wentworth guessed there were three in the cab. He saw the unmistakable muzzle of the Thompson jabbing out the back window of the car and then everything moved in slow motion. He saw a fiery flash burst from the muzzle and he dove to the sidewalk, grabbing a 12 year-old newspaper boy who was hocking the daily news on the corner.

The kid would have been walking Swiss cheese without Wentworth's quick action as the .45 caliber bullets walked up the side of his roadster with a pronounced clinking of metal on metal. The bullets then bit into the brick wall and shattered the plate glass window of Saul's Bagel Shop behind him. Fortunately, nobody was dining near the window when the assault took place or there would have been innocent victims sprawling over their fresh-baked bagels, smearing them with blood instead of lox.

Wentworth didn't wait for the speeding Packard to pass; he had already jumped up and was sprinting toward the retreating green car like a well-dressed cheetah. He saw the barrel of the smoking Thompson being pulled into the Packard, no doubt either being reloaded or being concealed in case any police were around.

He hoofed it toward the car, running in the middle of the busy avenue, his expensive wingtips slapping the concrete with a rapid, leather rhythm. Machine gun or not, he was taking these murderous creeps down right now—Merry Christmas to the New York Police Department all wrapped up with a bow, compliments of Richard Wentworth.

He was just about to jump on the rear bumper of the Packard when—*wham!*—a nun on a bicycle plowed into him, knocking him to the street. He was entwined in a black habit and bike frame. The nun groaned on the pavement, obviously the worse of the two in the collision. By the time Wentworth rose to his feet, the assaulting Packard had merged in busy Manhattan traffic and was gone. Wentworth helped the nun to her feet.

"You all right, Sister?" he said.

"Yes," she said, dusting off her black and white habit, then picking up her red bicycle. "The Lord watches out for us all."

"I certainly hope that's not the case for everyone," Wentworth said, leaving the puzzled nun, headed back to his bullet-riddled roadster. *Because those bastards' days are really numbered now,* he thought. How did those guys know who he was and where he would be? Something was definitely fishy. Then the name Fred N. Rasool popped into his mind, like the bright marquee on the Bijou movie theater. Yes, it had to be. He *must* be in on it. But why would he alert Wentworth if he were conspiring with these sabotaging sons-of-bitches? It was time to gain some answers...

And it was time to find out those answers as The *Spider*.

Jackson drove Wentworth toward Fred N. Rasool's aircraft plant down on the waterfront.

Wentworth fingered a button under the left side of the limo's rear seat. The entire section—cushioned back, seat and all—rotated forward. The back revolved and a rack of clothes hung waiting, illuminated by a small light.

With swift and ceremonious skill, he removed the clothes that made him Wentworth and quickly donned the dark tweed suit, stringy wig, false fangs, silk mask, and black fedora that made up the *Spider*. He then strapped on his two chrome-plated .45s nestled in shoulder holsters. He also strapped on beneath his arm a compact kit of chrome steel tools. Wentworth fingered the button again and the seat swung back into place.

The Master of Men was now ready for action.

Ten minutes later, the *Spider* ducked past the roast beef-faced guard and was inside the aircraft plant. It was a long, corrugated tin building surrounded by a chain link fence topped with razor wire. The night crew worked on the assembly line, riveting sheets of thin steel to the skeletal frame of an aircraft. He could see the lighted, windowed office above that overlooked the production. He saw Fred peering out the window, looking down on his graveyard shift workers. Fred looked worried.

With almost superhuman stealth, the *Spider* managed to slink past the industrious workers and drifted up the stairs to the office with undetected ease. Fred sat at his desk. The office was dark except for a single green banker's lamp on his expansive desk. Though it was cold outside and the temperature in the office was moderate, Fred seemed to be sweating. Wentworth could see droplets along the man's crinkled brow.

"Terrified?" The *Spider* said.

Fred looked up, shocked to see the unsettling image of The *Spider* looming above him, the fedora brim shading the cool gray eyes behind the mask.

"What are you doing here?" Fred said, reaching out to touch a button just under the lip of his desk, obviously a silent alarm. "This place is restricted."

"Don't touch that button," the *Spider* said. With a flick of his arms, The *Spider* moved back his cloak and pulled out his two pistols. "You will answer some questions."

"I don't have to answer anything," Rasool said. "You don't belong here. I have... powerful friends."

The *Spider* dropped the piece of paper Rasool had dropped into Richard Wentworth's hand 48 hours ago. "What's this about? Lie and you'll be sucking wind through an extra hole in your fat head."

Fred grew more nervous and sweated like an overheated pig. "These men... they left it... I told—"

"What you told was a lie," The *Spider* said, his voice almost a hiss. "Trying to make Wentworth take the fall."

"That's not true at all," Fred said. "Wentworth is a friend of mine. We served in the Great War together. We're simpatico." Then the expression of Fred's face changed to that of glee. Like he had remembered the punch line to some private joke. "Enter," he said with a stern tone of command in his voice.

The door in the back of the office slid open and three men dressed in black marched into the room in an almost uniformed order. The men all stood at the same height of five-foot-eight with black, slicked back hair. They were Asian in appearance.

"I'd like you to meet some clients of mine," Rasool said with his trademark smile and summer breeze on red velvet laugh. "Meet Veni, Vidi, and Vici," Fred said, guiding his hand to the stoic, silent men dressed in black.

Veni, Vidi, Vici—Latin for "I Came, I Saw, I Conquered," The *Spider* thought. *Clever.* "Which is which?" he asked.

"These Rangoon boys don't use their real names when they work," Fred said.

Rangoon, The *Spider* thought. *So they* are *Burmese. What the hell are they doing here?*

"America's about to enter a war with Japan," Fred said. "I can't tell you how I know—but it's happening, sooner than you may realize. They'll need more planes. *Both* sides will." Fred smiled.

It all started to make sense to The *Spider.* Rasool was a war profiteer and a traitor, hedging his bets against the US. No doubt blowing up his own aircraft plant would garner some incredible insurance money so he could rebuild a bigger and better one to supply the armed forces, ironically to fight planes that he manufactured for the enemy. Yes, it made sense, sure, for a madman. "Think the *Spider's* gonna let that happen? Think again."

"Already did," Fred said. "You're wanted by the police for countless murders. So what're a few more charges of sabotage and treason added to the count?"

The *Spider* said: "Expect me to watch you blast your own plant— and other military targets—and not do something about it?"

"My Burmese friends are more convincing than me," Fred said.

And with that, Veni, Vidi, and Vici—the Rangoon Raiders—leapt into action. One executed a flying sidekick, launching himself up and over Rasool's desk, and pointed a spiked boot tainted with a fast-acting poison toward The *Spider's* heart.

Unfortunately for Vici, he counted on a common opponent standing in the line of his kick. The well-attuned *Spider* moved with incredible speed, darting his body to the right. Vici only succeeded in kicking air.

As the Burmese terrorist landed on his feet, he caught a bone-shattering back kick delivered by The *Spider* to the rib cage that sent him reeling to the bookshelf along the office wall. The assassin hit it. Volumes of notebooks and ledgers tumbled down on him in an avalanche of paper and bindings. Two .45 shots into the man's skull from the *Spider's* pistols insured the assassin stayed down... permanently.

Then the *Spider* blasted Rasool.

"The bomb goes off in sixty seconds," Fred said, clutching his chest where The *Spider's* bullet penetrated. A flower of blood blossomed on his white suit near his heart. "Tell Wentworth, if you live... people change." He staggered out the door the Rangoon invaders had entered—obviously a back entrance, or in Rasool's case, a rear escape.

The *Spider* was too busy with the lethal Veni and Vidi to pay much heed to his former friend's escape. In the back of his mind, the bomb was counting down. Ten seconds had already elapsed. He needed to alert the workers down below, vacate himself, and turn these remaining two into crab Rangoon rolls before the inevitable explosion.

Veni pulled out a katana sword—and like a cyclone of whirling death—spun toward the *Spider*. The blade caught the *Spider's* cloak, neatly slicing off an end. The *Spider* had one advantage that he didn't last night—he wasn't taken by surprise. The sword blade narrowly missed The *Spider's* face. He leveled his pistols again—

Crack! Crack! Crack! Veni's head burst apart like an overdone chicken. Blood and brains coated the window of the office.

The remaining Rangoon Raider, Vidi hesitated for a moment—a

moment that proved fatal.

The *Spider* filled the man's body with round after round of .45 caliber lead. "That's for the roadster." As the last terrorist fell in his tracks, The *Spider* hit the silent alarm under Rasool's desk.

The *Spider* then hurled toward the door. He glanced out the blood-caked window and the workers down below were running out of the building, alerted by the alarm. The *Spider* dashed down the back stairs and out into the street just as Rasool's aircraft plant erupted into a ball of fire that rose like a fiery flower into the December night.

The blast knocked him back to the snowy ground.

He saw Rasool's corpse. His eyes wide and staring into the sky, his hand feebly over the fatal bullet wound in his heart.

The *Spider* burned his telltale vermillion *Spider* insignia into Fred's skull with his lighter. "Yeah, people change, Rasool," he said. "And not always for the better."

"What brings you here in the dead of night, Wentworth?" Kirk said, waiting by the fire truck as firefighters battled the flames of the corrugated tin structure that now looked like an exploded aluminum soda can belching fire.

"Fred is a friend of mine," Wentworth said, climbing out of his patched-up Hispano Suiza roadster. "Came to see if I could help."

"Your friend is dead," Kirk said. "Killed by The *Spider*. He most likely did this, too."

"Don't be so sure," Wentworth said.

Nestor Reynolds, the NYFD Fire Chief strolled up to the men. "Looks like this was sabotage. Found some bomb fragments next to a gasoline drum. And we found three bodies up in the office. Pretty burned up but they're Asian guys. No ID. They're packing an arsenal of weapons, too."

The Fire Chief handed over a folded piece of paper. "Luckily this wasn't a victim of the fire." Kirk took it and unfolded it. It was a map of the munitions factory layout in Westchester County written in Burmese.

The name Fred N. Rasool, Wentworth thought, shaking his head in disbelief. *If you rearrange the letters around, it spells 'fool's errand.'* He chuckled.

"What's funny?" Kirk asked.

"Looks like The *Spider* bagged these bastards for an early Christmas present to the New York City Police Department," Wentworth said.

Kirk eyed his friend with suspicion. "And what do *you* know about it?"

Wentworth offered only a grim smile.

Just Wonderful
by C.J. Henderson

"Intreat me not to leave thee, or to return from following after thee: for whither thou goest, I will go; and where thou lodgest, I will lodge: thy people shall be my people, and thy God my God."

Bible, Ruth

"You're wonderful. You're absolutely wonderful." Apollo could remember the first time his mistress had said the words. As he lounged, his large head heavy in her lap, everything in his world was as right as it could be, the memory of the treasured phrases flooded back to him. Not in the way a person would remember — of course — but in the way a dog remembers.

"Just absolutely wonderful."

He had been a puppy. A thing — still useless — lumpy, all legs and tongue. Frisky and wriggling, barely a few weeks old. Just aged enough to be able to leave his mother. To meet the new pack with which he would run. Those with whom he would spend the rest of his life.

"Just wonderful."

He had heard other speech during his brief life up to that point — other words, other voices. But it was that one word, spoken by his mistress, which finally captured his attention. Which made him care about anything beyond his own needs. He had known in a moment that, gently nestled within the arms of his Nita Van Sloan for the first time, that he was home. That he was in the one place where he would always be safe. Where he would always be loved.

His Nita's hand moved across the great hound's ears, gently scratching, the thing the massive Dane loved more than anything else. Sometimes in lazy circles, wide and slow — sometimes in rapid back-and-forths — from their base to their tips. Both were pleasing. Both let Apollo know he had done well. That he could still win approval.

That he was worthy.

Apollo strove to be worthy — to be a good dog. Yes, he had been trained by his Nita, and her companion, the Richard, to be everything a hound should be within human company — loyal, obedient, fierce. But for the massive white Dane, such was more than mere duty. Apollo loved his mistress. Beyond self. Beyond understanding. She was the center of his universe, his reason to arise in the morning. She meant everything to him. And she always would.

As the massive hound rested within his Nita's arms, panting heavily, his mind drifted over his years with her. He remembered his first steps, overly large paws attempting to balance his gangly body. She had been there, cheering him, applauding — her eyes filled with respect for his mighty accomplishment. Her heart filled with love.

It was not the first time.

He remembered their walks, long walks, thousands of hours of marches through city streets, along boulevards, through parks. There were others, like the Richard, with whom he walked from time to time. But it was those with his Nita he remembered. Her hair, always nestled under a hat, until they reached their destination. A bench, a clearing, some place where they could stop and rest. His Nita would remove her hat, shake her hair in the open air, and Apollo would know it was his cue to come to her. To wait for her extended hand. Palm up, she would hold it out and say;

"Slip me some skin."

When so commanded, he would lift his paw and slid it across her open hand. It was not a trick to be performed. It was not done for the amusement of others. She had never even asked him to do so when the Richard was around. It was a private thing. It was theirs alone. And, when he did so, the action would always delight his Nita, no matter how many times the routine was performed. And, once it had been accomplished, he knew he could then do his favorite thing.

He could kiss his Nita.

Always carefully, balancing his formidable one hundred and fifty pounds on one paw, he would reach forward and lick her face. Her lips, her eyes, her cheeks, her nose, all of them tasted, all of them moistened. It was another private thing, a special ritual between the two, never witnessed by others. It was the moment, when shared between them, that assured the great hound that he was loved.

Not that it was all that passed between them. Not in the least. There was so much more, so many things which allowed Apollo to know he was the luckiest dog in the world. Like bath time.

Unlike many dogs, Apollo loved his baths. He thought of them as he lie there in his Nita's arms, wondering if he would be getting one soon. His mistress took such great care when she washed him. The water always the right temperature, the shampoo always one which left him clean and ready — outside smells which might reveal his presence to others washed away. She would work on his ears and scrape the burrs and crust that gathered in his hair. She would rub him all over, and when she pronounced him "clean at last," he would shake, spraying her with water. And she would laugh.

Every time.

And then there was dinner. Wondrous, wondrous dinner. His Nita could not always be there to feed him. Some times such had to be handled by others. His food was always fine, tasty — well proportioned. But, when his Nita brought him dinner, it was always something special. The hound did not have any concept of what might have been different between a meal brought to him by the Richard, or the Singh, from those placed before him by his beloved mistress, but they were. The chunks of meat were not necessarily tastier or more plentiful. The gravies were no richer. They did not have to be. All that mattered to Apollo, all the great hound needed for his happiness to be complete ... was her. His Nita — his mistress. The woman he loved.

For so many reasons.

As he luxuriated under her gentle scratching, his weary head resting against her chest, his mind floated over the years. He remembered chasing after balls and sticks, retrieving them from fields and forests, lakes and oceans. He remembered waiting by her side for her to bring down game, birds, rabbits — whatever — then racing forward on command to retrieve whatever she had slain. Tasting the blood so as to share in her kill.

He remembered great swims, and romps down the sides of mountains. He remembered snow, covering his paws, as high as his chest, breaking his way through it, dancing across it, snapping at tossed spheres of it. And he remembered rain. Long walks in the rain. His Nita smelling of rubber shoes and coat, hair hidden beneath its hat, him at her side, the two of them, walking in drizzle or downpour.

His Nita loved the rain. Loved to sit and watch it out the window. Loved to walk in it. And since he loved her, he sat next to her when she stared at the rain, and he strode by her side when she chose to walk through it. She was his and he was hers. Where she went he did. No matter where. No matter what. Even into blood and chaos.

Especially into blood and chaos.

Sometimes, they did not even have to go searching for it. Like that night. That night when he had heard the sounds coming from outside. There in her apartment. Yes, there were always sounds in the hallway. Others lived in the same building. But these had been different. These had not been the noises of the neighbors whose sounds it was his business to learn. These were sounds which made the fur on his back stand up. That would make him growl low and hard if he were a stupid dog.

Stupid dogs, he knew, barked and threatened. Smart dogs were silent. Smart dogs waited. Smart dogs hid themselves in the shadows.

If there had been time, he would have raced to his Nita, warned her.

But it had been an accident he had even been in the front of their apartment to hear the wrongness of those in the hall, to smell it. Apollo knew the sound of keys in locks, and he knew the sounds of forced entry. Someone who was not supposed to enter was about to do so.

It was all he needed to know.

"All right," came a whisper as the door opened, words propelled by breath heavy with garlic and whiskey, "move. Let's get the bitch."

Four of them. Not for a moment did the great hound worry about the odds. He did not count them to calculate whether or not he would attack, but only to decide how best to do so. Then he saw that they had guns, and all thought left his mind.

"Jesus Christ!"

The scream had erupted from the first man to enter, words of confusion jabbered after the first of his companions had already fallen, his neck ripped open. Blood pumping madly from his first victim, Apollo pushed against the dying man with all his weight so he might turn in mid-air and attack anew. Before the invaders even quite realized what was happening to them, the Dane had fallen upon the last to enter. Knocking him to the ground with his weight alone, Apollo had then ripped into the man's groin, shredding his trousers and all that rested beneath.

As the second man screamed, his life gushing out between his legs, the great hound stood, scrambling around to handle the rest of the invaders, but he was too slow. Throwing himself at a third, his body caught part of the blast leveled at him from his intended victim's sawed-off shotgun. Stunned, a yelp of surprise escaping his maw, the Dane fell in an awkward heap, slamming against the floor with brutal force. But far more painful to him than his wound, was what he witnessed next.

As his Nita entered the room, gun drawn, the first thing to catch her eye was the sight of her beloved Apollo on the floor, writhing in agony. It was but a momentary distraction — a thing of less than a second — but it was enough. Rough hands grabbed the woman, pulling her off balance. To her credit, she got off a pair of shots, driving both bullets through the shotgunner, spitting at his body as it fell. But, it was not enough.

The remaining assailant managed to spin the young woman toward the wall. She struck it violently, losing her grip, her automatic falling from her hands. The man followed up his attack with ruthless efficiency, knocking his victim across the back of the head with his own weapon. Then, as she slumped, too dazed to react, the monster got an idea.

He and his associates had made their move when they did purposefully. The man who had hired them, who wanted their target for himself to do with as he pleased, had studied the apartment complex and all its occupants for weeks. As the only surviving assailant stared down at his victim's near unconscious form, he knew that their entry, overwhelming loud as it had been, had not been heard by anyone. The building was too plush, too well built, for noise to travel. And, the neighbors, all gone.

The man looked to his companions, dying and dead. He thought about their employer, a smug, heartless, arrogant toad of a man. And then he looked at the woman whose arm he still grasped, soft and beautiful, every inch of her a part of the most desirable female form he had ever beheld, and his mind formed a terrible plan. The fool to whom he was supposed to deliver the woman now at his mercy, he did not deserve such a prize — whether he had paid well for the privilege or not.

"At least," the thug chuckled to himself as he first closed the door to the hall, then began dragging Nita into the back rooms, "he don't deserve no first crack at her."

The man began to laugh cruelly then. He laughed as he stripped the clothing away from his victim's body. Laughed as he lashed her ankles to the posts of her bed, spreading her legs apart invitingly. And he laughed as he removed his own clothes and began to move toward the bed.

It was the laughter that was his undoing.

In the front foyer, Apollo heard the nasty, guttural cackling. Knew what the tone of it implied. Understood what was going to happen because he had been weak. Because he had been slow and clumsy. Because he was worthless. A bad dog. An unworthy dog. Useless.

Forcing his eyes open, he listened for a moment, summoning his strength. Then, he heard his Nita's voice, and he began to pull himself forward. Inch by inch. Leaving his blood streaking the carpet. Inch by inch. Feeling the fibers reaching up, digging into his wound as he dragged his torn body along. Inch by inch.

Inch by inch.

As the pain flooded him, made his limbs shake, urged him to howl in agony, the great hound closed his eyes once more. Biting down hard, grinding his teeth, Apollo forced himself to concentrate on nothing other than reaching his sweet Nita. On being by her side. On protecting her. On joining the hunt. He had taken two. She had killed another. He had not done enough. He had to do more.

And then, the Dane reached the wooden lip that covered the space where the different floor coverings met. It was nothing. A trifle. Normally. Indeed, the great hound did not even think of it as he approached. But then, the oozing wound in his chest and side rubbed against it, and his world knew fire.

Nearly did Apollo whimper in pain. Bolts of agony burned through him at that moment, and in his brain he knew that every further inch he moved forward would hurt the same. Or worse. And then, he heard the man's laughter turn to words. He heard his Nita screaming at him. He knew that he had no choice than to continue forward.

"You're wonderful. You're absolutely wonderful."

Dragging his torn and bleeding body over the lip, Apollo threw his memory as far back as he could, remembering the first time his mistress had said the words.

"Just absolutely wonderful."

He had only been a puppy. A thing — still useless — lumpy, all legs and tongue. Barely a few weeks old. Just old enough to meet those with whom he would spend the rest of his life.

"Wonderful."

As he pulled himself into the bedroom, the great hound kept his eyes closed. He ignored the sounds of his mistress and the thing which had her. Instead, he remember his Nita's hand moving across his ears, gently scratching, sometimes in lazy circles, wide and slow — sometimes in rapid back-and-forths — from their base to their tips.

"So wonderful."

Tasting his own blood within his throat, Apollo did not stop. He crawled, remembering his training. Remembering that a good dog was loyal, obedient and fierce. He thought about his Nita, cheering his first steps, their thousands of hours of walks, his baths. And he remembered chasing balls and sticks, and all their hunts ... and his meals. All the wonderful meals. He remembered steak and bacon. He remember fried chicken stripped from the bones, and pork chops, wonderful pork chops covered in fat. And gravy. Thick and warm, poured over everything.

And he remembered his Nita, her hand extended;

"Slip me some skin."

And then, he reached the bedroom door. Opening his eyes, he saw his Nita, unable to move, struggling against the man who had come to steal her. Struggling, because he had not been able to protect her.

Slowly, silently, his legs trembling, blood more than dripping from his scores of wounds, the great hound rose. Making it to his feet, Apollo took one step, testing his strength, then another. His teeth grinding, knowing he did not have the power left within him to cross the room and climb atop the bed, the Dane sucked down as much air as his bruised lungs could handle, and then he launched himself forward.

Two bounding steps he knew were all he could manage, but they were enough. Filling the air with a howl of vengeful hate, Apollo threw himself into the air, slamming against the intruder. His nails raking his Nita's exposed flesh, he landed squarely on them both, his one leg collapsing under his weight, snapping it between himself and his target.

His jaws locking on the man's head.

The intruder screamed for all the seconds he had left to live. Blind rage flooding him, the Dane snapped his terrible jaws closed, shredding one of the man's ears away instantly. Chewing viciously, Apollo shredded the man's eyes, sliced his nose away from his face, broke his lower jaw away. Finally, knowing he had reached the limit of his strength, the great hound shifted his jaws and tore away the man's throat, severing his spinal column.

Then, spitting away the offensive meat and bone, having nothing left to give, Apollo collapsed. Her hands no longer held by her tormentor, the dying hound's mistress pushed away the garbage between her and her beloved Apollo. She had not cried while being held captive. Could not possibly have given her vulgar captor such satisfaction.

But, his presence removed, her legs still bound to her bed posts, Nita Van Sloan pulled the Dane to her as best she could, tears flowing down her face. Whispering to him that everything would be all right, Apollo lounged in comfort, his large head heavy in his mistress' lap, everything in his world as right as it could be.

"Wonderful. You're so wonderful."

He was a good dog.

"Just wonderful."

He was.

The Gray Reapers
by Matthew Baugh

No one really noticed the men who would become known as the Gray Reapers when they arrived at Westwood Cemetery. There were three of them, dressed in charcoal gray suits, with gray hats, ties, and shoes. Their shirts and gloves were a lighter shade of gray, and even their skin was an ashen hue that lent a macabre touch to their expressionless faces.

The one man who paid attention was gravedigger Rupert McCoy. He had been up since before dawn, chopping through the frozen ground with his shovel to make ready for the Collins service. He stood at a distance, leaning on his shovel and watching the family and friends as they listened to the pastor's solemn words.

He saw the three men enter and thought they were mourners, though they didn't wear black and one carried a large briefcase. The strangers moved to the entrance of a nearby family crypt and the two taller gray men stood as the third knelt and opened his briefcase.

The mourners seemed oblivious but the sight made Rupert anxious. He didn't want the dignity of a graveside service disturbed at his cemetery. Shouldering his shovel, he headed toward the men.

As he approached, Rupert could see that the case had unfolded into an electronic device. Rupert had been a radio operator in the Great War and thought the device resembled the kind of portable set he had used in the Army, though with a more complex set of dials. The kneeling gray man took two metal rods from the case which were connected to it by wires and drove them into the ground. He turned a knob and sparks began to jump from the rods into the frozen ground and Rupert caught the smell of ozone.

"Hey!" he cried and hurried his pace. The two men standing watch moved into his path and drew strange weapons from their coats. They looked like a cross between a sickle and a short sword, having a blade shaped like a question mark with the outer edge of the curve sharpened. He paused, shaken as much by the men's expressionless faces as by the weapons.

The pastor's voice stopped as the members of the funeral party turned to stare, but the strange confrontation only lasted a moment. Then, a pounding noise from the inside of the casket claimed their attention. The mourners looked on in horror as the wood of the coffin lid splintered and the deceased man pushed his way free.

The man's wife, a distinguished looking woman of about fifty, gave a cry of mixed hope and horror. The pastor caught her by the shoulder, trying to restrain her, but it was too late. The corpse lunged at the woman; seizing her with inhuman strength, it buried its teeth in her neck. Blood fountained as the dead man tore the helpless woman's throat out. Then the monster stepped forward swinging its arm at the pastor. Hooked fingers struck the man's ample stomach with terrible force, piercing cloth and flesh. A moment later the monster tugged his hand free, pulling a length of viscera with it.

The mourners panicked, but even as they began to flee, the dirt of a dozen graves began to churn and hands emerged, poking up through the soil like strange, grasping flowers. The hands were followed by heads, then bodies, as decaying corpses in tattered clothing dug themselves out of their graves.

Rupert McCoy had seen enough. He raised his shovel and advanced on the Gray Reapers.

"I don't know what you're doing," he said, "but stop it now!"

One of the swordsmen stepped forward. Rupert swung his shovel but the man sidestepped it effortlessly and slashed out with his sickle-sword. The shovel fell to the frozen earth with Rupert McCoy's hands still attached.

He fell to his knees in shock, barely hearing the cries of horror around him.

Ram Singh pulled the town car to a stop at the graveside. The police had cordoned off the cemetery but, recognizing the car as belonging to the Commissioner's friend, Richard Wentworth, they had let it through. Ram Singh stepped out of the vehicle, then opened the rear door for Wentworth and his fiancée, Nita Van Sloan. He followed the couple as they moved to greet Stanley Kirkpatrick by a crypt, supervising the investigation.

"Hello, Kirk," Wentworth said, shaking the Police Commissioner's hand.

"Richard, Nita," Kirkpatrick returned. "What are you doing out here?"

"You know that I keep a police band radio," Wentworth said. "When I heard the call, I had to come."

Kirkpatrick nodded, knowing that cemeteries had to be on his friend's mind. It had only been three days since they had buried his chauffeur, Ronald Jackson.

"It's a real mess," the Commissioner said. He gestured at the scene where old corpses lay tangled with new ones. Even the fierce Ram Singh, who had seen death in a thousand macabre forms, couldn't help shuddering.

"So, what's the picture, Kirk?" Wentworth asked.

"You can see," Kirkpatrick said irritably. "Some lunatic found a way to raise the dead and the result is eight murders and a dozen more people in the hospital. It's just the sort of thing The *Spider's* always involved in."

"But The *Spider's* dead, Kirk," Nita said. "Ronald Jackson confessed to being The *Spider* and he was killed a week ago." The lovely brunette said it so matter-of-factly that Ram Singh almost believed she meant it. Of course, that was absurd. Nita knew that The *Spider* was really Richard Wentworth. Kirkpatrick had to know it too, the man was no fool. For some reason though, the Commissioner pretended not to know.

"I'm afraid that won't wash, Nita," Kirkpatrick said. "The *Spider's* been seen since then, even at the World Series. As far as I'm concerned that clears your chauffeur's name."

"I'm glad to hear that," Wentworth said. "That doesn't really answer my question though. How many bodies were reanimated?"

"We found eleven empty graves, though we've only recovered ten bodies so far," the Commissioner said. "Whatever did this, it only seems to have a temporary effect, thank God."

"And what do you know about the men who did this?"

"Not much. There was a gravedigger who got a good look at them but he's in shock… they lopped his hands clean off and he's probably not going to make it. He said they were gray, clothing, skin, everything. 'Gray reapers' he called them."

"Why reapers?" Wentworth asked.

"They had some funny sort of weapon," Kirkpatrick said, handing Wentworth a piece of paper. "He was able to describe this thing but couldn't give us a good description of the men."

Wentworth studied the sketch.

"This is a *khopesh*," he said. "It's an ancient Egyptian sword."

"You're saying this is the work of ancient Egyptians?"

"Would that be the strangest thing you've ever seen?" Wentworth asked with a laugh.

Kirkpatrick scowled and didn't reply.

"What do you think the motive was?" Nita asked.

"General carnage," Kirkpatrick said. "Maybe a mad scientist making a test run with his new death device. How the hell am I supposed to know?"

"Well, I don't have much to offer," Wentworth said. "Would you let me know if this happens again?"

"You'll know when I release an official statement," the Commissioner said, looking annoyed. He moved away to talk to one of the detectives.

Wentworth smiled as he watched his friend go, a knowing, superior expression that Ram Singh would have found insufferable on another man. On his master he found it wholly appropriate, for Richard Wentworth was superior to other men. That was why the Sikh served him so willingly, why Nita endured year after year of unending engagement with no hope of marriage, and why Jackson had willingly given his life to preserve his master's secret.

"I think the motive is much more commonplace than Kirk suspects,"

Wentworth said. "All we need to do is discover the identity of the eleventh dead man. If my guess is right, we'll find he was the man who was being buried today."

"What do you mean?" Nita asked.

"The older corpses were left behind, I assume because they weren't needed, but these 'Gray Reapers' made certain they took this man's body with them," he replied. "That tells me that he was valuable to him."

The police were able to keep the first appearance of the Gray Reapers quiet, but they struck again in Pennsylvania, and then in New Jersey. By the third attack there was no keeping the matter out of the papers. Banner headlines screamed:

GRAY REAPERS RESPONSIBLE FOR FUNERAL MURDERS!

"Kirk's leaked out some of Rupert McCoy's testimony," Richard Wentworth said as he read the morning papers in his penthouse apartment. "They've picked up on the 'Gray Reapers' name. Judging from the story, I'm afraid Kirk's on the wrong track."

"Sahib?" Ram Singh asked, clearing away the breakfast dishes. Wentworth sat at the table reading the paper while Nita hung on his every word.

"What do you mean?" she asked.

"He can't find a motive so, according to the paper, he's blanketing all the funerals in the state."

"But you have found the motive?"

"I'm close to it," Wentworth said, smiling. He paused to light a cigarette and the pause served to electrify the moment. Ram Singh didn't understand it, but he could see how it affected Nita as well. The woman leaned toward her fiancé, eyes half closed and lips parted in the sensual expression of a lover expecting a kiss rather than an aide waiting to hear her chief's plans.

"Well?" she asked.

"In each of the attacks, the police have recovered all of the rogue corpses except for those about to be buried. Besides Collins, the missing men are

Ryerson Jeffries, Kendall Northcutt, and Rance Concord. They were part of a six-man expedition to Egypt back in 1926. I believe that they must have discovered something important and that is why someone is collecting them."

"Collecting them?"

"Yes, darling. Someone has resurrected them prior to making off with them."

"But they've been raised as mindless zombies," Nita said. "What earthly use could they be now?"

"None, unless there's more to the process than we know," Wentworth replied. "Perhaps they can fully revive the ones they abduct later."

"And the zombies?"

"A residual effect of the device they use," Wentworth said. "A useful one too. What could cover their getaway better than a horde of blood-thirsty zombies?"

"Raising the dead, how horrible," Nita said with a shudder.

"Not horrible," Wentworth said, his eyes burning with excitement. "Imagine if we'd had that power when we lost Jackson. Think of the good that could be done as man's last enemy--death itself--is defeated."

"If they can do that, Sahib, then what do they need with these men?"

"I don't know, Ram Singh, but we have a chance to find out tomorrow," Wentworth replied. "Henry Mercer, another member of the expedition has also died. We will be attending the funeral."

"Darling," Nita said. "Raising the dead ... is it possible?"

"There are many stories in history, from the Bible to the Voo-doo practices of Haiti. There are also some intriguing modern experiments. I've been reading a monograph by a Dr. West of a prominent New England university which suggests that a reagent made of certain plant extracts can activate even desiccated nerve tissue."

"But if the flesh has rotted ... and what if the body had been embalmed?"

"West claimed that the revived tissue seemed to be oxygenated directly by contact with air, removing the need for blood. Though, he admits this is only a crude mockery of life. In actual resurrection, he says you need a fresh corpse and must expend a great deal of effort in reversing the undertaker's preparations."

"It all sounds mad," Nita said, shuddering again.

"More reputable scientists have affirmed it," Wentworth replied. "Savage himself claims to have revived an Egyptian mummy using a process that involved tana leaf extract. Sadly, the tana plant is extinct and he used the last known specimens of the extract in his experiment."

"But if someone else is raising corpses ..."

"Then there must be more of the plants," Wentworth finished for her.

Ram Singh stroked his thick beard. The tall Sikh stood at the rear of the crowd of mourners dressed in a Western suit and the turban of his people's tradition. His dark eyes scanned the vast sea of headstones and cenotaphs searching for a sign of the Gray Reapers. Wentworth stood on the far side of the crowd while Nita lingered near the middle of the crowd of mourners, near Mercer's widow. Ram Singh's gaze settled on Mrs. Mercer for a moment, a tall, stunning woman in her thirties with the dark eyes and hair of the Near East and a slender figure as straight as a flagpole. He saw the tearless expression on her face and admired her all the more for it.

Here is a woman of iron, he thought. *Ah, thrice-blessed the man who has such a companion.*

Near the entrance, four policemen, there on Kirkpatrick's orders, stood guard. They looked bored and ill at ease. He imagined that they resented the tedious guard duty but felt little sympathy. Any assignment, no matter how distasteful, should be carried out as if it were the most sacred order in the world.

"*Behold, I show you a mystery; We shall not all sleep, but we shall all be changed,*" the preacher read. "*In a moment, in the twinkling of an eye, at the last trump: for the trumpet shall sound, and the dead shall be raised incorruptible, and we shall be changed . . .*"

Ram Singh heard a noise, a faint rumbling as if something was burrowing through the earth. He turned his head, trying to locate the source, but it seemed to be coming from everywhere. The sound grew louder, and now the mourners heard it too.

"O death, where is thy sting? O grave, where is thy victory--" The preacher's voice stopped as, first hands and then heads began to sprout from more than a score of graves.

The mourners froze for a moment as the undead monsters pulled their way free of the grave-dirt. One of the police opened fire, emptying his revolver into one of the creatures to no visible effect. The corpse, an obese businessman who still had most of his corpulent flesh, grabbed the officer's neck with both hands and twisted until his head fell off and blood spurted from the decapitated torso.

That was all it took for the mourners; they scattered, trying to get past the ambulatory dead men and to their cars. Nita drew a small .25 caliber automatic from her pocketbook and took Mrs. Mercer by the arm.

"This way," she said, indicating Wentworth's big town car.

As they neared the car two of the reapers appeared from behind tombstones and rushed at them. Nita fired at the closest one, putting four shots into his chest with cool precision. As she turned to fire on the second, something hit her head from behind.

Careless, she thought as she fell to her knees. I let one of them get behind me somehow.

There was another blow and Nita slipped into unconsciousness.

As this was happening, Wentworth disappeared behind a large cenotaph. Ram Singh saw and understood that his master was changing into the guise of The *Spider*. Wentworth could accomplish this with the skill of a quick-change artist, but that still left the Sikh warrior to deal with the walking dead by himself for a few seconds. He pulled a throwing knife from his jacket and flung it to lodge in the chest of one of the corpses a dozen feet away.

The creature ignored the wound and continued its pursuit of a woman. Another of the mourners, presumably the woman's husband, interposed himself, trying to protect her. He held out a hand to stop the creature but the dead man grabbed it and, with one savage heave, pulled the arm from its socket. The man fell, clutching the bleeding stump of his shoulder and the woman screamed as the thing lurched for her again.

Just then Ram Singh split the monster's head with his huge, curved kirpan dagger.

"Curse me for the son of a baboon!" he said as the creature dropped to the ground. "I used too small a knife before." Ignoring the screaming woman, the big Sikh lunged at another of the undead creatures, severing its head with one stroke. He saw that three of the policemen were down already and the fourth was firing uselessly into the torso of an undead woman.

Just then a sinister, black-clad form appeared atop a massive tombstone. The *Spider*!

The big .45 automatics in his hands belched flame and lead virtually causing the undead woman's head to explode. The policeman fell back, a mingled expression of horror and awe on his face.

"By the ten holy gurus!" Ram Singh cried. "The head is their weakness."

The officer either didn't hear or was too panicked to respond. He backed away, stumbling into another pair of the monsters. They lashed at him with their nails, tearing open his shirt and digging bloody furrows into his chest. He fell with a scream as they continued to claw ever deeper until the white bone of his ribs showed.

The *Spider*, in the meantime, was too busy to help. Half a dozen of the walking dead had converged on Ram Singh and the Master of Man leaped from his perch into the thick of them. Ram Singh slashed around him, severing arms and splitting skulls in a berserker frenzy. The *Spider*, by contrast, moved calmly and deliberately. He seemed as terrible as the living dead themselves as every shot shattered a skull or severed a spinal column with devastating efficiency.

Ram Singh looked around, assessing the situation. All of the police and five of the mourners had died, but the *Spider* had reduced the number of their enemies to but a few. Then he saw the Gray Reapers. Three of them were leading one of the undead men away from the fight, a tall man in his early fifties, with iron-gray hair and blue eyes. Ram Singh started as he recognized the walking corpse as Henry Mercer.

The *Spider* raised a pistol, but the ammunition was spent, before he could do anything, a tall, gaunt, undead man caught him from behind, locking both hands around his neck to strangle him. The *Spider* knew that struggling was useless against the superhuman strength of the fiends, but flesh and bone were still only flesh and bone. Moving with dazzling speed he ejected his spent clips and slammed new ones home. His vision blurred as the grip deprived his brain of oxygen but, even as his consciousness started to slip away, he pointed his powerful pistols over his shoulders and fired.

Though he fired blindly, The *Spider's* keen awareness of the battlefield served him well. The bullets smashed into the thing's eyes to exit the rear of its head in an eruption of brain tissue.

As this was happening, Ram Singh faced his own danger. The mighty Sikh decapitated a corpse that was lunging at him and set out after the trio. The Grey Reapers saw him coming and two of them fell back, drawing their *khopesh* swords to meet him.

"Ah," the big Sikh said, grinning. "The jackals finally bare their teeth. Nothing pleased him more than a fight with blades. He slashed at the first Reaper only to see his blow parried by the curved weapon. The Reaper struck his own blow, which Ram Singh parried in turn. Then the other man joined in, his blade twirling in deadly arcs.

Ram Singh was forced to retreat before the deadly assault. These men were as skilled as any swordsmen he had ever faced. One-on-one and properly armed he had no doubt that he could beat them, but facing both, and with his shorter blade, he didn't have a chance. He smiled grimly, relishing the hopeless challenge. If he had to die, he could not imagine a better death than fighting in the service of The *Spider*.

He lunged forward, trying to catch the men off balance with the ferocity of his attack. The first Reaper parried his thrust while the second struck at him. Ram Singh pulled back but the hooked blade dug a diagonal gash across his chest.

He responded with a powerful overhead cut at the reaper who had wounded him. The man parried, but only barely, and the force of Ram Singh's blow drove him to his knees. But before the Sikh could strike again, the second reaper swung his sword, cutting into the muscles of Ram Singh's arm. With a cry of pain, Ram Singh dropped his knife and staggered backward as the Reaper raised his weapon for the deathblow.

Then Ram Singh heard the sound of a pistol behind him and a bloody hole appeared in the center of the man's gray face. The second Reaper rose, only to fall again a moment later, spurting crimson from half a dozen holes in his torso created by The *Spider's* bullets. As Ram Singh turned back to check the first Reaper he saw something strange. The gray skin of the man's face seemed loose. Ram Singh inspected him more closely and saw that the 'skin' was actually a mask made of some rubbery material that clung to his face like flesh. Underneath it the man had dark skin and Arabic features.

"I am sorry for needing your help, Sahib," Ram Singh said, looking up from his discovery. "I am but a weak lamb today, and it disgusts me."

"Fear not, warrior," the *Spider* replied, coming alongside the Sikh. "I have need of your service again."

The eerie figure pointed to the remaining Reaper who had reached a parked car and was attempting to force Mercer inside.

"My pistols are empty," The *Spider* said.

With a grim smile the powerful Sikh flung his kirpan with all of his strength. The curved knife turned end-over-end before striking the gray man between the shoulder blades.

Mercer took the opportunity to run. He had made it only about twenty feet when a retort was heard and he fell.

"They've shot him," The *Spider* said. He and Ram Singh raced to the man's side as the car sped off.

"I do not understand this," Ram Singh said. "How can a mere bullet strike down one of the walking dead?"

The *Spider* placed two fingers to Mercer's throat near the hinge of his jaw. "He is alive," he said.

"Alive?" Ram Singh repeated in disbelief. "But none of these thrice-cursed fiends is alive."

The *Spider* tore open the side of Mercer's shirt to examine the wound.

"Serious," he said. "He only has a few minutes." He shook the man roughly. "Mercer," he said. "Mercer, wake up!"

The man groaned and began to stir. The *Spider* shook him again and his eyes opened.

"What . . . what is this? Who are you?"

"Henry Mercer, you will answer my questions or I will give you to the Gray Reapers," the *Spider* said.

Mercer paled at the threat. "Please, no," he said. "Not those devils."

"I can protect you from them, but only if you answer my questions."

"Anything," the frightened man replied.

"Who are they?"

"They . . . we found them on the expedition; guardians of an ancient tomb under the Hill of the Seven Jackals. They are not Muslims, but a strain of priests of the old religion of Egypt who have an unbroken lineage going back to the days of the Nineteenth Dynasty."

"You took something from them, didn't you?" the *Spider* asked. "Something they want back at any cost."

"You . . . you know?" Mercer said, his eyes widening. Looking at him, Ram Singh judged that he had been a dynamic and energetic man fifteen years ago, but drink and a sedentary life had eroded him. He wondered how Mercer had won the hand of such a formidable beauty.

That made him think of something; he looked around for Mrs. Mercer. There was no sign of her but he did see Nita, her hand to her head, staggering toward them.

"Sahib, look!" he cried, pointing.

The *Spider* hurried to Nita's side and helped her the rest of the way. She had a bruise on her forehead but did not seem badly hurt.

"Mrs. Mercer?"

"A Reaper took her," she said. "I tried to stop him but he was too fast."

"My Auset!" Mercer said.

"We will find her," the *Spider* said, "but first I have to learn more. Tell me about the walking dead."

"There is a device," Mercer replied. ". . . something lost to the world for thousands of years. The guardians used it to defend their tombs from intruders."

"How do they control the dead?" The *Spider* asked.

Mercer tried to speak, only to fall into a coughing fit which left his lips flecked with blood.

"How do they keep the dead form turning on them?" The *Spider's* voice was a grim snarl.

"There . . . there is . . . talisman they wear."

"What did you steal from them?" The *Spider's* voice had the grim tone of a judge proclaiming guilt.

"Tan . . . tana leaves." Mercer closed his eyes. After a moment his breathing stilled.

"Is he--?" Nita said.

"Dead," the *Spider* said. "But he'll serve us better in death than in life. The Gray Reapers know that The *Spider* has Mercer, so they will strike at me to recover him."

"But how can they strike at you, Sahib?" Ram Singh asked.

"There is only one way," the *Spider* replied.

"Blast it, Wentworth!" General Barton Morrissey said. "This violates every military protocol I can think of."

"Do you trust me?" Richard Wentworth asked.

Ram Singh smothered a smile. The Army man was as hard as steel but the Sikh could see him weakening before Wentworth's masterful personality.

"That's beside the point," he said. "I have to play it by the book."

"It wasn't the book that helped you in the Argonne."

Morrissey tried to glare a hole in Wentworth but the younger man merely smiled.

"I trust you," the general said, "but this . . . this *Spider*. You want me to allow him to--"

"I know it's seems strange, sir," Wentworth said. "I was hesitant too, but his plan will work. He believes that they're going to come for Jackson to revive him--that Jackson has information they need. If you make it known that Jackson's military honors have been rescinded and that his body will be cremated, it will force them to strike on our timetable."

"They could strike before we're ready."

"I don't think so," Wentworth replied. "All of their raids have shown careful planning. That takes time."

"It has a chance of working," Morrissey said. "But we don't need The *Spider*. My men--"

"Have no experience in facing this sort of thing," Wentworth interjected.

"The *Spider* is the only one who has fought these horrors and beaten them."

"Just the same, the U.S. Army doesn't need help from some vigilante."

"'The enemy of my enemy is my friend.' Surely you've been in enough campaigns to appreciate the truth of that old saying, General."

"Alright," the general said after a moment. "I do owe you something for all those boys you saved. But I warn you, if this doesn't go as you say, my men will have orders to take down this *Spider*, and you'll have some hard questions to answer yourself."

"Don't worry, Bart, you have my word."

The funeral service was small, with a placid-looking, white-haired chaplain in a long cassock, two mourners and an honor guard of seven for the three volley salute. Still, Arlington National Cemetery saw services of all sizes.

On this day the hallowed fields saw something that they never had before. The chaplain paused in his recitation as the earth of a hundred graves began to churn. Like evil weeds, the bodies of the nation's honored dead began to claw their way out of what should have been their final resting place. The female mourner gave a cry of horror and her companion, a tall servant in a turban, caught her arm to steady her.

The honor guard fell back uneasily, leveling their M-1 Garand rifles and keeping between the mourners and the advancing horde of zombies.

Then a dozen of the Gray Reapers appeared, moving through the field of markers. They paused at one stone whose occupant had mostly freed himself. Two of the Reapers held his arms while a third emptied a small vial of liquid into his mouth. The dead man began to jerk spasmodically but the Reapers managed to hold on.

The chaplain had been watching this closely. Now he drew an automatic pistol from his robes.

"Take aim!" he cried in the tone of a commander of men. "Remember, the head should be your only target."

The honor guard fell into position, all pretense of hesitation gone. They fired a volley into the advancing dead, then another, and a third.

"Fire at will!" shouted the chaplain as he cast off his clerical robe to stand revealed as The *Spider*.

The turbaned servant opened the casket and The *Spider* took out a pair of Thompson submachine guns, passing one to the woman.

"Nita, help the soldiers, he said. "Ram Singh, we will go after the leader."

"Yes, Sahib," the turbaned man said. "These jackals scratched me before. Now it is my turn to teach them how a true warrior strikes!" He withdrew a sheathed sword and slung it across his shoulder, then a *katar* punching dagger and a set of *chakrams*.

Nita moved alongside the riflemen and laid down a withering barrage with the Tommy gun. The *Spider* used his weapon in similarly effective manner and the heavy slugs pounded undead skulls to powder, spattering desiccated brain matter across the well manicured lawn. Next to him, Ram Singh gleefully hurled one chakram after another. The foot-wide throwing rings boasted razor sharp edges that severed necks, legs, and arms when they hit. Between them they tore through the dead like scythes through wheat.

But the dead were not their only foes. The Gray Reapers drew their swords and made for them. Seeing them, Ram Singh drew his own blades, a long, straight *khanda* that flared at the tip for greater cutting power, and a katar with a two-foot blade.

"Come to me, o sons of dogs," he cried. "This time you will find me properly armed and ready to flay your mongrel hides.

The *Spider* cut down another five corpses and one of the Reapers before his Tommy gun clicked on an empty chamber. He discarded the gun and drew his big .45 automatics. Two shots took down two more Reapers, then they were on him. The first Reaper slashed at him and he managed to parry with the .45, but the impact drove the gun from his hand.

The swordsman moved closer and slashed again, but Ram Singh's khanda intercepted the blow. While the two blades were locked, he punched the Reaper in the chest, driving the point of his katar through his heart and out his back. Stepping past him, he used the superior length of his sword to split the next Reaper's skull.

That left two of the Reapers, the remaining swordsman and the leader who crouched over the body of the newly resurrected dead man. The *Spider* smiled grimly and scooped up a fallen khopesh and, leaving Ram Singh to duel the final swordsman, he stalked toward the leader.

"Stay back, I warn you!" the Gray Reaper said, drawing a small revolver. The *Spider* ignored the warning and continued moving forward, his face a grim mask of vengeance.

"Fool!" he said. "You think that you have the power over life and death? Your arrogance has doomed you."

The Reaper fired with shaking hands. The *Spider* managed to twist aside from the first bullet. The second caught him in the ribs but the *Spider's* indomitable will continued to drive him forward. He lashed out with his khopesh, severing three fingers from the leader's gun hand. The Gray Reaper cried out in a voice that was distinctly feminine.

The *Spider* dropped his sword and caught the Gray Reaper by the throat. She pulled away, leaving a mask of gray false-flesh and a golden chain with a small talisman in his hand. The face that was revealed belonged to Auset Mercer.

She clutched her mutilated hand to her gray jacket and backed away. The *Spider* made no move to stop her.

"You think you've won, don't you?" she said, forcing a laugh. "We will reclaim what is ours, and we will kill the fool who stole it from us."

"Your husband is already dead," The *Spider* said.

"No, you're lying."

She continued backing away until she bumped into one of the walking dead. The creature grabbed her, its bony fingertips sinking deep into the flesh of her shoulder.

"What?" she gasped, her good hand reaching for her throat. "My talisman! Where is my talisman?"

The *Spider* opened his hand and the golden charm fell from it to land at his feet. Three more of the walking dead joined the first and Auset Mercer began to scream.

"Sahib!" Ram Singh cried as he came alongside The *Spider*. He started to move to help the woman but The *Spider* laid a restraining hand on his arm.

The creatures began to fight over the screaming woman, their fingers ripping away cloth, skin, and flesh indiscriminately. The screaming stopped when a dead soldier ripped her lower jaw free from her skull.

The *Spider* turned and walked back to the resurrected man. Around him the soldiers of the honor guard finished putting down the last few living dead men. When he reached the man's side, the *Spider* knelt.

"I feel awful," the resurrected man said. "What happened to me?"

"Welcome back, Jackson," said the *Spider*.

Two days later the revivified Ronald Jackson sat in the living room of Richard Wentworth's penthouse apartment, surrounded by his friends. The *Spider* had sped him out of the cemetery to a hidden lab where he had pumped the embalming fluid out of his body and transfused him with blood. There had been numerous other treatments, but The *Spider's* research had revealed just what needed to be done. Between his care and the remaining tana fluid recovered from the Reapers, Jackson lived again.

"So I was dead?" he asked.

"The Sahib has already covered that several times," Ram Singh said.

"It's just so strange." He shook his head. "The idea that that woman had that kind of power."

"She was a member of the ancient cult that guarded the tana leaves," Wentworth said. She married Mercer at their command to try and recover the plants he had stolen."

"The cult didn't know which of the expedition members had the plants," Nita added. "When any of them died, they would steal the body at the funeral and resurrect them to gain the information."

"But... why not just kidnap them while they were alive?" Jackson asked.

"I think it was to drive home a point," Wentworth said. "They wanted their victims to understand that they could never escape from the cult... not even in death."

"But why resurrect me?"

"To come after The *Spider*, she had to know his identity," Wentworth said. "But as far as the world was concerned, you *were* The *Spider*. When I reappeared, I knew she would assume that I was a successor to the original *Spider*."

"And who better to spill the goods on the successor than the original?" Jackson smiled grimly. "You took a long chance on that, Major."

"I did," Wentworth agreed. "But it was the only way there would be even a chance of using the power of the Gray Reapers to revive you."

"Like Mark Twain said, 'the rumors of my death have been greatly exaggerated'... only in my case they haven't." Jackson shuddered.

"I hated to let them desecrate those sacred grounds," Wentworth said, "but it was worth it to get you back."

Author Biographies

MATTHEW BAUGH lives and writes in Albuquerque, NM. When not writing about pulp heroes, giant robots, and mad scientists he works as an ordained minister. He has published a number of stories including some for Moonstone anthologies about Zorro, The Green Hornet, The Avenger, The Phantom, and Sherlock Holmes. Currently, he is working on a short "The Ice Devil" featuring the Avenger.

JAMES CHAMBERS' stories of horror, crime, fantasy, and science fiction have appeared in numerous anthologies and magazines. *Publisher's Weekly* called his collection of Lovecraftian novellas, *The Engines of Sacrifice*, "chillingly evocative." His recent works include the novellas, *The Dead Bear Witness* and *Tears of Blood*, in the *Corpse Fauna* series, and the urban fantasy novella, *Three Chords of Chaos*. His work has appeared in Allen K's *Inhuman*, *Deep Cuts*, *The Domino Lady: Sex as a Weapon*, and *The Green Hornet Chronicles*. He has written the comic books Leonard Nimoy's *Primortals* and *"The Revenant"* in Shadow House. His website is: www.jameschambersonline.com.

RON FORTIER For the past thirty-five years Ron has worked for most of the major comic companies. He's best known for writing *The Green Hornet* and *Terminator: Burning Earth*, with Alex Ross, for Now Comics back in 348 The Green Hornet Chronicles the '80s. Today, he keeps busy writing and editing new pulp anthologies and novels via his Airship 27 Productions (www.gopulp.info) and contributing to Moonstone's Originals with brand new I.V. Frost adventures in both prose and comics. Visit him at www.airship27.com.

ERIC FEIN is a freelance writer and editor. He has written dozens of comic book stories featuring characters such as The Punisher, *Spider*-Man, Iron Man, Conan, Godzilla, and The Green Ghost. He has also written more than forty books and graphic novels for educational publishers. His short stories have been published in several Moonstone anthologies including Sex, Lies, and Private Eyes, The Green Hornet Casefiles, and The Avenger: The Justice Inc. Files. As an editor, he has worked on staff for both Marvel and DC Comics. At Marvel, he edited *Spider*-Man, The Spectacular *Spider*-Man, and The Web of *Spider*-Man, as well as limited series and one-shots including Venom: Carnage Unleashed and *Spider*-Man and Batman: Disordered Minds. At DC Comics, he edited storybooks, coloring and activity books, and how-to-draw books.

Long-time Moonstone stalwart **CJ HENDERSON** has written some 75 and/or novels, created numerous series, including supernatural investigator Piers Knight, occult Teddy London, and contributed new volumes to many existing series, including our own Kolchak: the Nightstalker. With hundreds and hundreds of stories and comics to his credit, he is known for writing everything from hard-hitting adventure to sci fi-military musical comedies. For further info on this deranged talent, feel free to check out his : www.cjhenderson.com

HOWARD HOPKINS (howardhopkins.com) is the author of thirty-four westerns under the penname Lance Howard, as well as six horror novels, three young adult horror novels, and numerous short stories under his own name. His most recent western, *Twilight Trail*, is a May 2012 release and his most recent horror series novel, *The Chloe Files #2: Sliver of Darkness*, is available now. He's written many widescreen comic books and graphic novels for Moonstone, along with co-editing and writing for Moonstone's anthologies about the classic pulp hero The Avenger, and he brought The Golden Amazon back for a new generation of readers in Moonstone's Originals comic book pulp line. Among his latest releases are the novel *The Lone Ranger: Vendetta* and the popular anthology *Sherlock Holmes: The Crossovers Casebook*.

RIK HOSKIN is a science fiction novelist and comic strip writer. Under the shared pen-name of James Axler, he has been the primary writer for the *Outlanders* book series since 2008 and has also contributed to its sister series, *Deathlands*. His comic strip work includes *Superman*, *Star Wars*, *Disney Princess* and *Winnie the Pooh*. He helped develop the pre-school *Spider-Man & Friends* comic strip which has been a worldwide success, and the *Wallace & Gromit* newspaper strip which reaches an estimated 8 million readers a day in the UK. He has also written for *Primeval*, *Shrek* and various Pixar and Disney characters among many others.

WILL MURRAY is a literary chameleon who has written Doc Savage in the style of Lester Dent, Destroyer novels in the styles of Richard Sapir and Warren Murphy, and dozens of stories and novelettes in many others styles--including his own. Murray has contributed to all three Moonstone Avenger collections to date. His most recent Doc Savage novel, Skull Island, pits the Man of Bronze against the Eighth Wonder of the World, the legendary King Kong.

Although he doesn't fight crime like Richard Henry Benson, author **BOBBY NASH** his days writing about characters who do. Bobby writes a little of everything including novels, stories, comic books, novellas, graphic novels, screenplays, and some pulse-pounding pulp just for good measure. "Lone Justice" was Bobby's first foray into the world of Justice Inc.'s head honcho, The Avenger. Said Bobby of the experience, "It was a nerve-wracking honor, not only because of The Avenger's pulp roots, but it's the first character both Jack Kirby and I have worked on. How is that?" Visit Bobby at www.bobbynash.com.

GARY PHILLIPS draws on his experiences ranging from teaching incarcerated youth, state director of a political action committee to delivering dog cages in writing his tales of chicanery and malfeasance. His latest efforts include the ebook novella *The Essex Man: 10 Seconds to Death*, a homage to '70s era paperback vigilantes, and is co-editor and contributor to *Black Pulp*, an anthology of pulp goodness with black characters in the lead. Please visit his website at: www.gdphillips.com.

DON ROFF is the bestselling author of *Zombies: A Record of the Year of Infection* from Chronicle Books/Simon & Schuster UK, as well as a spin-off audio book from AudioGO and wall calendars from Universe Publishing. In addition, he has authored over 14 books for Scholastic, Inc. For Moonstone Books, he wrote the story *"The House on Moreau Street"* which appeared in the *Sherlock Holmes Crossover Casebook.* Currently, Roff has scripted a supernatural thriller, *The Crooked Mile*, which is at the time of this writing in preproduction.

Based in Yorkshire, England, **I. A. WATSON** is the award-winning author of the *Robin Hood: King of Sherwood* trilogy and of the SF novel *Blackthorn: Dynasty of Mars*. He has contributed stories to the anthologies *Sherlock Holmes Consulting Detective* volumes 1-5, *Gideon Cain: Demon Hunter*, *The New Adventures of Richard Knight, Monster Earth*, and to half a dozen other collections. A full list is available at http://www.chillwater.org.uk /writing/iawatsonhome.htm He has considered becoming a masked avenger of the night but really prefers chronicling other pulp characters than being one – although all femme fatales are gratefully received.

AMERICA'S NEWEST ACTION SERIES!

The RED MENACE
#1 RED AND BURIED

a new novel-series from the author of "The New Destroyer: Adventures of Remo Williams

CUBA LIBRE

JAMES MULLANEY